THE
ORCHID
AND THE
EMERALD

TIMOTHY DAVID MACK

THE ORCHID
AND THE
EMERALD
SEARCH FOR THE CURE

BLACK STONE
PUBLISHING

First edition: 2022
ISBN 978-1-6650-4679-4
Fiction / Historical / General

Version 1

CIP data for this book is available
from the Library of Congress

Blackstone Publishing
31 Mistletoe Rd.
Ashland, OR 97520

www.BlackstonePublishing.com

For my wife, my best friend and faithful inspiration,
without whom this would not be possible,
and with whom all things are possible.

I drink to Life, I drink to Death,
And smack my lips with song,
For when I die, another "I" shall pass the cup along.
                              —Jack London, *The Iron Heel*

PREFACE

It was late summer 1992. Outside Puerto Berrío, at the edge of the forest on the high bank overlooking the river, the Englishman was buried.

We had just concluded partnership arrangements with several South American ecotour companies (one of my firms is an adventure travel agency) and were unwinding by kayaking down the Magdalena River. The river flows almost a thousand miles north through the western half of Colombia and is navigable for much of its length by kayak.

We came across the grave not far from the place described by the guide. Obscured by tangled vines and over a hundred years of jungle detritus, the small stone marker was scarcely visible in the dusk.

We approached close enough to discern the carved letters: J. H. CHESTERTON.

No stranger to harm's way, I was familiar with the final resting places of many unknown men. But the grave of J. H. Chesterton—a man buried far from his native land in a lone, almost unmarked grave—struck me. How had he died? And why had he come here, when it took months to sail from Europe, then weeks to travel by foot through the trackless jungle? Was he a soldier of fortune or a lone adventurer on an unknown quest?

Little did I know this small diversion would eventually consume years of my life. A more practical man would have passed by the place altogether. I had to probe further.

Finding a hotel with a fax machine, I sent a brief message to my stateside agent and was returned a thirty-page document the next day. What I read stunned me. Chesterton was a hunter. Not of dangerous animals, but of a single remarkable plant: the orchid.

I already knew the hunt for these singular plants went on for almost a century, ending only with the First World War. Among wealthy Victorians, an orchid atrium was a requirement, a place of illumination where one could converse over high tea while flaunting the latest exotic specimens from the far-off jungles of Borneo. The newspapers and journals of the day heralded each new shipment. This was the great "orchid fever."

Some searchers were motivated by greed. At one time, an orchid sold for a thousand times its weight in gold, a single specimen bringing enough at auction for a man to retire comfortably. Others sought scientific discovery, not unlike the hapless, real-life Joseph Jussieu of our tale.

Of all the adventurers, orchid hunters were the hardiest, the most daring, and quite possibly, the most mad. While today a hybrid orchid can be found at any corner grocery store, the orchid hunters of that day had to search in fever-plagued jungles for the most prized specimens. They were resourceful: the very best could live like the natives, speak obscure dialects, and survive for months in the most inhospitable places on earth.

But in spite of his considerable abilities, the life of an orchid hunter was in constant jeopardy. These men faced a host of dangers, not the least from one another.

An orchid hunter of the late Victorian era, Albert Millican, made a detailed list of his supplies before entering the jungle: "a stock of knives, cutlasses, revolvers, rifle." A mid-nineteenth-century expedition of eight orchid hunters went to the Philippines in search of rare orchids. Within a month one was eaten by a tiger, another was drenched with oil and burned alive, five vanished and were never seen again, and one walked out of the forest with seven thousand orchid specimens.

The peerless British navy combined with the industrial revolution led to an empire of plunder—an empire rooted in the bones of men like J. H. Chesterton. I followed his story to remote trails, sites of forgotten battles, long-abandoned gem mines, and places lit by the glow of phosphorescent orchids.

I had my own share of misadventures. I was lucky to survive a dicey moment outside a cantina in the mining town of Muzo, the very place where the intrepid Millican found his end at the tip of a fourteen-inch shiv over a century ago.

As I followed the footsteps of these bold explorers, my quest seemed to mirror their own, and I realized a strict historical account could never do justice to their thrilling lives. Instead, to better bring to life the incomparable tales of the Victorian orchid hunters, I present the nineteenth-century world through the eyes of two fictional young men, very different in origin and purpose, who face the dangers the actual orchid hunters might have confronted those many years ago.

And perhaps this story can serve as an epitaph, in some way, for our friend who still rests under his small stone by the side of the river.

Rest in peace, J. H. Chesterton.

Timothy Mack
Gozo, September 2004

CHARACTERS

FRENCH

Joseph de Jussieu, *French naturalist*

NORTH AMERICAN

Simon Bidwell, *New England shipowner*
Nathanial "Yankee" Bidwell, *woodsman*

BRITISH CROWN

William Cavendish, *sixth Duke of Devonshire*
Viscount Henry Palmerston, *secretary at war*
William Gunn, *orchid hunter*
Sergeant Angus MacPherson, *soldier*
Darius Acton, *naval captain*

SPANISH CROWN

Lieutenant Rodriquez, *commander, Barranquilla barracks*
Captain Ernesto Rodrigo Marquez, *king's agent / inquisitor*

DUTCH EAST INDIA COMPANY

Abel Veeborlay, *Dutch businessman*
Harold Hull, *businessman*

COLOMBIA
  Jaci, *member of the Tupi tribe*
  Robert and Theresa Sheridan, *Bucaramanga hoteliers*
  Pax, *William Gunn's dog*

SOUTH AMERICAN REBEL PATRIOTS
  General Simón Bolívar, *commander of all rebel forces in New Granada*
  General Santander, *Bolívar's general*
  Captain Daniel O'Leary, *Irishman on Bolívar's staff*

AMAZON
  Cauã, *Native American child*

BRAZIL
  John VI, *king of the United Kingdom of Portugal, Brazil, and the Algarves*
  Carlota Joaquina, *queen of Portugal and wife of John VI*
  Lady Julia Mendoza, *bodyguard and companion to Queen Carlota*

DUKE'S HOUSEHOLD
  Dr. Ferguson, *physician*
  Mrs. Hudson, *assistant gardener's wife*

THE ORCHID

I have discovered a forgotten treasure. Following a trail of clues hidden in ciphered texts, I was led to the corner of a Spanish library where I uncovered the lost chronicle of a Jesuit priest who traveled through South America over one hundred years ago. The priest makes a detailed account of sights that beggar belief: cities the size of Paris, carved from a wild jungle; tribes of fighting women, who are both beautiful and cruel; a river without end. Chief among these marvels is a natural elixir, what the priest calls, "the black orchid." It is a most rare flower, a genuine Holy Grail with the power to cure any ailment.

—Joseph de Jussieu, 1735 diary entry

Joseph de Jussieu wasn't going to leave South America alive. It was a suspicion he'd felt from the moment he'd stepped beneath the forbidding canopy that marked the entrance to the Sacred Land in his search for the black orchid. Now, with his hands tied to the reins of his donkey, her hind legs dangling off the side of the narrow mountain path as his own feet scrabbled for purchase, his suspicion had become a certainty.

"Help me, damn you!" Jussieu cursed the porter who stood back, leery of approaching the side of the path that seemed a touch away from disintegrating in the torrential downpour. The donkey brayed. The stupid, insistent honking competed with the noise of the storm and made it impossible for Jussieu to make himself heard. The servant hesitated, unable to decide whether the donkey or the Frenchman was the bigger ass.

The servant had been with Jussieu for over two and a half decades, ever since the Frenchman's colleagues had returned to Europe and the naturalist remained behind to continue his explorations. The two men had lugged the Frenchman's crates over mountains and down valleys, through swollen rivers and endless forests.

However, when they came to the cursed jungle, the servant had declined to enter. He waited on the border, expecting to never see the Frenchman and his donkeys again.

But Joseph de Jussieu did return from that land, a little paler, eyes a little wilder. Since his return, he had developed the habit of looking over one shoulder and rubbing the small of his back. He carried a canteen that he sipped from, the potion making him visibly more relaxed, the panic in his eyes ebbing for a few hours.

He drove them out of the jungle with a haste that bordered on recklessness. The porter warned Jussieu to wait until the weather cleared—one month, maybe two at the most—but the Frenchman had refused. He insisted on pushing ahead despite the danger of traveling over the Andes in the rainy season. After so many years idling in South America, Joseph de Jussieu was pressing for the coast, for a boat back to Europe, like a man possessed.

Lightning cracked directly overhead, immediately followed by growling thunder. The donkey's hooves pedaled madly, searching for traction. The narrow path crumbled beneath the animal, rocks and clay falling to the bottom of the ravine a thousand feet below. Digging his own feet into the mud of the rain-drenched path, Jussieu felt himself slide toward the edge.

"Grab that rope! Quickly, you fool!" Jussieu yelled after the thunderclap.

Coming to the realization he would be unable to plunder Jussieu's corpse if it were at the bottom of a ravine, the porter rushed to the European's aid.

The wind hurled pea-sized hail against their exposed flesh. Pulling together, they finally managed to haul the flailing animal onto the path. The servant pressed against the cliff face, but Jussieu grabbed the animal's halter. An unquenchable fire burned in the Frenchman's bloodshot eyes.

"Get your beast!" he yelled above the squall. He put his head down and pushed forward. The donkey advanced with hesitant, unsure steps.

But the Frenchman wasn't focused on the treacherous path—he was not afraid of the way ahead. He was gripped by an unrelenting terror, knowing what pursued them from the unknown land.

He again sipped the elixir from his canteen to muffle the cackle of unearthly voices.

As they struggled onward, the porter's sole thought was of the treasure Jussieu had obviously found in the Sacred Land. The squall intensified, the lashing rain blotting out all but the trail at their feet. A flash of lightning abruptly revealed a glade.

The Frenchman stopped. "Yes, yes, I know this place," he muttered to himself, rubbing the small of his back. "Stop!" he cried, whipping around toward the porter. He hastily took a draft from the flask, then pressed his palms to his eyes. When he let his hands fall, his face was calm, his eyes clear.

How could he secure passage home without exposing his invaluable trunks to the thieves in every port? He would have to push his fear aside. "I shall be gone a couple of days," he told the servant. "Wait here for me. Guard the trunks with your life."

As soon as Jussieu disappeared in the driving rain, the servant examined the trunks by the unremitting flashes of lightning. Every box was locked. *They must surely contain the most precious of treasures*, he thought. *Why else would the Frenchman risk so much? He even sleeps with them.*

At the port, Jussieu secured passage aboard a ship bound for Europe. He anxiously awaited the conclusion of the transaction, wishing every moment that he could hurry back to the glade and retrieve his precious trunks. When his business concluded early, Jussieu returned to the glade at last, thanking his good luck. When he entered the clearing, however, he froze, ignoring the rainwater that streamed down his back.

The clearing on the mountainside was empty. The trusted servant, the donkeys, and the trunks that contained his diary and an irreplaceable trove of scientific specimens gathered over the previous decades—all were gone.

He darted from one end of the clearing to the other, circling back again and again until he fell to the ground in frustrated exhaustion. He tore at his hair and wept.

Neither the servant nor the trunks were ever seen again.

Jussieu returned to France from the wilderness where he had just wasted thirty years of his life. Shortly after his arrival, he was committed to an insane asylum on the outskirts of Paris. He would never leave. He died eight years later, alone, trapped in his cell with the memories of his precious trunks, lost somewhere in that impassive green jungle on the far side of the world.

CHAPTER 1

A FRESH START

APRIL 1818: DERBYSHIRE, ENGLAND

William Gunn gaped as the estate of the sixth Duke of Devonshire crept into view of their private coach. Even from across the river and its arched stone bridge, Chatsworth "House" appeared impossibly grand. It could have easily encompassed William's regimental training grounds and housed his entire former regiment, with enough room left over for the servants' quarters, stables, and hunting lodge.

William smiled as he watched his daughter, Sarah, caress the drapery inside the coach, finer than any fabric she'd ever felt. She was so absorbed that she hadn't yet noticed the castle looming outside her window. The look on his four-year-old daughter's face when the duke's luxurious carriage had trundled up to their grimy South London flat—appearing like some kind of inner-city mirage—reassured William he'd done the right thing.

After the war ended, the only lodging they could afford was a flat in a run-down section of London populated mostly by former soldiers and unemployed factory workers. With the English victory at Waterloo and the end of the Napoleonic Wars, thousands of former soldiers returned to England, where they drifted to the larger cities seeking work in the new factories. But many factory jobs had already disappeared, and soldiers found themselves unemployed, injured, and forgotten as they barely survived in the dangerous and squalid slums of every large city.

William was no exception. Endless months of fruitless job hunting had depleted his family's meager savings. He had promised his wife, Miriam, he would never give up Sarah to an orphanage. With a young child and winter fast approaching, William had resorted to his last, desperate measure: he had petitioned his former commanding officer, Arthur Wellesley, the Duke of Wellington and field marshal of the combined European armies, for his assistance in securing a position.

Even though the Duke of Wellington had enthusiastically agreed to help his young aide-de-camp transition back into civilian life, William couldn't help feeling vaguely ashamed that he'd begged his former commander for help; not only that, but he still didn't have the slightest idea of what he'd been called to Chatsworth House to do for the Duke of Devonshire. He'd known only the military life since he was a boy: long marches and searching for a spare bit of dry ground to make camp. He wondered what possible use he would be on an estate. Was he here only as an act of charity? To settle a debt between dukes?

One look at his daughter, however, and any misgivings evaporated. It was the happiest he'd seen Sarah since the passing of her mother six months before.

The drive to the great house seemed to stretch on forever as they rode past fountains and elevated statues and a mock temple to Apollo. William averted his eyes from the main facade, where the windows gleamed in the light of the setting sun like the scales on a dragon. Departing from the coach by the servants' entrance, Sarah and William were met by a smartly dressed young man who acted as if they were one of a hundred father-daughter pairs he had shown inside that day. He admitted them to a foyer lined with coat hooks and bade them wait, before disappearing down a long corridor. Feeling as if they were peering inside a beehive, William and Sarah watched the continuous stream of servants and maids who came and went from the kitchen across the hall.

Oblivious to the activity, a cat slept between the legs of a stool. Sarah bent down and attempted to coax the creature out from the kitchen. Miriam would have told her off for being a nuisance, but William had never had the inclination. Especially now. He smiled as he watched his daughter, intent on the cat, who seemed just as intent on ignoring the child.

"What do we have here? Are you a little mouse?"

Startled, William looked up and saw that the voice belonged to a cook. She stood by the servants' entrance, an empty pail in her arms. She looked to be in her early thirties, about ten years older than William, and had strong forearms and a bluff demeanor. William could tell she was the kind of person who would brook no nonsense from anyone, but now she was smiling at the young girl. Sarah looked up at her, eyes wide. William's daughter solemnly shook her head.

"No? Well, you could be." The cook sighed as she looked at the sleeping cat. "Tom is so lazy we'd have more luck catching mice with a butterfly net. Here, try this." Reaching into one of the pockets of her apron, she pulled out a pinch of herb, and showed the little girl how to hold it out.

Like a sleepwalker, Tom the cat ambled between the legs of the kitchen staff, carried toward Sarah by the scent in her hand. Sarah allowed him to nuzzle her palm as she rubbed his back, causing her feline companion to arch.

"Thank the kind woman, Sarah," William prompted.

Sarah said nothing.

For the first time, the cook looked at the father, who stood awkwardly by the coats. By his strict posture and broad shoulders, he had clearly served in the war.

The cook instinctively dried her hands on her apron and introduced herself. "Mrs. Hudson. You'll be the new man, I expect."

"I'm William Gunn. And I am the new man . . ." William trailed off, hoping Mrs. Hudson might provide him with some clue as to what kind of man he was expected to be on the estate. But instead, she was studying him, with an expression strangely like regret.

William's blond hair was tied tightly back, revealing his smooth clean-shaven face. He was even younger than the last one, Mrs. Hudson thought.

"William Gunn," a solemn voice intoned. The footman had returned, accompanied by a man of unapproachable majesty and unmistakable identity—the head butler. The butler continued his address, "My name is Smythe. If you would." With a gesture no less magisterial than a duke's, he indicated for William to follow him.

William went to collect Sarah, but Smythe stopped him with a word. "Alone. Your daughter will be looked after."

The footman approached Sarah, but Mrs. Hudson had already placed her hands on the girl's shoulders. She smiled easily. "Don't worry, my Annie can look after her."

The footman looked uncertainly to the head butler. Impatient, Smythe nodded and turned on his heel.

William knelt in front of her. "I'll be back soon," he said, stroking her hair away from her face. Sarah turned her face down and mumbled something only her father could hear.

"She can manage without you, Mr. Gunn," Mrs. Hudson said, watching the man with a curious eye. He spoke to his daughter as if he were afraid she was going to disappear. "Go on—it won't do to keep His Grace waiting."

William gave a look of gratitude to Mrs. Hudson and reluctantly followed the butler deeper into the great house. Smythe led William to a pair of broad oaken doors—*This must be the duke's study*, William thought. But instead of showing him in to introduce him to his benefactor, Smythe turned sharply past, continuing further into the house.

"You will be an apprentice gardener." Smythe spoke without looking over his shoulder, expecting William to keep up. "You will see Mr. Turner, our head gardener. He will instruct you in the fine art of tending to greenery." Smythe gestured toward a window. "Our gardens are second to none, and we are constantly making improvements and acquiring new specimens, so you will be kept quite engaged."

William quickstepped to keep pace with the butler while trying to avoid running into him should he change direction, which he suddenly did, leading them both into a service corridor. "Are you sure this is what was assigned for me? When will I speak with the duke?"

From over his shoulder, Smythe shot a frown at William. "When he calls you," he said slowly, as though concerned William might understand less than was desirable for someone employed to hold a pair of gardening shears.

Smythe added as an aside, "There will be other tasks more suitable for you. In time."

"I want to thank His Grace—this means the world to me," William said, suppressing an underlying sense of foreboding he couldn't quite define. This was so much more than he could ever have envisioned. A good job in a good house. A place for Sarah to grow.

Smythe had returned to looking bored. "Turner knows his business, so pay attention and you will be up to speed in no time."

The head butler stopped abruptly, making an about-face. They had come to a door that appeared conspicuously clean. Its handle had been polished to a gleam, clearly by someone desperate for it not to appear what it was: the entrance to the gardeners' shed.

"Remember, Mr. Gunn, this is not a battlefield, this is Chatsworth House." And with that, Smythe departed to return to his own duties, which seemed no less significant than the maintaining of the planets in their orbits.

Uncertain whether it was the battlefield or the great house where the consequences were more grave, William wiped his hand on his pants leg and reached for the door handle.

CHAPTER 2

PORTENT

Seldom, very seldom, does complete truth belong to any human disclosure; seldom can it happen that something is not a little disguised, or a little mistaken.

—Jane Austen, *Emma*

Hearing the door open, Master Gardener Robert Turner looked away from the rake he'd been polishing with a zeal that suggested it was to be used strictly for ceremonial purposes. His mouth formed a scowl that William, frankly, would have been disappointed not to see on the Scotsman's face. The master gardener reminded William of a man he'd served with.

"You're here," Turner said by way of introduction. "On His Grace's direction, you'll begin as an apprentice, which I must tell you is unusual enough, seeing as how it passes over laborer duties." Turner's eyes went wide and he looked pointedly at William, as if to emphasize the irregularity of such a decision. Turner himself had begun at Chatsworth as a laborer, then moved on to apprentice and assistant gardener before finally managing a staff of over two hundred; his bent posture reflected the many hours he'd spent fussing over the extensive gardens.

"But I do suppose you are a bit older, having served our country. And you do have a wee one to feed." Here Turner's grimace deepened, which he may have intended to be a grin.

"Any questions you have, don't be afraid to ask. Remember," the master gardener added tersely, "there are no stupid questions, only the fools who don't ask them. If I'm not available, as I often am not, then ask the assistant gardener, Ben Hudson. Ben's wife is a cook, so he's used to doing what he's told. Ha!"

William flinched at the sound of Turner's laugh, which erupted from the man like a musket shot. After both men had recovered from the gaiety, the old Scotsman continued, "One last thing—be careful who you trust."

Unsure how to respond to such a comment, William simply nodded. Turner paused, seemingly dissatisfied with his new apprentice's reaction, until finally the codger waved his hand, dismissing the former soldier and himself in the same stroke. "Attend to your duties, Apprentice Gunn."

But Robert Turner's gaze followed the young man as he went outside toward the apprentice's shed; then, with a shake of his head and a heavy sigh, the old Scotsman returned to his tools.

William did his best to put aside his doubts as to why the duke had hired him and focused instead on learning all he could about his new position. He was delighted when he was assigned a small home not far from the Hudsons' cottage. The former British officer worked stubbornly to acquire the practical experience he had missed while away at war; William promised himself he would never accept as a given his employment on the estate. He was fortunate to have Ben Hudson, the assistant gardener, for a mentor. Being the father of two young girls, Ben felt kindly toward William, and helped him at every opportunity. Luckily, William found gardening to be something he had a knack for. The work relaxed him, producing a peacefulness he hadn't realized was possible.

William kept Sarah nearby, asking her to never stray too far from where her father worked. Ben told his new charge there were few dangers lurking about the grounds at Chatsworth that a child could fall prey to; William just smiled, and politely but firmly said that he would prefer it if his daughter stayed close, if it was all the same. Ben left it there. William would find someone soon, Ben reasoned, a woman who could be a mother to Sarah. That would settle him.

Ben's youngest daughter, Grace, was overjoyed to have a little girl her own age join the house. They immediately became fast friends, gathering stalks of grass together into small bunches and using them like brooms, playing "kitchen maid" while Mrs. Hudson's eldest daughter, Annie, kept an eye on them. Mrs. Hudson often watched the girls play when she wasn't busy in the kitchen.

One day, Ben was showing William how to trim the hedges on the side of the house near the servants' entrance. William noticed that Annie had ushered the children away from where the gardeners were working. "Why doesn't Annie let the girls play closer to us?"

Ben started to explain, when the sound of a horse in full gallop cut him short. Leaning forward in his saddle, the rider tore up the drive, urging his mount on faster with his heels. The horse's nostrils flared, mouth frothing from exertion. He pulled up short at the main entrance, scattering gravel, and jumped to the ground. A groom seized the reins and held the lathered animal, allowing the rider to rush into the house.

"That's why, lad, it's best to keep the children back a ways. That sight isn't uncommon around here." He held up his hand. "The duke gets a lot of visitors, and it's best not to ask any questions."

A few weeks passed, and with each day William grew more confident and capable. He was helping to fix a fence gate near the big house when a fine carriage arrived that caught his eye. Usually Smythe would ensure that the servants were arrayed in a perfect line to greet arriving aristocrats, but this time there was just the head butler.

A slim young gentleman with a high forehead stepped out of the carriage. He paused to adjust his spectacles before proceeding into the house.

"His Lordship, the Viscount Palmerston," Ben remarked, noticing that his apprentice had put down his shovel as his attention drifted to the new arrival, "that's who that is. Big man in the government, so I've heard. Comes by to see the duke quite often. In fact"—Ben winked—"the missus says he comes to Chatsworth more often than most of His

Grace's lady friends. Old childhood chums, I believe." The assistant gardener let out a deep breath. "Still, a bit strange. But then again," he said with a smile, "no one's paying me to think, are they?"

But perhaps the most peculiar visitor was a rather striking caller who arrived at the estate on a late-June afternoon. For several long moments the silver-haired gentleman with a dark beard had scrutinized Sarah as she played nearby before continuing on his way, careful not to be seen by anyone outside the staff. He hadn't noticed William working in a nearby flower bed.

The other servants deflected any questions William posed concerning the mysterious gentleman or the duke himself.

William waited for that fateful day when the duke would summon him and reveal the real reason he had been hired at Chatsworth. But his employer remained aloof, and William's time in the gardens became more demanding as the days grew longer and the estate moved deeper into summer. Soon his anxiety faded and William relaxed, settling into the rhythms of life on the estate, with its little dramas among the staff. There was the budding romance between a groomsman and a scullery maid; the latest trouble with Porter, the blacksmith, and his horrid wife, who were forever loafing or cheating the rest of the staff. William stopped waiting for the other shoe to drop.

On a quiet summer evening, when the duke had left the estate on one of his frequent absences, Mrs. Hudson was able to join Ben and William outside. They watched the girls play and waved good night to some of the younger staff who were walking into town for a dance. The sun had gone down, but the sky was still illuminated, producing that golden hour which can make the English countryside look like the Mediterranean. Ben and his wife shared a pot of tea while William stared at the beauty that surrounded them. He wondered how it was possible that he could feel so lucky and unlucky at the same time and if everyone felt that way.

Mrs. Hudson glanced at her husband. Taking his cue, Ben coughed and interrupted his apprentice's reverie. "What's your story, soldier? How did you make your way here to Chatsworth?"

"Fraud." William smiled. Somehow, everyone on the estate had already deduced that he had served in the war. He'd attributed that to his being a youngish chap who stood over six feet tall and was both lean and muscular. He was less aware of his bearing, how he moved with the self-assurance and loose grace of a professional soldier, not usual in others his age. William had avoided discussing his time on the Peninsula with anyone; besides, he wasn't much of a storyteller.

"What I mean to say is, how did you catch the duke's eye?"

William shrugged. "I was an aide to the Duke of Wellington; he commended me for my service at Waterloo. I took advantage of his favor and petitioned him for a position outside the service. He must be well acquainted with the Duke of Devonshire, for it wasn't long after when I received my summons to Chatsworth."

Mr. and Mrs. Hudson shared a look. "I suppose we owe you a great debt. If not for you, our Annie would be speaking French."

Sarah had approached while they were talking and wordlessly put herself in her father's arms, letting him hold her. He'd hoped the fresh air at Chatsworth would do her good, but she still tired easily.

William spoke, "I followed my orders and trusted the men above me to make them right. I know my place—whatever is owed, is entirely on my side."

These words seemed to agree with Ben down to his core. He nodded and said, "If you work hard and put your faith in those above you, the good Lord will make sure it all works out in the end."

Mrs. Hudson said nothing.

Sarah turned her face into her father's shirt and coughed. "My head hurts," she said. The coughs deepened, becoming ragged. Suddenly William felt as if the blood had left him; he jumped to his feet, still holding Sarah in his arms.

Ben asked, "Did she swallow an insect?"

"It's not that." William's face was distraught as he studied his daughter. Sarah's lips turned blue as she struggled for breath, deep hacking coughs shook her entire body.

"What is it?" Mrs. Hudson stood to get a better look at the child's condition. "Let me feel her forehead."

Mrs. Hudson furrowed her brow. "She has a fever. I've never seen a fever come on that fast."

"I have." William was grim. "It was the same that took the life of her mother, eight months ago."

His wife, Miriam, had not been the only one to become ill. Sarah, too, had been afflicted by the same sickness, but Sarah had managed to pull through, though her battle had left her in a severely weakened state.

She would have wilted had they remained in the flat in London. William was certain. This desperate knowledge had driven him to beg his former commanding officer for help and seize whatever opportunity the great man could provide. William had hoped their move to Chatsworth would grant Sarah the chance to recover. It had appeared to work—until now.

Putting these thoughts aside, William threw himself into caring for his daughter. He moved Sarah's bed into his room and tried to keep her comfortable.

But despite everything he did, Sarah continued to decline. Several days into her fever, William heard a knock on the door. Opening it, he was greeted by a gust of wind-driven rain. Framed in the doorway was the mysterious silver-haired gentleman whom William had caught staring at Sarah on his way into Chatsworth. Now he stood facing William, water cascading freely down his dark beard in the torrent.

"William Gunn?" the man asked, peering into William's home.

William hesitated, unwilling to let this stranger in.

The man held up his large black bag. "I'm Dr. Ferguson. I was sent by His Grace to attend to your daughter."

CHAPTER 3

EXPERT OPINION

William was overwhelmed, "Doctor, you are most welcome, please come in." He took the doctor's dripping overcoat and led him to the bedroom.

The doctor opened his bag and took out several instruments.

"Hold her steady while I have a look."

He examined Sarah, shaking his head and muttering to himself every so often. The child was agitated and had trouble breathing. Her skin was pale and clammy, and she cried softly as she tried to turn. The doctor had William bring warm water, which he used to administer a potion. After several minutes, Sarah calmed, settling into an uneasy sleep.

"Perhaps it's best if you and I have a cup of tea now," Dr. Ferguson said quietly, laying his hand on William's shoulder, "and let your daughter rest."

Sitting at the kitchen table, the doctor cradled the warm cup gingerly, as if holding a small bird with a broken wing. He looked directly at William. "This is not ague. I believe your wife and daughter share a most unusual condition, typically seen only in the tropics—a malady that is passed from mother to daughter through the blood."

William stared. "How do you know about Miriam?"

Confused, Dr. Ferguson spoke slowly, "The duke contacted me once your position at Chatsworth had been decided. He related the details in your letter to me."

William was stunned. In his letter to Arthur Wellesley, the Duke of

Wellington, he had included an account of Miriam's death and Sarah's condition in the hope it might move the duke to pity. He was proud where his own honor was concerned, but when it came to his daughter's well-being, there was nothing he would not do. He hadn't realized that Wellesley would share the information with the Duke of Devonshire, or that Devonshire would send his own personal doctor to care for Sarah. William's estimation of the aloof nobleman rose.

The doctor hesitated. "You must know, even if Sarah recovers tonight, this illness may return at any time. There is no known cure."

William swallowed and said nothing, doing his best to overlook the doctor's horrible *if.*

Ferguson stayed through the night, and by midmorning had Sarah's breathing under control. Her fever, however, remained high. Again the doctor administered his potions, each appearing to strengthen her a little more.

"It was pure luck and fortune His Grace directed me to stop by. If I had been anywhere else," the doctor said, "I'm afraid this illness would have taken your daughter." He removed two vials of colored liquid from his bag and handed them to William.

"Be sure to give her the amber liquid every hour until sundown today. Then give her the red liquid every other hour tomorrow."

William gingerly placed the medicine on a shelf in the corner.

Ferguson put his bag down. "William, I must caution you. These medicines will only help this time. I'm afraid an attack of this nature may occur again; if so, then there is a very good chance Sarah will not survive it."

When William spoke, his voice was heavy. "What's to be done?"

Dr. Ferguson rubbed his eyes. He was exhausted. "I'll search my library for answers—but the important thing for you is to not give up hope. Your daughter is alive."

Ferguson attempted a smile. "I will return to Chatsworth in a month; I can check on her condition then. In the meantime, you may want to do some reading of your own. A great many cures have been discovered by gardeners, you know."

The doctor left them. Sarah's recovery persisted in the days following Dr. Ferguson's visit. For all the world, she appeared like a healthy,
happy child again.

William could see his wife in Sarah's smallest gestures, in the way she
gently handled a flower or held his hand. Reminders of Miriam no longer
caused his breath to catch in his throat, but now brought a warm smile.
That this beautiful, strong child might be infected with some sort of a rare,
recurring malady from a distant land seemed absurd in the bright sunshine.

For his more experienced gardeners, the duke had made available the
latest volumes on horticulture and herbology from his extensive library.
Mr. Turner gave William access to these beautifully illustrated botanical
volumes, which William studied at every opportunity, intent on learning
as much as he could about his chosen field. He paid particular attention
to those plants which formed the basis of natural cures.

One afternoon, William was tending to some rather fussy exotics,
when the sight of a profusely sweating young laborer running toward
him grabbed his attention. "Mr. Gunn! Mr. Gunn!" the lad shouted.

William recognized the master gardener's grandson. "Whoa, slow
down there, Davy." William felt sorry for the young lad, whom it seemed
his grandfather was hard on, probably to dispel any accusations of favor-
itism. "What can be so blooming important to have you charging around
in this heat?"

Breathless, the boy gasped, "It's Grandfa—" He hesitated. "It's Mr.
Turner, sir, he wants to see you straightaway!"

Sitting at his desk in the master gardener's shed, Mr. Turner stood
when William approached. With him was Dr. Ferguson. William gave
a start at the sight of the physician, who looked like a mortician in his
customary black dress. Before he could blurt out the question that had
been uppermost in his mind since the doctor's departure, Ferguson
shook his head. "I'm sorry, Mr. Gunn, I've failed you—the cure for your
daughter's illness simply does not exist in Europe."

William paused, caught short by the doctor's statement. *In Europe*—where else did Ferguson have in mind?

"However," Dr. Ferguson spoke quickly, sensing that William had already moved ahead of him, "I have met with an expert here at Chatsworth on the matter of tropical maladies and their cures. He believes he may have found an answer."

William was skeptical. "An expert? At Chatsworth?"

"He has traveled widely and studied much on the subject of horticulture—even more than yourself, if Mr. Turner's account of your recent studies is to be believed."

"Aye." Turner puffed up proudly. "Mr. Gunn's progress has not gone unnoticed."

"And he knows of a cure for Sarah?"

Dr. Ferguson pursed his lips. "That's not for me to say. He'll tell you himself."

"Who? Who is it?" William could not stop himself.

The doctor held up a hand. "Save your questions—they'll be answered soon enough. Follow me."

Mr. Turner caught his arm as he passed him. The old Scotsman cocked his head and squinted at William through one eye. "Just mind yourself, lad, and learn all ye can."

Heeding the master gardener's advice, William approached the big house with a mixture of curiosity and trepidation.

He was surprised when Ferguson led him not to an ornate drawing room, but around the house and toward another, far more peculiar building adjoining the estate.

Moderately sized, the front half was of typical whitewashed stone construction; the back half and dome, however, were not the thatched roof and substantial walls one was accustomed to. The walls and sloping roof were made entirely from panes of pale-green glass, held in place by cast iron framing and laminated wood. William tried to spy into the interior of the cottage, but the glass was practically opaque due to its coloring, the condensation, and the mineral buildup.

Ferguson led William into a passage. The door closed behind William, immediately silencing the sounds of the outdoors, and the doctor proceeded to an inner door. On crossing the final threshold, William felt as if he had stepped into another world.

The air was thick with the sickly sweet odor of vegetation in bloom. The glass walls and roof were heavily misted. William removed his jacket to relieve the stuffiness and undid the top button of his shirt, running his hand around his collar. The light had a greenish, submarine quality to it that made him imagine this was what it would be like at the bottom of the duke's fishpond. A riot of color met his gaze: purples, reds, yellows, delicate whites. William sniffed one and fancied he could detect cinnamon and licorice.

Ferguson guided him under the apex of the domed roof toward a table and chairs positioned beneath a large umbrella. Smythe the butler was already there, laying out a setting for tea and scones—for three.

"Ah, William Gunn, at last we meet. I assume you know who I am," said a man lying almost prone in one of the chairs, as if to test if it were possible to be both fully reclined and still remain seated. He had that easy, youthful air which is peculiar to the uncommonly rich. He stretched languidly and stifled a yawn, still holding the newspaper sheet that he had been reading. The others slid off his lap and floated like giant gray snowflakes to the floor around him, barely touching the tiled floor before the butler gathered them up.

"Please take a seat," said William Cavendish, the sixth Duke of Devonshire, to his newest gardener.

CHAPTER 4

THE DUKE

Smythe eased a chair out from the table and looked expectantly toward William Gunn. The duke tried not to smile at the bewildered expression on his apprentice gardener's face. The duke reached into his breast pocket and retrieved a letter, which he proceeded to unfold. William thought he recognized the richly embossed stationery.

When his butler had left, the duke said, "This is your letter of recommendation to me from the Duke of Wellington. Arthur was quite eloquent, which is unusual for a duke." He accompanied this last statement with a wink. "He assured me you're a man who exhibits very desirable qualities on the battlefield." Tapping the side of his nose with a curiously Mediterranean flair, the duke added offhandedly, "Great valor, in fact, on several occasions."

William blurted, "With respect, Your Grace, I was only doing my duty. It was nothing another soldier wouldn't have done in my place."

"I beg to differ. Your mission at Waterloo?" The duke's gaze turned shrewd. "Were you aware that you were not the only rider Wellington sent to warn the Prussian general? He dispatched a man every half hour. Yet only you succeeded in reaching the Prussians and delivering the message."

Dr. Ferguson took his place beside the duke at the table. Cavendish gestured to the open seat. "Would you like tea?" the duke asked William.

In spite of the duke's warmth, William could not suppress the tingling he felt in his gut telling him he was in danger. Ascribing the sensation to his soldier's paranoia, William cautiously took the proffered seat. The tea he declined.

The duke's eyes grew solemn. He said gravely, "My doctor tells me that Sarah's condition has improved, but it is only temporary."

"This is true, Your Grace, but before we speak I-I must thank you," William stammered, "for my position here, and for your permitting your own personal physician to attend my daughter—"

Cavendish waved his hand, grimacing with embarrassment. "Say no more, William. You and Sarah are family here at Chatsworth. Your daughter has quickly entrenched herself as the staff favorite, and according to Turner, you're the least foolish apprentice he's ever had the chore of teaching—which is the Scottish equivalent of singing hosanna, I believe."

He smiled; his expression was open and welcoming. William felt himself relax a degree.

The duke spoke hesitantly. "You must forgive me if I am circumspect—I do not mean to be. Consider it a habit, developed over many years of holding that commodity which other men most value, what they would die for, would kill me to have.

"Information, William," the duke explained. For the first time, the duke was no longer smiling. He studied William. The former soldier didn't blink. When the duke spoke again, he had a glint in his eye. "Mr. Gunn, as a fellow plant enthusiast, I trust you with this information. Very few are privy to what I am about to tell you."

"Nothing you say to me will I repeat elsewhere," said William in an even tone. "You may tell me anything."

"I have recently obtained an interview of incredible value. It took place between a Parisian doctor and a resident of his institution. A 'mad-man,' I believe he is called.

"The poor fellow was named Joseph de Jussieu, and there are records that he was a scientist who traveled and worked throughout South America for decades before returning to his native France a broken man—in every sense of the word. Although he was quite obviously deranged by that time, the details he provides of his journey agree with those of other plant hunters.

"He speaks of an orchid, the only one of its kind, its petals as black as Newcastle coal. This rare specimen is protected by a fierce warrior tribe who keep all outsiders from seeing it, much less obtaining a specimen. I myself have heard rumors of this plant on my travels. Every story mentions the same fabulous quality: the black orchid has the power to cure any ailment."

William shifted in his chair. "A plant, you say?"

"That's not unusual, William," Dr. Ferguson chimed in, detecting the skepticism in William's voice. "As long as there has been sickness, people have searched for plants to effect cures. I have seen evidence in my own practice that for every disease which afflicts the human race there is an antidote, somewhere in nature, which can cure it."

The duke smiled slowly. "Come. Why don't you see for yourself."

Without waiting for a response, the young duke proceeded to stroll about the conservatory, examining his plants as if it were the first time he had seen them.

"Orchids are the elite of the floral kingdom. They possess beauty, a delicate and aromatic fragrance, and a singularity of structure incomparable to any other family of plants.

"Did you know," he continued, "our intrepid plant hunters only recently acquired our first orchid specimen—and quite by accident? Their mistake is turning out to be a most uncommon tropical treasure." While the duke described the conditions favorable to orchids, large drops of condensate plopped to the floor of the sultry greenhouse. William almost felt as if he were in a jungle.

"The well-being of these new plants is a tremendous challenge. There are few in Europe besides myself who are really familiar with their native habitat . . . or their special needs."

"I will do my utmost to care for these specimens, Your Grace," said William, almost reverently, "should your plant hunters return with a specimen of this black orchid, as I fervently hope they shall, for my daughter's sake."

"Ah. Yes." The duke spoke without looking away from the plant he was inspecting. Its leaves were damaged by rot. "My previous man wasn't quite up to the responsibilities of the position, I'm afraid." He felt around the stem of the plant, as though palpating the soil. "I find that whenever you remove an element from its natural environment and place it somewhere foreign, the grip on survival becomes . . . tenuous."

With a single violent tug, the duke uprooted the entire plant. His face a mask of disgust, he let it drop to the tiled floor. "Hence . . ." The duke made an expansive gesture, which William took to refer to the large glass structure that enclosed them, and proceeded on his way as if nothing had happened.

The duke led William across the room and stopped in front of a plant which seemed to be suspended on a piece of bark, its roots exposed to the air. It was crowned with a delicate and beautifully colored blossom, unique in its size and shape.

"Ah, here we are," the duke said. "The crown princess of our collection. We've kept its blooming quiet, at least for the moment. You're the first stranger to see her. She's the first orchid to be domestically flowered in Europe."

The sun behind the flower lit the three stamens like the spokes of a wheel, flaunting colors ranging from light lavender to apricot to peach. Two showy petals jutted from the nexus of the stamen, displaying an inviting dark lavender and delicate pink. Extravagantly large and heavily fringed, the exquisitely scented tropical wonder suffused this corner of the conservatory with a delicate fragrance.

"I want you, William," the duke said, looking evenly at his assistant gardener, "to travel to South America, find the black orchid, and bring it back to Chatsworth."

Before William could raise an objection, the duke added, "Not as a meaningless trophy to rot in my collection—but for your country. You see, with this orchid our doctors can devise a treatment for our troops—your compatriots who are suffering from every manner of malady this world can throw at them." The duke placed his hand on William's shoulder. "Do not think they are forgotten."

William could not meet his gaze. He was in turmoil. He couldn't refuse his benefactor, but he could never leave Sarah. Especially not now that he understood the severity of her illness.

No. For however long his daughter had, he would be by her side.

William's voice was steady when he replied. "Your offer is most kind, and it makes my answer more difficult. But with all due respect and appreciation I must refuse, Your Grace. I cannot leave my flesh and blood. Sarah is all I have, and I'm all she has. No one could care for her as I do, and I gave my word to my wife before she passed. Ask anything else of me, but please, not this."

The duke studied William closely. "No one can blame you, old man. You have done more than your duty for king and country. Entirely understandable."

In the days following his meeting with the duke, William was unable to sleep. He had humiliated the duke by refusing him. To erase the indignity, it was only a matter of time until the duke chose to remove him and Sarah from the estate. Outside Chatsworth, his daughter could never receive the medical care she required.

William tossed in his sleep, questioning his decision over and over. The options left to him were almost too unbearable to contemplate. Work in the mines seemed the only reasonable course. But even when compared to begging on the streets, the mines were hardly a promising alternative. William had heard the stories of miners who had been crushed, drowned, or suffocated; for the lucky ones, the constant grueling labor drove them to an early grave. There was always a need for strong men in Wales, William knew, because Wales had a way of breaking them. Worse still, if he worked in the mines, he would be forced to send Sarah to live with an aunt whom neither of them had ever met.

Yet if dismissed from Chatsworth, he would have no choice.

A week later the summons from Mr. Turner came early in the morning, while William was at work. Usually very direct in his conversations,

Robert Turner was having difficulty looking at his apprentice gardener. William knew the purpose of his summons.

"I'm afraid I have bad news for you," Turner began. "It's unfortunate, but we find ourselves overstaffed at the moment. I fear we must let you go.

"The severance should tide you over for a while. Chatsworth is highly respected—our recommendation will count for something. And it's my understanding you may stay in the cottage for a reasonable period while you look for other accommodations."

William said, "I'm afraid I don't know what to say, Mr. Turner." *It's not like it's unexpected.*

"Aye." The master gardener appeared to age, the lines in his face prominent in the early-morning light, the Scottish brogue more distinct than ever.

"Don't say I didn't warn ye, laddie."

CHAPTER 5

DECISION

William sent a letter to Miriam's older sister, Sally, preparing her for the arrival of her niece. It was hard to figure out how much Sarah understood. He had spoken to her about the move and the train ride they were to take, but he couldn't prepare himself for the moment when he would leave her behind. He didn't know how he would master himself—but he must. For Sarah's sake, and Miriam's memory. It was the best he could do for his daughter.

A knocking at the door stirred William from his reverie—he had no idea how long he had been standing there, holding Sarah's dress; it was the same one she had worn for her journey to Chatsworth. William was surprised when he opened the door and found Dr. Ferguson waiting outside.

"Just stopping by to have a quick look at Sarah," Ferguson said, and brushed past William on his way into the cottage.

"Your daughter appears a little more tired than usual this evening. Her eyes are slightly bloodshot." Ferguson spoke in the way of doctors, making his statements sound like questions.

William said, "Maybe she's a bit worn out from being outside all day—she was playing in the garden as I worked. And I thought the redness in her eyes might be from something that's blooming at the moment."

"Perhaps. But I will err on the side of caution, I think, and give her this extra tonic. I'll be staying at Chatsworth House tonight. Please don't hesitate to find me if anything seems amiss."

"Doctor," William said as he absently brushed the front of his trousers, "I don't know if you've heard, but Sarah and I will be leaving shortly." He added, "It's not our choice."

Dr. Ferguson did not meet William's eye. "I'd heard. I'm so very sorry to hear of your dismissal. I shall miss you both."

William gripped the back of his chair so hard his knuckles were white. His voice broke as he said, "It's not me I'm worried about, Doctor, it's Sarah. While we were here in Chatsworth, I could count on you if something happened. And with so much help from everyone, it got so I could put her condition out of my mind. But out there . . ." William's heaving shoulders betrayed his turmoil.

The doctor's resistance broke—he set down his bag and met the other man's gaze. "William, listen to me. You don't need to leave Chatsworth." He held up a hand to forestall William's instinctive rebuttal. "With Sarah here, I could continue to observe her condition and treat her if the need arises. I know Mrs. Hudson would be more than happy to take her in and raise her until your return. It's not as good as having her father here—but really, William, does a world exist where your daughter can always be by your side? We both know the answer is no. Where are you sending her now? The orphanage? Or to a family who barely knows her?"

"She'll stay with Miriam's sister. It's not what I wanted, but it's better than having her father dead in the middle of a jungle halfway around the world."

"Instead of dead at the bottom of a Welsh coal mine? Is that really so much better, William?"

William's eyes flashed, and for a moment Dr. Ferguson became aware of the imposing figure before him, but then the soldier shrank and returned to his forlorn posture. It had taken a mighty effort for William not to grab the doctor and shake him like a ragdoll. When he spoke, he sounded defeated. "Then damn it, man, what should I do?"

Dr. Ferguson put a comforting hand on his shoulder. "The duke is an understanding man. If you went to him and told him you accept his mission for the black orchid, I'm sure he would accept Sarah at Chatsworth. In fact"—Dr. Ferguson withdrew a slip of paper from his jacket—"I know he would."

"What's this?" William stared at the document.

Ferguson handed it to him. It was a contract. William read the duke's distinctive longhand: *Your daughter will have a nanny and tutor assigned for her care, along with access to the entire facilities of my estate. Mrs. Hudson and her girls can visit Sarah anytime they wish; they will have the run of the house. Should something untoward happen to you—though I am certain it will not—Sarah will be well looked after for the rest of her life.*

The doctor stepped away. "I'll leave you to think. But don't think too long."

William barely noticed the sound of the door closing. He looked again at his packing, and Sarah's dress. Peeking out from one of its pockets was a hint of yellow. Reaching within, William pulled out a daisy. His daughter must have seen William pull the flower from a bed in the garden and hid it in her dress pocket as a keepsake. A reminder of her father, the gardener.

William choked back a sob.

There was no choice. There was only the mission.

CHAPTER 6

THE MISSION

They sat at a small mahogany drop-leaf pedestal table in front of the fireplace in His Grace's wood-paneled library. Smythe understood that the duke required strict seclusion until otherwise indicated. William sat at the table to the right of the duke, awkwardly clutching a glass of claret. Considering what was at stake, William didn't feel at all presumptuous by accepting the powerful aristocrat's offer of a glass of wine.

The duke was still. The silence was broken by the odd crack of wood splitting in the fireplace.

"This black orchid," William spoke first, tentative.

"Yes?"

"It can cure any illness?"

The duke spoke evenly. "So the stories say."

"Then I want my Sarah to get the first treatment."

The duke smiled quizzically, as if delighted by his new friend. "But of course, William," he said. "That is why you were chosen."

He added, "I will give you the details when I'm certain of your commitment, but this task will involve your being away for some six months, at the most."

"Depending on what, Your Grace, if I may ask?"

"On whether you survive—not to put too fine a point on it." The duke spread his arms wide. "But come now, William, we believe in you.

You've been specifically chosen because you have the greatest chance of success. And His Majesty will be eternally grateful."

"His Majesty the King?" William said, finding it hard to believe His Majesty spent his days wondering what William Gunn was up to.

"None other. But I must caution you that everything we discuss from now on is in the strictest confidence, and must not be discussed with anyone—ever. Is that perfectly clear?"

"I don't understand, Your Grace," William said, "are we still speaking about obtaining a plant?"

"There is a little diversion we would like you to undertake first. A rather simple task, actually. You delivered an important message to a general once before—we would merely like you to do this again."

Tapping the side of his nose with an index finger, he continued, "You'll convey a short message to Simón Bolívar on behalf of His Majesty King George.

"His Majesty is willing to quietly encourage discharged British veterans to join General Bolívar's forces, transport those troops to South America, and provide arms, ammunition, and intelligence, all in exchange for Bolívar's support for an exclusive trade agreement with Great Britain. Secreted on your person will be documents to that effect, which you will deliver to the general.

"Do you understand the importance of this, William?"

"I think so, Your Grace. You believe that with my military background I have a fair chance of carrying out this mission."

The duke raised his glass. "You're the perfect person to carry out this task.

"You'll be well trained and will travel as a civilian—a hunter of plants—but officially you will have a commission as a British officer, a captain in the First King's Dragoon Guards—we thought the cavalry fitting."

Somehow, William wasn't filled with confidence.

"We have information that Bolívar will be leaving Angostura. He intends to take the battle to the Spanish on the plains of Venezuela. Therefore, entering New Granada from Colombia will be the safest route for you.

"A specially fitted merchant ship will transport you to the mouth of the Magdalena River. We have contacts there to help you locate Bolívar. Once you reach the general, you will deliver His Majesty's documents. Then you will be free to search for our black orchid."

The duke made it all seem simple and straightforward. The Magdalena River, Angostura, plains of Venezuela—hell, William barely knew where South America was. But he only said, "I believe you mentioned the doctor will continue to see my daughter and that Mrs. Hudson will look after her while I'm away?"

"Of course. I have no children of my own, William—Chatsworth is my family, along with everyone who calls Chatsworth home."

The duke refilled William's glass. "Any questions, Captain Gunn?"

"Just one: Exactly who is this Bolívar fellow?"

CHAPTER 7

ℙORT & ℬRANDY

In a quiet corner of the smoking room at Chatsworth, the Viscount Palmerston, secretary at war, had brook trout, plum pudding, and a hock. Opposite the Viscount sat William Cavendish, the sixth Duke of Devonshire, with a kidney pie and claret.

Palmerston set down his wineglass. He looked over his spectacles. "Are you trying to start another war?"

Palmerston—known as Henry or "Pam" to his friends—was a young man with a high forehead and a weak chin. Behind spectacles perched on an Irish nose peered a pair of dark-brown eyes.

The duke chewed, thinking. "Bloody place is going downhill, Henry. Give me that French chef we had—what was his name? Bernard? Miss him, even if he was third estate." He cocked his head and stared absentmindedly, as if examining the molding on the mantelpiece. "Wonder if he managed to keep his head through all that?"

Not to be distracted, the viscount leaned forward, looking intently at his friend as he asked, "Hart, what do you know that you haven't told me?"

The Duke of Devonshire smiled at Palmerston's use of his childhood nickname. The glow of the coals in the low-burning fire brightened with a draft from the entryway. "The Spanish empire," the duke said, tapping the outside of his nose with his right index finger, "is falling apart. Specifically, their empire in South America."

He examined his fork closely. "I understand Bolívar's recent freeing of the slaves has contributed immensely to his popularity. Did you know they're calling him the 'Great Liberator'? South America without the dons represents *such* a magnificent opportunity."

Palmerston spoke carefully, "The Spanish are our ally, and we cannot conspire or act against them."

"Of course not. And yet"—the duke paused to wipe his fork with a napkin—"our national interest now demands that we move away from this relationship. Quietly."

Palmerston studied his inscrutable friend. He'd known the Duke of Devonshire since boyhood, and yet, if asked, he would not have hesitated to say he was better acquainted with the lady who served tea in Whitehall. "What do you have in mind?"

The duke paused as he carefully folded his napkin, hiding the stain he'd left behind. "We should make Bolívar an offer known only to him: We promise discreet British support for his rebellion—men, military supplies, intelligence—and in return, he will grant us special trade status. Effectively, we will have won ourselves an entire continent without shedding any blood. That should be popular among your constituents." The duke couldn't help it if his smile turned into a sneer. Palmerston knew his friend's political views—William Cavendish thought the country had gone to the dogs after the signing of the Magna Carta.

Palmerston looked doubtful. "But what can we offer to stop those grasping Americans from taking what Spain leaves behind?"

"I have it in good confidence President Monroe is contemplating a prohibition on any further foreign interference or intrusion into their hemisphere."

Palmerston scoffed, "The British navy is master of the seven seas."

"Precisely. Without our navy, Monroe's prohibition will have no teeth. We offer our navy to prevent intrusions into their affairs; in return, they will recognize our preferential trade rights in South America. When Bolívar wins, we not only gain access to an incredible market, but we strengthen our ties to our American cousins. And possibly prevent another war."

Palmerston took off his glasses to rub his nose. "You realize, Hart, that if we're not successful in obtaining new markets quickly and peacefully, there will be riots in the streets—and not just in Britain."

"I am very aware that could easily lead to armed conflict across three continents and an ocean," the duke said. "With carnage the like of which has never been seen before. It will make the Peninsular War look like a Sunday stroll—if we hesitate. Which is why we must put our piece in play *now*."

They paused. Smythe shimmered into the room—the duke's other guest had arrived. With a flick of his hand, the duke dismissed his butler.

The viscount was the first to break the silence. "Bolívar is fighting a war to the death in a wild land. Everything we've worked for is at risk—who in God's name will you send to deliver our message?"

"No need to worry yourself with that detail, Henry," the duke replied impassively, watching the door as his latest guest entered. "We've found the perfect man for the job." He looked up. "Tell us, Dr. Ferguson, how did you convince William Gunn to accept the mission?"

Dr. Ferguson took his seat beside the secretary at war. He accepted his customary snifter of brandy from Smythe. "I only told him the truth. Mr. Gunn would do anything for his daughter." The doctor looked away to study the fire. "Tell me, Your Grace, do you always use family men?"

Cavendish yawned. "Nearly always, my dear doctor. Relates entirely to motivation. They have reason to stay focused on the mission—'preservation and return,' I call it. A family man exists to take care of those who are close to him."

The duke shook his finger at Ferguson. "Don't sell yourself short, Doctor," he said, "that Jussieu fable tipped the scales significantly in our favor."

Ferguson put down his glass, a thoughtful frown marking his face. "I would say so, Your Grace, but rest assured, that was no fable."

Palmerston scoffed. "You mean that black orchid he's always going on about? Why, it's just another jungle myth: fabulous treasure guarded by an immortal beast, no one ever returns—all that rubbish."

Dr. Ferguson spoke respectfully, "As you know, the doctor who served the duke's father related a similar story to me, and begging Your Grace's pardon, he *was* quite convincing."

The duke responded brusquely, "No matter. We had to be flexible. Time is pressing." His gaze hardened. "Do you understand me, Doctor?"

Ferguson paused, uncrossing his legs as he did so. "As I mentioned some time ago, Your Grace, once a child experiences the serious fever and shortness of breath, a recurrence is highly likely, and that episode will almost certainly be fatal."

The duke carefully sipped his own drink. "When?"

"Anytime. Ten years. Tomorrow."

The duke frowned, irritated. "That certainly is a complication."

The doctor was aghast. "You gave your word the girl would be cared for."

Cavendish waved his hand, dismissive of the doctor's sense of propriety. "You can be very middle class at times, Ferguson. It's so tedious."

Ferguson continued to stare at the duke in a manner that Cavendish found most disagreeable. The duke sighed. "No, good Doctor, of course we will not turn her out. We have a signed agreement. She must be kept at Chatsworth."

Palmerston leaned forward to offer an encouraging word, "You realize, Doctor, there's a knighthood waiting in acknowledgment of your outstanding service. Along with a permanent position at Trinity, should you ever decide to retire. All confidential, naturally."

Dr. Ferguson nodded distractedly, and stood, glass in hand, to approach the fireplace. He stared into the flames as if attempting to discern an image at a great distance and said a prayer for the poor fool they had just sent to his certain demise. "God help William Gunn," the doctor breathed into his brandy, soft enough so that neither of the other two men could hear him over the crackling of the fire.

CHAPTER 8

ᴅEPARTURE

After nearly four months of training and preparation, it was time for William to depart Chatsworth—and Sarah—for South America. William had missed Sarah's constant companionship while he'd trained for the mission, but now he'd be facing six months overseas. Or, he might never return. Saying goodbye to his daughter had been the most difficult thing he had ever done—it had taken more courage than facing enemy fire. He had woken her up to say goodbye, but she had insisted on stumbling after him, following him outside the house and up to the coach that would take William to the port, still rubbing sleep from her eyes.

"Everything will be fine. I will be fine," William explained to Sarah. He put on a brave face. "I will return with the medicine to make you well again." Sarah clung to William's neck until Mrs. Hudson and Annie gently took her, then she held tightly to the older woman and softly sobbed.

"I'll be back soon," William said, holding out his hand in a solemn wave, before stepping into the coach.

When the duke's coach was at the end of the long gravel drive, William shifted in his seat so he could catch a last glimpse of his daughter. She was still in Mrs. Hudson's arms, waving slowly, like a queen. Watching Sarah disappear over the curve of the arched bridge, William felt regret, because he knew that his last words to his daughter had been a lie.

The trip to the port of Bristol took several days by coach. William's resolve to meet the great challenges ahead of him increased with each passing mile. At the busy seaport, the coach came to a stop at a rather small brig secured to the dock. William climbed the gangway of the *Voyager*, carrying a trunk which held his clothes and personal articles. He wore a silver locket around his neck—inside were locks of hair from both Sarah and Miriam.

The seaman manning the gangway called out, "Ahoy, be you Captain Gunn?"

"I am," William said. He added quietly, "But for the duration of this voyage, it's Mr. Gunn, if you please."

"Welcome aboard, Mr. Gunn." The old salt removed the clay pipe from his mouth. "The name's Tom; I'm the quartermaster. I'll find some hands to stow your gear. Will you be needing your kit during the voyage?"

"Other than my trunk, I'll just need this," he said, pointing to the box that contained his firearms. "It needs to be stowed high and dry."

Tom returned the pipe to his mouth and hooked his free hand into the waist of his canvas pants. "Jimmy, the ship's boy, will come by and help you learn yer way around. I'll see you to yer cabin now, if you'd like." Tom bent over to pick up William's gear.

"No need for that, but much thanks just the same." William hefted his trunk onto his shoulder. In a waterproof tube, he had a writ of passage signed by His Majesty and maps of New Granada, Peru, and Brazil. He would finish his outfit by obtaining orchid-shipping supplies in South America.

Tom said, "You're quite the sturdy fella. We could always use another strong back on deck."

"If I can be useful, I'm always willing to lend a hand."

On the way to William's cabin, Tom explained that this ship typically carried several commercial passengers in addition to its cargo. In fact, one of their paying passengers for this voyage was traveling to the same port in South America as William: a Mr. Hull. "He's in the trading line, he is. A civilian type of gent," Tom said with a look of distaste.

After depositing his trunk, William made his way aft toward the stern, feeling confined by the low overhead so common to smaller ships. He saw a doorway polished to perfection; this had to be the captain's cabin. He knocked and hoped he hadn't marred the finish.

"Enter," a voice called from within. William turned the latch and saw a man who couldn't have been much older than himself, with a shock of red hair, a sun-freckled face, and serious green eyes. The captain had taken off his uniform coat and rolled up his sleeves. He held his quill pen as if looking for the best plan of attack on a desk covered in stacks of papers.

"Welcome," said the captain, "I'm Darius Acton."

"Sir, I'm William Gunn, captain in the First King's Dragoon Guards."

"So, you're Captain Gunn—or shall I say 'Mr. Gunn' for our voyage?"

"You're correct, Captain. I see I'm expected."

"Indeed. In addition to my orders, I've been informed as to your specific needs. I've only advised those members of the crew who need to know. To most of them you are a plant hunter headed to the interior of New Granada. We'll be carrying a few commercial passengers to supplement our disguise as a merchant vessel. To avoid arousing suspicions, we'll make regularly scheduled stops in the islands on the way. Has the quartermaster shown you to your cabin?"

"Yes, sir."

"My orders include ensuring you receive seamanship and naval warfare instruction while you're on board. Since most of your nautical activity will be coastal in nature and you have limited time with us, we'll focus on near-shore maneuvers."

Acton continued, "Once we reach South America, I'll be your contact for a short while." He hesitated "If you don't mind my asking, when we arrive in Barranquilla, what are your immediate intentions?"

"I'm in the private employ of the Duke of Devonshire, to acquire a most rare specimen for his collection of orchids."

Acton held William's gaze a moment longer before smiling and shaking his head. "I wish you luck with that, Mr. Gunn. Where you're going, I have seen far more . . . *impressive* men disappear. It's a lawless place, you understand?"

But William did not take the captain's bait. He questioned Acton in return, "How many of the men that you've taken to South America have returned?"

"One," the captain said matter-of-factly, "and that man lay on the dock at Santa Marta wrapped in a bloody sheet under a cloud of flies."

SOUTH AMERICA

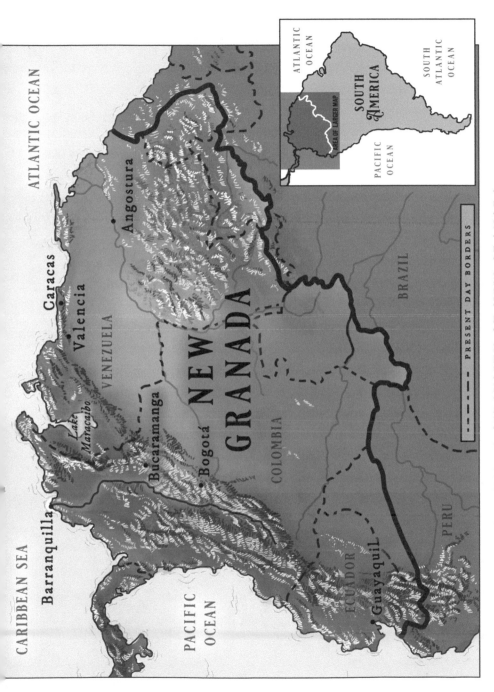

SPANISH VICEROYALTY OF NEW GRANADA

CARIBBEAN SEA

ATLANTIC OCEAN

Barranquilla

Caracas

Valencia

Angostura

PACIFIC OCEAN

Lake Maracaibo

VENEZUELA

Bucaramanga

NEW GRANADA

Bogotá

COLOMBIA

BRAZIL

ECUADOR

Guayaquil

PERU

- - - - - PRESENT DAY BORDERS

ATLANTIC OCEAN

SOUTH AMERICA

SOUTH ATLANTIC OCEAN

PACIFIC OCEAN

AREA OF LARGER MAP

LATE EIGHTEENTH CENTURY, MUZO EMERALD MINE
CENTRAL COLOMBIA, SPANISH VICEROYALTY OF NEW GRANADA

Tired at the end of a long, hot day, Victor Martínez, manager of the Muzo emerald mine, sat in the shade of a tree waiting for Garcia, the company representative. Garcia was on his way back from his "tour" of the pit—in reality, a carefully curated journey arranged by Martínez and his assistant, Diego, to hide from the company everything they didn't want to be seen.

It was hard enough managing a mine with six hundred thieving bush peons and two dozen bored, drunk soldiers; now Martínez had to contend with this horse's ass from Bogotá watching his every move. So long as he received his quota in gems each month, Garcia would be happy.

A figure strayed in front of the setting sun and cast a shadow over the mine manager. "Do you have a drink?" Garcia had returned and was clearly suffering in the dank tropical heat.

"Of course, sit down. I'll have something brought." Martínez raised his hand, and a young Indian boy who had been standing nearby ran off.

"Where's your guide?" he asked apprehensively, noticing that Diego was nowhere to be seen. It wasn't like his assistant to neglect his duties.

Garcia wiped his face with a wet handkerchief, not accomplishing much of anything. "He was called to the pit, so I made my own way back. It's baking out there."

Shouting came from the mine. Martínez jumped to his feet and hurried toward the commotion, followed closely by his guest.

A crowd of laborers had gathered on the narrow working terrace about a third of the way from the top. No one was working. The mine manager's hand drifted to the pistol on his belt—it didn't appear to be another insurrection, but it was odd the way the shift supervisors and the workers stood idle, gawking at a lone man still working in their midst.

Diego was digging into the shale face with his bare hands. Suddenly he stopped. He stood and held something aloft but was too far away for Martínez to recognize what it was.

Garcia said, "What could he be so excited about? It's too damn hot to get excited about anything."

But Martínez didn't move; he waited for Diego as he made his way to the top of the pit.

Diego ran to the last ladder. He awkwardly climbed the rungs with one hand, clutching the object tightly with the other. Finally at the top, he rushed to Martínez, where—unable to contain his excitement any longer—he opened his fist and revealed what he had found.

"*¡Madre de Dios!*" Victor Martínez breathed.

In the palm of his assistant's hand, sparkling in the last rays of the setting sun, sat the largest uncut emerald in existence.

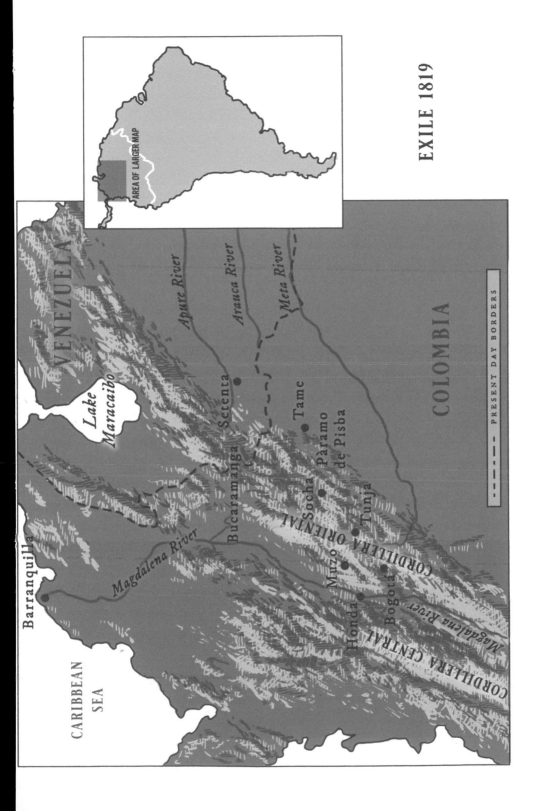
EXILE 1819

CHAPTER 9

XILE

I have loved justice and hated iniquity;
therefore, I die in exile.

—Pope Gregory VII

1819: FOOTHILLS OF THE CORDILLERA ORIENTAL

Nate woke slowly, his mouth cotton-dry, his mind fuzzy. He shook his head, hoping to drive away the dizziness.

His back hurt. Must have been a hell of a night.

He rubbed the sleep out of his eyes, raised himself on his elbows, and immediately sank back into the softness of an overstuffed bed. Where the hell *was* he?

He looked up. The early-morning light revealed a gentleman with a rather severe countenance staring down at him, one gloved hand clasping the hilt of a drawn saber, the other holding a plumed hat of some sort.

A painting.

Good thing, or he'd be in serious trouble.

A small movement drew his attention to the attractive woman in bed beside him. Her ebony hair almost covered the white pillow on which she was resting. Although her eyes were closed, he knew she was awake, partly by the small smile on her lips, but mostly by the movement of her hand under the sheets.

"Sorry, darling," he said, the previous evening's romp coming back to him, "but Don Fernando and José Antonio are due back today, and I don't think it would do for your husband to find me warming his bed."

"How about warming his wife?" she purred.

He was growing hard again under the heat of her hand. Knowing they didn't have time for this, he drew her hand away. Gently kissing her palm, then her wrist, he placed it back on her stomach.

"You're no fun," she said, her satisfied smile brightening, showing she felt exactly the opposite.

"My back tells me we had plenty of fun last night," he said. Then under his breath he muttered, "From what I can remember." In the future, he'd have to be more careful about how much of the local aguardiente he drank.

In his midtwenties, tall and lean, Nathanial Yankee had straight dark hair that was pulled back and braided tightly, like that of the Wampanoag warriors who had befriended him as a youth. His merry, sky-blue eyes were set in a rugged face burnished bronze from constant exposure to the outdoors.

She said sleepily, "You know how Fernando loves to show off to the llanero officer everything his plantation has to offer—including his mistress and her sister. I don't expect them here until this afternoon." She emphasized this last point by throwing the sheet back.

His breath caught in his throat.

With slightly parted lips, she wet her fingertips and ever so softly rubbed her nipples, bringing them erect as she looked at him. Then she took his hand and brought it between her thighs. She whispered, "Not until *late* afternoon."

He found himself stiffening. *Oh, what the hell.* He leaned over, and her arms encircled his neck, drawing him to her.

The evening was darkening as Nate Yankee and Colonel José Antonio Páez rode away from the plantation, followed closely by the colonel's manservant, Pedro Camejo.

"You are playing a dangerous game, my friend," Páez warned. "Every woman you sleep with thinks you will come back with this fabulous emerald you tell them about—'El Jefe.' El Jefe, my ass. Ha! They wind up with glass beads and a promise."

Nate replied, "Excuse me, sir, but you and Don Fernando just spent two nights frolicking with his mistress and her sister."

Páez took no offense and even chuckled. He was the leader of the llaneros, seasoned riders who made up most of the cavalry in Bolívar's rebel army. They were known for their fierceness in battle and sported scraggly beards and long hair. "This is true," he said, before adopting a more serious tone. "I don't want to ruin a good thing. You know this man, he trusts you, and we very much need the supplies he has pledged. Don't forget, Señor Yankee, the general values your skills as a forager and scout."

Frontiersman Nathanial Yankee had arrived in South America almost a year earlier. He had chosen the revolution in New Granada as the place to make his fortune, believing opportunities could be found in such turmoil, at least for a resourceful man like himself. He had a hunch, however, that time was running out on this particular racket. Besides, he would never acquire a fortune by trading gems—the key to wealth in this country was in its soil. His plan was to gain an audience with Bolívar, who promised generous land grants to the foreign soldiers of fortune under his command.

Páez rode silently for a short while. Then he said, "We are a passionate people, you know."

"You can say that again," said Nate, rubbing his sore back.

Both men laughed, Páez slapping his thigh the way he did when he was genuinely amused.

He leaned toward Nate conspiratorially. "The general has something of great importance he wants to tell us." He added quietly, "It had better be good, because the Spanish are kicking our asses."

Páez spurred his horse and Nate followed. They rode hard across the savanna toward the Arauca River; their destination was a meeting in the abandoned village of Setenta.

Patriot General Simón José Antonio Bolívar had been leading a revolution against the Spanish empire since 1813. However, a well-equipped army led by the Spanish General Pablo Morillo had recently driven Bolívar's army west, pinning them here, against the foothills of the Andes. Morillo could wait while they starved during the lean winter months, and then finish them off at his leisure. The revolution was hanging by a thread.

Nate and Páez rested little and ate less. It was not uncommon for llaneros to be in the saddle from well before sunup until long after dark.

They arrived in Setenta on a wet May afternoon after a week of riding. Nate was surprised by the meager forces assembled there. He had expected the main body of Bolívar's army to be more impressive. Many of the soldiers were barefoot and armed only with pikes and lances. How could these men hope to defeat the Spanish army in Venezuela, which included mounted dragoons and experienced Peninsular War veterans equipped with the latest muskets and artillery?

Páez teased, "Are you surprised, my Yankee friend? Expected to see an honor guard, perhaps? I'm afraid you won't find many ladies to entertain in this hole. You'll have to stick to chickens, if there are any about."

They pulled up their mounts at a ruined cottage. The junior officer and soldiers who were milling about came to attention. An enlisted man who stood barefoot in the muck took their horses.

Moving with the confident fluidity of a seasoned frontiersman, Nate followed the colonel through the opening where the front door used to be. The little cottage was filled with Bolívar's most trusted captains.

Páez roared a welcome that was answered by a chorus of similar greetings and accompanied by embraces and backslapping from his fellow officers. Fighting a guerrilla campaign, Páez's llaneros had seen the greatest success of any of them against Morillo.

Feeling out of place, Nate disappeared into the gloom at the back of the room. He leaned against the fragile back wall of the old hut and pulled his broad-brimmed hat low, trying to be as inconspicuous as possible. Bolívar was late.

While waiting for the general to arrive, tensions built as opinions were aired and strategies debated as to what Bolívar would say. The smells of rotting straw and sweat mingled in the damp air. The constant rain spilled through large holes in collapsed sections of the roof, ensuring the assembly remained sodden. There were no tables or chairs; the officers argued while standing, or sitting on the bleached skulls of oxen.

What had struck Nate as a bright idea at the time—getting paid to put his wilderness skills to use foraging supplies for Páez's llanero army—was beginning to look pretty dim. They hadn't been paid in months, were running low on supplies, and it never stopped raining. And he had yet to see General Bolívar, even from a distance.

To make matters worse, come spring, the Royalist army from Spain under the veteran General Pablo Morillo would be able to cut them to shreds.

Nate hoped the Great Liberator had another miracle up his sleeve.

Suddenly the room quieted. General Simón José Antonio Bolívar had arrived.

Somehow the general managed to look like he had just stepped off a dance floor. He was dressed in a dark-blue jacket with gold braid and red epaulettes, his spotless uniform betraying no evidence of days of hard riding through pouring rain over muddy ground.

As Bolívar turned, several strands of hair escaped their careless confinement. His dark and penetrating eyes hinted at great intelligence and passion.

"Gentlemen," he began with a smile, "thank you all for coming. It is truly unfortunate General Morillo could not supply us with more favorable accommodations for our meeting."

Though Bolívar was not tall or physically imposing, he had a dignity of manner and a sophisticated military bearing that commanded attention.

He paused, looking up at the sagging roof. "But perhaps in the near future we will not have to rely so much on his Spanish hospitality." Hoots and laughter showed him that his officers' spirits had not flagged.

When they quieted, Bolívar continued. "We have fought for over ten years to wrest control of our country from the Spanish. We have had many successes, but since the arrival of Morillo's army we have not been able to secure a decisive victory."

The general looked around the assembly. "And for some reason, our once fierce caudillo friends in the north have become afraid to venture out of their strongholds to challenge the Royalists." It seemed his gaze lingered on Nate for just a heartbeat.

"Every day we run lower on food and supplies. If we stay here, with winter rains coming, fever and sickness will deplete our forces further. And when the dry weather does come, we will be trapped between Morillo's army and the mountains in the west. By then he will have gathered his strength and will take us apart, piece by piece."

Murmurs of protest and restless movement greeted this image of impending doom.

"Or," he said, raising his voice, "we can do the impossible."

The room fell silent.

"There." He flung his arm out, pointing to the west. "*That* is where we will go."

Confused stares and furrowed brows met this pronouncement.

Then Bolívar drew out his saber and directed it around the room. His voice rose even higher as he proclaimed, "We will not only do the unexpected, we will do the *impossible*. We will cross the mountains into New Granada."

Once again, he drew their attention toward the distant peaks, this time with his sword. The Andes Mountains formed a six-thousand-mile rampart down the western edge of South America, where the altitude varied so extremely that perennial snows and bone-dry deserts lay just a few miles from each other. Bolívar roared, "We shall go over the highest pass in the Andes and attack the Spanish where and when they least expect it—we shall seize the viceregal capital of Bogotá from those vile bastards!" His voice reached a crescendo. "And in one bold stroke we shall break the Royalist power in America *forever*!"

Nate was spellbound. At that moment, there was no question in his mind that Bolívar was a visionary—either that, or he was insane. Crossing the thirteen-thousand-foot-high Páramo de Pisba pass into New Granada would exceed both Hannibal's and Napoleon's crossing of the Alps, which had occurred at much lower elevations and in milder seasons.

Páez was having none of it. He stood and shouted, "You're mad! First you'll have to swim across the flooded plains just to get to the mountains. If you don't drown, then you'll freeze to death. No one crosses those mountains in winter." He sat and said dismissively, "My llaneros will have none of it."

Neither Bolívar nor his other commanders were offended by the llanero officer. With his unyielding support in the past and countless victories over the Spanish, Páez had earned the right to speak his mind.

"José Antonio," Bolívar said calmly. "This is precisely why we are going to be successful. It is inconceivable to the Spanish that we will do this. They will be totally unprepared."

Colonel James Rooke, an Anglo-Irish officer, was the first to stand. "Anywhere you lead, my General"—he drew his sword with a flourish—"I will follow."

Prompted by the show of loyalty from the foreign officer, the rest of Bolívar's commanders stood and, one by one, pledged their support for the plan. They would follow Bolívar anywhere.

In the end, even Páez relented and supplied Bolívar with a volunteer cavalry division commanded by his fiercest lieutenant, Juan José Rondón. While Bolívar would attempt to enter New Granada with the main army, Páez agreed to keep Morillo's forces occupied in Venezuela.

With that, the meeting was over. Colonel Páez called from across the room, "Nate, maybe you want to go with Juan José and see some mountains for a change? Maybe earn yourself a piece of our land."

Nate felt uncomfortable with the attention he was now receiving.

"This is the gringo I told you about, General," Páez called to Bolívar. "A good forager, but watch him around your women."

"We would be happy to have him join us," the general said, perhaps a little too quickly for Nate's liking.

"Are you certain, José Antonio?" Nate asked Páez. He was wary; this felt too much like a setup.

"Sure. I can spare you." Páez gazed toward the Andes. "My llaneros will need you if they're to have any chance in those mountains."

CHAPTER 10

THE NEW WORLD

The night before they arrived in South America, Captain Acton asked William to dine with him in the captain's cabin to mark the end of the voyage. When they had finished their meal that evening and the steward had cleaned the table, they shared a bottle of port. The captain unbuttoned his shirt collar.

He said, "I believe I have information which concerns you. Do you remember the gentleman who boarded in the West Indies?"

William was puzzled. "You mean the London coffee merchant?"

"The very one. Well, last evening I had him along to dine with a couple of the other passengers who recently boarded. It seems our gentleman merchant recognized your companion, Mr. Harold Hull."

Acton's tone made William sit up.

The captain continued, "In addition to his other trading activities, our Mr. Hull is somewhat notorious on the continent as a plant hunter and collector. I've been told he has a reputation in these parts as a conniver who will go to any length to get a leg up on his rivals. Rumor has it he's not above hiring local thugs to take out a competitor."

The realization struck William like a direct hit from a blunderbuss. A confidence man had taken him in.

He reflected on the many pleasant conversations he'd had with Hull during the uneventful crossing. William had been careful not to reveal any information related to his mission to deliver the duke's message to Bolívar. Hull, however, had been able to patiently extract some details relating to William's hunt for orchids. It wouldn't be difficult for a man who was familiar with the region to deduce William's route.

The duke had stressed to William the sensitive nature of this work. He realized his lapse in judgment could jeopardize the mission—and Sarah's life. He felt a complete fool.

"I'd been told you knew how to handle your affairs," Acton said with just a trace of scorn. "Just make damn sure nothing happens to Mr. Hull until he's left my ship. Good night, Captain Gunn."

William thanked Acton and went to bed that night grateful for some of the more primal skills he had picked up while serving His Majesty.

Still some miles from land, William noticed the silt-laden coffee-colored waters of the Magdalena River swirling in the Caribbean.

A screaming host of pelicans welcomed the ship as they arrived at the bay of Sabanilla. There was a single wooden pier. It was small and weathered, suitable only for shallow craft. Behind the ivory-bright sand beach was a tangle of scrubs and twisted dwarf pine trees. Vultures circled high overhead. The odor of silt and rotting vegetation competed with the salt-laden ocean breeze.

William remained on deck as the *Voyager* anchored. He would have to be on his guard. This was a lawless place—and already he had an enemy. He cursed himself for his carelessness and wished he had some indication of where Hull would sneak off to. He had honored Acton's wish not to spill the blood of a passenger who had been promised safe passage, but he knew the con man would be impossible to track once they made landfall.

Several men came out to unload the ship. One manned a small boat tied up to the pier. Two others waded out to a skiff anchored close to shore. A skeletal pig chased after them to the water's edge.

Tom the quartermaster was waiting for William as he left the ship.

"William, I'm sorry to see ye leave, but I have a parting gift. Ye'll be wanting to stop this evening in the Hotel de San Martín." The old quartermaster gave a conspiratorial wink. "Captain Acton said to tell ye it's a favorite for orchid hunters."

William pressed a wad of notes into the old sailor's hand. "Much thanks, Tom—for everything. And with the grace of God, I'll be seeing you again."

He was anxious to get on with his mission. Whatever time was left for Sarah was quickly running out.

CHAPTER 11

BOLÍVAR

Slavery is the daughter of darkness: an ignorant people is a blind instrument of its own destruction.

—Simón José Antonio Bolívar

The sun set behind the Cordillera Oriental, the easternmost range of the Andes Mountains running through Colombia. A damp chill crept over the ruined village and settled among Bolívar's army. The men grouped around small fires, drying their soaked belongings as best they could. Seen from above, the flickering lights of their campfires resembled a multitude of fireflies.

They laughed and played cards. Behind the jokes and gambling was the unspoken fear of men who had survived the flooded llanos and were now going to attempt to cross the towering peaks of the Andes.

Nate sat alone. Having realized what he had committed to, he was not exactly in the mood for the endless card games and nervous joking. It wasn't that he was overly afraid for his own safety—as a wilderness expert, his chances of surviving the journey were better than most. However, for many others it would mean certain death—and he wasn't ready to let these ill-prepared troops get him killed up there.

If he waited until the men turned in and the campfires burned low, it wouldn't be difficult to make his way past the sentries.

"Private Yankee?" a voice spoke behind him with an Irish lilt.

"Who's asking?" Nate eyed the tall ginger-haired stranger with the round, beardless face. He looked to be about the same age as Nate.

The officer held out a silver flask. "Mind if I join you?"

"Suit yourself." Nate accepted the flask and shifted to make room on the moss-covered log, wondering what the man could possibly want with him.

The officer sat mindfully, adjusting the scabbard of his saber and careful not to soil his uniform with any campfire grime. Nate took a draft of the Irishman's spirits, the joyous liquid scorching his throat and spreading its fire throughout his body.

The officer chuckled as Nate rubbed the water from his eyes. "I'm told it's an acquired taste." The stranger matched him with a serious drink of his own—without the drama—then raised the flask a second time. He wiped his mouth with a white linen handkerchief.

Nate grinned at the Irishman's fussiness.

"My dear grandmother, God rest her soul, always said, 'You must look the part, Daniel.' Advice I took to heart." He replaced the cap and set the flask on the ground between them. He stretched his legs toward the campfire and offered his hand. "Daniel Florence O'Leary."

Nate had heard of this man: O'Leary fought with the Albion Legion, one of Bolívar's units composed mostly of British and Irish troops, mainly Napoleonic War veterans. O'Leary had distinguished himself and risen through the ranks of the army to eventually become the personal aide-de-camp to Simón Bolívar. Aside from his reputation as a fighter, O'Leary was known for being especially devoted to Bolívar. Anything Nate said to him would be repeated to the general.

Nate hesitantly grasped the outstretched hand. "Nathanial Joseph Yankee, but I'm called Nate."

The officer said, "Times are frequently tough in Ireland, Nate, and we Irish are often forced to leave the land of our birth. Too frequently we wind up fighting other people's wars in places we've never heard of. Then there are men like myself, who are lucky enough to find themselves involved in something worth fighting for, and with someone who's worth following. Why have you joined us, Yankee?"

Nate remained silent. Never one to place his trust in strangers—or friends, for that matter—Nate wondered if the Irishman had guessed that he was going to desert.

O'Leary recapped the flask and put it in an inner pocket of his uniform jacket. "I'll let you ponder your answer, Private, while you saddle up."

Nate looked questioningly at the officer.

O'Leary stood. "You've been summoned for an audience with Simón José Antonio Bolívar."

Lanterns hung on poles around the perimeter of the army's headquarters, their glow illuminating to the edge of the forest. A group of officers sat under a weathered canopy, drinking and playing cards. When O'Leary approached with Nate, a man dressed in a white shirt and uniform slacks rose from the card players to greet the two young men.

"Ah, Daniel, thank you for escorting our American friend. Private Yankee, I believe?" Bolívar asked with a smile and a small bow.

Although Nate had been at the meeting earlier that day when Bolívar announced his decision to cross the Andes, he was not prepared for the general's immediate presence.

"Sir, at your pleasure," he answered with a deeper bow.

The general faced the officers; they stopped their game and gave him their full attention.

"Gentlemen, may I present Nathanial Yankee, our one and only North American patriot. Come, Nathanial, please join us." Gesturing around the table, Bolívar said, "You know Colonel Páez and Lieutenant Rondón, and these are Colonels Rooke, Soublette, Mendez, and José Antonio Anzoátegui. You have arrived just in time to lose all your hard-earned money to Rooke."

Colonel Rooke acknowledged the compliment with a smile and a nod.

Nate bowed amiably to the group of officers, who were relaxed but still in their uniforms. Atop the roughly carved table was a dish of cold, half-eaten potatoes and a map held in place with empty wine bottles.

"Was that your beautiful tenor that entertained us a short while ago?" Rooke asked.

Before Nate could answer, the general said, "Of course not. The Puritans of New England do not indulge in such frivolity, am I correct?" Bolívar made a stern face, gently mocking. "They are a serious people. However, Private Yankee, I believe if you survive long enough among us you may pick up a song or two."

"Or a woman or two," Soublette countered.

After the laughter subsided, Bolívar clipped on his saber and put his hand on Nate's shoulder. "My American and I will now go for a walk under the stars. But don't worry, we'll return shortly to take our money back from Rooke. Daniel," he said to O'Leary, "you'll keep the cards warm, I trust."

Bolívar steered Nate out of the light of the camp. They walked along a track toward the forest edge, the path visible in the moon's silver light. The banter of the officers faded to a murmur.

Nate was on edge. Páez's generous offer to join the llaneros, as well as his ready acceptance into the circle of officers, began to strike him as very strange; Bolívar was legendary for his ruthlessness. Nate tried to recollect any perceived slight or inadvertent misdeed, to anticipate where the blow might fall. *How much does Bolívar know?*

"How did you know I'm from New England?" Nate asked. From his deep tan and stocky build, most people he'd met outside the United States assumed he was one of those frontiersmen who was born in the woods and raised by bears.

Bolívar grinned and shrugged. "Do not look so surprised. You have an accent."

Before Nate could think of a response, Bolívar linked his arm with Nate's and continued their walk. It was a South American gesture that Bolívar had (correctly) guessed that the mysterious Puritan would find uncomfortable.

"Unusual men, New Englanders. God-fearing men. Men who fled

Europe for the freedom of New England so they could practice their religion in peace. And, once there, became great slavers. That impressed me, I tell you."

Bolívar stopped and tightened his grip on Nathanial's arm. "And now, Nathanial *Bidwell*," Bolívar said, emphasizing Nathanial's true surname, "it is time for you to tell me why you are here, don't you think?"

Nate felt a sharp jab in his side. A man had appeared behind him and was pressing a blade against his ribs. It was Bolívar's servant, José Palacio. José removed Nate's facón from where it had been concealed in its sheath.

Seeing the look on Nate's face, Bolívar chided, "Don't be so surprised. How am I supposed to drive the Royalists back to Spain if I don't even know who is in my own army? It is essential for me to know as much as I can, about my enemies, and especially about my friends."

Nate said tensely, "It's just that I'd rather have left the name of Bidwell behind, General."

"Every foreign soldier in my army has a story he'd rather forget. In fact," Bolívar paused, "this is the main reason we are having this little walk. Maybe you are a spy, maybe you're not. Or maybe you were, but no longer serve your former master."

The sharp blade didn't help Nate's concentration. Mind racing, he decided that some version of the truth would give him his best chance for survival. He replied, "My apologies, General, I should have come to you directly. My reasons are mercenary—I joined in the hope of getting a land grant." He quickly added, "That is, once we are successful in ridding your country of the Spanish."

Bolívar contemplated the line where the sky met the distant coastal plains. The general's shoulders began to shake, and he erupted into laughter.

Gaining a measure of control, he slowly shook his head while looking at the ground. "Yes, I can see you are indeed a mercenary. You come here and put your life in danger for money. Meanwhile, I have a fortune, and I give it all away for the cause of freedom."

He nodded to José, who moved back a step but kept his knife drawn.

Nate had not yet recovered from his shock, when the general leaned toward him, his finger pointed at Nate's chest. "If you are purely a mercenary, I have an offer that should appeal to you. A second chance. An opportunity to prove who you really are, Yankee, or Bidwell.

"I want you to join a select group. A company of mountaineers will cross this damnable pass in advance of the army, avoiding all contact with the enemy and traveling as quickly as possible."

Is Bolívar forcing me to accept a suicide mission?

"You are to reach Socha early enough to prepare the people for our arrival. We *must* have provisions, warm clothing, and shelter ready for the army. If we are to take Bogotá quickly, we must ensure as many of our troops survive as possible.

"Surprise and speed." Bolívar pounded his right fist into his left palm for emphasis. "That is what will bring us victory. And should you be successful, I will make you an officer. You will lead the llaneros, and there will be a land grant for you."

Did he really have a choice? Nate gave a small bow. "I accept your very generous offer."

Bolívar smiled widely, deepening the wrinkles that radiated from the corners of his eyes. "Someday, Lieutenant, when this is finished, I will entertain you on my plantation. Your land grant will be next to my estate in the most fertile area on this continent, the Bucaramanga hills. Together, we will grow the best coffee in Gran Colombia. Let these thoughts keep you warm as you cross the mountains."

He led Nate back to the lights and distant laughter. "Come now, the night is short and you will start at dawn. But first we must win our money back if we're to properly entertain the women of Santa Fe de Bogotá . . . once the capital is ours."

Somehow, Nate didn't find his promotion to officer reassuring. He finally understood the reason for Bolívar's success: the man was crazy.

CHAPTER 12

ℜETRIBUTION

He who leads the upright astray in an evil way will himself fall into his own pit.

—Proverbs 28:10

William walked purposefully toward the dense scrub that marked the end of the beach while the porters stripped to their waists and packed the mules with goods from the *Voyager*'s skiffs. He was intent to rendez-vous with Mr. Harold Hull at the Hotel de San Martín that evening.

The new continent greeted William with a multitude of sensations, not unlike those from the Duke of Devonshire's stove house. In the shade, he was overwhelmed by the earthy scent of jungle vegetation. Tropical rot suffused the moist air, mingling with the odor of perspiring humans and their pack animals.

He had to clear his goods through customs. From their makeshift offices, half a dozen brokers offered to assist the disembarking passengers. William waved them off; the duke had told him a Mr. Veeborlay would be his Barranquilla contact.

Beyond the beach, in the shade of a twisted tree, stood a shed with a tin roof. Several soldiers sat in the shade, dozing. The other passengers were already gone by the time William reached the customs house. He walked through a door propped open by a rock, into a stuffy one-room office.

The sleep-eyed representative of the Spanish Viceroy of New Granada rose from his rickety chair. The man opened a large official-looking binder with a dirty cover, picked up a pen, and asked in Spanish, "Who are you, why are you here, where have you come from, and where are you going?"

Having served in the Peninsular War, Gunn, like so many other veterans, had become fluent in Spanish. The man half-heartedly scribbled William's answers then asked, "Is there anything you would like to declare, Mr. Gunn?"

"No," he said.

"Is that your baggage?" the clerk asked, nodding in the direction of the cart outside.

William looked out and saw that a soldier had taken an interest in his goods. With his writ of passage with the seal of the British Crown, he wouldn't have had any concern, but he had concealed weapons among his possessions. He stepped outside, the customs clerk close behind.

The snooping soldier's neat uniform and polished boots stood in contrast to the attire of his compatriots, who were still napping under the tree. Just what William didn't need: a junior officer striving for a promotion.

William asked, "Can I help you?"

"Open them," the junior officer said.

William decided not to waste time and opened the chest containing the Manton pistols, Baker rifle, knives, and ammunition.

The Spanish junior officer gave the clerk a hard look and called to the soldiers.

The clerk protested, "But, sir, you said you had nothing to declare."

"And I don't," William said, producing the writ of passage signed by King George.

The clerk looked at the document, then looked at the officer.

"It is in our language, and it says he is a plant hunter, here on behalf of the British sovereign, looking for medicinal plants in our forests."

The Spaniard laughed. "You are under arrest."

William said, "You cannot delay a representative of His Majesty on official business. We are allies."

The officer barked an order, and the soldiers aimed their muskets at William.

"Miguel, Lieutenant Rodriquez, what is this?" An unimpressive man dressed in a white linen suit approached. He was overweight and sweating and would have had a dangerously white complexion to match his clothing if his face weren't as florid as a bleeding tomato. He took his straw hat off to reveal a head of wispy blond hair.

"Did I not tell you I had a most important client coming in today?" said the strange-looking man, who appeared to be as suited to his present environment as a jellyfish washed ashore. Oblivious to the muskets leveled at William, he chided the officer, "This is my client, Mr. Gunn, and his papers are perfect. He is here on behalf of His Majesty King George. The Spanish and English are friends."

William stood stock-still, hands in the air, feeling like a fool while this unknown gentleman bargained for his freedom. Not quite the welcome to South America he'd envisioned.

The lieutenant pointed to the cart. "Señor Veeborlay, your client has enough weapons to start his own revolution."

Veeborlay smiled and strolled into the shade with the Spaniard in tow. The Dutchman said, "I understand your position, and the difficulty of this situation."

The officer said quietly, "One of the first passengers off encouraged me to detain this man. I didn't know he was one of yours."

The agent passed a thick envelope to the officer. "I am sorry I missed your son's birthday. How are Fatima and the boys?"

The soldier slid the envelope into his jacket. "She complains. She says she doesn't see me enough. You know how it is."

"I do, indeed," said Veeborlay, not bothering to strike a sincere tone.

The Spanish officer ordered his soldiers to lower their weapons. The Dutchman passed a similar envelope to Miguel, who departed with the officer.

The duke had told William everything had a price in the New World. (This had not been shocking to William, as it was the same in the Old World—the only difference being that the Old World was more expensive.)

Alone together, Veeborlay finally gave William a once-over, glancing at the Brit as though he were an afterthought. The agent possessed that air of distraction which seemed endemic among light-skinned Europeans who'd inhabited the tropics for too long. He shook William's hand. "Call me Dutch," he said, "I've been expecting you."

William waited by a two-wheeled cab while Veeborlay paid for his goods to be moved to the nearby town of Barranquilla, where he would stay until a reliable guide to the interior could be arranged. No stranger to the dangers facing a traveler in a foreign port, William kept his Baker rifle, John Manton pistols, and a fighting knife close on his person.

He was momentarily surprised when the Dutch agent climbed in to drive the cab himself.

"I'm indebted to you," William said, settling into the passenger's seat beside him. "I was going to contact you when I was in town."

Veeborlay was blunt. "How the hell did you manage to get on the wrong side of the Spanish so soon? You've barely even made it ashore, Officer Gunn."

William fixed the agent with a blank look. *How does he know I'm an officer? What else does he know?*

"You mistake me," William said, "I'm just a simple plant hunter."

Still holding the reins, Veeborlay raised his hands to placate the twitchy soldier, "I am innocent of subterfuge, William. I happened to see the hem of a red coat when your belongings were shifted. Not to worry—I ensured the garment was properly stowed. Above all else, His Majesty sees to it that my loyalties remain with Britain. After all"— Veeborlay smiled—"I may want to retire to sunny Cornwall someday."

William knew his luggage had been tightly secured; he suspected the hem of his red coat had taken some persuasion before coming to light.

Veeborlay inspected his new companion. "Come now, what did you do to deserve that Spaniard's attention?"

"A friend from the voyage." William grimaced. "Mr. Howard Hull— you wouldn't happen to be acquainted?"

Veeborlay said flatly, "You choose your friends very poorly, Mr. Gunn, very poorly. You must do something about that." Veeborlay looked straight ahead, focusing on his driving.

"I know."

Gradually, William's thoughts turned from Howard Hull to the present. He spoke evenly. "The duke said you were reliable, Dutch, not just for making arrangements, but with information of interest to the Crown."

The Dutchman smiled ambivalently. "What information can a modest shipping agent such as myself offer a simple plant hunter?"

William suffered for a moment, struggling to decide how much to divulge. Everything about this man reeked of duplicity, but he was definitely the agent the duke had described, the one with information regarding Bolívar's whereabouts; and the sooner he found Bolívar and delivered his message, the sooner he would be on his way to discovering the black orchid and curing Sarah. Time was running out for his daughter—he had no choice. "I need to intercept Simón Bolívar as soon as possible."

Veeborlay didn't break his concentration from the road, pushing their horse along at what felt like a breakneck pace on the narrow path. "Word has come to me that Bolívar has joined Santander. They may cross the Andes soon, very soon, and move on the capital."

"In the middle of winter? Is that possible?" William asked.

"If you know Bolívar, anything is possible."

William had learned enough about Bolívar in preparing for his delivery of the duke's message to believe that a man with the general's experience would not sit in the rain waiting for Morillo to destroy him.

The Dutchman held the reins with one hand to scratch his chin, William noticed with alarm. "The fastest way is up the Magdalena. After that"—Veeborlay shrugged—"I can give you the name of a man who should be able to help."

"And transport?"

"Flotillas regularly go upstream. The rains have not yet begun, and the northeasterly is still blowing. The sooner you start, the better. I'll ensure there are sufficient provisions waiting for you and your men before you arrive at the dock."

"Men? What men?" William asked, surprised. "I'm traveling alone, as a plant hunter."

Veeborlay laughed. With a trace of scorn, he said, "Are you serious? Do you know *anything* about New Granada?"

William was defensive. "I was well briefed on the warring parties and the disposition of both the Spanish and the rebel forces."

The Dutchman spoke loudly over the rattling wheels, as if he were ticking off the items on a grocery list. "The warring forces are the least of your worries. There are armed bandits and deserters everywhere who would steal the eye out of your head before you knew it was missing. There are headhunters and cannibals who use poison darts that prick like a gnat but kill you before you can think to scratch, bugs that eat you while you sleep, and venomous snakes disguised as vines. No. If you ever want to reach Bolívar alive, you don't want to travel alone—not up the Magdalena."

"Well, how do you suggest I find proper companions if I'm leaving tomorrow morning?"

The agent smiled and pulled the buggy to an abrupt stop, causing William to grip the sides of the cab to keep from pitching onto the road. "You can meet them in my room." Veeborlay nodded toward their stop: the Hotel de San Martín—the very place where Howard Hull was staying.

William gave Veeborlay a hard look. The businessman shrugged. "He likes the arepas here. And it will give you a chance to impress your new recruits. Ask for the room under my name; they'll be waiting for you."

As William stepped down, Veeborlay leaned out for one last word, "But be careful—don't forget the Spanish control this region."

As a soldier who had been in harm's way for much of his adult life, William was no stranger to violence, but unlike some men, neither had he developed a taste for it. He would have preferred to live in a world where such things were not necessary, but until the world changed, William would do what needed to be done . . . and was thankful he was good at it.

The San Martín was a two-story affair: the upper floor contained rooms for overnight guests and although the ground floor had a few rooms at the back, most of the lower floor consisted of a large dining room with a long bar, a score of tables for diners, and a piano in the corner.

The dining room was crowded, smoky, and noisy. An old man was playing an unrecognizable tune on the piano. At a table on the far wall, a customer sat by himself, eating.

William entered, armed with a brace of pistols and carrying a rifle. The fat bartender looked on with mild curiosity. Ignoring his stare, William strode across the room, his eyes riveted on the fraudster.

"Why, it's William," Hull said, feigning surprise. He put down his knife and fork, hurriedly swallowing. "Terribly sorry I didn't have a chance to say goodbye at the harbor, old chap, but my contacts set up a meeting with the factory boys up-country, and I really had to be off straightaway."

Without a word, William put a pair of Manton pistols on the table.

"I give you the advantage of reaching first," William said. "It should be a fair fight, but one of us must die."

"Please don't hurt me!" Hull pleaded. "I don't know what they've been telling you, but there's no truth in it." His hands dropped beneath the table. "I wouldn't do anything to harm our friendship."

"Last chance," William said, offering the pistol to Hull once again.

William saw a change in the imposter's features: Hull's eyes hardened, and the false smile transformed to a barely concealed sneer.

Harold Hull rose halfway; with his left hand he pushed the Manton away. At the same instant, his right hand began to clear the table.

It never got any further.

In one swift motion William shot the coward through the eye. Hull remained crouched. A small pistol clattered to the floor from where it had been hidden in his right hand. His mouth opened and closed soundlessly—either in silent protest, or perhaps trying to talk his way into heaven.

The lifeless body of Harold Hull pitched headfirst into his dinner and knocked the table over with a crash.

With a measured pace, William stepped over the body and picked up the small weapon. Looking at the corpse, he realized his own pistol had pulled slightly left and down. He noted this for future use since he hadn't had a chance to test the new pistols before departing England.

He walked over and settled with the bartender. The occupants of the pub returned to their conversations, and the old man resumed his tune on the piano. A big man bent over and went through the pockets of Harold Hull's lifeless body.

William had a quick drink, then decided he was ready meet the men the Dutchman thought were so special.

CHAPTER 13

COMPATRIOTS

On the ground floor in the back of the Hotel de San Martín, a copper-colored Indian wearing a blue and gray woolen poncho stood silently outside the room reserved by Veeborlay. William slowly pushed open the door and found four men waiting for him in the room.

He entered and closed the door behind him. All four men immediately stood to attention. They appeared to be British ex-army, dressed in a mix of civilian clothing and fragments of recognizable uniforms. They deferred to a big man who, from his bearing, appeared to be a noncommissioned officer. William recognized him as the man who had gone through Hull's pockets.

One man had a Baker rifle slung across his back. The youngest held a small monkey with a white face.

"What's this?" William asked the group in Spanish.

The big man stepped forward and answered in heavily accented Spanish, "I ask your excuse, sir, but we like to unite with you."

William smiled. "The last time I heard someone butcher the Spanish language that badly was on the Peninsula, from the mouth of a Yorkshireman."

The others grinned and the big man looked sheepish. "Sergeant Angus MacPherson, Fifty-Second Oxfordshire, sir."

William said sternly, "I don't know who you think I am, but there's to be no saluting, and I am to be addressed at all times as 'mister,' not 'sir.'"

The men straightened noticeably.

"If you and your men are to travel with me, Angus, everything I'm about to say is confidential unless I indicate otherwise. Is that understood?"

"Aye, sir. And please, sir, Gus will do."

"I travel as a captain commissioned in the First King's Dragoon Guards on a writ signed by His Majesty."

The sergeant's eyes opened wide, his attention riveted on William.

"All you need to know is that I am a botanist explorer on a scientific journey, collecting specimens for Sir Joseph Banks under the protection of the British Crown. If you accompany me, you come as my laborers, nothing else."

William grinned. "It'll be impossible to disguise you, but stow those uniforms and get into local garb. Your background will remain as honorably discharged soldiers working for the Crown. If anyone asks, we're armed to protect ourselves and for provisioning in the wild. But"—William instinctively lowered his voice such that the sergeant had to lean in to hear him—"I will lead you to General Bolívar."

The door opened slightly, and Veeborlay leaned in. "A Spanish patrol just entered, most likely drawn by your little quarrel with the late Mr. Hull. I suggest you gentlemen regroup in a less conspicuous location, perhaps at the hotel stable. You can leave through the back door." He ducked back outside.

William looked at the big man. "Mr. MacPherson, take the men to the stable. I'll meet you in the furthest empty stall in two minutes. Make yourselves scarce."

William reloaded the pistol and checked his rifle, then left the room, quietly closing the door behind him. He took a careful look around the corner.

Four soldiers stood near Hull's body while their officer was half-heartedly questioning the bartender. William backed off and left by the rear door.

The big man and the soldiers were waiting in the dim light at the back of the stable.

"An officer and four soldiers," William whispered, "armed with muskets. The officer has a pistol. They don't appear to be overly excited.

"Sergeant," he asked abruptly, "who was your commanding officer at Salamanca?"

The red-faced Yorkie answered instantly, "We was temporarily commanded by Lieutenant Colonel Moore, sir, with General Colborne having been evacuated after being wounded and all at Rodrigo. But the general came back, sir, to take over again at San Sebastián."

"Well, Sergeant, it seems you do know your way around the Peninsula after that campaign."

"A bit too well, mister, if you know what I mean."

"I do. And Waterloo—I heard the Fifty-Second was part of the final charge?"

"Aye, sir."

MacPherson said, "They're good solid lads, seen some warm work— Tommie at Hougoumont, Campbell at the Sandpit. We decided we'd be more likely to get where we're going if we stick together. Problem was"— the sergeant grinned with embarrassment—"once we got here, we had no idea what to do next. So we've been waiting and were about to go upriver just in hope, when I happened to meet Mr. Veeborlay. He told us he knew a British officer who would set us right, so here we are, sir."

That bloody Veeborlay, William thought, *he knew before I ever arrived that I was a British officer.*

But Dutch was right. These men were trained war veterans; they could be most useful.

"Let there be no mistaking the seriousness of my mission, Sergeant. It will not be compromised. I've shown one man the short path to hell and won't hesitate again. The men will answer to you, and you'll keep them in line."

The sergeant began to reach into his jacket pocket. "Sir, I have something I think might be of interest to you."

A voice called from outside in broken Spanish: "Enemy patrol."

William grabbed the big man's arm and quickly pulled him further back into the darkness behind several stacked bales of hay. The others followed, trying to hide as best they could. William held his pistol, Gus a sizable bayonet.

From the shadows, they could hear an order to halt barked in Spanish; the tramp of booted feet stopped abruptly. A harsh voice demanded, "You—half-breed—where are the English? We know they are here."

A quiet voice answered in halting Spanish, barely loud enough for them to hear, "Short time, men go to river."

The Spanish soldiers made a perfunctory effort of searching the stable, not bothering to come past the first couple of stalls. One stopped to drop his breeches and water the wall while the others continued looking about. Gus tensed. William put a restraining hand on the sergeant's arm.

The Englishmen waited until the voice outside said, "Soldiers gone."

Leaning against the stable wall was the Indian who had been standing outside the door to the hotel room where William first met the British soldiers. His face now concealed under a wide-brimmed hat, the blue and gray ruana wrapped around him, crossed legs hidden under shapeless cotton pantaloons, he was seemingly asleep. Gus and William looked at each other.

William said to the form, "Thanks for the warning, but how did you know they would leave?"

The man looked up without expression. He slowly parted his poncho to reveal a pair of loaded pistols, cocked and ready.

William and Gus both smiled.

The Indian spoke, more fluent in Spanish than he had let on with the search party. "My name Jaci, from the Tupi, by the Big River. You go to fight the Spanish?"

"We intend to kill many Spanish."

"I join you."

"Very well, Jaci, welcome."

William turned to Gus. "Sergeant, it appears the Spanish are searching for me."

"Begging your pardon, sir, but that's what I wanted to tell you before that patrol appeared."

"What are you getting at?"

"Well, I happened to check your dead bloke to see if there might be anything of interest."

"You don't say." William didn't appreciate scavenging the dead, but knew the reality of life.

"It's not like that, sir. I wasn't after money, but information. And"—the sergeant proudly held out an oiled envelope—"I came up with this."

William opened the envelope and quickly scanned its contents.

Gus said, "It shows that fella you done in, as far as I can make out, was an agent of the Netherlands, acting for what's left of the Dutch East India Company."

Acton's right, this place is a den of vipers, William thought. He folded the envelope and put it in his breast pocket. "Thank you, Gus, you did well. I'm afraid we'll hear from them again. But for now, take Jaci with you, keep hidden, and I'll be along shortly, or I'll get word to you. Be prepared to leave Barranquilla at short notice."

William quickly made his way back to the room by the rear entrance of the hotel. Veeborlay was looking out a window, partially obscured by a heavy curtain.

"The patrol was asking for the Englishman who killed the man in the hotel," Veeborlay said.

"I know; the Indian sidetracked them to the river."

"Ah, I'm pleased you met the Tupi. He could be very useful to you—absolutely hates the Spanish."

"Have you any idea why the Spanish have taken an interest in my altercation?" William asked.

"No. Ordinarily, a fight between two foreigners would be completely ignored by the authorities." Veeborlay sounded concerned. "In the morning, make sure you are at the Magdalena dock at six o'clock sharp. Whatever happens, you must leave before sunrise. I'll have a fully loaded boat waiting for you. And I'll make sure a rumor reaches the Royalists that you're planning to board a schooner out of Sabanilla tomorrow—keep them busy running after shadows. It seems there may be more to this Mr. Harold Hull than we thought."

William said nothing about the information Gus had taken off the dead man.

When William arrived at the dock the next morning, Jaci was already at the landing, an eight-foot-long blowgun in hand. Gus and two of the others soon approached with their kit.

"Where's your third, Gus?"

"Tommie will be here shortly, Mr. Gunn, he had to coax Charlie out from under the bed."

"Charlie?"

"His monkey."

"Does he intend to keep that monkey?" William asked.

"Attached himself to Tommie at a cantina the evening he arrived, sir. Can't separate them. Tommie even sleeps with him. No harm, though."

William shook his head. "Get your gear stowed and be ready to depart as soon as the other passengers are settled."

The Dutch agent had reserved room for them on a fifty-foot-long *champan*, a large flat-bottom dugout made of balsa, that came fully manned, with fourteen crew members. Over the middle of the *champan* ran a twenty-five-foot-long enclosure covered with woven palm fronds. Twelve of the fourteen crew members stood on top of the enclosure with long, stout poles of guaiacum wood they would use to propel the dugout upstream against the current. In addition to the punters, a steersman stood in the stern and a crewman sat on the bow to test for depth.

"Tommie should be here by now," Gus said. They had finished stowing their gear and most of the passengers were aboard.

"Go and drag him back here, monkey or no monkey," William said. "We have to leave—it's almost sunrise!"

Twenty minutes later, Gus arrived with a most contrite Tommie, Charlie sitting on his shoulder.

Gus apologized: "Royalist soldiers detained him, but Tommie convinced them he was harmless, and they let him go."

"Both of you get on board right now," William said, "and keep that damn monkey out of the way!"

"What is it, Mr. Gunn?" Gus asked as they scrambled aboard.

"They didn't let Tommie go because they believed he was harmless—they followed him. Look!"

A squad of armed Royalist soldiers rounded the corner, led by an armed officer on horseback.

"Stop! You are under arrest!" The officer's voice could be heard in the distance.

Standing on the bow, William ordered the helmsman, "Cast off *now!*"

The helmsman looked from William to the approaching Spanish soldiers and said, "No leave, not ready."

William leveled his rifle at him. "You're ready now. Gus, give those soldiers something to think about."

The big sergeant barked, "Greenie, put one over their heads."

Campbell swung his rifle around, aimed briefly, and fired. The round whined just over the heads of the approaching Spanish. The officer's horse reared while the soldier fought to control the animal; the rest of squad halted.

On the *champan*, orders were shouted, lines released, and the boat slowly drew out into the brown current.

The Spanish ran to the dock. The officer dismounted and yelled an order. The soldiers hastily formed a line and knelt.

The punters marched down the boat, planting their poles, working her upstream, and rapidly drawing her further out into the Magdalena, the incoming tide helping to overcome the slow-moving downstream current.

"We're still too close, sir, they'll shred us at this distance."

"Keep your men down, Sergeant, and let's hope their aim is as bad as the cheap aguardiente they drink."

William ducked under the meager protection of the shallow gunwale and wondered how the Spanish knew to follow Tommie.

The Spaniard raised his sword high overhead, and the soldiers raised their rifles.

The officer dropped his saber.

"Fire!"

CHAPTER 14

ASSASSIN

Nate felt like he had barely closed his eyes before the mountaineers woke him to begin their ascent.

The path began as a narrow goat track barely visible in the predawn gloom. As the group climbed higher, they entered the perpetual fog of the cloud forest.

Nate traveled with a dozen or so mountaineers from Casanare. These men were from the plains nearest the foothills and were more familiar with the alpine country than their compatriots from the central llanos or the coastal towns. Almost all of them had lost loved ones to the Spanish Royalists.

The Casanares wore clothing similar to those of the altiplano Indians: cowhide sandals, broad-brimmed hats, woolen trousers, and multicolored ruanas. There was little to distinguish the mountaineers from one another by their dress as they wore their hats low over their faces to keep out the driving rain and sleet.

Accustomed to traveling the wild paths of the mountains by himself, Nate usually proceeded carefully, observant of his surroundings. Now he was forced to sacrifice care for speed. The group seldom rested, the mountaineers most familiar with the trail taking the lead and the remainder following close behind, their attention riveted to the narrow path. The spine-chilling drop-offs on either side were a constant, dizzying reminder of the need for vigilance.

Once on the other side of the mountains, they would have to secure enough resources to save what might be left of the army when it descended, or Nate could forget his land grant and any dreams of a plantation. But first, they had to survive the dangerous crossing themselves.

They seldom spoke. Late on the first night, the rain and sleet paused and the sky cleared. A fantastic staccato display of near-continuous lightning illuminated a bank of clouds to the far north. The persistent light caused a young Casanare ahead of Nate named Santiago to make the sign of the cross.

"It's only the Faro de Maracaibo," said Nate. The Maracaibo Beacon was a natural lighthouse, producing fantastic lightning strikes with such regularity that it had been used as a beacon for centuries, visible from hundreds of kilometers away. "Páez told me that years ago it led to the defeat of the last expedition of Sir Francis Drake, an English pirate, when the lightning illuminated the outlines of Drake's ships. This tipped off the nearby Spanish garrison, which defeated the surprise attack."

Santiago looked doubtful as he stared at the far-off display.

On the second day of their climb, their progress slowed when they encountered ravines that had been carved into the mountainside by runoff.

To traverse these gorges, they were forced to prepare *taravitas*[1] before pulling themselves over. They left the ropes in place for the troops who would follow behind. Nate was the last to be pulled over on one such crossing. He concentrated not on looking down but at the mountaineers struggling to drag him over. Nate swung helplessly over the water that crashed onto the rocks below, soaking him with rising spray.

Finally, he reached the other side and gratefully shook the hands and clapped the backs of the smiling men, knowing it was one more crossing out of the way. As they picked up their packs, Santiago put his hand on Nate's arm, holding him back.

When they were alone, Santiago revealed the cable that had kept

---

1 Taravita: a hammock suspended from a rope and used to ferry people, animals, and material over a chasm.

Nate alive a few moments before. The cords had been almost completely severed. Nate had been within a few strands of falling to his death. He returned Santiago's knowing look.

"Who did this?" Nate asked.

The Casanare shrugged. They repaired the damaged section and resumed their climb.

Who would want to kill me? He discounted an inadvertent insult, as that would have been settled with gaucho knives. The matter would have to wait, but from now on he would be even more vigilant.

Several hours of steady climbing brought them to another ravine. This one was wider than any other they had crossed, the opposite side hardly discernible through the spray kicked up by the torrent. They hadn't rested in over a day and a half. The stress of the forced climb, the many crossings, the bitter cold, and the altitude were starting to take a toll.

They rigged the hammock for the crossing and transferred all the packs and men to the other side, with the exception of the American and a smaller Casanare whose name Nate didn't know.

Nate had casually observed from his place at the back of the group that the short mountaineer had hung back until he was directly in front of Nate.

As the Casanare prepared to enter the hammock he appeared to fumble with the rigging. Nate moved closer to assist.

In a single motion, the Casanare drew out a hidden dagger and swiftly drove the blade toward the American. But it never struck. Nate was prepared to deflect the thrust, but the attacker slipped on the wet boulder and fell backward into the torrent.

In that brief moment, Nate glimpsed the face of his assailant. Given a split second to decide, he plunged after his attacker, into the foaming maw of the cataract.

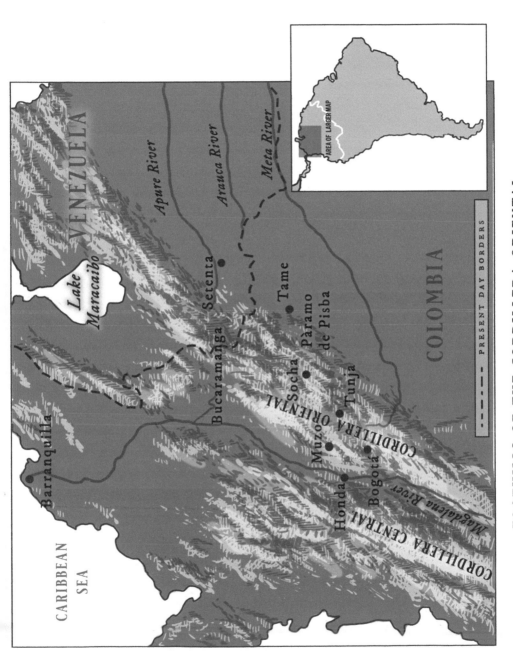

FOOTHILLS OF THE CORDILLERA ORIENTAL

- - - PRESENT DAY BORDERS

CHAPTER 15

THE MAGDALENA

William and the others hunched down in the boat, braced for the Spanish volley. Lead balls ripped the air close to starboard and splashed into the muddy Magdalena.

Abel Veeborlay stood out of sight on the dock behind Lieutenant Rodriquez. He watched the *champan* bearing the foolish British officer grow smaller as it made its way upstream. "Well done, Lieutenant, just close enough to keep them honest."

Rodriquez narrowed his eyes. "Your plan better work, Veeborlay. I let them go because you said this was best. I could easily have arrested them here. You know we have ways of making a man talk."

"I told you there's nothing to worry about. Word was sent upstream yesterday." Dutch wiped his wet brow with a white handkerchief. "The inquisitor will find out exactly what's in this British officer's message to Bolívar . . . without causing an international incident."

He clapped the officer on the back. "Then it shall be *Captain* Rodriquez, and with a bit of luck, perhaps a transfer for you to Bogotá, or even Spain."

William tried to understand how the Spanish could have ambushed them on the docks with so little advance warning. He didn't know Gus and his soldiers well enough to speak to their loyalty. Figuring they wouldn't be overheard from where they sat, he said, "Tell me about these men, Sergeant."

Gus gestured at the squad. "There's Paddy—that's Private Prescott, sir, from the Fifty-Second; he was in my unit." Paddy was young and red-faced, of medium height, with a nose which had obviously been on the receiving end of a fist or two.

"Have to watch him around the drink," the sergeant said, "but he's a good man in a scrap—fights like the devil."

Paddy accepted the compliment with a gap-toothed smile.

The sergeant continued, "Aboard ship, we sussed out Tommie— that's Flynn, sir—and Campbell."

"Thomas Flynn, Private, sir," the boy said, "Coldstream Guards, Queens Company." The monkey peered over his shoulder. The youngest of the lot, Tommie was tall and slender, almost lanky. He met William's appraising stare with an amiable nod and a pair of cheery gray eyes.

The other man introduced himself. "James Campbell, Corporal, Ninety-Fifth Regiment of Foot. Infantry rifle regiment." Campbell returned William's gaze with a judicious bow of his head. A young man of medium height with a powerful build, he wore his hair long to cover an ear half-bitten off in a bar fight. He had the self-assured air of a marksman who had known success.

Gus said, "Campbell and Flynn are close. They made a pact in Europe to watch each other's backs. They sailed over the ocean to this place together."

"I'd like to know why you left the Ninety-Fifth," William asked Campbell. "The Green Jackets weren't disbanded after the war."

"Best option at the time, sir." Campbell grinned "I sort of got involved with the wife of a Frenchie—a big-shot attaché or something like that."

"Quite a group, Gus," William said, figuring they simply couldn't have divulged any information that would have allowed a patrol enough time to attack.

Veeborlay. William had suspected the Dutch agent of double-dealing but couldn't believe he would stoop to outright betrayal. Still, he believed the information the agent had provided him was reliable; it agreed with what he already knew regarding Bolívar's location in Venezuela. It was also the only lead he had.

Their *champan* made good progress the first days of their journey upriver. The punters methodically planted their poles, marching with a steady rhythm toward the stern, beating time with songs sung in low African dialects.

The soldiers didn't mix with the rest of the company on board, but sat in the stern playing cards and chatting or dozing. Tommie asked Jaci to show him how to fish, an afternoon's activity that resulted in several good-sized bocachica and moncholo for dinner. The Tupi amazed them by bringing down a duck in flight with his blowgun. After that, they all wanted a try.

William suspected Veeborlay might have exaggerated the dangers of traveling in New Granada.

He awoke to find that a network of plants had formed an impenetrable green wall along both sides of the river. When they poled closer, they discovered the wall's colorful lace to be an untold number of wild orchids, clinging to vines and branches. The duke's stove house paled beside the spectacle.

William had worried that the mystical black orchid would be impossible to locate in the South American wilderness. Witnessing this incredible number of orchids, however, he believed the legendary black orchid must be among them. Surely, Jussieu had been mistaken in describing the remoteness and scarcity of the plant—orchids were everywhere.

The Caribbean breeze soon disappeared, and the heat on the river increased, along with swarms of hungry mosquitos. The ceaseless high shrieks of monkeys became irritating.

The monotonous green foliage parted sporadically, revealing solitary settlements, the dwellings little more than palm-thatched bamboo sheds. There was no sign of habitation. Corn plantings withered in the heat, the jungle consuming whatever had been left by the people who had tried to live there.

One night William lay awake in his hammock, unable to sleep for the constant complaining buzz of mosquitos.

In the hammock next to William, Tommie slept, his arm curled around his small capuchin monkey. Disturbed in its sleep, Charlie moaned, so like a human William turned to look. The monkey adjusted its position, putting its arm over Tommie's hand, and settled once again.

Closer to dawn the jungle was still, and William finally fell asleep.

Then the rains came. One afternoon, the land shimmered with such steam that even drawing breath was a labor. The deep song of the puntsmen lulled them into drowsiness as the dugout glided near the crocodile-infested bank, the creatures motionless like scaly logs. A flock of parakeets flew low over the *champan*, their plumage blinking lime and scarlet with every wingbeat. A troop of monkeys foraged along the shore, picking at fallen fruit and seeds.

Jaci and William sat close to the bow. The others tried to rest in the shade of a canopy rigged over the stern. The smell of drying fish encouraged them to remain outside. As usual, Jaci was alert, studying the jungle.

"See anything?" William asked.

Jaci smiled and said nothing.

William hadn't asked Jaci why he hated the Spanish so much. The most he could glean from their brief conversations was that Jaci's tribe had welcomed the Franciscan priests, who were the first settlers. Then soldiers came, looking for gold and other valuables. The Tupi did not speak of his family or his tribe. William concluded he had good reason to seek revenge.

"Have you ever seen a black orchid, or know where they might be found?" William ventured quietly.

William waited while Jaci appeared to come to a decision. On the point of the *champan*, the bowman measured the depth to make sure they stayed in the channel.

The Indian moved closer to William, and said quietly, "Every other year, shamans go upriver. Many months pass. Sometimes they do not come back. Sometimes they come back with red bark and black flower, dried. Red bark is for fever everywhere; black flower is for the one killing fever."

Transfixed, William asked, "Do you know where the priests go?"

"Only they know. They go upriver, far—many months. But then Spanish come. Everything gone now." Jaci went back to watching the bank.

William was about to persist, when Gus exclaimed from the stern, "JUMPIN' BALD-HEADED MOSES!" At the same instant, a nearby monkey troop burst into an excited chatter, fleeing into the trees. In less than a heartbeat, a crocodile had snatched a monkey in its jaws; it clenched the struggling victim about the chest with its two massive sets of teeth.

Paddy leapt to his feet and pointed. "Did you see that?" Gus grabbed the back of his shirt to keep him from falling into the river. Charlie screeched and frantically jumped about in the stern, trying to hide behind Tommie. The puntsmen paused in their song, their poles dragging, idle for a moment in the current.

The passengers watched spellbound as the predator slithered into the muddy Magdalena and rolled several times, the twitching monkey limbs resembling those of a small man, briefly visible, before disappearing into the deep channel. The dust from the attack settled in the air.

Jaci hadn't moved throughout the attack. William felt reassured by his presence, the only native of this strange environment, perhaps affording those with him a degree of protection.

The puntsmen resumed poling, their melody once again filling the close afternoon as the vessel continued its steady progress.

In order to ride out a vicious thunderstorm the next evening, they tied the *champan* to the shore and set anchor. The storm lasted so long the boatsmen decided that was where they would spend the night.

The men were restless. As trained soldiers, they were comfortable seeing the enemy before them, rather than coping with this constant sense of danger that frowned on them from all sides. Tommie had reached the end of his tether. "I don't care what anyone says, after what we saw yesterday, there's no way I'm hanging my arse over the side so's I can be dinner for some big lizard waiting in that dirty river. No way." He sat irritably, the air now thick with clouds of the Magdalena's mosquitos.

The procedure for answering the call of nature on the boat was to sit on the stern and allow the current to carry the waste away. But on this evening, Tommie wasn't having any of it.

William sympathized with the protest. Private Thomas Flynn, the youngest member of their group, was easily the most good-natured and agreeable member of the crew. But after the difficult passage, they were all feeling worn down. Even though Jaci advised against it, they decided to tie up their hammocks and nets onshore to make themselves more comfortable. Maybe they would get that night's sleep they all so desperately needed.

"All of us will sleep onshore from now on," William said, "close to each other under our nets. We'll keep a small fire, and slop on this awful bug stuff that Dutch gave us. If anyone needs to relieve themselves, do so no more than twenty paces away, and not out of sight. Our guns will be loaded, primed, and kept dry; knives, at the ready."

Jaci stayed on board the *champan*. He again cautioned the others against moving ashore, but their decision had been made.

The men settled in their hammocks around a small fire, listening to the rumble of the thunderstorm.

"Are you awake, sir?" Gus said softly on the other side of William. William stifled a sigh. "Yes."

"A lot going on out there. Do you find this a strange place, Captain?"

"Perhaps the strangest place I've ever been, Gus."

"Good. I thought it might be me. I'd rather be back in the ditch at Waterloo than spend another week on this stream to nowhere; at least there I knew who the enemy was."

"I know what you mean."

From somewhere on the other side of the river came the sound of wild pigs crashing through the brush in search of food.

Gus said, "He's certainly taking his bloody time at it, he'll be lucky if his arse isn't ate to nothing by the skeeters the way he's going."

Suddenly Jaci called out with urgency, "Come to boat, now!"

Before William could react, a low guttural snarl came from the jungle, followed by a piercing cry. A sharp silence followed, almost as startling as the outburst. Nothing stirred.

"Private Flynn!" he called.

"Tommie!" Gus and Paddy yelled.

Nothing stirred. The howler monkeys were silent for once. Even the insects had halted their chorus.

Jaci appeared beside them, machete in one hand and an unlit torch in the other, frowning with concentration.

"Jaci, what's happening?"

"Soldier gone."

"Gone? What's he talking about—gone? *Gone* where?" Campbell said, visibly shaken, a note of panic creeping into his voice.

"Jaci," William said quietly, "what do you mean, he's 'gone'?"

"*Yaguareté*," Jaci said with finality.

The jaguar, the ultimate predator in South America. The animal had been discussed, briefly, in William's training in England. In the duke's well-appointed drawing room, a warm cup of tea in hand, the subject had seemed barely relevant. Now it had returned to haunt the British officer.

The chief boatman approached William to say they had to leave immediately, before the squalls could return and make further delays.

William ignored him. He ordered Corporal Campbell to stay behind while they searched for Tommie. Campbell protested, until a glare from Gus silenced him.

William selected the corporal to remain behind not only for his skill as a marksman but because he was wary of what they would find in the jungle. He said quietly to Gus, "Bring a shovel," and then to Campbell, in Spanish so it would be understood by all, "Corporal, shoot the first bugger who picks up a pole."

Jaci lit his torch in the campfire and handed it to William. He began to hack a path through the tangle of vines and brush. A short distance in, the Tupi took back the torch and held it close to the ground, then raised it to look into the trees. William came forward and saw the animal print in the soft ground. It was larger than a grown man's hand, dwarfing any dog print he'd ever seen, even those of a mastiff. They started off again. William was surprised to see Jaci not following the tracks but looking up into the trees.

Jaci halted at the edge of a large stand of very thick brush.

"There," said the Tupi, pointing to a tree in the center of the thicket, where in the top branches there appeared to be a nest of some sort.

"What are you showing us, Jaci?" William asked tentatively.
"Tommie."

It took Jaci a few minutes to climb the tree to remove what remained of Tommie's body while they waited at the base of the trunk, guarding against the killer's return. The Tupi had brought along an old canvas coffee sack in which he wrapped the remains after removing them from the big cat's cache.

Jaci said to them in his quiet way, "*Yaguareté* kills quickly, but you do not want to see your friend." Later, when they were alone, Jaci explained to William that a jaguar kills differently from other cats, which go for the throat. The jaguar, with the most powerful bite of all, goes for the skull. William understood.

The ground fought their every attempt to dig a decent hole, so they settled for a shallow grave at the edge of the river for their friend and compatriot. A solitary monkey watched them from a nearby tree. It disappeared as they approached, and they did not see the creature again. But as the *champan* pulled away from the bank into the Magdalena, a mournful cry rose from somewhere in the dense jungle.

The loss of the popular Tommie, and the horror of his sudden death, brought the company close to despair. Hardened to the violence of war, William still felt lost in this strange land, with its unfamiliar dangers and overwhelming sense of gloom. The green mocked his feeble attempt to understand it.

And then, abruptly, they had reached the end of their journey on the Magdalena. They gratefully left the damned river behind them.

Once in the foothills of the Andes, they ascended a mule track, passing into the shade of the cloud forest. Instead of trying to sleep in their soaked clothes, they opted to continue walking as long as they could see.

The Tupi showed them the best way to remove leeches and other parasites. To relieve the rashes caused by their wet clothing, he cut the stems of an odd-looking plant that had spikes instead of leaves and released a sticky whitish liquid that relieved the inflammation. William thanked whatever power—if it was Fate, Fortune, or just bloody-minded revenge—that caused the Tupi to join his mission.

The men were somber, still feeling the absence of Tommie, and even Charlie, whose presence they had grown accustomed to.

After two days of hard, steady climbing, the rain tapered off and the steepness of the path decreased. The deep forest gradually gave way to plantations, their neat rows of coffee and sugarcane circling the hills. Beyond these estates the city of Bucaramanga opened before them on the plain, the high blue peaks of the Andes towering in the distance.

Numb with exhaustion, the diminished company stumbled toward civilization.

CHAPTER 16

PÁRAMO DE PISBA

Plunging into the ice-cold river jolted Nate like a bolt of lightning. The water slammed his chest like the hand of an angry giant, pinning him against a submerged boulder and flooding his nose. He choked as the powerful current tore at his clothes, and he struggled frantically to reach the surface.

The intense cold numbed his limbs and clouded his mind. Uncontrolled spasms seized his muscles. His feet found a ridge in the boulder. Starved for air, his chest ready to burst, he gathered his remaining strength and made a last desperate shove. Miraculously, he broke free. A colorful blanket whipped by him in the thunderous torrent. He seized its edge and kept a firm grip in the hope it was still attached to his attacker, even as the flow carried him rapidly away.

He surfaced in the calmer water behind the roots of a tree, dozens of feet below the crossing. The current tugged at the blanket still in his hand. Grasping tightly, he pulled on it with all his strength.

It seemed an eternity before he knew he was winning the struggle. Gathering in the garment, he saw the arm and leg of the unconscious attacker.

Turning the body over in the frigid water, he found himself staring at the face he had glimpsed before his plunge into the torrent. He'd been right. His attacker was a young woman. With her loose cloak and the wide-brimmed hat of the mountaineers, he had at first mistaken the slight Casanare for a young man. Quickly untangling the cloak, he lifted her out of the water and climbed the bank.

Reaching a clear, flat area surrounded by thick undergrowth, he laid her on the ground. Water trickled from her mouth, and her dark skin had taken on a cold bluish hue. He shook her angrily by the shoulders. "Why?" he said. "Why did you want to kill me?" Her head lolled, spittle collecting at the side of her mouth. She wasn't breathing.

Nate turned her on her side and struck her between the shoulder blades with his hand. Her entire body jerked spasmodically, and she coughed up brown vomit. She gasped and coughed again, expelling less water each time, until she could breathe regularly.

Nate scrutinized his would-be killer.

With her light cotton underclothes plastered to her skin, it appeared that a couple of red welts were the worst damage she had sustained. He looked at her face closely, trying to see if he could possibly remember where he might have met her before.

She shivered. Nate covered her with his cape. Even wet wool would help keep her warm. Her skin was cool and clammy to the touch; to restore her circulation, he vigorously rubbed her arms and legs.

She began to regain consciousness. When she came to and saw Nate, she weakly sought a knife that was no longer there.

Santiago and the others could be heard working their way through the tangled brush to reach them. Nate gripped her arm and said quietly, "You're going to tell me why you tried to kill me before they reach us, or I'm going to throw you back in. Do you understand?"

She stopped struggling.

"Hey, you two decided to stop for a swim? Don't you know we don't have time for this pissing about?" Coming through the brush, Fernando, one of the oldest of the mountaineers, smiled at them through broken yellow teeth. The would-be assassin jerked away from Nate's grip.

He wouldn't confront her in front of the mountaineers. Some of them had to know who she was and that she had tried to kill him. They might even help her if he decided to press the issue. He would wait until he could speak with Santiago. Nate felt he could trust him.

The others added to Fernando's greeting, expressing their relief that the two were safe and their small group was still whole. Two of the men retrieved the remaining dry wood they had carried with them, and a fire soon warmed the small copse.

"Julia, you didn't know you had an angel looking over you, did you? And a Yankee angel at that," said Santiago, arriving with their packs.

She looked confused as she drew closer to the fire, steam rising from the wet wool blanket, which she hugged tightly. "What are you talking about?" she said. "No one needed to save anyone," she insisted irritably.

"He saved you—the American," Fernando explained, and he pointed toward Nate, who also moved closer to the blaze. "When you slipped and fell in, he jumped after you."

Another mountaineer added, "We only knew there was trouble when the sling went limp. We thought you were both gone."

A pot of water heating on the coals began to whistle. One of the Casanares threw a fistful of leaves into the pot to soak. Nate and the girl were handed the first tins of strong coca tea. Portions of the bitter leaves floated on top; they were meant to be chewed and spat out as one drank.

Nate lifted the cup to his mouth. Uncontrollable spasms caused him to spill some of his drink. He forced himself to take several slow deep breaths. The realization of how easily he could have been trapped under the current made him reconsider the leap as one of the more questionable choices of his life so far. The violent trembling subsided.

Revived by the tea and the fire, Nate and Julia changed into the dry clothes they had brought for the *páramo*. Nate noted how the mountaineers averted their eyes when the woman dressed under her ruana.

The Casanares did not mention the incident again. They spoke to the girl only once, deferentially, when they asked if she thought her uncle and cousins would be surprised to see her descending from the *páramo* this time of the year. She nodded distractedly but didn't say anything.

They resumed their journey. The woman avoided looking at Nate and took the lead. He wondered who she could be—the daughter of someone important? Why would she be sent to kill him? He needed to talk to Santiago; if he could trust anyone, then he was the best bet. Nate slowed until he was just ahead of the Casanare. He stayed at that position, waiting for a chance that never came.

On the afternoon of the next day, they rose above the tree line to discover a frozen waste. Their arrival was greeted by a staggering blast of icy wind. Unprepared for the assault, Nate was nearly knocked off his feet. He lifted his head to see a barren snow-white moorland.

The small group had reached the dreaded Páramo de Pisba pass. This was the area of high plains that lay between the active volcanos of the Andes. It was a zone of frozen salt beds, caustic lakes, and broad empty heath.

Nate hesitated; as Santiago passed him, he grabbed his arm. Nate spoke over the gale. "Am I in danger?"

Santiago shook his head. "No," he gasped, "at least not from any of us. Ask O'Leary."

Nate nodded, exhausted from the effort. *Why would the Irishman betray me?*

Dizzy from exhaustion and a lack of nourishment, each breath became a labor; Nate sensed from the others' concentrated quietness that they were experiencing the same lethargy. He trudged on, senselessly following the Casanare directly in front of him. As the dark wings of night settled over them, his mind wandered . . .

At first Nate didn't know how or why he was being shaken. His mind resisted returning to the frozen wasteland. Santiago shouted in his face, "Look, look!"

With a superhuman effort, Nate roused himself and raised his eyes to follow Santiago's pointing finger.

A brilliant orange-ribbon sunrise lit the clear frosty morning. They stood on the uppermost verge of a narrow valley that sloped down toward a hint of green in the distance. They had marched all night and crossed the Pisba pass.

"We've made it!" Fernando exclaimed. The older man's quick breath whistled through the gaps in his teeth.

The sight instantly revived Nathanial, even as he thought of the extraordinary task of securing provisions for whatever remained of the army when they arrived.

"Thank God it's downhill," he said, and staggered on.

Three days after Nate and the mountaineers entered Socha, the army proper began to arrive. The survivors came in groups of two and three, staggering on swollen feet. Frostbitten and emaciated, their clothes blasted into rags by the bitter alpine wind, they resembled an army of scarecrows. Assisted by the mountaineers and villagers, they struggled down the mountainside, the bloodstained path they left behind grim evidence of their determination.

O'Leary was one of the first from the main army to arrive. The eyes of the weary, limping Irish officer were locked on the broken ground in front of him. He stumbled, and Nate caught his arm. O'Leary stared at Nate wide-eyed, as if seeing a ghost.

"You must have smelled the coffee, sir," Nate said with a cheeriness he didn't feel. "I certainly hope there's more than your ragged lot left, or we're in trouble."

The Irishman collected himself and managed a wan smile. "That coffee does sound promising."

Nate led the exhausted officer to a campfire burning outside a small hut near the edge of the village and poured him a large mug of steaming black coffee, generously fortified with the local aguardiente. He needed the Irishman alert for a while longer.

Looking around to ensure that no one was within earshot, Nate held O'Leary's arm in a vise grip. "*What the hell is going on?* Why is a young woman trying to kill me?" he said, his grip tightening even further.

Daniel O'Leary was no fool, he knew that in his present state he could easily be killed by the American, and no one would assign his death to murder, not when the pass behind them was littered with the corpses of so many exhausted men and animals.

O'Leary drew a deep breath. "Her name is Julia Magdalena Teresa Portillo—a Casanare. I've been told her father was at Valencia when the slave army took the city. She was with him, and only eleven or twelve at the time."

This drew Nate's attention. The slaughter at Valencia was well known.

"She's fiercely anti-Royalist and has no trouble killing the Spanish. Because of her beauty, the general occasionally uses her as a spy, if the danger isn't too great."

"And why is she trying to kill me?"

After taking another deep drink, O'Leary murmured, "There are some in the command who wish for you to disappear. There are rumors you're an agent sent by the Americans to offer a deal to Bolívar to abandon the revolution."

"That's ridiculous. You're telling me Bolívar believes this nonsense?"

"It doesn't matter. The reports alone have caused the caudillos to withhold their support for the general."

"Am I still in danger? Would I be better off deserting?"

The Irishman gave Nate a hard look. "That's one thing you don't want to do. It would only confirm the rumors; then there would be no shelter for you here, on this side of the world." He added, "But you did save Bolívar's favorite spy—and found the poteen, thanks be to God. I don't believe you're in any immediate danger. And you'll have plenty of chances soon enough to prove to Bolívar you're a patriot."

Nate was not exactly reassured. There had to be an easier way to get some land.

Weary survivors trickled into the village, shepherded by the locals. Horses pulled makeshift stretchers carrying men with feet blackened from frostbite.

When O'Leary's knees buckled, Nate caught him under his arms.

"It's time you had something to eat," said Nate, "I'll see to the others."

O'Leary couldn't have protested if he wanted to. Nate left to ask one of the villagers to bring some food to the officer. When he returned, the Irishman was sound asleep on the ground.

This army wouldn't survive a battle with a well-fed and well-rested Spanish force. Nate would bide his time until that first engagement and, in the chaos, slip away to find his South American fortune elsewhere, far from suicidal crusaders or would-be assassins.

CHAPTER 17

A SHORT REST

Topped with a clay tile roof, the hacienda stood in the middle of a field of coffee. Several cows grazed in an adjoining paddock.

William wasn't sure of the greeting they would receive when they arrived. But at the moment there weren't any other options. They were too exhausted to continue without a rest. Besides, he desperately needed local information, both on the Spanish military situation and Bolívar's latest movements. Veeborlay wouldn't risk losing the stipend he received from the duke by misleading him about the Sheridans. Nevertheless, William ordered his men armed and ready as they approached the homestead.

In a small garden at the side of the house, a woman knelt in a trove of vegetables. The climate varied little in the protected valley, resulting in a year-round growing season. The woman's silver hair was tied back under her blue broad-brimmed hat. She looked up and brushed a stray lock back into place.

"Lost your way?" she called out to the five disheveled travelers stumbling up the path. She smiled. "It certainly looks like you could use a hot bath."

"Ma'am." William removed his hat. "That's most kind of you. I'm on a botanical mission from England and was guided to you by Abel Veeborlay in Barranquilla." He paused, still off balance at the sight of this well-preserved English woman tending her garden in the middle of the Andes. "I must ask"—William hesitated, returning his hat to cover his head from the sun—"how is it you're not afraid of us?"

"Come now," she chided, "Robert and I have been cheering for you boys since you left Barranquilla."

Robert and Theresa Sheridan, it turned out, were singular for their hospitality—and this in a city known for its friendliness and generosity.

After breakfast, Sergeant Angus MacPherson and the other recruits lay peacefully in the long, soft grass under the shade of a fruit tree, protected from the midmorning sun. The men were in a pleasant, satisfied stupor, having bathed in clear, hot water and consumed an English breakfast of steak and eggs, fresh fruit and juice, and warm bread with lathers of butter and cream washed down by strong, aromatic black coffee from freshly ground local coffee beans. Jaci sat nearby, having earlier accepted some fruit and bread, but declined the invitation to go inside the house with the others.

William and Robert took their coffee in the study. A landscape painting hung on the wall above a polished oak desk; the large windows opened onto a garden filled with colorful orchids.

Robert Sheridan was tall, thin, and tanned, the streaks of gray in his black hair the only clue to his age. He ran the main assay office in the region, along with a general store that carried an extensive stock of mining and agricultural supplies. He also owned a small hotel adjoining the store and rented rooms to miners and ranchers when they came to town.

He would often join these men for conversation. They came from every corner of the region for supplies and were his sources of information. The other main source was the Spanish commander of the local garrison, who occasionally visited his home for lunch. After a few drinks, the Spanish officer became a regular fountain of gossip.

William said, "Dutch spoke very highly of you, said you were in touch with the goings-on in New Granada."

Sheridan ignored the opening to provide information. "A word to the wise, Captain. If a playing field had three teams, Abel Veeborlay would find a way to be on all three. After all"—he sipped his coffee—"he is a

Dutch businessman. And although he usually relays reliable information, I certainly wouldn't trust him if my life were on the line."

Robert added, "I heard there were five men in your group, but now I see only four."

William rubbed his eyes and realized just how tired he actually was. "Coming up the Magdalena, I lost a man. He was taken at night by a wild animal."

"I see." Sheridan scrutinized the English officer a bit more closely. "When you set foot on this continent it's important to understand that your main enemy is not the Spanish. It's everything around you." He waited a moment before adding, "Pay close attention to the Tupi. He'll help you survive."

"Hard-learned lesson," William said, "my first command, first casualty."

"There'll be more," Sheridan said. "This is your first time in the tropics?" It was more of a statement than a question—William's sunburned face, blistered hands, insect bites, and stained clothing gave him away as a greenhorn. "It'll take a while, but I expect you'll pass for one of the duke's tropical plant hunters before long."

As if he could read William's mind, Robert added, "Believe it or not, news reaches us quickly here. After spending twenty-five years in Bucaramanga, you tend to blend into the scenery, particularly if you run the only hotel in town."

"Moving here must have been difficult," William said.

"At first," Sheridan acknowledged, "but once we set straight a few of the rougher characters, we were left pretty much to our own devices."

William wondered at Robert Sheridan and his wife. They had tamed this wilderness, and then defended themselves against bandits, stray army deserters, and wild animals for years so that now they were as if a drop of old England had fallen on the hillside. Still, William had to be on his guard. He didn't know the extent of Robert's relationship with the local Spanish militia.

Recalling the flowering orchids he had seen earlier, William took a chance. "Have you ever heard of a black flower of the type growing in your garden?"

Sheridan gave him a strange look. "I have. Humboldt, the plant hunter, stopped here years ago and filled my sons' heads with stories of a flower that could cure any illness. That flower was the black orchid. My son John was obsessed with it. After his brother came down with an unyielding fever, John left for the Amazon to try to find the plant."

William waited breathlessly for Robert to continue, but the other man seemed lost in his thoughts. Finally, Robert recovered. "We never saw him again. The last we heard, he was with the Muzo tribe on the upper Magdalena. That was years ago."

"I'm sorry, Mr. Sheridan."

"Don't be," he said, "this can be an unforgiving land." Sheridan looked directly at William, emphasizing his words. "But the black orchid is just a myth. If it were real, you could spend five lifetimes searching for it and never find it, even if it were under your very nose."

"I'm bound by my duty as a father to try," William explained. "My daughter's life is at stake."

Robert Sheridan opened a drawer in his desk and withdrew what looked like a silver chain necklace with a gold medallion. He held it out to William, who recognized the pendant as a medal of Saint Christopher, a well-known protector of travelers, soldiers, and mariners. It was beautifully crafted, depicting a man in ancient clothing with a staff in one hand and carrying a small child on his shoulders. The gold was warm and heavy in William's hand.

"We gave one to each of our sons for their confirmation. John was wearing his medal the day he left. This was his brother's, and I'd like you to have it. The Spanish say, '*En San Cristóbal confías*': Place your trust in Saint Christopher."

"Thank you, Mr. Sheridan." The British officer hung the chain around his neck. He felt the warmth of the gold medal against his chest. "And if I should come across any information of your son John, I'll send you word."

Robert smiled, and produced two long cigars from the top drawer of his desk. He lit William's and then his own, drawing deeply on the dark-brown roll. They watched the pungent blue smoke rise toward the ceiling.

"If you're looking for Bolívar, you're going in the right direction. Against all expectations, Simón Bolívar has crossed the Andes with his army in the middle of winter. The Spanish here are like a hive of disturbed bees, to say the least. My guess is General Bolívar will be in Tunja this time next week, to capture the Royalist armory there. Most of the Spanish soldiers have already left to reinforce General Barreiro. You won't have much time to rest if you wish to intercept Bolívar."

William was elated but kept a poker face. "Suppose I'd like to arrive before him, and take Tunja?"

"With only four men? You're either keen or mad—or both."

"We're all veterans, Mr. Sheridan—the Peninsula and Waterloo. That boy out there under the tree"—William nodded in the direction of Paddy—"was at Waterloo, the other at the Sandpit, and the big fellow was in Spain and Portugal before Wellesley ever arrived. The Tupi will put a dart in your eye at fifty paces."

"Then I'd say any Spaniard left in Tunja is in for one very hot spell. I think I can help you get there in time to impress Simón José Antonio."

Robert offered William detailed directions and a hand-drawn map just before they left for Tunja. "Although we live here, William, we have stayed English in our hearts. Our loyalty will always be with king, country, and," Sheridan added, "with the duke.

"But one last note of caution, Captain." Robert Sheridan's years were evident in his knitted brow. "If the path to the black orchid leads you to the Amazon, take special care. If you found your journey from the coast a challenge, the Amazon is a *much more* dangerous place, even for those experienced in the ways of the wild. The perils are countless, from starvation and drowning to the predations of wild animals or the poison darts of headhunters. There, the simple sting from an insect can be deadly, and the most superficial cut can lead to gangrene. Then you must pray there isn't an earthquake." He paused to see if his words were having any effect.

William said nothing. The more difficult the test, the more trying the circumstances, William had found, the more resolute he became. He would never allow himself to fail. He did not know where it came from, if it was from experience or the parents he had barely known—but he knew it was not strength or what those who have never fought in battle call "courage." He was stubborn, that was all. That was enough.

Robert understood him. The agent smiled. "In that case, Officer Gunn, never *ever* let your wicket down. Good luck and Godspeed."

William's company traveled all day and into the night when the weather allowed. On a clear dawn six days after leaving Bucaramanga, they descended toward the city of Tunja. The name of the Great Liberator—Simón Bolívar—was on everyone's lips. They met a group heading back to Bucaramanga who told them the troops had left Tunja some time ago to join the main Spanish army.

The bare outline of the plan conceived at the Sheridans' developed in William's mind.

They stopped at the bottom of a hill not far from the town, where they rested under a small copse of trees. Tunja looked like many garrison towns they had taken in Spain or Portugal during the Peninsular War.

William had learned from Wellington never to engage in a battle if you weren't absolutely certain of winning, even before the first shot was fired. And he had no intention of wasting the lives of his men, nor of jeopardizing his chances of saving his daughter's life.

"You men stay under cover of these trees. Let's take a walk, Gus."

Gus pointed to James. "Corporal Campbell, keep an eye on that road from the north. Keep us covered with that Baker."

William and the big sergeant walked to the edge of the road, which was deserted at that early hour. The western gate of the walled town of Tunja lay less than a hundred yards directly ahead.

The sky brightened with the coming dawn. William sniffed the air; a familiar scent gave him an idea.

A short way along the deserted road, from around a bend, came the distinct sound of cattle. The two soldiers stopped when they saw a farmer herding his cows toward the milking shed.

"I guessed if anyone was up and about it'd surely be a farmer," William said.

"Aye, you'd be right there, sir."

"Let's say good morning, Gus, and see if perhaps he needs a hand herding."

A little while later, they returned to the men waiting under the trees.

"Look sharp there, and listen carefully to Captain Gunn's plan," Sergeant MacPherson barked.

"We've had a nice chat with a nearby farmer," William said, "who just happens to supply the Royalist garrison with milk and eggs."

"Hasn't been paid in months," interjected MacPherson. "Sorry, Captain," the big man said, embarrassed he had interrupted an officer.

"Never mind. The farmer has had plenty of opportunity to observe the garrison grounds and—as the sergeant pointed out—plenty of reason to dislike the Royalists. A small door on the outside of the wall leads directly to the parade ground next to the armory. Two armed Royalist soldiers stand guard at all times inside the building; a conscript guards the small door through the city wall."

William nodded to MacPherson. The sergeant said, "Not to worry, the guard on duty is the farmer's nephew. The farmer says all the conscripts are itching to join the patriots, including his nephew. The boy will open the door for us at a pre-arranged signal."

"Gentlemen," began William, "an opportunity has presented itself for us to impress General Bolívar with the mettle of the British soldier. We are going to secure Tunja for the patriots." He retrieved his pack and took out a securely wrapped bundle. Releasing the tie, he found a scarlet jacket festooned with ribbons. "It's time for you to don your uniforms."

In this light, they might pass for proper troops—William was banking on it. And since the British and Spanish were allies, he was counting on this ploy to confuse the guards just long enough for them to succeed.

"We'll go along the south road in groups of two, not so fast as to attract attention," William explained. "Jaci, remain here as the rear guard. Campbell, you watch the barracks door. Should anyone appear, make them wish they'd stayed inside. Any questions?" In that moment, a group of professional soldiers now faced him, grim and poised. He was quite proud of his small troop.

The sergeant ordered, "Prime and ready your weapons."

William hoped these veterans would perform their best in the next few minutes. He walked across the road to the wall and knocked on the door twice, followed by a single rap. Campbell stood by, Baker rifle trained, the others well positioned. The wooden door swung partially open.

"Gentlemen, king and country." William moved forward, followed by his men.

The first thing William saw as he stepped through the city walls was the farmer's young nephew holding the door open, his face split with a wide grin.

"How many men in the barracks?" William asked quietly in Spanish.

"Only four, like myself, from Tunja," the young man answered in a boy's voice.

"When we are almost at the armory you will cross to the barracks—not too quickly—and tell the others to stay inside until I order them to come out."

The young man nodded and the British soldiers formed up.

"Forward, march," William ordered, and they began to cross the parade ground in perfect formation. Even from a distance he could see the guards squinting into the sun, trying to make sense of the movement coming toward them. William had counted on the element of surprise, knowing that the guards might think they were Royalist messengers returning with news or orders.

One guard raised his hand to shade his eyes as he tried in vain to see who these men were.

"Steady now, double time," William called out.

Confusion among the guards gave way to agitation as the soldiers in scarlet stepped up their relentless approach.

Then the guards raised their guns.

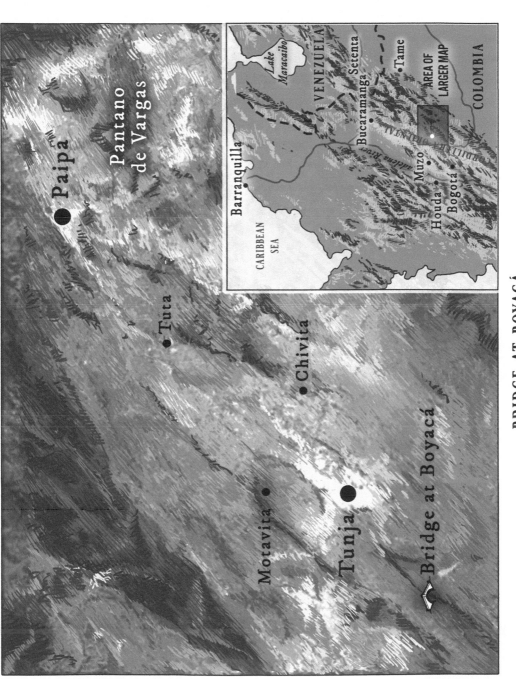

BRIDGE AT BOYACÁ

CHAPTER 18

MEETING

"Lieutenant Yankee, welcome to the llaneros once again," Major Juan Mellao said, grinning. "It's our privilege to have an American patriot along, especially as you Americans have so much more experience being rebels than us Venezuelans."

Nate rode alongside the major at the head of a column of patriot horsemen, traveling on a dirt lane in the gray predawn light toward the town of Tunja. Bolívar was with the main force a two-hour ride behind them. The Liberator intended to take Tunja before General Barreiro realized what was happening; he could then use the location to launch an attack that would destroy the Spanish army once and for all. Bolívar had gambled everything on this roll of the dice.

He had ordered Nate to accompany the llaneros on this reconnaissance mission of the crucial Spanish garrison; this would keep the American far enough away from the main army for the time being.

Ever since crossing the Pisba pass, Nate had been looking for a chance to bolt. A skirmish at Vargas Swamp almost two weeks before had presented the best opportunity, but at the height of the battle, O'Leary had charged into the melee, blocking Nate's escape and earning the Irishman a slash across the face from a Spanish blade. Ever since Bolívar's victory in the swamp, the countryside had been crawling with men looking either to join the patriots or to sabotage them. If Nate tried to escape now, he'd stick out like a sore thumb. He would have to bide his time and watch his back.

As the rosy wisps of dawn touched the eastern horizon, the town of Tunja gradually appeared in the valley below. A rider came up the hill, approaching at a gallop, clods of mud flying from the hooves of his sweating stallion.

As he neared, Major Mellao called out, "Luis, it better be good news that has you running that fine horse into the ground."

Drawing alongside the major, Luis swung neatly off his mount. The scout gasped, "It is just as you said, sir: the Spanish have abandoned the town. The entire garrison left the day before yesterday to join Barreiro. And, Major, they left stores, weapons, ammunition, and"—his eyes widened—"real medicines."

Mellao's eyebrows lifted in disbelief.

"But, Major, this is the strange thing," the scout spoke before Mellao could reply, "when we arrived the guards had already been dispatched."

"What! By whom?" Mellao said, with surprise. "We're the advance force."

"By a uniformed British officer and a group of irregulars. The officer says he wishes to present Tunja to General Simón Bolívar on behalf of His Britannic Majesty King George."

Major Mellao was uncharacteristically speechless; he stared from the scout to Nate and back again.

Reaching a decision, Major Mellao turned on his mount and said grandly to his column of waiting horsemen, "Lieutenant, it's time we put these New Granadan horses through their paces." He raised the sword in his right hand and, catching Nate's eye, winked at the American before shouting to the cavalry behind them, "For the Republic!" and swept his arm forward.

With a collective yell, the column surged forward, racing toward the waiting town.

Mellao rode as he always did when approaching a fight—flat out. Nate felt the excitement build as they approached the east gates. At Mellao's signal, the horsemen split into four squads, three diverting to surround the town, while the major led the remaining riders directly through the gates.

Although they believed the people of New Granada were ready to overthrow their Spanish masters, nothing had more disastrous consequences in war than letting down one's guard.

Nate remained with the first squad, riding behind the major as they entered the town. They thundered down the empty streets, their horses' hoofbeats echoing off the close walls. It seemed they had taken the town completely by surprise.

The officers focused on the tops of the houses, wary of a potential ambush. They moved through narrow lanes cloaked in shadows until the street widened onto the town square.

They had ridden straight into a trap. The plaza was filled with what seemed to be the entire population of Tunja, all frantically shouting, their noise deafening in the square along with the tolling of bells from a startlingly white cathedral.

The patriots were overwhelmed. It took Nate several moments to realize the crowd's roar consisted of shouts of "Bolívar!" and "The Liberator!"

Even more of the town's citizens poured from the church and from the double-storied mansions that fronted the square around them. Men and women of different races and fashions joined together in the welcoming chorus, many of them weeping with joy. The entire square was a vibrant, excited mass of people yelling and singing and throwing flowers to the riders while waving colorful pieces of fabric and makeshift Republican flags.

Two figures stood alone on the top steps of the cathedral, one conspicuous in a bright scarlet tailcoat, immaculate black breeches, and the spotless black boots of a dragoon, the other dressed in the garb of a Roman Catholic bishop. Below them appeared to be an Indian dressed in the native fashion, his eyes continuously scanning the crowd.

The officer caught Mellao's attention and directed a confident, open-handed British military salute. Mellao looked at Nate, as if to confirm what he was seeing. The bishop bowed slightly to acknowledge the major, his features creased by a frown.

Major Mellao and Nate dismounted at the bottom of the steps, the crowd parting around them. Nate remained slightly behind Mellao, feeling an instinctual aversion to the British officer's red coat.

The crimson-clad officer descended to meet them, his arm linked securely through the arm of the bishop. The Indian didn't move.

"Major," the officer said in Spanish, slightly bowing from the waist. Mellao stared at him as though he might be dreaming and wake up any moment frozen in the Pisba pass.

William hesitated, then continued, "Captain William Gunn of His Majesty's dragoons," he said, and presented the bishop standing beside him, "the Bishop of Tunja, whose close company I have maintained to ensure that word of his town's liberation does not reach our Spanish friends." The bishop looked miserable. Mellao guffawed, increasing the bishop's discomfort and causing the rest of the llaneros to break into fits of laughter.

When the laughter subsided, William continued, "And the mayor of this fine village is being detained, along with this bishop's priests, in the garrison jail under the watchful eyes of my compatriots."

Mellao finally spoke. "You need to explain exactly who you are, Captain William Gunn, and how you came to be here at this time."

William leaned forward to speak, but Mellao held up his hand and said quietly, "Not here. We will speak elsewhere."

As they made their way through the city, Nate marveled at the cosmopolitan dress and manners of the people in a city as remote as Tunja, which was accessible only by mule path over treacherous terrain yet seemed to be roughly the size of the city of Washington. Nate had quickly realized that the American colonies were drab second cousins in comparison to the Spanish cities of South America. He wondered how these people had built their libraries, museums, and universities in such an isolated place.

Navigating the crowds that thronged the streets, they arrived at the garrison. Inside the barracks, William related his capture of Tunja. "Fortunately, I had good intelligence that the Spanish soldiers guarding the town had left to reinforce General Barreiro's troops further north."

"But how did you manage to cross the parade ground without alerting the guards?" Nate asked, incredulous.

William ignored the question.

Mellao spoke, "I am also interested in your strategy, Captain Gunn."

The British officer answered him, "I ordered the men to assume parade formation, and we simply marched directly to them. Seems they didn't know how to react. Then the silly buggers got a bit nervous and raised their guns. We were forced to kill them. Unfortunate, actually, but unavoidable."

"Two less Spanish soldiers to worry about," Mellao said, "and most important, you've captured their armory." He paused, deciding on the best tack. "Now, perhaps you will tell us why you and your men happen to be here, at this time."

"I'm afraid that's a rather long story, and I must insist that General Bolívar be the first to hear it," William said, as courteously as possible.

"I'm afraid," Nate said, not attempting to be courteous, "you can't meet the general until you tell us."

William looked at Nate with an unwavering stare. Mellao stepped between them, "I must agree with my American lieutenant. Until your audience with the general, you and your men are to remain confined in the garrison. The people thank you for your service." Major Mellao bowed with a sarcastic flourish, as did Nate, before both turned and strode off, leaving William and his men to join the other prisoners.

The sound of carriage wheels signaled the arrival in Tunja of the first wagons carrying wounded patriots from the fight at Vargas Swamp. The troops in the square grew quiet as the wagons rumbled through.

Daniel O'Leary entered the square on his dappled mare, a white dressing fixed around his head. Nate met him halfway across the cobblestones.

"We have to stop meeting like this," O'Leary said, sliding off his horse, "or next time you'll be picking me out of one of those damned carts."

"Nice haircut," Nate said.

The Irishman fingered the fresh bandage covering his forehead. "I got it saving some moron who managed to get his squad into trouble."

Nate replied, self-conscious, "I haven't had the chance to thank you for that."

"No thanks are necessary, Lieutenant. Could have happened anywhere."

Nate led O'Leary through a neat adobe house to a tidy, bright courtyard beyond. A group of men in colorful ruanas and wide-brimmed hats were gathered there.

"Gentlemen," he said lightly, "this is Captain Daniel O'Leary whose head, thank God, is as strong as his liquor."

The Casanares laughed at Nate's formal Spanish. Reunited, they stood and embraced the captain with much gratitude.

The mountaineers continued their card game, and the two officers took their coffee at a nearby fountain, under the shade of the trees.

Nate grew serious. "I owe you an apology."

Taken aback, the Irishman asked, "What for?"

"I had you figured wrong from the start." Nate took a breath and looked at the officer squarely, saying, "I thought you were Bolívar's chief ass-kisser." He held his hand up to avert O'Leary's wrath. "But I've come to realize you're an extremely courageous and intelligent soldier, one who got us out of a particularly tight spot in that damn swamp fight."

"Listen, Yank, I know where my bread is buttered, and it's not in Ireland. And if I do the general's bidding, I do it because I believe in him and in the patriot cause." O'Leary smiled. "As much as my own future."

Nate said, "I imagine I'm on my own if I do anything stupid again."

"You're a bit overly keen at times, but you certainly *do* get noticed." O'Leary's hand unconsciously touched the wound. "You must want that land grant quite desperately."

"I'm just trying to convince *our side* not to kill me," Nate replied. As O'Leary had likely blown his only opportunity to escape, the American felt it prudent to shore up his standing with the patriot army.

"As far as I know, you're not in any danger from that quarter. The cavalry performed well at Vargas, although it was just a skirmish."

"It was thanks to Julia's uncle we had a cavalry at all."

"*Julia* is it?" O'Leary said slyly. "Do you fall in love with every pretty face who tries to kill you, Yank?"

Nate smirked. "It's not the craziest thing a woman's done to get my attention."

"Ah, yes, the trail of broken hearts left behind by Nathanial Yankee," O'Leary soliloquized to the laughing Casanares, "the Casanova of the cordilleras, who has a mistress behind every hill—'loving off the land,' as they say."

In fine spirits, O'Leary carried on, "We've been receiving such good information, I suspect your Julia may be romancing either General Barreiro or Colonel Jiménez at this very moment—and pining for you desperately, of course."

He toasted Nate, "To lady spies and land grants!"

Nate toasted and drank.

The Irish officer grimaced. "What *is* this we're drinking?"

"Just coffee."

"Oh." O'Leary poured the rest into the fountain; the water briefly ran brown.

"God, I miss Ireland."

CHAPTER 19

THE BATTLE OF BOYACÁ BRIDGE

A dog barked in answer to the cock crowing in the distance. Rubbing his eyes and looking around the open square, William remembered where he was. After General Bolívar had arrived in Tunja, he'd freed the British officer and his men. William's men had been reassigned, camping with the army just south of the town, and he had yet to meet the busy general.

He had spent the night sleeping close by the small house where General Bolívar was billeted. The general had sent his apologies the previous evening for not being able to spare a moment for William due to the impending military action. This was perhaps the most important hour in Bolívar's long fight for independence. Time was critical.

William was disappointed. Perhaps taking Tunja was not enough to impress a seasoned commander such as the Great Liberator. Or maybe Bolívar was delaying their discussion until after this upcoming battle, to see how the new British officer performed before considering any proposals from the British government.

Fine with him. Might not matter anyway, if Bolívar's ragged outfit was defeated in the upcoming action. In any event, he'd do his best. His mission was to deliver the message, nothing more. Then his hunt for the orchid could begin.

William stood to stretch the sleep out of his stiff limbs. He walked to the marble fountain that graced the center of the small plaza and plunged his head into the water. Hearing a sharp cough behind him, he snapped around to see the grinning face of Santander's aide-de-camp, a popular officer named Morales.

"I hope I'm not disturbing the Englishman's morning bath, but the general desires the honor of your presence—preferably sooner than later," Morales cautioned him in English. "He wants you to see his strategy firsthand."

William joined Bolívar and his officers at the top of San Lazaro, a hill located about a mile and a half outside of Tunja. They walked to a vantage point with an unobstructed view of the valley to the west, leaving footprints in the sharp morning frost. The early-morning light revealed two villages in the distance, along with a narrow road running like a ribbon down the center of the valley.

Through a small spyglass, the general scanned the valley for several moments before pointing to the furthest hamlet.

He smiled. "Gentlemen, have the buglers assemble the troops in the main square, and move out as soon as possible. In about four hours our army will be waiting for Barreiro at the valley of the Teatinos River."

Turning to Santander, Bolívar said, "Francisco, I am assigning the American and his cavalry to you for this battle. Some of his men have been here before and will be familiar with the terrain. He will be one of your aides until we meet the Spanish, at which time he will rejoin his squad."

William spoke, "General, is it possible to have my men assigned to Colonel Santander?"

"I'm afraid that's quite impossible, Captain. They will fight with the British Legion. But you must stay with Santander; I want you to report to your monarch what you witness today."

William and Nate accompanied Colonel Santander, along with his aide-de-camp, Major Miguel Morales. William wasn't sure who was the more extravagant in their dress: Morales, with his blue waistcoat and sash, or the American dressed in animal skins.

It remained a mystery to William why the American colonies had fought to separate from Great Britain. At the very least, this "Lieutenant" Yankee was an irritant.

They followed the road as it snaked toward the Teatinos River, the rising sun revealing the hills to their right. The general had been correct—the buttress to their right perfectly concealed the patriot army from the Spanish.

About midday the road curved sharply around the bottom of the ridge. The distant report of musket fire echoed from the valley below.

The road fell steeply, ending in a small crossing over the Teatinos River known as the Boyacá Bridge. Once over the bridge, the road continued toward Bogotá. Santander's skirmishers reported that the bridge was held by Barreiro's vanguard, but the main body of the Spanish army was still further up the valley.

Colonel Santander ordered his aide, "Major Morales, it's time for you to tell General Bolívar the Spanish have arrived and they have split their forces. Tell him that I intend to gain the heights above the bridge to prevent them from reuniting."

Morales turned his mount to go, but Santander grabbed his reins and leaned toward him, speaking with intensity, "Miguel, be hasty."

Santander stroked his goatee, intent on the river below. He turned to Nate. "Lieutenant Yankee, you will rejoin your unit and advise your Captain Taylor to assemble his Second Guides in the lower field above the bridge. He will be our anchor on the right flank."

Nate swung his steed around and galloped back up the hill. The cavalry passing him were moving quickly toward the front.

He drew up alongside his commanding officer, Captain Taylor, and related Santander's orders.

"Thank you, Lieutenant." Captain Taylor turned and raised his voice. "Forward canter." Following the cavalry in front, Taylor's company began to move so they could position on the far right above the small bridge held by Barreiro's crack troops.

William Gunn rode with Colonel Santander, leading their fast-moving column toward Boyacá Bridge. Santander had just received Bolívar's assent, permitting him to attack the bridge and to keep the Royalist army split at all costs. Bolívar would mount a simultaneous attack on the main body of Spanish forces that were just entering the upper end of the valley.

Although this was not William's war, Bolívar had placed him in a position where he had no choice but to fight. At least the patriot army

THE BATTLE OF BOYACÀ BRIDGE

August 7, 1819

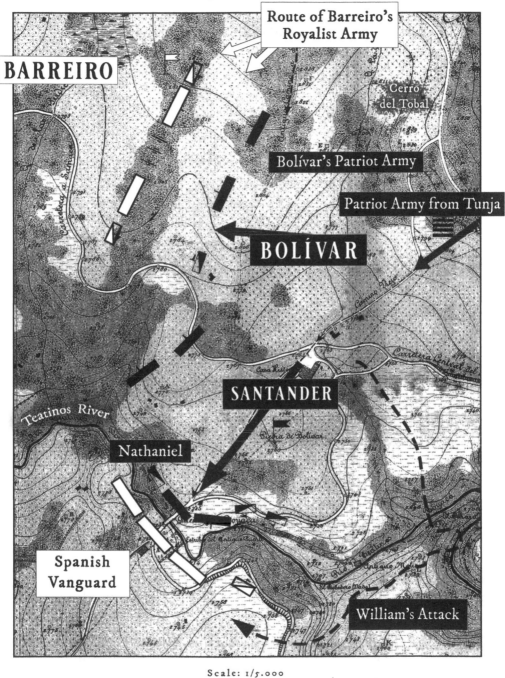

Route of Barreiro's Royalist Army

BARREIRO

Cerro del Tobal

Bolívar's Patriot Army

Patriot Army from Tunja

BOLÍVAR

SANTANDER

Teatinos River

Nathaniel

Spanish Vanguard

William's Attack

Scale: 1/5.000

M.100 50 0 100 200 300 400 500M

Legend

▬ Patriots		≡ Patriot reserve troops
▭ Royalists		▰ ▰ ▶ Forward movements
⊢ Republic Command (Bolivàr)		
⊢ Royal Command (Barreiro)		

held the better position—they would be attacking downhill against a divided enemy. William scanned the area ahead, looking for any additional tactical advantage that might be present.

Drawing ever closer to the valley bottom, a swale branched off to the left, its route to the stream below marked by a few small trees.

"Colonel, I do believe troops could be led down that gully and perhaps approach the bridge from behind, without being seen."

Recognizing the experienced advice of the British officer, Santander didn't hesitate. "Take a squad and surprise the Spanish from behind. I will hold back the attack until I see you have engaged the enemy."

On the far right flank, Captain Taylor commanded, "The division will attack on Colonel Santander's signal. Until then, *we hold our positions.*"

Nate could see the fear on the faces of the enemy at the bridge. Already exhausted from their forced march and cut off from the main body of their army, the Spanish light cavalry was now desperately attempting to deploy over the narrow bridge.

Their tired horses piled onto one another. The cavalry that did manage to cross would have their backs to the swollen Teatinos River, which was spilling its banks from the recent rains.

Emerging from cover, William moved into position behind the Spanish who were holding the bridge. He breathed deeply and prepared his troops for the surprise attack. He felt the weight of the Saint Christopher medal hanging about his neck.

Knowing Jaci was not familiar with this sort of warfare, he indicated for him to attack from the least vulnerable place on the right side of the line.

"This fight is for my people," Jaci said determinedly. "My life means nothing."

William said, "We don't have time for this. I order you to stay on the right."

On the other side of the river, Nate noticed activity behind the Spanish. Santander must have sent patriot forces to attack the rear of the enemy.

The Spanish cavalrymen crossing the Boyacá Bridge suddenly paused—it looked as if they might turn around. The patriot force must have been discovered.

Without the element of surprise, the patriots behind the Spanish would be cut to pieces. Nate was hesitant to place himself in needless danger at the very front of the line, but he saw an opportunity to make a favorable impression with Bolívar.

If he led a charge now, he could draw the Spanish cavalry away from the exposed patriots. Once the general heard about his courageous act—placing himself in harm's way to save the day—he would have to be rewarded. Feeling his mount's readiness, he reined the restive horse back a pace; it pawed at the dry ground, pricking its ears.

Nate didn't know whether his recklessness was an inherited family trait or whether it had appeared of its own accord from the losses he had experienced. In any case, he knew he did not fear death as much as he feared failure.

Nate allowed an irrational rage to build inside him against the men he faced across the field, as if they were somehow directly responsible for keeping him from his destiny. If he was going to do this, he might as well do it right. *What the hell—no one ever got anywhere by playing it safe.* He opened the bottom of his jacket and checked his pistol. He felt capable of extreme action.

Nate took a deep breath, stood high in his saddle, raised his saber, and bellowed, "Forward! Charge!"

Letting the reins out, Nate gave the large black horse its head. The stallion extended its neck, bolting down the green hill under the sapphire sky with an ever-increasing pace. Nate drove the animal, the ground thundering from the hooves of the horses charging behind him, the roar of their riders accompanied by the jingle of metal bridle chains and weapons, the thunder of close-packed horses in full gallop, in wild exhilaration at the vigorous downhill dash.

"What in God's name are they doing?" Santander asked, incredulous at seeing his far right flank break into a charge without his giving the order. Although he was also baffled, Morales knew better and kept silent.

"That fool is ruining the only chance we had of drawing their dragoons away from the bridge. And if we don't join those idiots soon, the chasseurs will chew them up and be free to attack Bolívar."

The colonel didn't hesitate. Addressing his aide, he said, "Order a general charge immediately."

The raucous cries of attacking cavalry carried over the bridge to William's position. A section of the patriot far right flank had broken into a hard charge toward the Spanish chasseurs. The rest of the patriot line hesitated, then joined in a general charge, racing down the slope, the right flank far out in front. The Spanish dragoons on William's side of the river hurried to cross the bridge to meet the advancing cavalry.

"Blast!" he spat.

"What?" Jaci wanted to know.

"Some bloody fool on the right flank has advanced early," he answered. "We'll never draw their cavalry back now."

He called loudly to his infantry, "Fix bayonets!"

Just before the clash with the Spanish cavalry, Nate felt a calm, slow-motion certainty, as during the final moments of a hunt. Focusing on the enemy uniform directly in front of him, everything else blurred, becoming muted in the background. Relying on an old Wampanoag tactic, he drew his raised saber back, leaned to the side, then quickly pivoted his horse around the slower Spanish horseman whose cut went wide. It was a fatal miss—Nate swung up and over, severing the man's sword arm.

Wheeling about, Nate lost sight of his squad. Only then was it obvious that the furious charge had penetrated too deeply. Not checking his forward momentum, Nate had miscalculated and driven his squad right through the Spanish dragoons. Now their backs were to the stream. Spanish uniforms were everywhere.

The rest of the patriot cavalry was seconds behind, but those precious seconds could mean doom for his men. He looked around—each man was fending off several mounted attackers at once.

William saw that the patriot horsemen who had charged prematurely were in danger. Their uncontrolled gallop had taken them through the Spanish cavalry. Now surrounded, with their backs to the river, the Royalists hacked at them from three sides.

"To the bridge, to the bridge!" the British officer roared, pointing with his saber. The patriot Cazadores, all veteran elite infantry, understood William's order, even though it had been shouted in English. The charging warriors followed William like a blue flood to the center of the fray.

William's large stallion trampled several confused Spanish infantrymen before a furious dragoon met him.

William closed on his attacker more quickly than his opponent anticipated. Using his steed's momentum to turn his horse in a tight pivot, William cut the Spanish dragoon with a ferocious slash. His opponent fell beneath the fighting cavalrymen, mortally wounded.

The action here was most hot; every foot was contested.

Sensing movement, the American spurred his horse to rear. He wheeled as he descended, driving his saber forward to impale a charging dragoon. Nearby, an attacker stood poised to slash a llanero. Nate blasted the Spaniard with a dragon pistol and the man's skull disappeared in a red cloud.

The sharp clank of steel on steel signaled the welcome arrival of the main body of patriot cavalry. Attended by the sound of their enraged bellows, the neighs of their mounts, and furious splashing, the charging patriot horsemen drove the Spanish cavalry into the swiftly moving stream.

The bridge was pure chaotic carnage, horses crowding in a fierce crush where men were dying, swearing, cutting, and drowning.

William fought desperately. The Spanish right flank was beginning to fold back, moving to attack his squad from the rear while his men were pressing the action at the bridge.

William whirled to cover this new angle of attack. The Spanish charged forward in overwhelming numbers, their gray bayonets flashing. William was one man on a horse against a hundred. They would remember him. Screaming a primal war cry, the British officer lifted his saber high, his horse rearing.

Behind him, he heard a great roar rising from a multitude—the Spanish ahead of William halted, then broke and ran. William wheeled his horse about.

Santander's infantry battalions had arrived. The colonel had waited until this critical moment to throw the full weight of his patriot infantry at the Spanish. Their straw hats and white shirts swarmed the bridge in an all-out bayonet assault as they mobbed the remaining Spanish infantry, sweeping them away like the tide demolishing a sand castle.

For Nate, the end of the battle came as swiftly as the first clash—a frenzy of feinting and killing, when, all of a sudden, he looked around to find only his dazed and exhausted compatriots. They were survivors, surprised to find their brotherhood of cavalry partially intact. A few riderless horses wandered, wounded and confused; others lay prone either atop or beside their dead and dying troopers.

His own horse stood quietly, head down, blown. Nate rubbed his eyes, feeling exhaustion mingled with the elation of a victorious warrior who has survived combat.

In the face of the relentless onslaught of Santander's infantry, the Spanish at the bridge surrendered. They threw down their arms as their commander lay crumpled on the bridge, dying.

On the higher ground behind them, Bolívar's regulars and the experienced British Albion Legion had routed the main body of the Spanish army.

It took less than two hours for General Simón José Antonio de la Santísima Trinidad Bolívar to defeat the only Spanish Royalist force standing between him and Santa Fe de Bogotá, the Spanish viceregal seat of wealth and power in South America.

While he waited for the senior officers to arrive, William rode to the edge of the stream. His mount stepped cautiously through the crimson bodies. The contorted positions of the corpses about the bridge were like so many dolls left askew.

Looking over the span, almost hidden under the heap, he noticed a familiar face.

Jaci had died killing the Spanish commander. Absorbed in avenging his family and tribe, the Tupi had ignored William's orders to stay on the edge of the action. Instead, he had attacked the Spanish commander amid the slaughter on the narrow bridge.

Jaci appeared calm. In contrast, the face of the Spanish invader, fallen in a land far from home, betrayed a much more painful and bitter end.

William did not rejoice at his triumph. For the first time, he wondered why any of them were there at all, and if it would not have been better if men preferred the comfort of home to winning glory on alien soil.

CHAPTER 20

฿OGOTÁ

The patriot army arrived in Bogotá two days after their lopsided victory at Boyacá. Crowned with laurels, Bolívar led the column, preceding his generals in a victory march. Crowds thronged the streets and waved from the rooftops as the city turned out to welcome him, not as a conqueror, but as a liberator.

William and the junior officers were billeted at several private residences down the street from the palace, near the barracks. Bolívar's adjutant had stopped by and requested his presence at the palace ball that evening. Twenty-one-hundred sharp.

The members of his squad had just arrived on leave from the Albion Legion. From where he sat on the bed, William said, "Gentlemen, it's good to see you all in one piece."

"Compared to Waterloo, just a stroll in the park, sir," Gus said, "though Paddy did get a scratch helping take the Spanish artillery." Paddy had a fresh bandage around his left arm and another around his right ankle.

"I'm glad to see that not only have you all survived, but you've earned a place at the table, so to speak." He asked Prescott, "How are the wounds, Private?"

Paddy replied, "Just nicks, sir, no bother. But we heard what happened down below at the bridge, sir. We'll miss Jaci."

"It's the fault of that bloody American, if you don't mind my saying so, sir," Gus declared.

James Campbell chimed in, "Too right! Thanks to Jaci I'll always remember how to remove them leechers."

That made William smile. "Thank you, gentlemen. I'll remember you when I'm at the palace this evening. I have a feeling I'll be meeting a general."

The festive air did nothing to raise Nate's spirits. Santander blamed him for attacking before he had given the command and had stripped Nate of his commission—and any chance of a land grant—after the battle. Nate had been ordered to the viceregal palace that evening; after taking the city, Bolívar had commandeered the palace as lodgings for himself and his senior officers.

Watched by his messenger, whom Nate suspected had orders to guard against his escape, Nate arrived at the former viceregal palace along with a train of carriages bearing the entire aristocratic gentry of Bogotá. Ladies and gentlemen dressed in their finery crowded the entrance for what Nate guessed was an extravagant ball in honor of the Great Liberator.

"Private Yankee." Major Daniel O'Leary met Nate at the top of the steps.

Nate saluted and said, "I see word gets around quickly."

"Making the wrong decision on a battlefield can have serious consequences," the Irishman chided, "particularly when a commander's orders are ignored."

"So I've been told."

They walked into the portico between the pillars outside and the ballroom entrance. The city's wealthy and powerful continued to stream past to pay homage to the general.

"Looks like the Royalists turned into patriots overnight," Nate mused.

"Don't be so cynical, Nathanial," O'Leary said distractedly, both men straightening as a group of beautiful, dark-haired young women passed by them. One cast her eyes back at the American, shamelessly staring as the rakish soldier lifted a brow.

O'Leary glanced sideways at Nate. "She was looking at both of us.

"Come on." He took Nate's arm and led him away from the music and lights. "Too bad you're going to miss the party."

"What did you think of the battle?" Nate asked, hoping to learn as much as he could from the Irishman before meeting with Bolívar.

O'Leary was wistful. "It was pure magic—Barreiro's best men trapped below at the river while Bolívar threw our veterans at the Spaniard's center."

"So you could see the action at the bridge?"

"I saw everything, including Santander's right flank break far out in front and descend on the Spaniards like the hammers of hell." O'Leary stopped beside a closed door with a polished brass knob. "Whatever were you thinking?"

"I don't know," Nate said. He scanned the corridor, but there was no one close by. "I saw a chance to prove myself to Bolívar."

The Irishman chuckled. "Well, you definitely got his attention. Wait here. General Bolívar will arrive shortly."

Nate's suspicions deepened when the Irishman took his hand and said with some finality, "Good luck, Private, and goodbye."

Nate didn't have long to wait before the general arrived.

Two armed soldiers in dress uniform preceded Bolívar down the hall. The general was engaged in conversation with the British captain, closely followed by Santander and Morales. As they drew near, Bolívar looked up.

"Ah, Nate, thank you for coming—I request your patience for just a while longer."

William froze, glaring at Nate. This was the first time since Jaci's death that he had encountered the American. His face reddened and he clenched his fists.

Bolívar put his palm on William's back, saying, "Let us continue inside, Captain."

William regained his composure and ignored Yankee, leaving him outside as they entered the drawing room. Within, a richly embroidered Persian carpet covered the center of the polished floor and led to a purple velvet chair behind an immense desk.

"Please take a seat, William." Bolívar indicated a less elaborate armchair facing the desk. He sat on the purple throne. Santander sat beside him, while Morales walked behind William to sit on one of the divans lining the wall. Morales stretched, anticipating a good show.

"To business." Bolívar gestured to Santander. "Francisco, if you please."

Santander spoke to the British officer. "The message you delivered to us from your sovereign was a request: that we recognize Great Britain as a favored trading partner. In return, His Majesty would encourage discharged soldiers from the British army to join our forces, and provide us with arms, ammunition, and intelligence."

"Discreetly," Captain Gunn clarified.

"Discreetly," Bolívar repeated, although in the silence that followed William wasn't sure if it hadn't been a question.

"Yes, sir," William said, just in case.

Bolívar spoke quickly, breaking the tension. "I thank you for bringing this offer to the people of South America. I wish to congratulate you personally, Captain, on your courageous action at the recent battle. Your performance strongly reinforced my positive opinion of the British soldier. It is with great pleasure that I accept His Majesty's offer. We have reviewed the documents you provided and will send an emissary shortly to visit with your king and formalize arrangements."

William bowed, relief flooding through him. His mission was complete. Now he could begin his search for the black orchid.

Bolívar spoke, "I wish you the best of luck with your next task; any assistance that is mine, I offer. But before you leave, Captain, I would have you stay just a moment longer."

He spoke to the guard at the door. "Show the private in."

As Nate entered the room he saw Bolívar, seated behind a luxurious desk, flanked by Santander and attended by the British officer.

"Please approach, Private Bidwell."

Nate stood to attention in front of Bolívar, surprised the general had used his real name. "At your service, General."

He stiffened, expecting the worst, but maintaining a distant hope his performance in battle (after disobeying an order) had vindicated him.

Bolívar said, "Some time ago, the Spanish spread a rumor that the Americans had brought me an offer on behalf of the Spanish king. An offer to betray the revolution in exchange for the viceroyalty."

He continued, "Neither that pisspot Morillo nor that son of a bitch Boves could dislodge us from Venezuela; but all it took in the end was a lie. *Someone* leaked the news that a deal had been made."

Sensing his life was hanging by a thread, Nate spoke quickly, "General, the lie came from Secretary of State Adams and that horse's ass Onís. America wanted Florida, and the Spanish were willing to give it up. But they wanted something in return."

William Gunn's hand moved to his sword. "Traitor!" he spat at the American.

The guards restrained William before he could stain the palace furnishings with the mountain man's entrails. The American watched the struggle calmly.

Bolívar held up his hand. "Captain Gunn, please control yourself."

William was escorted from the room, embarrassed that he had lost his temper.

Bolívar asked Nate, "Tell me, Private Bidwell, are you Adams's emissary?"

"I was asked, and I refused. They made it clear they would make my life in the United States . . . unpleasant if I didn't cooperate, so I came here. Of my own accord.

"I believe my actions at Pisba, Vargas, and Boyacá speak for themselves, General," Nate said firmly.

Santander lifted his eyebrows at this, but said nothing.

"I admit your assistance in provisioning the army after crossing the pass was most welcome—but your presence was one of the reasons we were forced to cross the mountains in the first place. And Vargas . . ." The general looked thoughtful. "It took my heroic Irishman to plug the gap you left."

Bolívar leaned on the top of the desk. "However, your actions at Boyacá convinced me you have no intention of betraying us. No, I do not believe you are capable of representing anything larger than yourself, *Bidwell.*" Bolívar enunciated the American's real last name as though it were an insult; stranger still, Nate reacted as if it were, his eyes flashing. Morales wondered if it were more than just convenience that led the American to leave his name behind.

Bolívar smiled, softening his next words. "While you may be at home in the jungle, on a battlefield you are an idiot."

Nate said, "But, General, you knew this—Páez told you who and what I was."

A sudden realization dawned on Nate. "You could never publicly execute an emissary of the President of the United States. *That's* why you sent me over the pass—you planned to kill me there. When that failed, you promoted me, knowing I'd get *myself* killed."

Bolívar's expression didn't change. "You have a great imagination, Private. You disobeyed General Santander's orders, and Francisco José is a man for whom orders and the law are everything. I respect his command; you must leave."

Nate glared at the general. "You sent the girl to kill me." It was as much a statement as a question.

"This conversation is over," Bolívar said dismissively. "I have someone waiting for me. Goodbye, Mr. Bidwell, and good luck finding your fortune."

Morales escorted Nate from the room.

William Gunn stood just outside, waiting to apologize to the general. He brooded on the recent battle and Jaci's unnecessary death. The American was to blame: he had charged the Spanish lines before William could properly arrange his forces. Jaci would still be alive. Now William was alone in his search for the black orchid.

When he saw the American, he mocked, "Is it just a fool who disobeys orders and charges the enemy before we can mount a proper attack? Or a traitor?"

Morales held Nate firmly by the arm.

Nate said evenly, "If it wasn't for me, their dragoons would have chopped you to pieces."

William spat, "You Yankee bastard! If it wasn't for you, a man worth ten of you would still be alive."

"You lobsterback son of a bitch, that's your last insult. I will have satisfaction."

"That would give me the greatest pleasure." William turned to the Republican officer. "Major Morales, if you would be so kind as to be my second."

CHAPTER 21

UEL

Major Morales and Sergeant MacPherson accompanied William to the area selected for the duel—an isolated location on the north road out of Bogotá. It was the same place Barreiro's officers had conducted their contests of honor. When they arrived, an unearthly mist swirled about the haunted spot.

"Quite a chill in the air this morning," Morales said.

Gus shivered. "Probably the ghosts of officers with poor aim."

Although grim when he arrived, William couldn't help breaking into a smile.

Gus remained by the side of the road watching out for the American and his second. When Nate and O'Leary arrived, he led the group ninety paces into the evergreens, where the ground was clear and flat. The patriot army doctor arrived, and all was ready.

The rules were discussed, then each challenger's second stepped off seven paces from the center and marked the boundary by driving his sword into the ground.

"Please proceed to your mark," Morales called out.

The American and the British officer walked to their swords. When Nate faced William, the fourteen paces felt a lot closer than he would have liked. From this distance the small scar on the British officer's chin was visible.

Morales loaded the pistols while O'Leary watched. The Irishman shot a knowing glance at Nate—they would be dueling with rifled pistols, a weapon which favored the British officer. O'Leary took one and brought the weapon to the American.

"I'll say it again, Bidwell, there's very little basis for your challenge," the Irishman spoke softly, "even now, if you'll allow me to express your regrets, I'm sure the Englishman will accept."

"No one calls me a traitor." Nate said the words, but they felt hollow. He knew he was staring at almost certain death. But, he reassured himself, he had been in tight spots before. His thoughts drifted, his mind seeking relief in the time before the trouble, when he had lived with the Wampanoag. The Irishman's voice brought him back.

"Then there's nothing else for it," O'Leary said, handing the pistol to Nate. "God be with you." And before turning away, he reminded Nate of the Manton's responsive trigger: "Squeeze, don't pull." Morales delivered the other pistol to William. The major stepped back and said, "Gentlemen, you will note your pistols are not cocked. They shall remain so, until the signal is given."

O'Leary tried to stop the duel again, this time directing his plea to the British officer, "As second to the challenger, I request an apology from the challenged on behalf of my principal."

"Belay that request," Nate said.

"No need to belay anything," said William. "It's my pleasure to give the offended an opportunity for his honor to be satisfied."

Morales directed a look of resignation at O'Leary and called out, "You will not fire until the count of three has concluded."

Nate waited until the British officer was in position, then hefted the pistol. The weapon felt strangely light. He breathed deeply, his nerves settling as he focused.

Confident but troubled, William stood at the marker and felt the comfortable Manton in his right hand. He had fought in two duels before, one on the Peninsula and one just before Waterloo. They had both ended the same way. He turned sideways, presenting the smallest possible target.

Morales called, "Gentlemen, cock your pistols." Two distinct clicks could be heard.

Nate wasn't given to introspection, but even he couldn't help but marvel at the series of incidents which had led him here to a duel in Bogotá with a British officer whose first name he didn't even know. And if he shot the man and killed him, what then? What meaningless fortune would he set as his new target? A target to be pursued at a cost he could only measure in hindsight, in moments like these, staring down the barrel of a gun.

An owl roosting in the trees overhead hooted its indifference to the human drama unfolding below.

"Take aim, gentlemen."

Both men raised and sighted their weapons.

"One."

Nate shifted slightly to get a better angle. Time slowed. His hearing sharpened.

"Two."

"Sideways, man, protect yourself! Sideways!" O'Leary called to the American.

William released his breath and settled on the fine target presented by the man standing a mere fourteen paces away.

"Three."

Both guns spoke simultaneously, a single loud report that tore the air. The pall of blue smoke mixed with the mist, forming a dense fog.

The owl flew off.

Stirred by a breeze, the haze swirled, then blew clear. The duelists had not moved. To the onlookers, it appeared as if they were frozen in position.

William lowered his pistol, his ears still ringing.

Pistol still raised, Nate sank to his knees. A bright red stain spread across the front of his white shirt.

CHAPTER 22

JUNGLE SECRETS

Captain Ernesto Marquez watched as William's small party took the northwest road out of Bogotá, toward the Magdalena river town of Honda. The lithe Spaniard had an aristocratic nose and the intense eyes of an eagle. Ever since receiving word from the Dutchman in Barranquilla several weeks ago, the Spanish agent had been waiting patiently for the Englishman to appear. This was his first and best opportunity to send an unmistakable message to Britain.

He pondered methods. He was especially enamored with his Chaumette breechloader pistol, which accepted rifled rounds and was very accurate. Marquez had had his pistol custom-made some years ago—it was truly a work of art—and he so wanted to murder this Englishman with it. If he used this gun, he could make it appear as though a rebel officer had executed the Englishman.

But he had his orders: he must first capture Gunn and discover what the British officer had offered Bolívar. Then, as with most things in life, this affair was really quite simple: eliminate the British officer and pin the blame on Bolívar.

This wasn't supposed to be necessary. Bolívar should have been neutralized at Boyacá, and William Gunn captured. The viceroy's torturers would have discovered everything the Englishman knew, and he—Captain Ernesto Rodrigo Marquez—would have taken care of the rest.

Instead, the rebels had forced His Most Catholic Majesty's Viceroy to flee the city disguised as an old woman. Disgraceful.

Then there was the other matter. Marquez did not like cleaning up other people's messes. If Harold Hull hadn't gotten himself killed before reporting to Veeborlay, they would have been able to communicate some progress to the Dutch East India Company.

The Dutch money Abel Veeborlay had offered Marquez only increased the Spaniard's desire to discover why the heathen British king had sent an officer from England halfway around the world to this hellish jungle. *What could be so important?*

Making men talk was a task Captain Marquez was not only good at but relished. Trained by the Inquisition, he had far surpassed his mentors in techniques and methods. The Englishman's luck had run out.

William was thankful for the pack donkeys Bolívar's quartermaster had provided to assist him in his search for the black orchid. But he had his doubts about the mestizo guides.

Manuel and Tito were not inclined to conversation. They replied to most of his inquiries with grunts and nods. He sorely missed Jaci— William's temperature rose whenever he thought of how the American's treachery had resulted in Jaci's death. He hoped he could find guides who were even half as knowledgeable as his Tupi companion.

The lack of human interaction made him feel low. He'd gone from the close camaraderie of his first command to wandering alone in the wilds of South America.

The truth was he missed the company of Gus and the others, now more than ever. But it would also have been terribly unfair to accept their offer to join him, and thereby jeopardize their land grants from Bolívar. This was his mission alone. He would see it through, wherever it led.

Robert Sheridan had said that the Muzo tribe might hold a clue to the location of the black orchid. In addition, he had told him that the last known whereabouts of the tribe was somewhere on the west bank of the Magdalena. The only thing these useless guides could tell him was that the tribe had left the Muzo area a long time ago.

But William still believed the quickest way to find the black orchid would be among the multitude of wild orchids lining the riverbanks. At Honda he could pick up transport down the river, hunt for the black orchid at each stop, and inquire about the Muzo tribe as he went.

If he didn't come up with any leads after several days, he would prospect inland from the western bank, among the foothills of the Cordillera Central. It was rumored that orchids were prolific on both sides of these steep mountains.

By late afternoon, they were ready for a rest.

William decided to leave the river at the first downstream stop, based on the advice of the guide Manuel that strange orchids were found toward the foothills in this area. William and the guides took a small road heading in that direction.

They saw only two other travelers, much earlier in the morning; one passed them going toward the river, while the other overtook them and soon was out of sight.

They had yet to come to a stream or a cistern. William had been so long without a drink of water that he couldn't even sweat.

When he saw the pond, all he could think of was quenching his thirst—bugs and scum be damned. Life in Gran Colombia had a way of stripping away the veneer of civilization he had embraced on his return from Waterloo.

Plagued with thirst and kneeling down to drink, William caught a fleeting glimpse of Manual's reflection in the rippling surface.

The cudgel struck the right side of William's head where the jawbone met the skull. Manuel always considered this strike a small mercy to his "customers," at least those he did not hold any particular grudge against. This blow, dealt quickly and forcefully, sent the recipients quickly into unconsciousness.

Before they departed with his belongings, Tito delivered a quick kick to William's ribs. One of the pack animals, spooked by the sudden action, bolted and disappeared deep into the jungle.

Manuel scolded him, "Did you have to do that? Now we have only one donkey for our trouble. Idiot!"

Concealed in the brush, Marquez watched the two men round the bend in the road, arguing, oblivious to their surroundings. The Spaniard was surprised the British officer had allowed these two morons to lead.

After a few moments passed and the Brit still hadn't appeared, the Spaniard began to suspect the guides of duplicity.

He had originally planned to dispose of them quickly. No longer. The brigands would regret interrupting his plan to capture the British officer. It would be so much the worse for them if they had actually killed the Englishman.

When the moment finally came, they would welcome death.

William awoke with a massive headache. He was parched, having lain unconscious in the sun for hours. To make matters worse, a host of mosquitos had feasted on his exposed skin.

He crawled to the edge of the pond and drank through cracked lips. He sipped slowly at first, being careful to take small swallows of the filthy brew. As he stood, the throbbing pain in his cranium intensified. A glance told him most of his belongings were gone.

The quartermaster had warned William that the army couldn't spare their best guides, but the British officer never thought the two he wound up with were going to be actual brigands. He could kick himself for trusting them.

The thieves must have been in a hurry, for they had not looked under his shirt—the locket pendant with Sarah's and Miriam's hair and the medal were still around his neck. Bending to gather up an overlooked blanket, a sharp pain in his side caught his breath. He ran his hand over his sore ribs; he was sure one or more were bruised.

With the pain throbbing through his skull, it was difficult to take stock. He would have to find the main road, make his way to the nearest town, get assistance, and restart his search. And never again trust another person in this godforsaken place.

He made a cloak from the blanket to block the curiously blinding sun. Without food, shelter, or supplies, and with time running out to save his daughter's life, William Gunn plunged into the shadows of the enveloping jungle.

CHAPTER 23

MUZO

It had been a fortnight since the duel.

The British officer's bullet had gone straight through Nate's shoulder. At first, Nate had felt nothing and had heard nothing, just the ringing in his ears. But then a strange creeping weakness had invaded his legs and his vision had blurred, he became light-headed, and blackness overcame him.

Luckily, the Englishman's ball had passed through his shoulder. The wound had now healed to the point where his complaining was starting to annoy his comrades. They felt he should be more thankful he wasn't badly hurt and for Bolívar allowing him to stay with the llaneros while he recovered.

His thoughts were interrupted by the sound of a horse and rider approaching.

Only when the rider dismounted and began to walk toward him did Nate recognize Daniel O'Leary.

"The doctor says you're quite well healed, Bidwell. It's time you left us."

"I suppose I should thank Bolívar, but all I'm getting out of this in the end is a sore shoulder."

"You're lucky to be alive, but I think you know that," O'Leary said. "The quartermaster will see to provisioning you. So where to next, Yank?"

"Back to the second oldest profession in the world."

"Let me guess. Trading gems?"

"I always said if I ever found myself this far south, I'd have to visit the Muzo mines."

"Santander's aide used to live in Maripi, not far from Muzo. All he can talk about are the emeralds of Muzo. From what he says, it's just about a week or so journey northeast of here."

"The most sought-after gems in the world, Daniel. Back home around the docks when I was a boy, I'd hear sailors speak of the emeralds of Muzo with the same awe as the rubies of Ceylon. I reckoned they were fairy stories, like the Arabian Nights or something."

"I've heard that the Spaniards guard the mine quite closely. The Indian laborers aren't even allowed to leave the site—they live and work there, a couple hundred of them."

When Nate looked surprised, O'Leary added, "No one leaving the mine means no smuggling, right?" He smiled. "Maybe you'll find El Jefe."

"The lost emerald?"

O'Leary asked, "Isn't it supposed to be the most valuable gem in the world?"

"Right," Nate replied derisively, "a perfect emerald larger than a grown man's fist. Worth a king's ransom. It's a lot of nonsense, Captain—it doesn't exist, except in people's imagination. Like the pot of gold at the end of the rainbow."

"Now that's *real*, Yank—every Irishman knows that," O'Leary said, enjoying himself.

"El Jefe sounds more like an Irish fairy tale than anything else," Nate said, not taken in by O'Leary's wit. "All I hope to do is pick up a few quality stones and make enough money trading them up north to buy my way back home."

"So that's the long-term plan?"

"Been a while since I found anything to commit to," Nate replied. "And it never was my idea to come down here in the first place—despite the rumors. I was dragooned out of the States onto a ship bound for Cartagena. Seems I was expendable to some people, but luckily it didn't work out that way."

"I understand Muzo can be a dangerous place," the Irish officer said, mounting his horse. "Especially if anyone finds out you fought for Bolívar."

After ten days in the rain, tramping over mountains, across freezing *páramos*, and through steaming tropical valleys, Nate was relieved to finally be approaching the town of Muzo.

Native Colombians were typically very friendly and welcoming. But as the American approached the emerald country, a noticeable sullenness entered into his interactions with not only the people but the land itself. Perhaps the threadbare rope bridges on the trail to Muzo contributed to the peevish nature of the population. But it was more than that. An indefinable heaviness sat over the area.

"At least I still have you, Jenny." He found himself talking to the mule and laughed. He realized he was in serious need of company.

Dealing in precious gems elsewhere was straightforward. In any sizable town in Colombia and Venezuela, there would be a store or plaza where stones could be traded at a particular time of the day. If you knew your business and had some capital, there were always deals to be made.

But this was the first time Nate had tried to acquire gems at an actual mine. His plan had been to bargain with the mestizos who worked the tailings. If nothing turned up, it might be possible to approach a friendly guard.

He hesitated at the edge of the town, under a cloudy sky. He was unsure of the direction to the mine and decided a hot breakfast at a café with the locals wouldn't go astray. He set off down the main street, hoping to find a place in the village.

The street was deserted at that early hour. A breeze descended from the surrounding hills, swirling about the lone stranger and his mule. A skeletal pig rooted through some trash and a couple of mangy dogs wandered aimlessly nearby.

Muzo might be the most miserable place on this continent, with its ramshackle huts and single mucky lane serving as the town's main thoroughfare. Located in the center of the fabled gem-producing district for nearly two hundred years, Muzo nonetheless looked as though it had been thrown together the week before. The prospects of a refreshing bath and decent meal were fading rapidly.

A few hardy folks emerged from their homes. A man leaving his shack gave one of the dogs in the road a hard kick for no apparent reason. A silent glare met Nate's polite request for directions to the mine.

He passed a couple of small open-air cantinas, deserted at this hour, their thatched roofs looking ready to disintegrate with the slightest gust. About halfway to the end of the small town, Nate had almost completely lost hope, when he detected the aroma of coffee wafting from what looked like a log shack that opened onto the street. Supported by sturdy wooden corner posts, it was one of the few structures with a tiled roof. A ribbon of blue smoke drifted upward from a chimney.

He tied the mule to a post that would be visible from inside. Before he entered, the American frontiersman checked his powder, slipped the dragon back into its holster, and loosed his facón in its sheath.

Careful not to hit his head on the low roof beam, Nate entered. The air was dry and warm. The room was lit by one small window. In the semidarkness, the floor and tables appeared clean. There were three people inside—not bad for this early hour. One of them should be a talker.

A sad-looking man with greasy black hair, mostly hidden under a dirty white bandana, and wearing a sort of apron, which might have been red at one time but was now stained dark brown, poked a bed of glowing coals in the corner fireplace, throwing up small yellow flames as the sticks on top ignited. He went back to preparing breakfast for the regulars.

A short man in a flannel shirt standing close to the fire conversed with the cook while another man sat at a table, perched on the flat side of a cut log. The man at the table scooped food into a mouth framed by a bushy black mustache.

A pot of steaming hot coffee sat invitingly next to a jug of chicha on a high table across from the fireplace. The cook placed cornbread on the table, along with a pot of eggs in boiling water.

He went back to frying something that looked like capybara.

Nate said firmly, "Coffee and eggs."

The cook looked up from the fire, surprised that another customer had come in. "Help yourself," he said gruffly and nodded toward a narrow shelf holding several cracked and chipped ceramic mugs, "and there is bread, some butter. Not much else. Too early."

"I won't require anything else—except perhaps some advice." Nate kept one eye on his mule as he got his breakfast.

"I'd like to buy some emeralds," Nate said loudly, "I hear this is the place."

At his table, a spoonful of eggs briefly hesitated on its way to Bushy Mustache's mouth.

The cook sighed loudly. "There's no trading here—it's not allowed in town. It only encourages smuggling."

Without turning to look at Nate, Bushy Mustache belched out, "Which is punishable by death." He took a large swallow of weak liquor and wiped the back of his hand across his mouth. He stood, wiped his hands on the front of his trousers, and walked over. "I can help you. Maybe you like El Jefe, huh? Big as your fist and green as death."

Nate hid his amusement. *What a horse's ass.* He'd met more men like Mustache in his father's orbit than he would care to recollect. Over by the fire, the man in the flannel shirt put on his hat and walked out.

Nate asked, "How much?"

The man picked at his teeth. "Two silver reales for directions to the mine; I'll even draw you a map."

Nate was not inclined to stay in Muzo any longer than necessary. "Let me think about it while I eat."

Mustache grinned, his smile blemished by several burnished silver teeth. "Of course, you cannot leave without some of José's *chigüiro*. It would hurt his feelings." Nate didn't like his smile.

Nate rode out of town in the early afternoon. He didn't pay for a map; the way to the mine would naturally carry the most traffic, and the road should be well tracked. He did learn from a smithy, who overcharged him for a bridle bit, that the mine was about ten kilometers to the west. He was determined to get there well before dark.

Leaving town, the main street strayed to the southwest though cultivated fields. After a half hour's travel, the road entered a thick forest.

"Bit quiet in here, isn't it, Jenny?" he mused. The shadows ahead swallowed the brown sweep of track. "Be a lot more settling if we could see further down this road."

He led the mule along for another quarter of an hour or so. In that time only one wagon passed, going back toward town; the driver cast his eyes down and didn't speak. Nate wasn't surprised at the lack of traffic but did wonder where the ambush would take place.

He knew that men like Mustache didn't make a living without getting their hands dirty. He also knew his leaving Muzo had been watched. There wasn't much he could do, though, beyond having his weapons primed and ready. A man couldn't do more than weigh the risks and take every precaution. It was up to fate after that.

He came to a fork in the road. The left branch was the smaller of the two and wound quickly away to the south; the right fork was wider and turned directly north.

In the dense woods and tropical mist, it was difficult to see. A light rain began to fall. He was told the road to the left eventually met the Río Itoco and, from there, followed the river upstream to the mine. He strained, trying to see into the gloom ahead.

But that road looked less traveled. The smooth surface was pitted with sprouting weeds. No one had gone that way in a while.

The route to the right, however, had multiple wagon ruts worn into the path, which made sense if this were the road to the mine. He dismounted and led the mule down the rutted path. Wide enough for wagons to pass, the trail was firm underfoot, as though from constant traffic—a good sign. Several horsemen had passed recently.

Giant ferns rose overhead, and the dense banks of vegetation enclosing both sides of the road fashioned a dark-green tunnel.

Something was not quite right—it was much too silent. The noisy chatter of birds and tree-dwelling animals ceased. Jenny showed a sudden, unusual reluctance to continue. He had a bad feeling about this.

He coaxed the mule down the track and drew back the blanket covering the animal, revealing the pistol and blunderbuss. Whoever was out there was in for a nasty surprise. This was not his first encounter with thieves.

Through the haze, he could just make out the downed tree blocking the road.

He'd expected this from the moment he entered that dismal town. It was always the same, with the same result. Where would they come from this time? The vegetation was too thick on either side of the road.

He nonchalantly turned around, calm and deliberate, keeping Jenny by his side. The mule kept pace with him.

He came around the turn and saw them waiting at the crossroad. Five of them. With machetes.

CHAPTER 24

DELIRIUM

"Father, is that you?" Sarah said. "You've been away for so long."

Sarah was older than he remembered, her long brown hair braided down her back. William reached out to take her hand, to reassure her.

He stumbled and fell. Pain surged up his arm.

"Bloody hell," he swore, the agony building in his wrist, driving away the vision of his daughter. With his unhurt hand, he wiped the sweat from his eyes.

Everywhere he looked was the same sea of green. He was unable to make his way back to the road after being betrayed by his guides and had wandered with a vague plan in mind of contacting a tribe who might assist him.

But something was wrong. He was always too hot, even after he stripped off most of his clothes. The bug bites had ceased to concern him; the mounting heat and acute dizziness were too distracting. He dreamed he had a snake in his hand, not remembering if he was bitten, or even where the creature came from.

He decided to rest, to lay down on the bed of soft ferns in his English garden. When his head stopped hurting, he would continue searching until he had found Sarah, and they would be together. He would not leave her again.

"William, this is not a time to rest, nor a time to give up. You must continue your search. Our daughter is depending on you—her very life is at stake. Even now she is in danger."

He sat up. "Miriam, is that you?"

"Yes, William. I am always here—you know that. Now have faith, husband. Be steadfast, as always."

He found relief in the visions that were becoming ever more frequent. But now he was growing convinced that they were not visions at all, but real—more real than the green nightmare surrounding him.

CHAPTER 25

JUST DESSERTS

The thugs walked toward Nate, slowly and deliberately shortening the space between them. The five of them brandished machetes.

"Hey, Yanqui, you want our emeralds?" the big one in the middle, obviously the leader, shouted. "Here they are."

Another yelled, "But first we'll take something from you." Nate recognized Flannel Shirt as the speaker. The man ran a finger along the edge of his blade.

Wonder where Mustache is. Maybe on the hill, covering them with a musket. This could get interesting. Nate stopped. Good to keep out of accurate musket range—allow them to come in close, and let his weapons do their work. As always, the fools never realized what his weapons were capable of.

They stopped. Behind them at the crossroads, a young woman in a shawl led a limping horse past, on the road back to Muzo. The leader—thickset, bearded, with long matted hair, and a head taller than the others—turned and spoke with her. Nate could just about catch what she was saying.

"My horse has gone lame. I need to get to town before dark. Can you help? I would be ever so grateful," she said. Beneath her shawl, her shapely figure was partially revealed by her light cotton dress.

They had all turned around. The leader said to his men, "Wait. First, we take care of business."

She called loudly, "Five of you and no one to help me?" She smiled and turned to leave.

Nate wondered what the hell a lone woman was doing out here. *She should run from this scum as fast as her legs can take her.*

Flannel Shirt took out a length of rope. "We'll make sure she doesn't go anywhere." Carelessly bunched together, the four brutes approached her. Their boss remained between them and Nate, blocking the American's view.

A large oddly colored rock came loose from somewhere on the steep slope. Bouncing down the hill and through the brush, the strange object launched the last few feet onto the road, where it rolled to a stop at the big man's feet.

Purple tongue protruding from his mouth, Mustache's severed head gazed up with unseeing eyes.

In the same instant, the air split with a single thunderous crack. The leader whipped around—a thick veil of smoke had enveloped his accomplices.

The commotion was too much for Jenny, who bolted into the underbrush at the side of the road. Hesitant to turn his back on his attackers, Nate ignored the loose mule and released the facón from its sheath, cursing his stupidity for not taking the guns from his pack on the animal.

The leader was still straining to see through the haze at the crossroads.

Flannel Shirt emerged, clutching his chest, coughing up red. Behind him, visible though the dissolving smoke, a mortally wounded man sank to his knees, staring at the ground as if searching for something important. Another lay in the dirt, flopping from side to side like a fish out of water. The fourth was unhurt. Recovering from his initial shock, he lunged for the woman.

A single shot rang out. The attacker fell at her feet, screaming, his hands clutching his thigh. Blood seeped through his fingers.

Nate calmly took out his knife and waited. The leader turned back to face him, his features contorted in fury. With his machete raised overhead, the big man charged, bearing down on the American.

Nate feinted, drawing the machete swing wide. A quick sweep-kick took out the attacker's legs, pitching him on his face. Nate slammed his knee into the prone man's back, keeping him facedown on the ground.

Nate reached down to grab the thief's chin. He could feel the struggling man's enormous strength. Nate twisted the head upward; a crunching noise, not unlike tramping over seashells, echoed in the close space. A watery gurgle and a rush of breath followed.

Nate rose, exhaling deeply. He retrieved his knife and walked toward the woman. She wiped the stained blade of her facón with the dark-blue bandana tied to her waist. The wounded attacker lay dead at her feet.

It was Julia, Bolívar's assassin.

She cut off any questions. "Not now." Adjusting her shawl around her shoulders, she said, "We must leave this place."

Luis and Santiago arrived, leading the horses. Luis cast a look at the big corpse down the road. "Good job, Nate—a nice llanero move."

"Learned that long before I met you, *amigo*," Nate replied. He shifted his gaze to the woman. "It seems you appeared at just the right time." *Strange coincidence.*

Julia stood with the reins of her horse in one hand, the other hand on her hip. Despite herself, she stared at Nate; she had seen him briefly at a distance that first week in Socha, but this was the first time she had a chance to study him up close.

Despite all he had been through, his eyes—the clear blue of a tropical sea—smiled back at her, full of intelligence and humor. Not much older than herself, he was clean shaven, his face tanned a mahogany brown, his long dark hair pulled into a braid that hung down his back.

During the fight, a necklace—composed of the enormous claws of an animal she didn't recognize—must have escaped from under his shirt and now hung loose about his neck. She sensed the power in his muscular arms, knowing the great strength it must have taken to kill a man with one's bare hands. She had never seen a man kill the way he had. She found his grin irritating.

"We can talk later," Julia said. "Right now, we must go. Mount up."

Nate was careful not to stare back but did not look away either. She had dark skin, golden brown eyes, and high cheekbones; her hair had grown and now hung to her shoulders in a silken auburn wave, the same color as a field of grain in autumn. He could imagine her as a spy, the seductress in a luxurious bed.

"I'm not in the army anymore. I don't take orders from anyone," Nate replied, sounding more pitiful than he'd intended.

She sprang lightly onto the back of the large gray mare. "You may join us or stay here to get yourself killed. It's your choice."

They took the south road toward the Magdalena port city of Honda. From there, Julia and the soldiers would take the main road directly east to Bogotá and report back to Bolívar.

Knowing he couldn't return to the capital, Nate hoped something would turn up before they arrived at Honda.

Under a gradually clearing sky, they rode quickly and silently. The trail ascended, the dense tropical vegetation eventually thinning into scrub oak forest. The sun dropped behind the high hills, and a hard chill crept into the air; the first sharp stars of night appeared. They found a clearing not visible from the trail and set up camp.

To avoid attracting unwelcome attention, they decided to eat their food cold by the light of the full moon. When they finished, Nate brought out a skin of aguardiente. He handed it to Julia. Without drinking, she passed it on to Santiago.

The llanero coughed as the fiery liquid scorched his throat. "The colonel must have given this to you. Everyone says he finds the strongest juice wherever we go."

"Hold on, are you talking about O'Leary? That Irishman's a full colonel now?" Nate shook his head in disbelief.

"He's the only reason you're still in one piece," Julia said. It was the first time she had spoken since the crossroads. "When O'Leary heard you were heading to Muzo, he asked for volunteers to intercept and warn you of the danger."

Luis interjected, "Colonel Julia was the first to come forward."

She cast Luis a sour look. "Colonel O'Leary decided a small, quick squad would be more effective," she lied, "and chose the three of us to find you."

Nate smirked, causing her face to flush in the pale moonlight.

"I owed you a life, that's all," she said testily. "Now we're even."

Nate nodded as he tried but failed to wipe the grin off his face. He changed the subject. "What was that weapon you used against the bandits? I've never seen anything take down three men with one shot."

Julia explained, "A special gift from Bolívar. A 'duck's foot' pistol. It's a prototype, from Europe." She took out a four-barreled caplock pistol and handed it to him. "It discharges four cartridges at once. The general believed that someday it might be of use to me."

Nate whistled. "I guess I'm lucky you didn't use this going over the Pisba pass."

Julia smirked. "It would've been too hard to hide under my ruana."

"Oh, I don't know," Nate said, his tone light, "you were hiding quite a few things under that ruana—I think there was room for one little pistol."

Julia arched an eyebrow. "Little?"

Nate hefted the ludicrous weapon, feeling its weight. "Compared to mine."

Julia matched Nate's smile as they tested to see who would look away first.

"You're lucky you left Bogotá," Santiago said, ending the moment nearly as effectively as if he had he heaved a bucket of ice water over them.

Self-conscious, Julia looked away. Nate scowled at Santiago. "I wouldn't exactly call winding up in an ambush 'lucky.'"

Oblivious, Santiago continued, "Santander disobeyed Bolívar's orders and killed the Spanish prisoners of war, including Brigadier Barreiro. Maybe you would've been among them."

Julia stared at Santiago for a long hard moment until he looked away. She took the aguardiente from the llanero's hand and left for her tent, taking a swig from the skin.

"That's mine," Nate called after her.

"I know." She looked over her shoulder at Nate, her hips swaying a touch as she disappeared from view. She left the flap open.

Nate and Santiago shared a look.

"She tried to kill you, amigo."

Nate was already standing. "Shut up, Santiago."

Nate considered the roof of Julia's tent. Julia faced him, lying on her side, using one of his arms as a pillow.

"Sorry about that," he said.

Julia squinted at him through her eyelashes. "Do you Americans always apologize after sex?" She smiled and patted him on the chest. "Don't worry, Yanqui. I take it as a compliment."

She rested her head again and closed her eyes, exhausted.

Nate considered the roof of Julia's tent.

"I usually last longer than that. Must be the altitude."

Feeling him move under her blanket, Julia groaned and rolled away.

"I thought you took it as a compliment," Nate said.

"No," Julia murmured. "I'm trying to sleep."

Nate considered her back. He was in a considering mood. "Why did you try to kill me?" he asked.

Julia turned back to Nate, moving on top of him. "If you insist on bothering me all night, I might as well give you a second chance."

They rose with the first light of dawn, the starry points of the Hunter still visible in the indigo sky. They ate a quick meal and set off for Honda. Having studiously avoided eye contact with them over breakfast, Santiago and Luis rode on ahead, where they loudly debated the relative merits of a mule over a horse. Julia grinned as she and Nate rode abreast.

Their horses matched pace, walking shoulder to shoulder.

Eventually, Julia pulled away. Now she was frowning at Nate. Familiar with these little plot twists in his relations with the fairer sex, Nate looked straight ahead and pretended not to notice.

They rode for a few moments before Julia said, "You must understand that Bolívar is squeezed between the great powers, all pushing their own interests." Her brow creased in concern. "There are spies everywhere."

"That's ironic, coming from you."

Julia ignored him. "You probably won't live much longer, the way you're going, so I'll tell you." She shifted in her saddle as if sitting on a burr. "The British have come to Bolívar offering their secret support. That's what Captain Gunn is doing here. But the Dutch East India Company has also offered assistance to the general."

"The Dutch? What do they have to do with it?" Nate asked.

"All I know is the Dutch are trying to manipulate Spain and Britain into another war, and maybe even involve the Americans. They think Bolívar would have to turn to them."

He looked at her. "How do you know so much?"

"The Dutchmen are no different than other men: they like to talk. Like Barreiro," Julia said spitefully. "He would say anything to impress me. In a way, he impressed his way to his own death."

Julia goaded him. "Now, *you* tell *me*: Why is a scout and gem peddler interested in such things? The mysterious Yanqui—so at home in the woods, yet so lost on a battlefield."

Nate explained, "I grew up spending more time with the Wampanoags than with anyone else. They taught me a lot about the wilderness. Their fighting is much more personal than your great armies with cavalry, flags, and all the rest," he continued, "it's a close-up, look-'em-in-the-eye affair."

"Where were you raised, that you to spent so much time with the natives?" She was curious. "You seem to have been in the woods your whole life."

"In New England, not far from Boston."

"Your parents?" she asked.

"My mother was from one of the oldest families in the colonies. I never knew her." He took a deep breath, "She died in childbirth."

"And your father?"

After a slight pause Nate said, "I'm afraid we had a falling-out. In fact," he continued with a wry smile, "we can't stand the sight of each other, to put it mildly. Never could."

They rode in silence for a while, the wind carrying the far-off sounds of a boar nosing in the underbrush.

"And that's the reason you left your country?" she asked.

"Among other things," Nate said.

"Are you sure you're not running away from a nagging wife or jealous lover?"

"No wife"—he looked at her closely—"and no lovers."

Julia laughed quietly. Although her laugh was brief and restrained, he liked the fact she was amused.

"You should laugh more often. The Wampanoag say it keeps a person young."

"I haven't had much to laugh about. At least after Valencia—but you've probably heard about that."

High clouds had moved over the rising sun, which now gleamed dully like a tarnished silver wafer pinned low in the sky. A cool breeze stirred the branches in the pine trees.

Nate pointed. "See that?"

"What?"

"The bark on that tree. See how it's scored, about seven feet off the ground?"

"Yes, now I see. What *is* that?"

"Bear sharpened its claws on that tree. They probably like to eat the sugar in the base of that plant over there." He indicated a clump of puya plants. "More dangerous than people realize. The bear is the only animal that will lay a false trail if it knows it's being followed, and then turn around and stalk its pursuer."

They rode in silence for a while, the sun now hidden behind the thick clouds gathering in the west. The woods were quiet save for the sound of tree limbs groaning in the breeze.

She spoke abruptly. "Everyone believed you were an emissary from your president. They believed you came to offer Bolívar a deal to betray the revolution."

She caught his eye. "Just the rumor was enough to threaten the shaky ties we have with many of the caudillos." She added evenly, "You were a liability."

They heard Santiago laughing at something Luis had said. Julia's horse gave a low whinny.

"Have you ever heard of El Jefe?" she asked.

Nate was silent for a long time, then replied, "The emerald?"

"Bolívar regretted his treatment of you and asked me to give you two documents. They concern El Jefe."

She took a leather pouch out of her saddlebag. Opening it, she withdrew a file containing two letters sealed with the general's stamp.

"You must promise not share these with anyone," she said, handing them to the American.

"You have my word." Nate broke the seal on the first document and read it. He looked up, his azure eyes narrow and inscrutable. Then he opened the second and quickly scanned through it.

"To your liking, I hope," she said.

He asked, "Where did they come from?"

"The viceroy's files. The coward fled so fast he left everything behind. O'Leary came upon the records and thought they were a fraud. But knowing that the general's family owned mines, the Irishman thought Bolívar would be amused. The general believes the dossier is authentic," Julia said, "and wants you to have it. He also said the Indian tribe who attacked the mine was last reported somewhere west of the river."

"This is not the first I've heard of El Jefe," Nate said thoughtfully, "but this is the first evidence I've ever come across that hints at its actual existence."

"What do the papers say?" Julia asked.

"The first was the mine manager's official report to Bogotá the day after the discovery. The second was written a fortnight later by an assistant superintendent"—Nate glanced again at the paper—"obviously under great stress. The paper's torn and stained, but best I can make out, he describes an attack, the death of the manager, and the loss of the gem."

"Do they say where the emerald is now?"

"No. But most likely with the Indians. If it exists at all." Nate asked sharply, "And tell me again: Bolívar wanted *me* to have these?"

"He said it was for your service, and so there would be no hard feelings between him and his only American patriot."

"Certainly sounds like the general." A plan began to take shape in Nate's mind. If these documents were authentic, and the tribe still had the gem, that made two lucrative leads, both having to do with the payoff of a lifetime, and that was too good an opportunity to pass up. Especially for someone who had no other options. Anyway, no one was in a better position than he was to find the tribe and get that gem.

Things were definitely falling into place. About time.

Julia was silent until they came to the place where Nate was to leave them. Only after he had taken leave of Santiago and Luis, did Julia approach him.

"This is goodbye. I wish you much luck in your hunt."

He said, "Here's to the next time."

She said, "If you can manage to stay alive, Yankee, which I strongly doubt."

"Thanks for the vote of confidence, lady." He smiled and followed his path to the west while the other riders continued south.

After a short distance, he heard her call out, "*Vaya con Dios*, Nathanial Yankee." To herself, Julia said, "Until we meet again."

In the former viceroy's place in Bogotá, Julia sat on a settee across from General Bolívar. She said, "I've delivered the documents, General, as you requested. I've also told him the last known location of the emerald tribe."

Bolívar leaned toward her and spoke with gentle attentiveness. "We both know King John will need British help before all this is through.

And the emerald will be the greatest of inducements, believe me. There's no other gem on earth like it. El Jefe will prove irresistible to a fortune hunter like our American."

"If he tries to leave with the emerald from anywhere in Brazil," Julia added, "the king will know."

"And if he tries to leave from anywhere in Gran Colombia," Bolívar said pointedly, "*I* will know."

"But does such a gem truly exist?" she asked.

"I believe it does. Don't worry. If the treasure is real"—Bolívar smiled—"the *Yanqui* will find it."

CHAPTER 26

PARTNERS

William swam in a sea of dizziness and pain—each muscle in his body ached, it hurt to breathe deeply, and his ears were ringing. He struggled to sit up and open his eyes; the blinding light hurt his head. Someone helped him into a sitting position.

A lively and familiar voice announced, "If it's not Captain William Gunn, the wandering Brit, back to the land of the living."

No. It couldn't be. That bloody Yankee.

"Now, my good Captain, let's not get ahead of ourselves, there's plenty of time to thank me for saving you—at the moment, let's just focus on you getting your strength back."

The infuriating nonsense from this damn American helped to clear his head. Trying to turn to see who was feeding him, he winced from the fierce pain that shot up his side.

When a person entered the wilderness for any length of time unprepared, it usually didn't turn out well. Gunn was no exception. Wounded, bitten, his body wasted, his face pinched in pain and fever, he'd been barely recognizable when the American first saw him two weeks ago lying naked and prostrate, dirty banana leaves keeping him off the bare ground. The right side of William's face had been swollen and his ribs darkly bruised; his dry breath had barely rattled between the officer's cracked lips.

"Better take it easy. Either someone danced a minuet on the side of your body, or a mule kicked you. Either way, I'd say you're the proud owner of a couple of bruised ribs." Nate poked a finger in William's side. "Could be quite painful for a while."

"Ow! What're you doing?"

"For the bullet," Nate said, rubbing his recently healed wound.

"That was your doing, Bidwell," William managed to rasp. "Where am I? And what the hell are you doing here?"

"I strongly suggest, your imperial majesty, that you continue speaking the King's English, as we have the chief's son for company. He's spent time with the missionaries and speaks Spanish." Bidwell changed to Spanish. "Cusi, the great white shaman has just rejoined us from the spirit world." A smiling young man approached hesitantly. "This is Cusi, the chief's only son. His name means 'joyful.'"

True to his name, a perpetually cheerful expression lit Cusi's face. He was short and thin, not long out of adolescence, and his voice broke with the edge of manhood. Like the rest of his tribe, he was light complexioned and wore a short cotton cloth about his waist. Being a youth, Cusi was not yet allowed to wear the heavy, dangling silver and gold earlobe ornaments of a warrior, or the gem necklaces of the elders and his father, the cacique.

Nate said in Spanish, "And to answer your question: We're deep in the jungle on the west side of the Magdalena, not far from the foothills of the mountains. I believe we are with the Muzo tribe.

"You should also know," Nate switched to English, "our lives hang by the merest of threads. The only reason we're both not with our ancestors at the moment is that this tribe thinks you"—Nate's eyebrows rose—"are some sort of great shaman from across the ocean. And that I'm your servant, or assistant. Or something. So, I suggest you start acting real shamanic, real soon, or our gooses are cooked."

Nate switched back to Spanish. "Cusi, please tell my master what has happened."

Cusi said, "Every year the turtles come, they lay eggs on lake shore. When this happens, many *otorongos* leave the forest to catch and eat turtles. When turtles leave, *otorongos* go back." Cusi's smile faltered. "This year, not all go back.

"For two full moons after turtles, almost all village dogs gone. Then one of the children. Then another, getting water for the meal. We try but we cannot kill the *otorongo*. At night, in the village, men and women are taken. And now, *otorongo* has taken the best hunters.

"When we find you," he said, to the British officer, "you speak with the gods. You have gold hair, and on your neck are *illa* and *khuya*. Since you come, *otorongo* does not kill. My father said this was because the creator brought you to us from far off with great medicine to keep *otorongo* away."

Cusi smiled again. "But then you become more sick and more sick, and cannot heal yourself. Our spirit man says, 'He cannot help us or himself. Dyus, the creator, sent him, not as medicine man, but as sacrifice to please the beast.'"

William's side ached, and he groaned. Someone changed the cloth on his forehead. Nate lifted a mug to the British officer's lips. Bits of vegetation floated on top of the concoction.

"What's that mess?" Damned if he was going to drink anything that Yank had cooked up.

"That mess, your worship, is a special Jesuit brew which brought you back from the brink. You had the worst case of ague I've ever seen. The drink's mainly grounds from the fever bark tree—and a couple of other herbs for good measure."

William said, "I suppose I should be grateful, but I'm damn certain that you didn't keep me alive out of the goodness of your heart."

"You're right there, Admiral. The only reason I'm still breathing is because these folks believe I'm your servant. You go, I go. Simple." Nate explained, "When the tribe's shaman wanted to put you to death, the chief was afraid because he couldn't be certain whether or not you *really were* a messenger from the creator. So, he decided to hedge his bets and leave you outside as bait, and let the jaguar finish the job. That couldn't possibly displease the gods. Clever. And that's the way I found you almost two weeks ago. One foot in the grave."

A flash of pain ran through William's skull. "Bloody hell."

"Please refrain from swearing in the presence of a woman, Gunn,"

Nate said. "At least show some manners to the person who was feeding and bathing you." Nate reached out, bringing an old woman into William's view.

"May I present Madam Jizcamox, with the healing hands."

A wizened old woman stood before William, her long silver hair tied in two braids down the sides of her head. A toothless smile lit up her brown wrinkled face. A pair of twinkling hazel eyes met his gaze.

He realized he was naked. "For God's sake, man, put something over me."

"Don't worry, Gunn, our healer has been quite impressed by your manhood. I can't be sure if it was the fever, a dream, or simply a need to pass water, but every time you were bathed you went full mast. Quite impressive. Do all British officers react to a bath in such a fashion?"

William mustered as much indignation as possible, considering his circumstances. "What a load of rubbish." Jizcamox helped him lay back into a reclining position and put a folded blanket at his head.

William said weakly in Spanish to the smiling old woman, "Jizcamox is a beautiful name. I am eternally grateful for your help." Cusi translated for her, then said they had to leave, but that he would return later.

Before she left, Jizcamox giggled, said something to William, and flicked his manhood.

"What—why'd she do that?"

"I know you're confused," Nate continued, "so I'll tell you what I know."

With some effort William sat up and glanced around. Finding they were now alone, he said quite deliberately, "Before this goes any further, Private, tell me: *Why are you here?*" He looked down, to the foot of the bed. A mangy dog looked up, panting happily. He stared at the dog. The dog stared back. "And what is that cur?"

The American explained, "The dog won't leave your side, which is as perplexing to me as it is to you. As for why I'm here, after I recovered from the bullet you put in me"—his jaw tightened—"I went back to trading gems; this tribe is known for its emeralds. Now it's my turn. What the hell are *you* doing here?"

"I don't answer to you, *Private*," William said.

Nate took a step forward. "Now you listen to me, *Gunn*, there's no army around here—we're in the middle of the goddamn jungle, if you haven't noticed, *not* in Piccadilly. And you can rot in hell for all I care. If I hadn't come along, you'd be a moldy pile of bones right about now. I only saved your lobsterback ass because I temporarily need your help. After that, we go our separate, merry ways."

"Put that way," William said dryly, "how could anyone resist? I'm listening."

Nate said, "I believe the animal preying on this tribe is a man-eating jaguar. Must be a particularly large male because they haven't been able to kill it, even with their poison darts and spears." Nate stretched. "But it's just your luck that ever since you arrived, Gunn, no one's been attacked. And that's where my idea fits in," Nate said cagily. "The jaguar is the most proficient and deadly killer in the Americas. Maybe anywhere. But I hunt these animals."

"So?"

"Have you ever hunted?"

William looked puzzled. "Birds, back home. Why?"

"First, we're going to continue the pretense of you being a powerful healer and I your obedient assistant. Then we make a deal with this tribe. They have a gemstone that I want, and they must have something you want, or you wouldn't be here.

"So," Nate said, "once they agree to help us, the great white shaman and his servant are going to hunt and kill the most dangerous animal in the Western world."

CHAPTER 27

ℰL TIGRE

He was a killer, a thing that preyed, living on the things that lived, unaided, alone, by virtue of his own strength and prowess, surviving triumphantly in a hostile environment where only the strong survived."

—Jack London, *The Call of the Wild*

Still shaky from the fever, William stood alongside Nate in the lodge. The lean gray dog sat at their feet. Following Nate's advice, William had Sarah's silver locket and the gold Saint Christopher medal hanging from his neck where they could be seen, trying to look every bit the dangerous warrior-healer the chief and the shaman respected.

Cusi translated while William outlined their proposition. The two men would rid the village of the voracious *otorongo* if the chief and the shaman would give them information on the location of the black orchid and the emerald.

Nate warned that if the white shaman left, the big cat would once again begin to prey on the tribe. It was providential that the previous night the deep-throated roar of the jaguar could be heard throughout the village. The animal had only quieted with the approach of dawn.

The chief agreed to help them with the search for the black orchid and the emerald, fully expecting both men's bodies to be decorating the jaguar's perch before long.

The shaman sat bad-tempered and silent.

In the middle of the night, William woke to the roar of the man-eater. Considerably closer and of a higher timbre than the previous night, the deep-chested tremor would rise and then end abruptly in a heavy rasping groan. The sound didn't frighten him as he supposed it might. Instead, with Tommie's death, he felt fate had pushed in and was now presenting an opportunity to even the score—a reckoning of sorts.

The hunters rose early the next morning while it was still dark.

"It was just pure luck I found your pack donkey wandering in the bush with your rifle and pistols still intact," Nate said. "They'll come in handy today."

"When exactly *were* you going to tell me you had my donkey?" William asked.

Nate shrugged. "Right now we need to focus on the hunt. We'll head for where the man-eater was last heard—that will be the best place to pick up his spoor."

They finished packing, and William followed the American down a barely visible track.

"Are you as good with that as you are with a pistol?" Nate asked, indicating the rifle.

"Passable. Why?"

"Well, if you're not too sore to shoot, that Baker's the best weapon we have for what we're doing. So, if you're comfortable with it, you take the shot while I cover you."

"Pain's not too bad, I think moving about is helping."

"There're a few things you should know, Commodore," the American said softly over his shoulder. "The jaguar's fearsome—the largest beast of prey in the New World. They can easily outweigh two grown men and have been known to drag an eight-hundred-pound bull through the jungle. It usually hunts on the ground, but watch the trees and even the water—it can kill virtually anywhere. If you're its prey, Gunn, you won't escape."

William asked, "Is a *yaguareté* the same thing as the creature we'll be hunting?"

Nate stopped and looked at him curiously. "Yes. You know the animal?"

"Coming up the Magdalena, my Tupi guide found the body of one of my men—well, just a boy actually—who had been taken one night by an animal while we were on shore. The next day"—William hesitated, attempting to separate himself from the raw emotions still surrounding the incident—"we found what remained of him hanging high in a tree. The Tupi called the killer a *yaguareté*."

Nate continued walking. He uttered quietly, "That's what the big cats do—hide what's left of their prey in a tree, so they can come back later and finish."

"I'll take the shot," William said decisively, "I'm a fair hand at shooting game."

"This is not a bird hunt. Pheasants don't turn around and eat you. It's important that you don't underestimate the danger. From a hidden crouch, this animal can leap thirty paces in one bound and be on you before you know what's happening.

"And a jaguar kills differently than any other predator: it crushes the skulls of its victims. I'm not trying to frighten you—it's important for you to know exactly what we're facing. It wouldn't help to have someone along with a tense trigger finger." Nate paused briefly. "But then again, the British skull is probably thicker than most."

"Then there's no doubt about the American ability to withstand a jaguar attack," William countered, "seeing as there's so little between the ears to crush."

"Just remember, Gunn," Nate said, unamused, "to the Indians, this animal's godlike, almost supernatural." He stopped again and rested the blunderbuss on his shoulder. "But it's just a big cat, and it *can* be slain."

"How do you know so much about all this?" William asked. "From what I can figure, you've been here maybe a little over a year longer than myself."

"If you must know, Admiral, as a child I spent most of my free time with the local Wampanoag Indians. They took a liking to me and taught me a great deal. When I arrived in South America, I got along well with the Indians, especially in the wild places in the north.

"I learned a lot in a year, Gunn. So pay attention to my instructions. We'll follow the big cat's tracks, with me in the lead." Nate spied the gray dog trotting alongside William. "He'll be useful for catching the animal's scent."

William scratched the dog behind the ear. "High time you had a name. Perhaps 'Paxon' would be fitting," William said, recalling the name of a very young master gardener from another estate, still in his teens, who had impressed William with his extensive knowledge of exotic plants. "Though Pax is easier."

The dog looked up and wagged his tail.

"Looks like Pax it is," William said.

"Gunn, don't move."

"What is it?" William whispered. He stood stock-still. He hadn't heard or seen anything.

"I thought as much." Nate then called in Spanish, "Come out! Now!"

From behind a nearby tree, Cusi emerged sheepishly, blowgun in hand.

"What do you think you're doing?" William asked. "Does your father know you're here?"

"I go with you to kill *otorongo*," the young Indian said. "I, too, am a man and a warrior. The animal took Radiant Dawn, she was my closest friend. I will not go back."

"Cusi," Nate said, "you're the chief's only son. Once your father joins your ancestors in the other life, the tribe will depend on you to be their leader. This hunt is too risky."

"A chief does not let other men hunt for him. If I must, I will follow you."

William and Nate looked at each other. The American shrugged. "Follow us with the dog on a lead," he said to Cusi. "If he makes a sound, you tell me. Don't let him go, whatever happens."

Nate checked that his pistol was secure in his belt. "The ancient Mayans had a saying, Gunn: 'A brave man is always frightened three times by a jaguar; when he first sees his track, when he first hears him roar, and when he first confronts him.'"

William picked up the Baker rifle, buckling the extra ammo and provisions around his waist. "Guess I have one fright left."

William and Cusi followed the American as he warily picked his way through the brush in a light mist.

Blood pounding, William used an old trick from his military days to slow his racing heart: He focused on details. Following Nate's lead, they would take three or four steps, pause to regroup and mentally chart out their next steps, then continue on. The trodden vegetation underfoot enveloped them with a fragrant aroma like crushed rosemary.

The sweet fragrance immediately brought to William's mind a vision of Sarah playing in the duke's garden on a warm day; Nate was reminded of the last time he stalked a large predator, well over two years ago, back in Massachusetts. Both men consciously forced the distractions out of their minds to focus on the dangerous work at hand.

The sky was considerably brighter when they arrived at the small lake. Turtle shells littered the shoreline; old, faded jaguar tracks were everywhere.

Nate spotted the new tracks in the sand, the largest paw prints he had ever seen. Much larger than those of either a wolf or a cougar, they were half again the size of a grown man's hand. Deep in the soft sand, they were the tracks of a killer. He followed them.

They carefully tracked the jaguar for almost half a mile before Nate spotted the animal on the opposite side of the lake in a clearing at the edge of the water, drinking. The hunters ducked in among the bushes to avoid being spotted.

Even from this distance, the jaguar was immense, his large head suspended on a massive neck, overdeveloped shoulder muscles bulging as he looked up, sleek strength rippling along his tawny rosette-checkered back and flanks.

Figuring this would be similar to hunting mountain lions back in New England, Nate hadn't mentioned this was his first jaguar hunt. With difficulty he now hid his shock—the animal he was looking at was much larger than any cougar he'd ever seen. Judging by its massive physique, he guessed it must easily weigh close to three hundred pounds, if not more.

A crane alighted in the shallow water not far from the jaguar. The big cat finished drinking and, with a motion like a horse trotting, disappeared into the jungle. The crane continued fishing and moved slowly along the shoreline.

"The bird was unafraid," Nate whispered. "The predator's been here before."

They carefully slashed and hacked their way through thorny vines in the steadily building humidity. Dripping sweat, they arrived in the early afternoon at the place where the beast had been drinking. A small sandy beach extended into the lake.

Pax sniffed around, walked into the water, and dipped to drink greedily.

Nate followed the jaguar's vast paw prints for a few feet into the jungle. "This must be a popular watering spot. See here," he said, pointing to the ground at their feet, "several recent sets of tracks come and go. But over there"—he pointed again, this time into the jungle—"the ground changes from sandy to hardpan, and the spoor quickly becomes difficult to follow."

William squinted into the dim light of the jungle.

Nate walked several steps and knelt, examining something carefully. He stood. "To go in there would be suicide," he said quietly. "Best we camp downwind. Right now, he's resting somewhere. But they're creatures of habit. When he comes to drink this evening, we'll take him."

They backtracked a good distance away, where the brush provided effective cover. They lay in the shade surrounded by the pervasive sounds of the tropical jungle until late in the afternoon when Nate said, "It's time to make a blind closer to the beach, where we can get a good shot."

Making their way through the thick brush, Nate abruptly stopped and crouched. Something was wrong. The sounds of the jungle had retreated.

Pax made a soft noise, not so much a whine as a quiet growl, deep in his throat. Nate glanced at the dog. Teeth bared in a snarl, Pax strained at the leash. Cusi's cheerful expression vanished.

The American's skin crawled. *Damn.* Somewhere close by, the deadliest predator on the continent was stalking them.

The British officer's well-honed battlefield instincts blazed with alarm. Nate silently stepped sideways and waved him up. Rifle at the ready, William had just reached Nate's side, when a quick movement in the brush to their right caught their attention.

The immense man-eater was already airborne, propelled by its massive hindquarters. William squeezed the trigger. Off its mark, the shot wounded the beast in the shoulder. An earsplitting explosion quickly followed, the medium-caliber shot from Nate's blunderbuss catching the jaguar in midair, the tight spread slamming into the predator's flank so close it knocked the beast several feet to William's side, lifeless.

Gunfire still ringing in their ears, they considered the carcass at their feet, well over eight and a half feet from the nose to the tip of the tail. Before either could speak, Pax snarled again and, with a violent jerk, pulled the lead out of Cusi's hand.

An enormous brown blur burst from a covert spot in the brush and leapt over Pax to pounce on Cusi. Its vast paws sank into his shoulders and pinned him to the ground with its great weight. A second jaguar had been lying in wait.

Nate struggled to free the dragon for a shot, but the pistol's firing mechanism caught in his belt.

With both hands on the animal's throat, the young man struggled to keep the enraged killer from crushing his skull. But the man-eater's jaws—stretching wider than a person's head and full of razor-sharp teeth and bone-crushing canines—sank relentlessly toward Cusi's face.

CHAPTER 28

BARGAIN FULFILLED

It is not down in any map; true places never are.
—Herman Melville, *Moby Dick*

The jaguar's jaws descended around the skull of the chief's only son. Pax lunged and sank his teeth into the exposed flank of the attacker. Snarling in pain, the ferocious jaguar turned to rip the dog to pieces.

The Manton spoke with a sharp report.

Nate looked up in time to see the enormous creature drop, motionless, killed by a single shot to the brain.

As soon as Pax had growled, William had reacted instinctively, withdrawing his only remaining weapon—the Manton dueling pistol. Without hesitation, the British officer calmly fired into the great head of the beast.

He stood with a dead man-eater to either side of him, one less than ten feet away, and the other even closer.

Nate exhaled, not realizing he had been holding his breath. The Brit had made probably the finest shot under pressure with a pistol he had ever witnessed. There wasn't the slightest tremor in the officer's hands. With a shock, Nate suddenly realized the British officer had intentionally put that bullet through his shoulder at the duel.

Picking up his rifle, Nate said, "Next time I challenge you to a duel, you son of a bitch, it's with bows and arrows."

That night, Cusi told the story of the hunt at a great feast attended by the entire village. To the boundless delight of the tribe, he elaborated every detail of the pursuit, proudly displaying his bandaged arm and the wounds on his shoulders for all to see. Cusi now sported the heavy, dangling silver and gold earlobe ornaments of a warrior, which his father had presented him earlier. The chief beamed as if his son had single-handedly eliminated every present and future threat to their tribe.

That there had been a pair of *otorongos*, preying on the tribe, hunting together, was practically unheard of. The enormous man-eaters lay dead on the ground, lending extra credence to the tale. It had taken four men each to carry the animals back to the village.

The British officer and the American sat slightly to one side with the chief and the shaman. The chief offered the liver of a tortoise to William, much prized for its fat, a sign of the cacique's great respect for the white sorcerer. Nate shook his head in amusement. The Brit was the furthest thing from a shaman he could possibly imagine.

They had fulfilled their part of the bargain, and it was time to talk. Cusi joined them so he could translate.

The chief took William's hand and spoke directly to him. Cusi told them how grateful his father was for the killing of the man-eaters. The shaman also said something and pointed at the British officer.

Cusi translated, "He says he knew you were a powerful warrior, sent to help them. He knew this because of the golden amulet." Nate looked questioningly at William.

The British officer shrugged.

Cusi said, "My father says you have fulfilled your part of the bargain. Now they will fill theirs and tell you what they know of the black orchid and the god-stone."

The chief spoke for several minutes. Every so often, the shaman would nod in agreement. At one point, the medicine man appeared to clarify something.

When they finished, Cusi said, "Many years ago, a white man came through here wearing the same charm you have. The medal was a powerful talisman to our people. The man was looking for a sacred plant. As long as we have been a people, this plant had been known as the most potent healer, but it is rare—*very* rare. The shaman said he was sorry, but his only son went with the white man to bring the plant back for the tribe."

"What's he sorry about?" William asked.

Cusi said, "The shaman's son took the tribe's god-stone to trade for the plant."

William said quietly, "They were never seen again. This is why the shaman was upset by seeing me. I must remind him of his misfortune, of the son he lost."

The American wasn't listening, he was shocked. "He lost El Jefe? His son lost an emerald the size of my fist? They must be joking. Or mistaken."

"Can you understand now, Bidwell," William asked, "just how much they treasure the black orchid?"

Nate ignored him. He asked Cusi, "Where can I find that damned plant?"

Cusi translated, "The chief will honor the bargain. In the morning I will take you to see someone who knows everything about the plant."

The next morning, Cusi arrived with two warriors. The warriors were there to ensure that only the white shaman went. No servants.

"Too bad, Yank," William said, "looks like you'll just have to trust me."

The chief's son led William along a small, winding path ascending a steep hill. The British officer was intrigued. He wondered if this was just another wild-goose chase, hardly daring to hope that he might finally be getting a solid lead on the location of the black orchid.

After several hours of climbing, they arrived at a shack at the edge of a clearing in the forest. A clear stream close by rushed down the mountain.

Cusi said, "You wait. Sit."

Cusi clucked once, and an ancient, wrinkled wisp of a man emerged from the hut. Pax wagged his tail, then ran up to the old man and licked his hand.

With tenderness and respect, Cusi assisted the man in making his way to sit near the Brit. When William moved aside to make room, he noticed the old man's eyes. He was blind.

Cusi said, "Capac, this is William, a great shaman come from far away. He killed the *otorongo*."

Capac felt William's face, then followed the chain around the British officer's neck to the Saint Christopher medal. When he rubbed the raised impression between his gnarled fingers, he smiled.

Cusi filled a wooden bowl with chicha from his gourd and placed it in the withered mahogany hand. The old blind man lifted the bowl full of fermented maize to his thin lips, drank deeply, then drank again. He put the bowl down carefully. Then he started to sign while speaking in his harsh language.

Cusi translated, "Capac has been here longer than any other. Seen much before they take my eyes." The old man smiled a broad toothless smile.

"My oldest brother left many, many years to go with the white man to look for the black orchid. When he came back, he was ashamed he left, and sorry he took the useless things of the white man. Disgraced, he would not live in the village. Only to me did he speak of what he had done, and of the Sacred Land."

His voice tinged with disbelief, William asked, "Cusi, wait. Can you ask him the white man's name? Was it Jussieu?"

Cusi translated dutifully, but the old man merely shrugged. Yet who else could it be? William remembered every detail of the story about the Frenchman and the orchid. He said to Cusi with great urgency, "We must go to the place where his brother lived."

The site was not much further up the mountain.

All that remained was a wretched roofless hut, and an overgrown, partially cleared field, with a few withered fruit trees. Pax closely sniffed at everything and everywhere, but nature had reclaimed all other signs of occupation by Capac's older brother. No trace of Jussieu's servant endured, nor remnants of the French scientist's writings. Another wild-goose chase.

William was growing angry for the faith he had placed in the natives, when a distant rumble accompanied by a faint vibration of the earth startled him. It subsided quickly, but left him unnerved; he'd heard of earthquakes, but had never before actually felt the ground shake. He wondered what it meant.

When they returned, the blind man was still sitting where they had left him, seemingly asleep. He looked up and spoke when he heard his name.

Cusi said, "Capac says Pachamama, wife of the dragon and the ruler of earthquakes, is angry. This is only the beginning."

This is no time for superstitious nonsense. He asked Cusi, "Does he know how to get to the black orchid?"

When Cusi asked Capac, the old man spoke for several minutes. "He said there are two ways to the Sacred Land," Cusi translated. "Most fast is to use the Spanish roads, lower down, below the mountains. Go south for many days until the sun sets behind the biggest hill, then go east seven days between two big volcanos, down through the jungle into the great bowl, take the snake-stream for many days, then come to Big River. But there are many enemies that way, and much danger."

"The Big River is the Amazon, Cusi?"

"Yes. The other way is slow, but no Spanish. Go by the south trail up to the high plain, walk until the sun sets behind the biggest volcano, then take the path down to the jungle. Cross many rivers and small valleys for six more days. Climb to the last, highest country. Walk toward rising sun, keep the sunset behind *ariq*, until you come to the edge. Go down, enter great bowl of Big River."

The old man spoke again, and Cusi translated. "Once on the Big River, you float for many days until meeting with big brown stream, then soon you see them on the side of the river."

"See who on the side?" William asked.

"That is all he knows. He says you are brave and with luck, you will keep your head."

"The only thing these directions will do, Cusi," William said, frustrated, "is get me killed. I need more information."

The British officer pressed, "Please tell him I seek this plant not for myself, but for my daughter, who is very sick and will not survive much longer without the black orchid."

The old man held out the empty chicha bowl. Cusi refilled it and gave it back to him. The dark-brown hand slowly lifted the bowl; he drank fully, smacked his lips, and put the drink down. Then he spoke, Cusi translating. "Many years ago, when I have eyes, the young white man comes seeking the plant. He goes with the son of the shaman. They never return. I am blamed for the loss of the shaman's son—so they take my eyes."

William watched the lids close over the empty eye sockets in satisfaction as the old man drained the chicha. He started to slowly rock and sing to himself.

"And only to me did my brother tell of the sacred boxes."

William was riveted. "What do you mean? What sacred boxes?"

Cusi said, "Never show anyone."

"I *must* see them," William insisted.

The old man was silent for a long moment. When Capac finally spoke again, Cusi said, "He knows you look for Sacred Land with or without his help. But if he helps—shows you these things—you might have better chance of living. He is old and has no fear if the tribe brings death to him. Not for you, but for your daughter, Capac will show you."

The old man stood and told them to bring torches. They started through the woods, Cusi holding Capac's hand.

What could possibly be left? The tropical climate would quickly destroy anything of value. But William had nothing to lose.

William asked, "What did he mean by saying I 'might have a better chance of living'?"

Cusi said, "No one who sees the Sacred Land and the black flower ever comes back. Monsters there live on human flesh."

"But his brother and the Frenchman survived."

Cusi said, "Come, we follow him."

They cut through the vegetation until the jungle ended at the bottom of a sheer mountainside. The rock face appeared unbroken.

Capac walked to a thick acacia bush resting against the base of the cliff. Despite the sharp two-inch thorns, he reached in and pulled the bush back. Behind was a split in the rock, several feet wide, high enough for a man to stoop down and walk through.

Not knowing what lay beyond, they bent down and cautiously followed the old man through the opening in the mountain wall.

While William met the blind man on the mountain, Nate went to the shaman to see if he could coax out of him any additional information about the emerald. He just couldn't believe the old priest had lost the gem.

A handwoven reed mat covered the dirt floor. In the pale light of the semidarkness of the priest's lodge, Nate recognized the skins of a jaguar, cougar, and huge anaconda adorning the near wall, while a pair of flayed monkeys stared with lifeless eyes from the top shelf of a roughly carved wooden rack off to the side. The other shelves held a variety of colorful minerals, dried butterflies, the skull of a small caiman, and the shells of a hairy armadillo and several turtles.

Most conspicuous was a shriveled human head. The stitched and permanently smiling face of the diminutive pate sported a thin mustache, a slight goatee, and long black hair. The trophy sat atop an upturned wooden bowl in the center of the shelter.

The American had spent time in the company of many different tribes throughout the Americas, most of which he got along with fine, although there might have been a few that would have been happy to get their hands on him. But Nate had never seen, or even heard of, a shrunken head of a white man.

The shaman interpreted the white man's fixation as admiration. He smiled and patted the top of the grisly object affectionately.

They shared a bowl of potent chicha, and through signing and a few words of Quechua and the common language, Nate illustrated his knowledge of herbs. He also admired the old man's collection of potions and questioned him about healing plants, learning enough to know that many of the shaman's cures were from the Amazon—a knowledge which would soon prove invaluable. He pretended to be interested in every sign the shaman made and every word he spoke, some of which Nate couldn't understand.

Flattered and charmed by the American, the old Indian decided to help him. He stood unsteadily and began to speak with his eyes closed, at times seeming as if he were in a trance; at other times, he became animated, even interrupting his narrative by singing a song while slowly shuffling.

It was difficult to interpret much of the old shaman's story. But Nate understood enough to confirm that the tribe had lost their most treasured and sacred object when the shaman's son took the fabulous emerald to the Sacred Land to trade for the orchid.

"The Sacred Land is where both the black orchid and our god-stone are waiting." The priest stumbled, and Nate reached out to steady him.

"Since the loss of my son, that way is forbidden to us."

So, El Jefe was real, and waiting for him somewhere in the vastness of the Amazon. Hopefully, the Brit has discovered enough on his little excursion up the mountain to lead them to this so-called Sacred Land.

CHAPTER 29

THE CAVE

Holding his torch up, William entered the cave. With its high roof, the large space was more accurately a cavern—an unexpectedly cool and dry one. Barely visible in the gloom beyond the torchlight were a myriad of finger paintings on the yellow-brown wall, stretching from one end of the cavern to the other. The drawings largely consisted of stick figures hunting various unfamiliar beasts. Animal bones littered the floor.

Cusi said, "The First Ones made these drawings, long, long ago."

William walked toward what looked like the back of the cavern, but as he approached, the light from the torch revealed a fissure running from the ground through the roof. It was almost wide enough for a man to squeeze through. It was apparent that the temperature drop and dryness came from the steady stream of cool air issuing from the crevice, likely from high in the mountains.

They heard a dull bang echo in the darkness, followed by another.

Not needing any light, the blind man had gone directly to the trunks his older brother had dragged into the cave many years ago and started opening them. As he lifted each lid, a thick layer of dust rose into the air. The man coughed.

William and Cusi walked to the first of the trunks. The leather bindings had rotted away, and the lid and sides had decayed to little more than a frame.

In these dilapidated chests, William groped through several inches of brown and brittle scraps of paper, at times uncovering an animal's remains or a small rock. In the process, he managed to preserve the odd page or two that hadn't immediately crumbled. He also found intact one small, barely legible, hand-drawn map. His disappointment grew, along with his fear that Jussieu's servant long ago perceived the contents as worthless and disposed of them.

They came upon the last trunk. Stored apart from the others, deeper in the cave, it was in the best condition. They had to unbind the leather straps still securing the top of the chest. The trunk itself was relatively undamaged. For some reason, Jussieu's servant—Capac's elder brother— must have stored this trunk in the cave earlier than the others.

William hesitated for a long moment. He'd come a long way to arrive at this point—all his hopes now rested on this last trunk. His hands shook with the tension of knowing his daughter's life depended on finding something substantial within to guide them. He said to Cusi, "You look."

The chief's son opened the lid.

The trunk was empty.

Back to square one. Cusi turned and walked toward the cave entrance.

William refused to leave. He couldn't let Sarah down. He knelt next to the trunk. By the light of his single torch, he bent down and ran his hands over the sides, then felt with his fingertip in the shadows around the edge of the trunk's base.

"Light, Cusi, if you please!" he shouted.

Driven by the urgency in his voice, Cusi hurried back. In the light of both torches, William carefully examined the bottom of the trunk.

"By God, there's something odd here." William pointed. "That far side at the bottom is a bit lower than this side." He took out his blade. "This trunk's in too good a condition for the floor to be broken."

William lightly inserted the sharp point at several places around the near edge, gently prying upward as he did so.

Deftly, he lifted the false bottom out and laid it on the ground. He held the torch closer.

There, in the bottom of the chest, snug against the side, was a brown object three quarters of a foot long, half a foot wide, and about an inch and a half thick, bound by a black leather strap. The British officer reached in and gently removed the package from its resting place of fifty years.

Heavier than leather and smooth in texture, the brown shell would flex, and snap back to its original shape. Feeling the strange material under his fingers, a thrill coursed through William. There could be no doubt that it contained something important.

He cautiously inserted the tip of the knife at one corner of the package and drew the sharp blade down until the interior was exposed. He reached in and carefully withdrew a dark tan, leather-bound manuscript. Scanning the first few pages, a smile creased the British officer's face.

It was the lost diary of Joseph de Jussieu.

CHAPTER 30

PROPOSITION DENIED

Outside the cave in the warm sunlight, William quickly skimmed the diary.

More valuable than gold, the record contained a compilation of the French scientist's discoveries accumulated over the course of thirty years of wandering the continent. And although it would take many years of close scrutiny to decipher the sum of the priceless information it contained, right now all the British officer wanted was the Frenchman's directions to the black orchid. Which he promptly found.

Grateful that the duke had insisted he acquire enough French to enable him to read the publications of French botanists, William set about deciphering Jussieu's directions. The Frenchman described two main routes one could safely take to the Sacred Land. They resembled the directions the blind man had given, but with more detail and specific landmarks. The scientist stressed that the preferable and fastest route was over the lower-elevation roads and bridges, through Spanish towns. He mentioned the other route—using the high Inca roads—as an alternative only if the lower way should be blocked. The trail over the high altiplano was seldom used, being a desolate, windswept upland full of hazards and much slower than the lower trail.

William memorized the directions and packed the diary and map back in their strange wrapping. He hid the package under his shirt.

"Cusi," he said sharply, "only I have the power to use these sacred objects. You must be careful never to tell anyone of this, or you will bring a great curse on the tribe."

"No tell the American?" Cusi asked the white shaman.

"Especially not the American," William said.

Before they left, William thanked the old man again.

"You must be careful," Capac warned, by way of Cusi, "my brother said there are many harmful things in land of the Big River, and small creatures are *most* dangerous ones. Warriors there use poison arrows, kill fast. Many deadly snakes in jungle—one can swallow whole cow. And many, many insects—must take tree bark powder every day, or get sick and die. Red bark powder."

If even half of what he said of the Amazon was true, this was going to be a lot more interesting than William ever thought possible.

"What old Capac didn't tell you," Nate said sharply, back in their lodgings, "was that *he* was responsible for the death of both men—the young white man and the son of the shaman."

"What are you babbling about?" William asked.

"While you were gone, the shaman and I had a little discussion. Your old friend on the mountain was the one who gave the men the directions to the Sacred Land. And he also planted the stupid idea to trade the tribe's most highly valued gemstone for a plant.

"Seems the shaman's son knew how desperately the tribe needed the black orchid," Nate explained, "and how fanatical his father was about obtaining the plant to cure a sickness spreading through the tribe at that time. Just so happens the emerald people consider the jewel to be their 'god-stone.' That means it possesses the spirits of their departed ancestors. There's no way the tribe would ever have parted with this gem, Gunn, under any circumstances. Capac was blinded and banished for his trouble."

"You came here to *steal* that stone, didn't you?" The realization just hit William.

"Suppose I did want that stone," Nate said. "Everything now points to it being in the same place as your black plant. You know how to get there, but I don't. You have to realize, Gunn"—Nate bent toward the officer—"if you go into the Amazon alone, your life's not worth a bucket of warm spit. That is"—he leaned back again, and grinned—"without my help. But before I go any further, tell me: Did you even have any idea you were being followed?"

"What are you talking about?" William answered peevishly. *What's this cur up to now?*

Nate ignored him. "How many companions were you traveling with before I found you?"

"Two treacherous bastards, guides provided by the quartermaster. If I ever—"

Nate cut him off. "They're dead. But there was another, who I believe killed them. Is this plant you're looking for actually worth something?"

"I imagine it might be."

"How many people here know about it?"

"Just Bolívar. Perhaps the Irishman. No one else."

"Soon after I crossed the Magdalena, I picked up signs," Nate said. "The men with you were tortured and killed."

"Those scum waylaid me, so they got what was coming to them," William said. "But I can't guess why someone would torture them."

"Perhaps that someone knows your mission and is following you, hoping to cash in," Nate said. "No worries, though, at least for the time being. Whoever he is, he seems to have lost the trail: I didn't pick up any signs of your pursuer from the point of the attack. Of course, at the time I didn't know you were the victim."

"How *do* you know what happened back there?" William asked.

"I told you, Gunn, in the wilderness I know what I'm doing, and that includes tracking."

"So, you're proposing another partnership." William didn't trust this bastard as far as he could throw him. He said sharply, "Once was enough. You seem to forget you were responsible for the death of my guide in the first place. So, I suggest you go to hell, Bidwell." William figured that with the detailed information he now had, he no longer needed this galling American.

Nate shrugged. "Fine, Gunn. But without me, you'll be crossing the River Styx a lot sooner than I will."

That night, for the last time, they slept in the hut at the edge of the village.

After several hours had passed, Nate determined the Brit was asleep and quietly stole outside to William's donkey. He was rifling furtively through the saddlebags, when he heard a click.

A pistol was pointed at Nate's head.

"Put it back," the British officer said, "or this time I *will* put one between your eyes."

"You can't blame me for trying," Nate said.

William kept the pistol trained on the American. "I knew you'd figure the old Indian wouldn't be of much help and that I'd have another source of information." The British officer held up the leather diary. "You were right: the Frenchman's lost diary. But you're not getting any information from me. And first chance that comes along tomorrow, Bidwell, we're splitting up."

"At the duel, Gunn, why didn't you kill me?"

"Just know it wasn't for your sake, Yank, that I let you live." The officer's eyes narrowed slightly. "Ever come near my belongings again, and I *will* kill you."

William turned away and went back inside.

Both men had a troubled sleep that night, doubt lingering in their minds. William convinced himself that with the diary, he could navigate his way across the Andes and down the Amazon to the Sacred Land. But he had less confidence in how to deal with the natives once he arrived there.

Nate, on the other hand, talked himself into believing that he had the skills to find his way to El Jefe without the diary. Handling the natives shouldn't be a problem—hopefully.

CHAPTER 31

ᴅEPARTURE

William awoke trembling. His daughter was breathless and couldn't call for help. Her pale skin was turning blue, yet no help came for the distressed girl. Unable to shake the vivid dream, William became determined to take the fastest route to the Amazon, using the Spanish roads.

Nate elected to avoid those busy roads, instead sticking to the lonely Indian paths. If a tenderfoot Frenchman could find the Sacred Land fifty years earlier, he certainly didn't need the Brit to show him the way. He would travel south through the jungle for several days until he intersected with the trail ascending to the *páramo*. Once on top, he could access the old Inca road network. Then, perhaps with the odd rumor or two gathered along the way to help guide him, he'd turn east, and find the way down into the Amazon.

"We'd better start out together, Gunn, or the tribe might get suspicious. Remember, they believe I'm your assistant, or something like that." He couldn't bring himself to say "servant" again.

Cusi arrived, and surprised William with a present: a sand-colored blowgun, perfectly smooth, inside and out. He smiled. "I made it from a reed from the land of the Big River. Bring you much luck."

The gift included a beautiful quiver resembling a dice box. It contained a supply of poison darts made from the end leaf of a palm tree, as well as the wild cotton and silk-grass thread that would be used to ensure the darts' airtight fit in the blowgun.

The chief had also been generous, supplying as much food as could be packed on their animals. The shaman added a good supply of dried herbs and tinctures.

Nate led the mule out of the village, and William followed with the donkey, Pax at his heels. At the end of a grove of fruit palms, they left the east path for the trail to the south; the American passed around a turn in the trail ahead, the British officer some distance behind him.

After Nate had passed, Capac suddenly appeared by the side of the path. William had no idea how the blind man got there, or why. He must have been waiting patiently in the jungle for William to arrive.

The old man put his hand on the officer's shoulder and spoke softly, at the same time handing him something wrapped in leather. Capac clapped William on the shoulder and retreated a step. Staring through sightless eye sockets, he waited for William to continue on.

The south trail rose rapidly, allowing a clear view back. William turned for a last look and saw the man in the distance, still standing at the edge of the jungle, small and withered. He appeared to be speaking to someone in the bush.

Curious about what an old blind man would travel all that way to give him, William unwrapped it. Inside was a plentiful supply of the finest, pure red cinchona.

When he looked again, Capac was gone.

CHAPTER 32

ℛESPECT

We confide in our strength, without boasting of it; we respect that of others, without fearing it.

—Thomas Jefferson

"Like I said before, Yank, this is where I leave," William announced. A small side trail broke off to the west, leading to the well-traveled roads and bridges used by the Spanish.

"Suit yourself," Nate said. "If it was up to me, I'd still rather have that diary. Think about it," he insisted, "this part of Colombia's crawling with Royalists. You're going to lose a lot of time when you're stopped and checked at every village. And what happens if you're detained?"

William steeled his resolve. "Any way you look at it, this route is much faster. And should the need arise, I have a letter of passage from King George."

Nate tried again. "You know, considering the recent successes of the British brigade at Vargas and Boyacá, I have a fair idea what they'll do with that letter if you ever present it. Trust me in this, Captain Fusilier of the Royal Whatevers."

"Don't worry about me, Yank, you're the one going to need all the luck you can get." He started down the path.

In the dim light of the jungle, William soon lost sight of the

American. He hadn't walked more than a hundred yards when he came to a three-way fork. All the paths appeared similar. He chose the middle route as it seemed to continue most directly toward the west.

Within minutes the path had completely disappeared. Attempting to backtrack along the way he came, William realized for the first time just how difficult it was to follow these barely marked trails. Bidwell made it seem easy. At his heels, Pax whined.

William worked his way back to the fork in the path. The threatening screech of tropical birds and the sonorous warning call of insects seemed louder than usual. He unexpectedly came upon another trail leading off to the right, one which he hadn't marked earlier. Was this the way he came originally? It was impossible to tell.

William felt his skin prickle. He realized he was lost. Twenty minutes alone in this damnable green mess, and he hadn't a clue where he was. Frantically, he looked around, desperate to spot anything familiar.

A low whoop directly overhead startled him. He looked up. A large monkey clung to a branch less than fifteen feet away and stared at him accusingly. The creature's voice rose in alarm, and the repeating whoops increased to a frightening volume, then just as suddenly dwindled off to a low moan.

What the hell did I get myself into?

He took the trail to the right, pursued by the monkey's cry. He hurried along, anxious to break into a clearing, to see anything recognizable. Scrambling heedlessly, without warning, he stumbled onto a jungle path.

A short distance ahead there was a stream crossing. Utterly disoriented, he glanced back, only to see a mule secured to a tree several yards away. It was Jenny. He had bumbled his way to the correct path. Bidwell was nowhere to be seen.

Mystified, he decided to have a look at the water crossing: Perhaps Bidwell thought it was overly deep or too dangerous and was exploring for another place to wade.

He approached until the entire stream crossing was visible. Although a bit deeper than previous crossings, it appeared entirely fordable, having a narrow beach strewn with logs—now he was truly mystified as to Bidwell's whereabouts. But the last thing he wanted was for the American to find him confused, hesitant, and looking like he had just run frightened through the brush.

He left the bank and started onto the beach. He was about to step over a log when he noticed the cold disc of the reptilian eye flip open. Lying at his feet, like the trunk of a fallen tree, apparently asleep in the shade at the verge of the water, was a huge reptile. Pax barked from the top of the bank.

The giant caiman was not asleep. The relaxed posture of the beast shifted as it prepared to spring.

In the same instant the alarmed British officer noticed the huge crocodile at his feet, a creature burst from the thick undergrowth onto the back of the monster.

In a singular motion, the American drove a heavy gaucho knife deep into the giant reptile just behind its eyes, buried the weapon to the hilt, and then quickly twisted it. Instinctively, the large croc violently threw itself over, flinging the woodsman onto the sandy shore. Almost caught under the thrashing death throes of the huge beast, Nate and William just barely scrambled to safety.

"Bloody hell." Watching the final kicks of the dying crocodile, William shuddered.

Nate waited half a minute to make sure the reptile was dead, then placed one foot on its head, yanked the knife out, and wiped it clean.

"Decided you missed Jenny and me, did you, Gunn?" Nate asked mockingly. "Can't be more than half an hour since we parted company." He smiled ingratiatingly. "We'll take your return to us as a compliment, like the prodigal son."

William never thought he would be glad to see the American, but at that moment he would take the devil himself. He looked at the dead croc. "What was that about?"

"That," Nate explained, "was waiting to make a meal out of you. Since the next closest place to cross is a half day upstream"—Nate put the facón back in its sheath on his belt—"I was about to claim *this* crossing when you came along. Thanks for distracting it for me."

"You used me as bait!" William said in disbelief.

"You were never in any real danger, Gunn."

William marshaled his anger. "While I was gone," he said, "it occurred to me that a partnership might lead to better results for both of us. If you had asked my permission to see the diary, instead of going through my things when you thought I was asleep, I might be more trusting."

"Can I see the diary now?"

William shook his head, marveling at the American in spite of himself. "Your self-assurance is almost admirable, Bidwell."

Nate asked, "What are you going to do when we get close enough to the Sacred Land and I don't need you anymore?"

"We'll cross that bridge when we come to it."

Nate scoffed, "Or burn the bridge. You wouldn't be the first who's tried to kill me."

"No. Nor would it be my *first* try, Yank. As I said, next time I might not be so generous with my aim."

"A partnership it is then," Nate said jauntily, wading into the water. "Just don't forget the pack animals, Gunn," he yelled over his shoulder. "They're all yours from now on. And with a bark like that, are you sure that's a dog with you?"

William described his plan for their journey, taken straight from the Frenchman's directions.

"Because we're taking the more difficult route south through the jungle," Nate repeated, "we follow the paths of the ancients over the mountains. We're to cross the *páramo* and keep the volcano to the sunset."

"Correct, Yank."

"It'll be slower"—Nate's smile broadened—"but no Spanish soldiers. You plan to keep spoon-feeding these directions to me, Gunn, a bit at a time?"

"That's the deal. I'll get us there, and you keep us in one piece."

It looked like Nate would have to depend on the Brit if he ever wanted to be sure to see the Sacred Land and El Jefe. And William would have to rely on the American woodsman to do his best to keep them alive. At least until they reached the land of the black orchid.

"Until we ascend into the more remote mountains," Nate said, "we'll travel as silently as possible. When I make this sound"—he made a flutelike trill—"it means we stop."

The low warble emanating from Bidwell was so birdlike and natural, yet distinctive, that it caught William by surprise. A call he couldn't replicate if his life depended on it.

Nate said, "We'll space ourselves about ten to twenty yards apart. I'll lead, and you'll go behind with the pack animals—just keep me in sight."

William asked, "Is that so the Indians won't smell the animals?"

"No—it's so they won't smell you," Nate said bluntly. "And we know where Pax will be."

The dog, at William's side as usual, wagged his tail furiously at the sound of his name. William glared at Pax. "Whose side are you on anyway?"

The ease with which the American moved through the dense jungle fascinated William. Like a silent wraith, Bidwell disturbed as little as possible, stooping under vegetation and stepping over or around obstacles. He teased out secret paths barely discernible in the thick undergrowth. Continually glancing up and from side to side, on occasion he would halt, listen briefly and, without speaking, be off again.

William marveled at the enormous trees around them, easily over a hundred feet tall, covered with vines, and bedecked to their summits with golden trumpet blossoms and violet, blue, and scarlet star flowers. Dark-emerald palms and lime-green ferns formed the undergrowth.

A symphony surrounded them, the overhead chatter from troops of brown monkeys and colorful toucans mixing with the sounds of wild turkeys scavenging in the undergrowth. A soft carpet of mosses cushioned their footsteps, and they passed unobserved by man or wild beast.

Although they walked cautiously all day, Nate was pleased with the distance they covered. "A few more days like today, and we'll be at the foot of the hills."

Nightfall brought swarms of mosquitos.

Preparing his hammock, Nate was stopped in his tracks by an odd stench. "What is that stink?"

William held up the remnants of Veeborlay's mosquito repellent. "From the Dutchman."

"He really didn't like you, did he?" Nate walked to the edge of a small stream and cut a succulent plant growing there. It instantly secreted an odorless, oily substance. "Rub this on, and get rid of that dung."

William hated to admit it, but if he didn't wind up strangling the tosser while he slept, this American might just be able to help him survive long enough to bring the cure back to his daughter in England.

CHAPTER 33

NEMESIS

In spite of Virtue and the Muse,
Nemesis will have her dues,
And all our struggles and our toils,
Tighter wind the giant coils.

—Ralph Waldo Emerson

Marquez absentmindedly picked at the tick that had lodged itself in his arm. *I must be particularly careful, especially now there are two of them. That other one—he is almost as formidable in the wilderness as I am. He must be watched closely.*

The tick came free, and the wound started to bleed. The king's inquisitor looked at his blood in a curious but detached way.

The Englishman has recovered very well. Most unfortunate I missed such a good opportunity in the jungle, when he was sick and lost. I shouldn't have let myself be distracted by those two mestizo fools. That was a weakness and will not happen again. I must remain true to my primary goal and discover what the British want with Bolívar.

He primed and loaded his weapons. Then Marquez recalled the pain he'd inflicted on those trash before they died, and he smiled.

The Spaniard idly scratched his goatee and went over the plan once again. *Together the British officer and the woodsman killed the man-eaters . . . I must be very careful.* Through his growing frustration, he knew there could be no mistakes next time.

Another chance to discover the British officer's mission would come; he just had to be patient. First, he would pay a visit to the old Indian and have a good talk. Then he would need assistance. There was too much at stake.

Lieutenant Francisco Rodriquez wasn't at all happy to see the man they called the inquisitor captain arrive at the fort. It wouldn't do to irritate Marquez. That devil's spawn had arranged Lieutenant Rodriquez's transfer to this shithole when he failed to arrest the Englishman up north. Now Marquez was depleting the lieutenant's isolated barracks to capture the same man.

When Lieutenant Rodriquez cleared his throat, his voice quavered. "I'll need a guide, sir." He swallowed. "I was transferred from the Barranquilla barracks and am not familiar with the *páramo*. There's been no need so far to patrol the high country."

"I don't care how many guides you take," Marquez said harshly. "You mount up within the hour, with or without guides.

"Find them on the high plains," he ordered. "Chew as many coca leaves as you need—eat the wretched stuff if you have to—but make damn sure you don't stop until you find them." His gaze narrowed. "Then pursue them . . . and make no attempt at concealment or confrontation"—a gleam came into the inquisitor's eyes—"just force them forward.

"The remainder of your garrison will accompany me. I'll be waiting for them in the forest. When they descend, they'll be trapped between us.

"And remember," he cautioned, "above all else, I will have the Englishman alive."

CHAPTER 34

ℙaths of the 𝕀ncas

Climbing the last few feet over a small hillock, they finally stood on the vast, windswept tableland nestled among the loftiest peaks of the Andes. A distant volcano was just visible, rising out of the southwestern mists. A place of frequent rains, this *páramo* was the source of water for the great rivers of the Magdalena and the Amazon. The high plateau abounded with springs, swamps, bogs, and small lakes.

It was also absolutely desolate, save for the ribbon of a road which snaked across the land to disappear into the distant horizon in either direction. Passing immediately in front of them and paved with smooth stones, the road was a scar across the barren land.

"Amazing," Nate said with a tinge of awe. "Back home, not once traveling from Boston to Washington, did I come across a road this fine."

"Do you know who built it?" William asked.

"The shaman said their ancestors long ago built a system of roads extending to the far south, west to the Pacific, and east to the Amazon. They say it linked over twenty-five thousand miles of roads, from the highest *páramo* to the lowest valley. The Spanish destroyed many of the roads lower down and used the stones for buildings and churches. But up here, the roads survive. They call it 'the Road of the Gods.'"

Although the Inca road was straight and mostly level, the biting wind never stopped blowing over the flat land. It was gracious enough to blow at their backs all day though, so it didn't impede their travel.

That evening, when the American was asleep, the British officer reviewed the Frenchman's diary by the light of the fire. He kept a loaded Manton pistol by his side.

On this route over the *páramo*, Jussieu advised that the best way to enter the Amazon was south of the llanos, taking the east path leading down through the forest to the jungle. The turnoff was marked by a large fissure in the ground, venting an unusual yellow-green steam. William rewrapped the diary and stored the parcel in his saddlebag. Pax lay at the foot of his bedroll.

Early the next day, they crossed a sturdy grass bridge constructed over a ravine. For part of the morning, they were shadowed by a huge bird of prey soaring high overhead, riding the air currents.

"*El buitre*," Nate explained, "largest bird in existence, the Andean condor. A good omen."

William waited patiently as the American watched the vulture until it disappeared over the far northern horizon. "Guess you want all the luck you can get."

Absorbed in staring at the horizon, Nate didn't hear him.

Anxious to make progress, William said, "Bidwell, let's get on with it."

The rest of the day was uneventful, until that evening when they were preparing to camp. William pointed. "Is that smoke? There. Back north."

The American didn't need to look. "They've been behind us since early yesterday. Seems half the damn country is chasing you."

"When were you going to say something? When we were shaking hands with them?"

"We're not actually being followed," Nate said sharply, "they're driving us."

"Driving us?"

"Into an ambush. They've made no attempt to hide their approach." Nate paused, then said thoughtfully, "It can't be up here, it's too open. The others will be waiting on the way down, wherever that is. There's time to figure something out," he continued sharply, "but you're going to have to tell me where we're going." He hated being kept in the dark, having to depend on the Brit for directions.

"There may be a shortcut," William said hesitantly.

"A shortcut?"

"There's another way, not in the diary. The old Indian said to avoid the place." William continued guardedly, "He was stubborn, called it the 'haunted valley' or something like that. No one ever goes there—supposedly it's damned."

Nate said, "Do you remember any of the Indian words he used?"

"I only remember one, and that was because he repeated it. The word was *anchanchu*."

"A mythical demon which spreads terrible sickness," Nate said. "I have little doubt we'd be in grave danger should we go that way. Besides, those behind us would know we've left the Inca path. Maybe something else will come up."

"They're moving fast," Nate said, gazing back.

They were crossing a long stretch of bog in late afternoon. Part of the causeway was replaced with a narrow, woven-reed mat. These were usually quite sturdy when maintained, but this one had seen better days.

"I'll test it before we chance bringing the animals over." Nate stepped gingerly forward. The structure felt buoyant.

Nate visually examined the mat as far ahead as he could. He said, "Seems fine." Further on, a darker section was slightly underwater. "But keep a good distance between us, so as not to overload any one section—some parts look to be rotting."

Nate went first with Jenny.

Then it was the Brit's turn. At first, William's pack animal refused to follow him. The donkey had to be encouraged, pulled, and coaxed along, resulting in frequent delays and tedious progress. Pax ran several yards ahead and waited.

Nate had already reached firm ground on the far side of the marsh; he peered through his spyglass at the men following them, when he heard a peculiar sound: Pax's yelp. The big Indian dog had an innate sense of trouble, which he expressed the only way he knew how: the strange exhalation that was his version of a bark.

William had been walking cautiously over an especially rotten part of the mat when his skittish donkey suddenly bucked and then leapt clear off the path onto what had appeared to be solid ground.

"What the devil," he said incredulously, amazed to see the animal plunge up to its belly in wet muck. The more the panicked animal thrashed, the deeper it sank, its flank disappeared first, quickly followed by its hindquarters. William had never encountered anything like it. Not wanting to lose the baggage, he desperately pulled on the reins. It was no use. However, the ground just ahead of the beast appeared stable enough to allow the animal to be dragged out.

Fully expecting firm footing, the Englishman jumped. To his shock, the ground gave way under his weight; his feet sank into the ooze. He struggled to yank them out, but the mud sucked at him like a giant parasite. He sank to his waist. In his struggle to reach the baggage, he sank to his chest. The more he tried to move, the deeper he submerged. Concern for his survival quickly replaced his fear of losing the baggage. He couldn't move his legs. He continued to sink.

Pax ran back and forth several times, then appeared ready to spring.

"Stay!" William ordered. The muck had reached his armpits and was rising fast, the pressure on his chest making it difficult to breathe. He called loudly, feeling the quicksand tickle the bottom of his chin.

CHAPTER 35

THE HOUSE DOESN'T ALWAYS WIN

Pax's bark grabbed the American's attention. The British officer and the donkey were foundering in the quagmire, both well on their way to disappearing.

"Stop struggling! Lay on your back!" Nate shouted.

"I have no back to lay on!"

"Quit moving your jaw so much then!"

The American seized a coil of rope and rushed back with Jenny in tow, hitching a loop as he ran.

The muck was now above the British officer's chin. William breathed deeply, spread his arms under the mud, and laid his head back. He immediately stopped sinking. *So much for saving the donkey and the packs.*

Eyes wide with fright, the donkey was now up to its withers, only a small portion of its neck and head showing. By the time Nate arrived, the writhing beast had disappeared entirely.

The American tossed the rope to William. "Thanks," the Brit gasped. "Bloody stupid of me."

"At least *I* didn't have to say it." Nate pulled the officer out far enough to allow him to slip the loop over his head and under his armpit. Taking a couple of quick turns with the rope on Jenny, he backed the mule away, slowly drawing the officer out of the cloying muck.

"We'll miss those pistols," Nate said with genuine remorse. The Brit's prized dueling weapons given to him by the duke were deadly in the Englishman's hands. "At least the rifle is stowed on the mule."

"Pisswater, Bidwell." William got up, oozing muck. "The real loss is the diary."

"We've other concerns," Nate countered. "Before you went for a swim, I had a look behind us through the glass. Those bastards are so close I can almost count 'em. And there's more than I'd like."

Looking at the mud-covered British officer dripping brown slop, Nate brightened, his face split by a wide grin.

"I'm glad you're enjoying yourself."

"I just had an idea. Stop cleaning off that muck, Gunn, and hand me your hat."

Nate said to Jenny, "Now hold still, girl, for a few moments, while we pretty you up."

"Don't you think we're close enough, Lieutenant?" José, one of the hired guides, cautioned.

"We're six against two," Rodriquez said grandly. "What are you worried about?"

José, a local-born mestizo, didn't want to infuriate the Spanish officer, so he didn't argue. But he thought, *This man is an idiot. Those two up there haven't given us any reason to think they're stupid. This lieutenant's haste could get us killed.*

For the past week, in order to gain on their quarry, the four soldiers and two guides had been forced to ride almost twenty hours a day. Lack of rest and high-altitude effects were beginning to show on both men and horses.

"Tired men make mistakes," the other guide, Paulo, stressed.

"If we're tired, they'll be worse," Rodriquez countered. "They don't know who we are, or how many of us are following. The harder we push, the more their fear will drain them. Believe me; I know men."

Lieutenant Rodriquez was sick of this country. If he wanted a transfer back to Spain, he needed to impress Captain Marquez. If there was any chance he could capture the Englishman before they arrived at Marquez's ambush in the forest, he was going to take it.

They arrived at the bog.

The lieutenant stood in his stirrups and peered ahead through the spyglass. "That's interesting," he said softly. "One is riding; he must be hurt. And there's no sign of the other pack animal."

"Look," he called to the guides. "They've already run out of food. They must have eaten the other horse."

José and Paulo shared a skeptical look.

"Men, we have them now," Lieutenant Rodriquez announced. "We're mounted, we outnumber them, and one is injured. Once we push across this bog, we'll attack. Remember," Rodriquez warned, "under no circumstances is the one with the yellow hair to be harmed. Kill the other."

CHAPTER 36

AMBUSH

Preoccupied with those he was pursuing, Rodriquez was unconcerned with his surroundings. His targets were clearly in sight through the spyglass, less than a half a mile ahead. They had slowed down and were doing absolutely nothing to protect themselves. This was almost too easy.

Those were the last thoughts Lieutenant Rodriquez would ever entertain. He never heard the shot, nor felt the lead ball rip through his skull.

Practically invisible in a suit of caked mud, the sniper had shot the Spanish officer as he rode past, close to where the donkey had drowned in the quicksand not long before.

Concealed on a small rise less than a hundred yards away, William had already primed the rifle again, packed another cartridge down the muzzle, and was sighting on the next rider in line when the Spanish officer's mistakes began paying bonuses.

Startled by the sharp report of the first shot, the horse just behind Rodriquez bucked its rider into waist-deep ooze. The panicked soldier, thrashing to get out, quickly sank to his shoulders in the quicksand.

William shifted his focus to the next rider in line. The horseman tried to escape but ran into the rider behind him.

The gun plate shivered against the British officer's cheek as he fired again. His target grunted and fell heavily.

The guides, José and Paulo, had prudently held back, and by the time of the second shot, they were well on their way home. They galloped north, closely followed by the last remaining soldier.

"Nice move, Bidwell." William begrudgingly acknowledged the American's idea, although vaguely ashamed by the notion of camouflaged combat. "Hard to believe a descendant of the great Spanish conquistadores would mistake a poncho, a hat, and a couple of pieces of wood for a British officer."

"Hard," Nate said with a grin, "but not impossible."

Despite himself, William couldn't help but grin back.

As they continued south along the Inca trail, the two men differed on how to proceed. William wanted to avoid the ambush in the forest by taking the shortcut through the forbidden valley.

"You say you've memorized the Frenchman's directions to a friendly tribe in the Amazon," Nate said, "one that supplied him with canoes. Then I opt we stick to that original plan, follow his directions, and fight our way through any ambush in the forest." He pointed out, "If there's the slightest chance we can get canoes, we must take it. If we don't get on the river as soon as possible after entering the Amazon, we're dead."

William replied, "Whoever's chasing us is no fool. Using those soldiers to drive us across the *páramo* into a trap shows he's a military man. In the forest, he'll have the time and resources to set up an ambush that's impossible to sniff out. Believe me, Bidwell," he urged, "in this, I know what I'm talking about. To go there would be suicide. I say we take the valley shortcut instead. I didn't tell you, but there was a loose map in the diary that I stowed in my pocket for safekeeping. It may show us something."

While William unfolded and looked at the old parchment, Nate fumed. "We can't go into that valley," Nate insisted. "You just don't realize what it means to have a taboo placed on an area. That's not done lightly."

"I prefer that to walking into an ambush, even if forewarned," William said. "We lost more than the Frenchman's journal back there—my pistols, and most of the gunpowder went down with the donkey."

"Maybe, but we still have the other guns, and some ammunition, plus what we took off the dead Spaniards. Don't discount the blowgun either," Nate persisted. "It's deadly in the right hands."

"The forest path is certain death," the British officer repeated emphatically. "This map's only useful after we're on the river."

"Believe me, Gunn, that valley is a *more* dangerous choice." Nate was obstinate. "If I must, I'll go on alone."

"What're you talking about?" the Brit shot back. "Without me, you have no idea where you're going. And that forest route is idiotic."

"Are you saying I'm an idiot?"

"What I'm saying, Yank, is you'll be a dead idiot."

The two glared at each other in silence for several long moments.

"Why not draw a straw?" William suggested in an attempt to break the stalemate. "Pick the short piece, and we go as originally planned through the forest. Pick the longer piece, and we descend through the forbidden valley to the Amazon." He added lightly, "What the hell, Bidwell, either way we're likely to wind up dead."

"Only sensible thing I've heard from you yet, Gunn."

William trimmed two dry pieces of grass, then held them up, seemingly identical, the end of each concealed in his palm.

Nate picked the one on the right.

They walked most of the day to find the trail to the forbidden valley. It was midafternoon when they came to a place where a barely perceptible path branched off to the left and was soon lost among the tall grasses and stunted trees.

"Are you sure?" Nate was skeptical. This looked more like a game trail, or perhaps a place where the Incas had left the road to relieve themselves.

"From everything the old Indian said, this is the way," William said without conviction.

Even Nate felt challenged at times to follow the wandering, erratic track. The shadows were already beginning to lengthen when the path stopped at the top of a narrow gorge. The deep scar appeared to be carved out of the heart of the high *páramo* by some colossal, crooked claw. If the path had not led directly to the edge, the valley would have been easy to miss altogether.

Sheer and narrow at its upper end, it gradually broadened to perhaps a half mile at its widest point. The furthest eastern extremity of the valley was shrouded in an odd fog, like a roof of clouds turned upside down.

Nate said drily, "Some choice."

A clearing far off near the horizon broke the endless march of trees. Using a spyglass liberated from the dead Spanish officer, Nate spotted a structure at the edge of the field.

"That's odd. It means that people are either there or were at one time. We should try for that cabin at the edge of the clearing. It doesn't look like much from here, but at least it's shelter."

William said, "We better get going if we're to make it before dark."

"When the Spanish discover we're not coming through the forest," Nate said, "they'll search for us. And when it comes to a fight, we can't beat half a garrison."

"They may not even know about this route," William said.

"If they did, they wouldn't be stupid enough to take it."

The path appeared to be the sole entrance to the valley, the sides of the opening so steep and scarred by rockfall as to prohibit entry elsewhere. Descending had a walled-in feeling, like entering a neglected garden of an abandoned cloister.

"Who's Sarah?" Nate asked as they began to pick their way down the slope.

"Why do you ask?"

"You talk in your sleep. You're keeping me awake at night."

"She's someone close to me," he answered.

As William's search for the black orchid dragged on, each night his daughter visited him in his dreams. Lately she seemed to be in some kind of institution, among strangers. He had heard of places where they put patients who had no hope of ever getting better, but he had never seen one. He worried that Sarah was ill or dying.

The path narrowed, becoming no wider than a couple of feet; descending required all their concentration. The ancient construction was carved from the mountainside over a precipice hundreds of feet above the valley to their left. To their right, the sheer face of the mountain loomed above them.

The track was so steep that they felt it would soon level off, but it continued sharply downward. They felt an indefinable heaviness grow with every step, an inexplicable foreboding. The slightest breeze from the east brought a vague, nauseating odor like eggs rotting.

The suffocating heat and humidity had been intensifying all day, dark clouds steadily gathering in the leaden sky. The broiling sun was well hidden behind the western cliffs when the path finally began to flatten.

They entered a woodland, airless and hot, consisting of a mixture of deciduous and conifer trees crammed closely together. Only the plodding of the mule's hooves broke the silence. A malaise overtook them as the afternoon darkened into evening.

Nate wondered how he had ever agreed to come this way.

Even William started to question whether this was a wise choice. The thick, surrounding woods could harbor any sort of evil—human or otherwise. He made sure his rifle was within easy reach. Maybe it was a mistake to ignore the American's advice about a native taboo. They should turn back while there was still time. To walk into a trap with your eyes wide open would be foolish.

"Much further to the hut?" William blurted out, his words puncturing the silence.

Nate's reply lacked confidence. "Not far."

A sudden fierce wind set the tops of the trees waving like the masts on a fleet of schooners caught in a hurricane. The sound of thunder betrayed an approaching storm, and the sky quickly blackened like churning bitumen. A few large drops of rain splashed down. Nate cautiously tightened his grip on the mule's halter, reassuring the panicky animal.

A bolt of lightning split the air, and the rain began to pour in earnest. Caught in the sudden torrent, they stumbled along with only staccato bursts of lightning to illuminate the path. It would be impossible to light a fire or make any kind of shelter. They had no choice but to continue on to the cabin—in a storm this fierce, it would be madness to attempt to spend a night in the open.

They lurched forward for what seemed ages, questioning all the while whether they were going in the right direction. Just as Nate began to worry that they might be lost, they stumbled upon a cleared field. In a flash of lightning, he saw the hut at the far edge. From this distance, the building appeared to be quite a bit larger than most rural shelters. Blue smoke issued from a chimney.

They slipped and slid their way over the channels of water that had formed in the ground, finally arriving at the front door of the cabin. Before they could knock, the door swung open, seemingly of its own accord. From the dark opening came the stale odor of decay.

From the gloom within, an unearthly voice chafed in English, "What kept you?"

CHAPTER 37

THE HAUNTED

"Enter!"

Cautiously, they stepped over the threshold into the dim room. The door suddenly slammed shut; a rusty bolt groaned into place. Dark figures behind them blocked escape.

The only source of light in the large room came from a small fire in the far corner.

A gauze curtain concealed the speaker, only his outline visible in the dim light. "Your lives are forfeit." The casual verdict made their blood run cold. Surprisingly, the words were spoken in English with a Manchester accent.

"Can I not beg you to consider otherwise?" William entreated, feeling there must be a human connection possible, especially with a fellow Englishman.

Nate was about to say something when William caught his eye. The British officer shook his head slightly from side to side. He pleaded with the concealed shape, "We ask leave only to pass through your land."

"Through to where?" A coarse barking sort of noise that could have been laughter came from the shrouded figure. "There is *nothing* after our land."

Becoming slowly accustomed to the gloom, they could detect many more beings in the shadows of the large room. An audible shuffling filled the space as the figures closed in on them. William glimpsed a handless specter, another shuffled on stumps, and yet another hobbled on a crutch. What manner of beings were these?

"We journey to the Sacred Land," William said.

"The Sacred Land? Well then, my English friend, surely you are *already* doomed. We'll do you a favor and end your suffering here and now and take your miserable possessions for ourselves. I like the dog." Pax lay near William, resting on his front paws, watching.

A large man angled into position behind William and Nate. With a full black beard, swarthy face, and fierce, closely set eyes, half his head covered in a stained turban, he held a pistol in one hand and a long curved sword in the other, the likes of which neither man had ever seen before.

Nate shifted uneasily. The Brit had better get this right or, he felt, their remaining time on earth was going to be quite short.

William measured his words carefully, his voice wavering. "My guide and I beg your pardon and your leave. We only entered your land in the most dire need, to avoid the pursuit of a Spaniard, most likely an inquisitor, who endeavors to prevent us from acquiring the black orchid." The loud mutterings from the shadows chilled William to the bone.

"The flower we seek not for ourselves, or for fortune, but as the cure for a mysterious sickness which afflicts my daughter, the same strange sickness that took my wife's life. Your consideration and your kindness in this are requested."

The shrouded figure sat unmoving. After several moments, the apparition slowly retreated into the shadows to confer with a knot of figures. Nate shot William a curious glance.

Their muted conversation ended, and the man moved back to the curtain.

"Inquisitor, you say? We await the arrival of any inquisitor here and, indeed, would welcome him with open arms." The vestige of a laugh accompanied the next uttering, "Those of us *with* arms. An inquisitor would make such delicious entertainment." With this, the silhouette cast aside the shroud.

Clearly visible in the candlelight, his lipless mouth and rotting gums stretched wide in a mirthless grin below a flat orifice where there once had been a nose. The man announced, "I am Adam."

The hairs rose on the back of Nate's neck.

William had guessed correctly.

Lepers.

"Come. Sit with me."

William took the spare chair at the table, while Nate remained standing. Pax followed and planted himself at William's feet.

Aside from the damage of the disease, working in the tropical sun had also taken an obvious toll on the man—his eyes betrayed his youth, but his skin was like leather jerky, and the hours spent in the fields had bowed his back.

A heavily bandaged man materialized out of the shadows and slid a platter onto the table. Tarnished black, the once-silver plate held a loaf of bread. With a hand missing several digits, Adam placed a battered tin cup in front of the Englishman and filled it with rose liquid from a jug. He poured some for himself.

Nate watched expectantly, wanting to hold his breath in the close atmosphere, but anxious of betraying any sign of revulsion. This was a test William must pass, and pass well, or they were dead men.

"Your health," the leper said ironically, taking a deep swig.

"To you and yours," the British officer responded, followed by a long draft. But he had not expected the smooth taste of fine wine and the surprise showed on his face.

"Better than you imagined, eh?" the leper captain said, scrutinizing William's every reaction.

William seized the loaf, pulled off a chunk, and promptly put the leper's bread into his mouth. It was still warm—the best bread he'd had in a long time. Nate was appalled, barely able to hide his shock.

The leper nodded slowly, his eyes riveted on the chewing Englishman. There was a noticeable lessening of the tension that had charged the room.

"I'm sorry we can't repay your hospitality," William said, removing another chunk of bread, "but we were deprived of much when we lost our donkey, including some very good tea."

"We know. Little escapes our notice here."

"Who *are* you?" William asked.

The leper leader considered for a moment. "You say you are searching for the black orchid for your daughter. She has a terrible sickness. This"—he stretched his arms out—"we can understand." This was met with a chorus of agreement. "Also, you don't fear our disease. You are foolish in your ignorance but are lucky. Those who prepared your wine and bread are not contagious.

"As for who I am: I am *no one*, abandoned by the captain of an English whaling ship, left for dead when they discovered I had the sickness. Marooned and forgotten"—he waved his arm around the room inclusively—"like most of us here." Throughout the room the lepers pounded their feet, swords, and pikes.

Adam shouted over the din, "We are a league of nations, English, Portuguese, Spanish, French, Indians, slaves, Chinese, and many others, bound by an incurable affliction." He waited for the noise to subside. "This valley is our world. Because we have been expecting you, this room tonight is filled with the clan leaders. This committee will decide your fate."

The leper washed down his bread with wine. "Had you been a soldier, a slave hunter, or a priest, you would be begging to die right now, or already be in hell with your brothers." He spread his ravaged hands in appeal. "You must understand, my people are not cutthroats." The gruesome grin reappeared. "Well, not *all* my people. We kill those who trespass as a precaution. We must remain unknown and feared. It is our only protection.

"We toil in the heat to grow whatever we can, but we also depend heavily on what fate sends our way. Soldiers, the rich, and any others we deem worthy of waylaying"—bitter laughter filled the room—"help us survive. That is the only time we leave the valley. We cannot let anyone remain alive once they have seen us, or in fear, they would come back with others and hunt us down."

He drank deeply again, and continued, "But you are special. You do not come seeking fortune, but arrive in need, to help another. To cure a sickness." A quiet murmur rippled through the room. "*That*, as I said, we understand. We ourselves have attempted many times to gain the Sacred Land to obtain the flower. None have ever returned."

"If we let you live and allow you to pass"—Adam leaned across the table—"you must never breathe a word of our existence to anyone. And all we ask in return is that if you find the orchid and survive, you must promise to somehow get the plant to us, if at all possible."

William looked at Nate, who nodded ever so slightly. "I give you my word." *As if we have a choice.*

"Swear on your daughter's life that you will do your best, should you survive."

"As a fellow Englishman, I swear on my daughter's life that should I be successful in getting the black orchid, I will do all in my power to get the plant into your hands, by whatever means necessary."

"Then we have a deal, my fellow Englishman," he said with a trace of sarcasm, "and you may pass through our land. But start in the morning, when the storm's passed, if you can endure a night under a leper's roof."

Several candles were lit, but the room remained in shadow, most likely by intention. Plain but clean food was brought. Many did not suffer themselves to be seen, but guttered out the door, some disappearing through the back exit.

Of the men who remained, the most memorable was the bearded one, over a head taller than either Nate or William. He introduced himself as Ajeet, a highly educated sailor, first mate on an East India Company Indiaman, pressed into service on a British warship after the Isle de France invasion almost a decade before. After escaping, he spent several years sailing on Yankee whaling vessels until being stranded on the coast of Peru once his disease was discovered. Although his hands were unscarred, he wore a turban to cover his decayed ears and scalp and walked with a slight limp. The manner in which he twirled his scimitar suggested he was well familiar with its use.

Mesmerized with the big dog, Ajeet fed Pax and gave him a drink. Pax in turn was as gentle with his hosts as he was menacing to jaguars.

There was little evidence of the violent storm of the previous night. From the knoll the cabin was perched on, they would have been able to see down the entire length of the valley if the far end had not been obscured by a yellowish-green haze.

"Before you depart us," Adam said, "there is a man here you must speak with. He's been to the Big River." He signaled, and a man reluctantly shuffled forward. "John, tell these men what you've seen."

The disease was advanced in the man, and he spoke weakly in English with a slight Scots accent. "Once you leave the valley, take the jungle path toward the rising sun. You'll come to the remains of the Inca path on the second day. Take it and pass over several gorges before ascending to the last high plateau." A fit of coughing seized him and racked his body with its spasms. The attack passed momentarily, and he continued, speaking through a bloody rag held to his mouth. "Travel for several days more on the high path to the east until you reach the Jaws of Death. Descend through there. That's the only way down to the Amazon." This was followed by another outburst of coughing into the bloody rag.

When he quieted, the ruined man gathered his strength to give a last bit of advice. "There's a fair chance you'll meet the Jivaro. Either they'll trade for a canoe, or they'll take your heads." John held up a withered hand. "Ask me no questions," he implored tiredly, "and tell no one you met me here." He shuffled slowly back to be consumed by the shadows. A last weak caution percolated from the darkness: "Remember: The Jaws are the only way into the Amazon."

As a farewell present, the British officer gave his sole spare shirt to Adam, and Nate gave his dragon pistol to a companion of Ajeet, a Frenchman named Philippe. The Frenchman, who kept his face hidden behind a mask, had casually remarked on the weapon, and the American gave it to him without hesitation.

The leper chief offered some parting advice of his own. Adam addressed Nate, his voice edged with an ominous tone. "Guide. A last caution. Avoid the low-lying areas further down our valley. The valley floor there is littered with the bones of trespassers and animals. And keep up your pace, you must leave the valley well before nightfall if you wish to leave at all."

Nate and William journeyed through the valley all morning, past cabins and fields of livestock, a fresh western wind at their backs. Although they never saw another person, the feeling they were being closely watched was always present.

"How did you guess they were lepers?" Nate asked.

"In Spain, our unit chanced across an isolated colony," William said. "Hard to forget."

"Clever story too, about your daughter."

William didn't bother answering. The American wouldn't understand anyway.

Around noontime the path entered a dark wood. The sun disappeared behind a ceiling of low gray clouds, extending the impression of traveling through a confined room. It was quiet except for the crows cawing in the treetops and the intermittent muffled cry of some distant, unidentifiable creature. There was no longer any sign of human habitation in the seemingly endless valley.

Most of the way so far had been generally level or slightly ascending. But after a while they had the distinct impression of drifting downward. William was mystified by the lack of orchids or any flowering plants in the strange forest. The fresh western breeze slowly faded, replaced with a clawing wet fog accompanied by an acrid odor.

It was near midafternoon when the American's eyes drooped, and he spoke, his speech slightly slurred, as if unnaturally weary. "We've been

descending for much longer than I'd like," he said, "and that stink is growing with every step forward. It's nearly choking me." He could no longer
blink away the narrowing of his vision, and a dull ache filled his chest.

Behind Nate in the tiresome grayness, the throbbing in William's
brain had grown almost intolerable. They were suffocating in the strange
rancid fog. But how could such a thing be true?

The American was about to say something, when a bloodcurdling
wail rent the air, the unnerving drawn-out cry originating from deep
in the gloom of the lower dell. The strange fog seemed to thicken and
fold about them.

"This way, quick, there's no time to waste," William ordered as he
rushed to a small clearing on a hillock to the left side of the path. In his
haste to follow, Nate tripped.

At first, he thought he had fallen on dry branches. But struggling to
stand, he realized his hands were caught in the broken bones and twisted
spine of a rotting corpse; the partially decayed rib cage had broken his
fall. This close to the ground, he could see many more bones, including
human skulls, scattered about.

"No time to get acquainted with your friend, Bidwell, they're
coming," William said grimly, spotting movement through the fog. He
helped the light-headed American off the ground.

A strange muted clicking and scratching came from the murky
shroud surrounding them, like the sound of a thousand claws on a hard,
polished surface. The noise spread in every direction.

They stood on top of the small rise and faced out toward the encircling gray mist, the Brit standing back-to-back with the American.

"Balls, Gunn. You may be willing to die for this noble mission you're
on, but frankly, I'd trust you more if you were in this for the money."

William merely grunted as he steadied the rifle on the shadows
dancing in front of them, his sword unsheathed on his belt. Nate held
the blunderbuss ready with numb fingers. Next to them stood Jenny
and Pax, prepared for battle.

"In the trees," Nate said, steadying himself against the mule, his
head swimming.

Above them, pairs of yellow eyes glowered, their eerie gleam penetrating the fog. Shapes moved through the foliage, hissing through terrible jaws.

Pax bristled, teeth bared in a challenging growl.

William said, "They're behind us as well." He shook his head, trying to clear it.

"We're surrounded," Nate said, raising the blunderbuss for the onslaught.

In the darkness, the creatures fell upon them.

CHAPTER 38

A GOD-FEARING MAN

Better sleep with a sober cannibal than a drunken Christian.
          —Herman Melville, *Moby Dick*

BOOM! A deafening report and bright flash split the gloom, revealing the glowing yellow eyes of huge wolves with scarlet tongues, tensed to pounce. Beside them, muscular felines jostled for position, gaping jaws dripping saliva.

Out of the mist appeared the turbaned Ajeet, glowing scimitar cleaving an arc through the abominations. Two powerful warriors—one masked—fought alongside the Sikh, widening the path through the murderous horde like scything weeds.

The attack of the brutes faltered, terror at their slaughter overcoming their thirst for blood.

William and Nate joined the melee. William fired at the closest beast, then waded into the confusion with his blade. Nate's blunderbuss spoke, brutally sweeping a wide curve clean of the fiends, the roar of the weapon cowering the remainder.

Any which could escape fled back to the dark places they had crawled from.

The men looked at each other. The big dog and Jenny stood still, panting.

"What the hell were those?" Nate gasped, leaning tiredly on the blunderbuss, the carcasses of the mutant killers scattered about.

William spoke to Ajeet. "You followed us."

Ajeet said, "We cannot tarry. More will come. Follow me."

He led them almost directly uphill, out of the dark dell. They quickly left the cloying fog, and the atmosphere became fresher. Their heads cleared with every step, and they felt revitalized. The dark roof of clouds parted, and they were surprised to see the sun still shining, although quite low on the horizon.

"The path can be deceptive," Ajeet explained, "and too often leads the unwary astray. Adam feared for you"—he flashed a brilliant smile—"only because we believe you are more useful seeking the orchid on our behalf than joining this graveyard here."

"What were those monsters?" Nate asked.

Ajeet looked at him strangely. "There were no monsters. Had you not been poisoned by the fog, you would have seen just a few starving dogs, pushed to madness by bad air in that low place. As you were also. They attack anything that enters the hollow."

Behind the mask, Philippe added, "We patrol to keep them at bay, and kill any which stray into our livestock."

"We'll see you safely to the far borders of our valley. There you can pick up the path to the east."

William and Nate continued on the forest path which Ajeet had brought them to several days before. The path was level and appeared to be well-used, although they had yet to encounter anyone.

Having escaped the Spanish ambush and negotiated the haunted valley intact, the British officer felt more optimistic than he had in a long time. To celebrate, he said, "How the bloody hell did you ever lead us down into that hollow?"

"I wondered how long it was going to take for you to say something," Nate answered. "It was *your* blasted valley. If you're so clever, you should have led us."

The Brit had prevented a disaster by his quick action in directing them to take defensive positions on that knoll.

Damned if Nate was going to admit it, though.

They traveled east on the jungle path, troops of monkeys and flights of toucans kept them company.

"Let's hope our luck holds," Nate said. "We still have to find our way into the Amazon, somehow get river transport, find the Sacred Land, escape with the treasure, and then find our way home. All this, while hopefully keeping our heads on our shoulders, where they belong, and not hanging in some chief's hut."

Their gradual ascent out of the steaming jungle led to a dense broad-leaf forest where the trees grew higher and closer together. The gardener in William admired the tall trees filled with orchids, some blazing tangerine and pink, others creamy banana and rose—any of which would have made an elite centerpiece for the duke's arboretum back in England.

Late that afternoon, in the upper limits of the thinning cloud forest, they came to a halt at the edge of the deepest ravine they had yet encountered.

The rope bridge crossing the chasm was over a hundred feet long. It consisted of a scant center rope with two waist-high cords running on either side. This was easily the most hazardous bridge they had yet encountered—in Nate's opinion, even surpassing in danger the worst crossings of the Pisba passage.

Vapor rose from the foaming torrent far below. William spoke over the roar. "What do you think?"

Looking into the abyss, Nate frowned. "Seems to me the mule will never go on her own. We'll have to carry our supplies over first, then rig a traveler and pull her across. Wait until I reach the other side, then come over. I'll make fast a rope over there and come back to this side to complete the rig for the mule. Then I'll go back across, and together we'll pull her over."

Nate made the slow journey across with the guns and some of their provisions.

William crossed with most of the rest. He was happy to be safe on the other side. *I don't envy Bidwell going back and forth again—once was quite enough.*

With the coil of traveler rope draped over his shoulder and the sling in his right hand, the American started inching back across on the center rope while holding on to one of the two waist-high cords with his left hand. He was in the middle of the ravine, when he stopped cold.

A tall man with a black goatee and broad-brimmed hat stood next to Jenny, stroking her with his right hand.

He was well-armed, a late-model rifle in his left hand, a pair of pistols secured in a wide waistband, a cartridge bandolier slung across his shoulder and down his chest, the stock of another rifle clearly visible in a pack on his horse. A large machete hung at his side.

"She's a good beast," he yelled across in English, "I can see by her brand she is Spanish. I owe you for keeping her so well for me." He shifted position and approached the rope bridge. "I was waiting for you in the jungle, but you outsmarted me. Very clever."

Nate tightened his grip on the cord with his left hand and let the sling fall into the ravine so he could grip the other with his right. He had been too complacent, thinking their tracker had quit. It was not like Nate to underestimate an enemy.

William slowly let his hand drift toward the saddlebag storing the weapons.

"Move another inch and your friend goes for a swim!" The Spaniard looked down and smiled. "That is, if he survives the fall!" He walked up to the waist cord on the right side of the bridge and drew out the machete. Without another word, he brought the sharp blade down and cut the rope clean through.

When Nate saw what the man was about to do, he shifted his grip to the other waist-high cord; now he clung for dear life while balancing on the center rope.

Marquez yelled across to William, "I know about the treasures you seek: the black plant and the gem. The blind *indígena* told me everything before he died."

"Was it really necessary to kill him?" William shouted.

"He was old—the pain was too much for his heart. But don't worry"—Marquez smiled—"I baptized the savage before he expired, and his screams showed his soul was purged of its black sins."

William snapped, "You're a sick bastard."

Marquez pointed at the American, hanging onto the damaged bridge. "If you want to worry about someone, you should worry about your friend out there, because if you don't tell me right now, what you brought to Bolívar from your king, I am going to send your infidel friend straight to hell."

William hesitated, knowing that war with Spain hung in the balance should he reveal this information.

The razor-sharp machete bit into the center rope Nate was standing on, the bridge vibrating from the impact. A few remaining strands were all that kept Nate from falling.

Nate urged, "For God's sake, Gunn, give him what he wants!" He tried to tighten his grip on the waist cord, but the rope was slippery, slick from the spray rising from the roiling waters far below.

"*Now*, Captain! Tell me what I want to know *now*"—Marquez raised the machete—"or he dies!"

His daughter's life was in jeopardy. Without Nate, William would never have a chance of reaching the black orchid. World politics be damned.

He shouted, "We've made a deal with Bolívar. My country will provide men, arms, ammunition, everything he needs to defeat the Spanish, in return for exclusive preferential trade rights."

"Thank you, Captain. Was that so difficult?"

With a flash of metal, Marquez cleanly sliced through the remaining cords, and like a condemned man falling through the opened trap of a gallows, Nate plunged downward, disappearing into the mist without a sound.

William stared at the place where Nate fell. He couldn't hear anything over the sound of the rapids. There was no trace of the American on the water.

Marquez yelled across, "You should just go home, Captain Gunn. Unlike you, I can use the Spanish roads and bridges and will arrive at the Sacred Land well ahead of you. There will be no orchid left and no gem—I'll see to that."

CHAPTER 39

TAKING STOCK

WINTER 1819

Simon Bidwell waited patiently in the back room of the Black Swan. Located in rural Massachusetts, the tavern was remote enough to ensure neither he nor his guest would be recognized. And since the tycoon occasionally provided the owner with an "indentured servant" at a good price, privacy was assured.

It was dark when his guest arrived. John Quincy Adams tied his horse to the rail at the side of the tavern. He walked around to enter the back room unobserved. He was alone.

Adams did not look forward to these clandestine meetings. Afterward, they left a bad taste in his mouth and the feeling he needed a hot bath. But he couldn't ignore the man's wealth and influence and still be secretary of state.

Bidwell was standing near the fire when the secretary entered the small room. The physical difference in the men was striking—Bidwell towered over Adams, his powerful build contrasting with Adams's almost portly shape. However, Adams's intelligent, piercing black eyes and stern face framed by blooming white side-whiskers contributed to an appearance as formidable as that of the powerful merchant. These men met as equals.

Never comfortable with pleasantries, the secretary nodded and drank the glass of Madeira the shipowner had poured for him. Adams set the glass back on the table.

He said, "It appears our ruse was successful. They signed the treaty earlier this year. The Spanish were pleased we had a man down there, sowing suspicion among Bolívar's caudillos."

Simon poured himself another glass and refilled Adams's. "We're doing them a favor by taking Florida off their hands. *They* should be paying *us* to take it."

The secretary of state answered, "It's only because the Spanish are so overextended, fighting rebellion in all their colonies, that they're more than happy not to fight us as well."

Ignoring Adams, Simon added, "And the Brits appear happy with their own trade agreement."

This drew a sharp look from the secretary.

"Don't be surprised, Mr. Adams, I know everything that's happening—or will happen—on both sides of the Atlantic."

"And your son?" Adams asked. "There's been no word in some time."

Bidwell spoke, "He knows how to take care of himself. He was certainly better prepared than any of those whiskey-swilling lackeys of yours who would otherwise have been sent."

Simon Bidwell walked to the fire. "I understand Monroe will be getting the support he seeks from the Crown, Mr. Secretary, for his dream of keeping the Europeans out of our part of the world—the Brits will be more than happy to keep the rest of the world for themselves."

He drained his glass. "Now let's see how long they can keep it from us."

CHAPTER 40

℞ESCUE

Nate slammed into the side of the cliff, feeling as if his arm was being pulled out of its socket.

The rope, wrapped around his arm, swung him into the rock and knocked the wind out of him. He hadn't time to celebrate contact before the rope began to uncoil. He grasped as tight as he could, desperate to arrest his fall, but the slick rope continued to run through his burning hands. The roar of the rapids in the gorge far below filled his ears.

His raw hands caught the final braid; he clung to the rope and called, "Mr. Gunn, if you please!"

William leaned over the edge and was amazed to find his guide alive, although rather precariously suspended above the chasm. But as Nate slowly swung, the cords of the rope holding the Yank rubbed on the sharp outcrop and frayed dangerously. To avoid parting the rope altogether, William tried to pull him up gradually. The closer Nate got to the edge, the thinner his lifeline became. William decided to heave more swiftly; his arms burned with the effort. Almost at the top, he saw the last cord about to split. "Your hand, quickly!" he shouted, lunging over the edge.

Nate reached up as the worn rope parted; William just managed to seize the Yank's outstretched hand but watched helplessly as the American dangled in thin air, his shaky grip slipping. Frantically scratching at the cliff face with his feet, Nate found a small rock ledge with his right foot, enabling him to reach up with his other hand; William grasped it tightly and pulled. When the American's shoulders appeared over the side, Pax gripped Nate's shirt in his mouth. Together, the officer and the dog dragged the Yank to safety. The Brit and the American collapsed backward, exhausted.

"If we're ever going to do that again, mate, you're going to have to lose some weight," William gasped out.

"Don't worry, Gunn—where we're headed," he gulped, "we're both going to lose some weight." Nate examined the rope burns on his bleeding hands. "And by the way, thanks." He rubbed Pax's chin. "You too."

After a brief rest, they continued to ascend the Inca road.

William said what they were both thinking, "That son of a bitch Dutchman sold me out to the Spanish. If ever I get my hands around his neck . . ."

But now their enemy was no longer faceless. And things could have been a lot worse. At least they were still alive, and although they would miss the mule, they hadn't lost all the provisions.

William asked, "Do you think the Spaniard's threats were real?"

"I think he'll be in for some surprises in the Amazon. Overconfidence may get him in trouble."

William added, "He's got a good lead and access to better roads. We're going to have to go hard."

"So let's not waste any more time. Let's beat that murdering bastard to this Sacred Land of yours."

CHAPTER 41

JAWS OF DEATH

COLOMBIA-BRAZIL FRONTIER

Toward evening William and Nate arrived on the last high plain leading to the Amazon. A volcano was visible in the west, its cone surrounded by a pall of smoke, like a fiery halo in the setting sun.

This plateau was higher than the others, and more fissured from strong seismic activity. Off to the south and southwest several more volcanos could be seen, some quite distant on the horizon, the steam rising from their cones plainly visible in the thin, clear air. The land was barren save for a solitary stunted tree.

To speed their journey across the *páramo* toward the Amazon basin, the dying leper had directed Nate and William to take one of the age-old Inca tracks. A cairn clearly marked the direction of the ancient path.

Unable to find a sheltered place to camp, and reluctant to descend back into the forest, they spent the night upwind of a sulfurous vent. The warm ground would occasionally vibrate, accompanied by a throaty growl from the fumarole. Late in the night, a loud rumble and slight shaking of the ground roused them. They held their breath for a moment, waiting for additional tremors.

"Bidwell, you remember the old Indian back there who gave me the diary?" William started.

"Huh?" the sleepy American grunted.

"He said something about these shakes. That the wife of some

dragon god or the other was angry. He said this was only the beginning—sort of hinted it was the end of his people. Could there be
anything to it?"

"Maybe," Nate said, and yawned. "When I rode with the llaneros
they told me that a few years back, just about the time your lot was burning our capitol down, a great shake almost leveled Caracas. I found out
later that Bolívar's house was seriously damaged—could have been the
end of the revolution right there, but he escaped. I guess a lot of people
were killed. On the plains, I rode past a couple of abandoned towns that
were mostly rubble, destroyed by that earthquake. Seems these things
happen, Gunn, especially around the Andes."

Neither of them slept a great deal that night.

The next day, their lungs were raw from the dry air mixed with the
fumes.

"What do you think he meant by 'Jaws of Death'?" William asked.
"There's nothing up here except the odd smelly hole or dried-up salt
pond."

Nate said, "I expect we'll know it as soon we see it. Something like
that should stand out."

The going became difficult. Streams of water from past rainy seasons
had eroded deep chasms in the fractured basalt. Accompanied by fissures
left by earthquakes and pockmarked with rifts and gullies, at times the
terrain was almost impossible to negotiate, causing time-consuming
detours. They regularly stopped to scan the area for the "jaws" the old
leper was so insistent they follow down into the Amazon, but they could
see nothing in the cracked and scarred landscape. By now, they had
learned to ignore the almost daily trembling of the ground.

Late in the afternoon of the third day on the high plain, the
road gradually deteriorated from the improved Inca path to a faded
track, and eventually disappeared altogether. And they were almost
out of water.

"I say we keep going as much as possible directly east," Nate said
with a conviction he didn't feel.

"That doesn't sound very bright," the British officer said. "We've been going east for over three days and haven't seen a damn thing. Before we completely run out of food and water, I say we split up and look for something resembling any kind of jaws."

"That would only get us lost or killed. Look." He pointed. "I may be mistaken, but that unbroken horizon suggests to me we're getting close to the escarpment."

The American was pointing to the straight line ahead that could signal the edge of the high cliff ending the *páramo*, and the beginning of the Amazon basin.

"From what I remember of his journal, Jussieu was describing a trail hundreds of miles from here," William said. "How do we know this is the same escarpment?"

"We don't, but it makes sense."

William saw he was probably right. The rigidly defined skyline hinted at a rapid drop in the land beyond. But Bidwell had been wrong before. William was starting to have serious doubts about the American's abilities.

They reached the cliff the next morning. The panorama which extended before them almost made them forget there was no way down.

Far below, beyond an amber fringe of grassland, as far as the eye could see stretched an endless ocean of verdant rain forest, sky and land melding together in the distant mist. All sound disappeared into that hollow emptiness, their small voices swallowed by the void. No sign of man pierced that primitive sky: no cathedral spire, no castle rampart, no factory smokestack. The green continued, unblemished by road, cultivated field, town, or village.

"Well, here we are," Nate said, awestruck.

Confronted with such an alien world, William was speechless. He could only stare. The curvature of the earth could be sensed in the extreme vastness of the expanse. He could never have imagined anything like this in his wildest dreams.

Nate said, "You sure about this, Gunn?"

"Although I've seen orchids everywhere in this country," William replied, "I've come to believe the black orchid is only found somewhere down there."

They continued to look downward. The sheer face of the cliff extended for a long, long way below them.

"God Almighty," Nate said, "it's so far down it's difficult to see the ground right below us."

William was unperturbed. "Back in England I learned the Amazon is one of the least explored regions on earth. Maps of it are mainly blank." He turned to the American. "But if we can just get down there, I know I can get us to the Sacred Land. I memorized Jussieu's directions. All you have to do is keep us alive."

Nate looked around. He said, "It's impossible to descend here. We're running out of time to find these Jaws of Doom."

"*Death*, Yank—the Jaws of Death," the British officer corrected.

"Right, those."

William observed, "The Frenchman's original path to the south of us went through high cliffs also, but he had the advantage of a pass. And if that Spanish bastard who waylaid us went that way, he's probably already floating down the Amazon."

"We'd lose weeks just trying to get there," Nate observed, "and then we still couldn't be sure of where we were."

"We're out of water," William said, upending the calabash.

Nate hefted his water skin. It was light—too light.

"Well, guide, where's the water around here?" William asked.

Nate ignored him. He got up. "Perhaps to the old leper, 'jaws' simply meant a ravine."

William said, "That makes a lot more sense than actual 'Jaws of Death.'"

Nate exhaled. "Maybe all this time we should've been looking for some fissure sloping down toward the Amazon. Some of the deeper gullies we passed early on looked like they drained to the east."

"Are you serious?" William replied. "Backtracking would take days."

"Not exactly backtrack, but head north. Maybe we can quickly come across the correct gully. And if it's deep enough, that's where we'll find water as well."

Leaving the faded remnant of a path, they struck northward. The uneven ground, difficult to walk on, absorbed their attention. They were forced to walk around a large salt lake, adding several hours to their journey.

Their shadows were long in the late-afternoon sun when Nate finally signaled a halt. "Hell, Gunn," he croaked through parched lips, "those channels I saw must have disappeared."

He sat down, dizzy from thirst, when something odd caught his eye. "What *is that?*"

"Where? What're you talking about?" William gasped.

"Out there." Nate pointed.

A lonely dead tree brooded over the blasted, barren landscape like a gray watchman. Slightly beyond this solitary sentinel, a rock face projected a short way above the ground. The only reason it was visible at all was due to the sunlight changing the color of the stone from the dull gray of its surroundings to a bright red. Seen from another angle, the scarlet streak would have been invisible.

"You're raving." William was too tired to stand.

"I'm going to look."

"This is it, Bidwell," the British officer said, and struggled to his feet. "I'm not going to die of thirst out here. This is the last time I follow you."

Pax trailed the men. He panted deeply, his dry tongue dangling from his mouth.

Carefully making their way over the uneven terrain, they passed the dead tree. The land dipped down before rising slightly toward what appeared to be a split in the earth.

Coming closer, they could see that the cleft steadily opened and deepened into a narrow chasm. What had first attracted their attention a few minutes ago—the opposite wall of the rift glowing fiery crimson in the full lowering sun—had now darkened to a dull burnt orange in the last dying rays of the sunset.

"Look at this bloody thing. It must be a hundred feet deep." Bending slightly, William peered into the fissure. The bottom appeared to slope smoothly down to the east. "I can't see the end; it's too dark."

"We'll rest here tonight and locate the entrance in the light of day."

At dawn they found the beginnings of the crevice. Located in a shallow bowl, two immense carved stone figures straddled the entrance.

"I recognize this one," Nate said, peering at a solemn stone form sculpted with thunderbolts in his hands, a shining sun crowning his head, and tears flowing from his eyes. "He's the chief god of the Incas. If you're heading into a place like the Amazon and want someone covering your back, he's a good choice."

On the other side of the opening, a grinning, horned demon holding a human skull in one hand stared down at them, the outline of a partially consumed body suspended from its mouth. The American's tone changed. "On the other hand," he said grimly, "this gentleman is Supay, the Inca god of death."

Passing between the two large figures, they entered the rift. The walls of the narrow opening were covered with bizarre pictographs: palm prints, animals, and various stick figures, many missing heads and limbs.

Nate hesitated. "I have a bad feeling about this."

William looked around. "This is our only choice. Or you can stay up here and die of thirst."

"You're right," Nate said decidedly. "Tallyho, old chum." He shouldered his pack and started into the gully.

The gray dog lay down and whined.

William whispered encouragingly, "C'mon, Pax. Can't stay up here forever."

The big dog stood and, with a noticeable lack of enthusiasm, followed his master into the chasm.

The way descended sharply, straight and true to the east. Huge basalt blocks were strewn everywhere—debris from the walls of the tight canyon.

"If this gully were any narrower, we'd have to climb over these boulders," the Brit observed. "I don't think I could do it," he said quietly.

As if speaking to himself, Nate added, "The question is, How did they get here?"

Weak and giddy with thirst, they reached out to steady themselves as they picked their way down. Pax trailed close behind, head low, his tongue almost dragging on the ground.

After a few hours, William said, "It's getting warmer in here." He was so dehydrated he couldn't even sweat.

"Damp, as well."

When Pax stopped to frantically lap at the wall, Nate looked more closely. "Some seepage. Not enough. If we don't find a spring soon, I'll be licking these walls next." The dog's tongue still hung out the side of his mouth.

The sky overhead began to brighten, illuminating the mysterious gorge and allowing a view of the path that plunged before them. Like a deep, roofless tunnel, the chasm appeared to be carved from the charcoal-gray basalt columns forming the walls, standing like so many silent watchmen. Every so often a gap in a column indicated where a block had dislodged and fallen, the space like a missing tooth in a smile.

Late in the afternoon, the walls had become very high, just a narrow strip of sky showing far overhead. Additional tiny seeps had appeared, so small as to dry up before reaching the ground, each one enviously eyed by the desperate men. Frail and dizzy, they could barely drag themselves along. They were dying of thirst.

The minuscule green opening at the end of the chasm didn't seem any larger than when they had begun their descent that morning. Light-headed, their tongues swollen, they no longer spoke unless absolutely necessary. At one point Nate tripped and lay on the ground.

William bent over him. "I knew you'd give out first, Yank," the British officer gasped raggedly. "Do I have to save your butt again?"

Raising himself slowly on all fours and then grasping the wall, the American pulled himself upright. He waved the Brit closer. William bent down and turned an ear to the American. "Kiss my ass, lobster-back."

Pax hurried past them, almost knocking Nate over again. They both stared at the big dog. Several yards down the path, Pax stopped with his nose near the wall. It sounded like he was drinking.

Nate staggered to the dog and dropped to his knees. A clear rivulet ran from a split in the rock to the bottom of the now steamy confines of the ravine. They soaked up the water with cloth and sucked what they could from the material, repeating the process until their immediate thirst was quenched.

Then they dammed the water and waited until the pool was deep enough to enable them to fill their flasks. They rested afterward, backs against the wall, savoring the cool moisture trickling down their throats. The still water of the deepening pool reflected the canyon walls and narrow sliver of sky overhead.

After a while it was not so much the beauty of the reflection which caught Nate's eye, but the ripples which began vibrating across the quiet surface of the pool. Pax whined—a strange sound, one they had never heard from him before.

"What's the matter, boy?" William interrupted filling his flask for the second time to look searchingly at the anxious animal.

It was unnecessary. Both men recognized the low thrumming that came from deep within the earth accompanied by a faltering vibration.

Suddenly realizing what had dislodged so many large blocks, they jumped to their feet. "We've got to get out of here—now!" Pax was already racing down the ravine.

The first tremor hit with a deep rumble, rolling through with enough force to knock one of the basalt columns over. Had they not been in the protective shadow of a huge boulder, the collapsing pillar would have flattened them.

"Bloody hell, Bidwell! We'll be crushed in here!"

Another wave of energy shook the canyon, dislodging even more basalt blocks.

"The opening!" Nate shouted. "We've got to get out—this is a death trap!"

William didn't need any encouragement. Propelled by the fear of sudden, crushing death, both men dodged the rocks crashing from above in a sprint for their very lives.

CHAPTER 42

MISSION ACCOMPLISHED

The Duke of Devonshire sat with Viscount Palmerston in the library at Chatsworth. The duke swirled the amber sherry around in his glasses as he listened to the secretary at war.

Viscount Palmerston said, "An envoy from Bolívar arrived with an agreement containing all the terms and conditions we desire. And it looks as if we're backing the right horse, so to speak. We've word of a significant victory: The Viceroyalty of Bogotá has apparently fallen to our 'Great Liberator.' We've no further word on Captain Gunn, but it certainly appears his mission was successful." Palmerston lifted his spectacles and rubbed his bloodshot eyes. "Men like William Gunn don't come along every day, Hart. We're fortunate. Frankly, I don't know where you find them."

The duke nodded his acknowledgment. "We shouldn't assume Bolívar's scouts are correct."

Palmerston said, "The last they heard, your man was wandering in the wild, in enemy territory, without a guide." The viscount gave the duke a significant look.

"Yes, but the latest reports put him in the company of an American. That's the oddest bit." The duke dabbed at an invisible spot on the gleaming table. "A wilderness sort, one of those chaps living on the edge of the forest. He was with Bolívar when our William arrived. Smythe," the duke called to the butler, "what *are* they called?"

The butler shimmered in. "Mountain men, I believe, sir."

The viscount asked, "What in name of the Almighty has ever led them to the Amazon?" After a moment he lifted his glass. "In any event, God help those men . . . if they're still alive."

William Cavendish stared into the darkness beyond the large window. "I'd say we've heard the last of Captain Gunn." He reflected, "Sarah may have to be moved somewhere better suited to a young girl."

"A boarding school, perhaps," the viscount suggested.

"Perhaps."

"And what will you do if her father survives?" Palmerston asked.

"Billy Gunn," the duke scoffed, "in the Amazon? No, we don't have to worry ourselves on that score."

Lifting his chin, he said brightly, "I believe you came to discuss that China situation. But first, a toast." He lifted his glass. "Mission accomplished."

CHAPTER 43

END OF THE WORLD

A journey of a thousand miles begins with a single step.
—Lao Tzu, *Tao Te Ching*

Nate and William collapsed on the ground and lay still, bruised and bloodied, not sure how many broken bones they had suffered. Panting from exertion, they struggled to catch their breath in the heavy, humid air. A final minor spasm shook the earth, showering them with a spray of fine powder and shards. The rock dust caught in the back of their throats.

Pax nuzzled William's hand, then stood back and issued that strange yap.

Nate looked at the dog and rasped, "You sure he's a dog, Gunn?"

William managed a brief rub of Pax's muzzle.

They had scrambled so far down along the broadening chasm that the sky was wide open overhead. "It looks like we're out of harm's way here," Nate observed. They cautiously felt their arms and legs to assess the damage. It appeared they'd managed to escape with only minor cuts and bruises.

"That was bloody close." William brushed off his shirt and smacked his trousers. The rock dust rose off his clothes. "But if that's the worst their earthmover god can do," William said, "we've no further worries from her."

Nate looked back at the collapsed rift. "Guess Jaws of Death wasn't such a bad name after all," he admitted.

The ravine ended only a few hundred feet above the Amazon basin. From behind a break in the clouds, the full force of the direct rays of the sun struck them. The blinding beams of sunshine briefly bathed the end of the chasm in golden light.

Nate pulled the wide brim of his hat lower, over his eyes.

Transfixed by the endless unbroken sea of green in the distance, they gazed out from their perch. Where the dry grassland ended, the rain forest stretched to the horizon.

Without shifting his gaze, Nate said, "You know, Gunn, I never told you what the Indians call this place."

"What's that?"

"End of the World."

William hefted his pack, adjusted the straps, and tightened his grip on the blowgun.

"Best get on with it, then. To the Big River and a race to the Sacred Land."

The British officer started down the narrow path which wound through the broken rock face to the grassland at the bottom of the cliff, his mind fixed on his daughter, Sarah, somewhere across the ocean, far, far, away.

Amazon River Basin,
South America

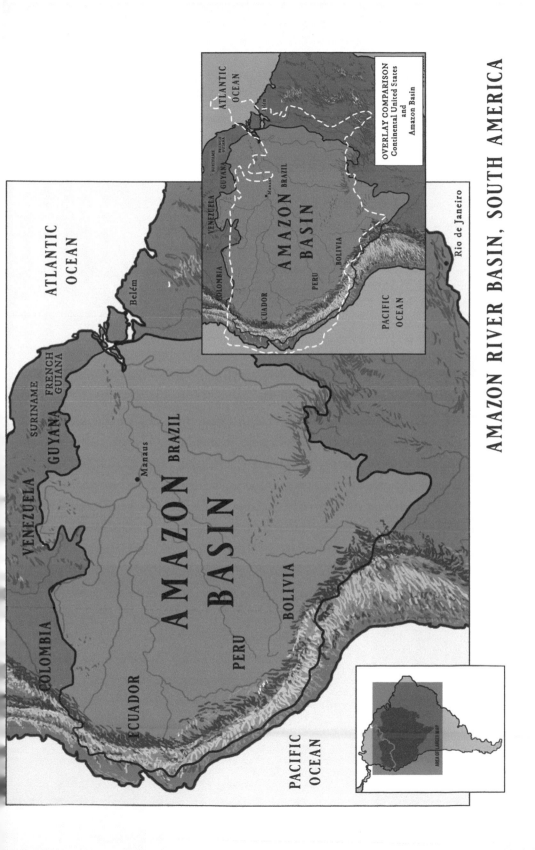

AMAZON RIVER BASIN, SOUTH AMERICA

1815: MIDNIGHT, DEEP IN THE AMAZON

The young man dashed through the rain forest. He was completely naked save for the gold medal that bounced against his chest. He did not pause, not even when a cloud obscured the light of the moon. When he tripped, the sharp cutty grass and branches slashed his bare skin. With the memory of his companion's screams fresh in his mind, he scrambled to his feet and plunged on. His pale white skin shone like a beacon in the dark.

This was their home; pursuing him would be like an afternoon stroll through an English garden.

They were gaining on him. Straight flight was futile; evasion was his only hope. If he could hide until dawn he might find the river, then escape.

He thought he heard whispering somewhere in the darkness. He froze and listened. Nothing. But then, close now, strange words sighed in the night. Ignoring the danger, he climbed. He knew deadly predators lived in the trees, but he had no choice.

He wedged his naked body into a gap between two large limbs. Far below, the man could clearly hear voices on the forest floor. He lay still, barely breathing. He clutched the medallion and prayed he was invisible behind the limb.

But other beasts prowled the Amazon.

Searing pain suddenly gripped the man's scrotum. Feeling as though he'd been shot, he doubled over in agony. He bit his lip until it bled but was unable to stifle a moan.

A bullet ant.

His trembling fingers located the mandibles of the stinging insect, still embedded in his swollen genitals. Assaulted by waves of fiery pain, it was impossible to control his shuddering limbs.

He wedged his body in tighter, hoping against hope that he could remain undiscovered. The medallion weighed heavy against his chest, dragging him down.

He did not feel the prick of the darts, but his pain vanished and he grew dizzy. His vision faded. Hearing ceased. Chest tightening, his limbs slowly grew numb as he struggled to draw breath.

But he no longer cared. From a distant warm place, a familiar voice called.

And then, darkness.

CHAPTER 44

$\mathcal{A}$MAZON

THE RIVER SEA

The Amazon River is the largest and longest river on earth, having a length approximately equal to the distance from New York City to Rome. Spanish soldier Francisco de Orellana gave the river its present name after reporting pitched battles with tribes of brave female warriors whom he likened to the Amazons of Greek mythology.

Ancient pre-Columbian peoples gave it the name "River Sea" due to its extreme width—one thousand miles inland, it is still seven miles wide. The flow of the Amazon is greater than the combined discharge of the next seven largest rivers of the world. The amount of water that flows from the Amazon into the ocean every day is enough to supply New York City's fresh water needs for nine years. This tremendous flow travels so far into the ocean before mixing that early sailors could drink fresh water from the Atlantic without being in sight of the South American continent.

In the distant past, before the tectonic shift which resulted in the creation of the Andes Mountains, the Amazon River drained the eastern highlands and originally flowed west. But the uplift of the Andes about twenty million years ago blocked the river's path to the Pacific Ocean and resulted in the formation of an immense inland sea. The waters eventually broke through to the east to pour into the Atlantic, resulting in the formation of the present Amazon basin. The Amazonian rain forest developed from the combination of rich, sediment-laden soil left behind and the abundant rainfall draining from the eastern Andean slopes.

The scale of the Amazon drainage basin defies the imagination. Containing over a billion acres, it is the largest watershed in the world, draining an area almost the size of the continental United States.

It is the world's largest tropical rain forest, representing half of the Earth's remaining rain forest. The forest canopy is so thick that when it rains it takes an average of ten minutes for the water to reach the ground. More than one fifth of the world's oxygen is produced here.

The Amazonian rain forest is also home to the largest ecosystem in the world, containing more than ten percent of all the living plant and animal species on earth. A single Amazonian rain forest reserve is home to as many species of birds as are found in the entire United States.

While over a quarter of all current Western medicines come from the Amazon, only one in a hundred plants in the rain forest has been scientifically tested for medicinal properties. It is estimated that well over three hundred new drugs of incalculable value still await discovery in the Amazonian rain forest. Of the more than one hundred pharmaceutical drugs derived from Amazonian plants, three quarters were discovered through documented use by shamans.

JANUARY 1820, AMAZON BASIN

The Brit and the American carefully picked their way down the cliff face. At the base of the escarpment, the prairie began. In the breeze descending from the *páramo*, the alpine grasslands undulated like a silvery green sea. Only the thin path that snaked through the high grass interrupted the illusion. Two posts flanked the narrow path, a strange bulge of some sort crowning each.

As they approached, it became obvious the lumps were shrunken heads, their withered features now mere parodies of human faces.

"Welcome to the Amazon," Nate said grimly.

William bent for a closer look, and what he saw made his skin crawl. Insects scuttled over and through the grisly, wrinkled objects, poking about every leathery opening.

"Makes me wonder," William mused, "if this is a warning, or a greeting."

"A simple hello would have been just fine with me," Nate said. "Keep an eye out."

When the path disappeared in the high savanna, they remembered the old leper's directions and followed a small brook nearby. The leper had said the brook would eventually become large enough for them to float a raft downstream to the Amazon River.

They followed the watercourse for several days, the brook eventually growing into a rushing stream. Midmorning on the fourth day, the high grass plain abruptly transitioned to the thick scrub and dense foliage of the Amazonian rain forest.

Walking beneath the impenetrable forest canopy was like being submerged in an ocean abyss where all color has been absorbed by the vast depth of water above, leaving only a tarnished silvery-gray hue to light the way.

In the quiet gloom, their breathing felt forced. Their footfalls were muffled by the spongy turf underfoot; the scream of a distant puma was followed by the startled voice of a multitude of birds. Evening came quickly to the rain forest floor.

It had been over a fortnight since the earthquake on the *páramo*. In the dim, trackless rain forest, Nate and William continued to follow the stream, both men hacking their way through the thick jungle growth along the banks. Branches lashed their faces, creepers clutched their legs, and thorny vines tore their arms. Breathing in the stifling heat was like sucking air through a hot, wet blanket.

Clouds of stinging, biting insects left bleeding wounds on their necks and arms. The men wore lace mesh over their heads—a nuisance, but essential to keep small insects from attacking the corners of their eyes.

"Looks like we're never going to meet those Indians with the canoes. Or anyone else out here," William said, pointlessly wiping the sweat from his eyes.

"Maybe you haven't noticed, Admiral Gunn," Nate said, "but this stream's still too damn shallow for canoes anyway. If we'd stuck to the Frenchman's original directions and taken the forest path, we'd have gotten those dugouts and been on the river weeks ago."

"Or we'd be dead," William said. "You're conveniently forgetting that's where the Spaniard was waiting to ambush us." He took a vicious swipe at a bush.

William had never before faced anything even vaguely resembling the Amazon. This was a universe unto itself: more desolate than anything he'd experienced, including the New Granadan jungle. Even Nate found the remote forests of his home country to be tame in comparison. There were no roads he knew of, nor permanent settlements for thousands of miles. And as if they didn't have enough to concern them, there were more jaguars in the Amazon than anywhere else in South America.

"There's no climbing out of this tangle, like we could in the Magdalena," William complained, breathing heavily, "makes New Granada seem like a Sunday afternoon on the duke's estate."

"Think of the jungle like your first sweetheart, Gunn," Nate said, adding, "the sooner it's over, the better." The American resumed cutting.

"I wouldn't know, Bidwell, I married my first sweetheart."

Nate hesitated. "Lucky you."

"Yours run away?" William ventured. "Or go into hibernation?"

"She was killed." The leaden finality of the statement clung to the wet air.

William resumed slashing a path through the vines, perhaps a bit more vigorously than earlier. He cleared his throat, and when he spoke his voice was unsteady. "I'm not really that lucky, Bidwell. My wife died not long after we were wed."

Nate asked, "Is that story you told the leper true? You know, about your daughter needing the orchid as a cure?"

"Yes."

Nate nodded thoughtfully. "My wife's death was a bit of a family affair." He stopped and examined the edge of his machete closely. "I suspect my father was involved."

William didn't say anything but kept cutting.

"These'll need sharpening soon," Nate said and resumed hacking at the vegetation.

Evenings they took the fever potion that old blind Capac had given to William so long ago, then removed the leeches and other parasites their bodies had recruited during the day.

The jungle at night was considerably cooler. William didn't know how the Yank managed to start a fire in the pervasive damp, but every evening the American somehow got a blaze going. Without the fire they would have been unable to see their hands in front of their faces. But even more disconcerting were the night sounds of the Amazon.

The chatter of insects would often be broken by a sudden deathly silence, the terrified creatures of the forest alert to a stalking predator. William waited, tense as piano wire, until the anticipated death-shriek broke the night. He asked Nate several times what the sounds were. Invariably, he received the same answer: "No idea."

After another sleepless night, William said, "This is like being trapped in a prison vault. We've got to get on the river."

"Relax, Gunn," Nate advised, "it's still too fast and shallow. This place isn't the enemy. At least there's plenty of food."

William had to admit that the American was keeping them well fed. He was good at foraging for edible fruit and had also killed several birds. They tasted like hell, but it kept their strength up.

Nate held up a banana. "Try to see things from a different angle, Gunn."

"Pray tell. What angle would that be?"

Nate peeled the skin off the banana. "Best as I can figure, everything here grows twice as fast as anywhere else, dies just as quickly, and then is eaten by something. For instance"—Nate held up the banana skin—"watch."

He threw the skin at the base of a tree a couple of feet away.

Within seconds, the ground near it moved, splitting into several types of insects that tore at the discarded skin. Two huge beetles at least four inches long were winning the struggle against an army of giant ants. One of the beetles was abruptly snatched in a lightning strike from a red and yellow banded snake, which retreated under its cover of fallen leaves as quickly as it had appeared.

William whistled softly. "Steady on!"

Nate probed under the leaves with a stick. "That one's so deadly the natives don't even try to treat the bite." The small colorful snake had vanished.

"So, what you're saying is I shouldn't worry, because I'm going to become bug food anyway?"

Nate shrugged. "It makes me feel better."

Easy for him. To the British officer, the American appeared to be as much a part of this ancient domain as Jaci had.

They sat close to the flames in order to dry out as best they could. As added protection against insects, Nate had sprinkled pungent ground-up erigeron to the coals at the edge of the fire. The smoke kept the swarms of biting pests at bay. More important to William, it also kept the vampire bats away.

Bidwell had told him that these bizarre creatures needed to suck half their body weight in blood each night simply to survive. To the Brit, they were second only to caimans and jaguars in terms of Amazonian animals to avoid. The giant black caiman, apex predator of the Amazon, was "good to eat," Joseph Jussieu had written in his diary, "that is, if it isn't eating you."

Pax never failed to patrol a circle around their camp, marking the territory with his scent as a warning to potential intruders. Afterward, the big dog would find a prickly bush, lean into the thick stubby branches, and vigorously rub back and forth, ridding his short fur of insect pests. Only when the men had settled for the night would he curl in a ball to rest near William's hammock.

Pax was always up before them, alert and watchful.

The next morning, while they breakfasted on manioc, bananas, nuts, papaya, and coffee, Nate peered into the forest. "The ground's becoming more level." He absentmindedly felt the sparse stubble on his chin. "We'll be able to take to the water before long."

Covered in insect bites and sweat, and with salt stains on his tattered clothing, the British officer was barely recognizable. William almost regretted dragging them into that accursed valley of lepers which had led them to this, but he knew that the Spaniard would have surely killed them in the forest. "We *need* to get on that water," William said, "we can't keep this up."

Sensing the British officer's anxiety, Nate said, "You're right. It's time we had another look."

They worked their way closer to the water and soon had a clearer view. Downstream, a great tributary entered from the southwest, effectively doubling the flow of the river and creating a large, swirling eddy.

"We're in luck," Nate said, feeling relief. "No problem floating a raft now."

"Wouldn't a canoe be faster and easier to steer?"

"You want to spend a week making a dugout? That's at least how long it'd take." Nate put his pack down and picked up a machete. "You've been worried about how critical time is. If you stop complaining and start cutting," Nate said sharply, "we can get a serviceable raft together by this afternoon. Then maybe we can get to your Sacred Land and find that plant of yours." *And maybe get El Jefe as well.* He intended to keep his plans close, as close as William was with Jussieu's directions.

A peculiar noise came from somewhere downstream.

"Where's Pax?" William scanned the area. He gripped his rifle. "I'm going to have a look."

Nate said, "I hope he didn't get on the wrong side of a snake . . . or a caiman."

William flinched at the thought of the big reptiles. He allowed the American to lead. They worked their way downstream along the edge of the pool, past the large eddy.

Pax burst out of the brush, tail wagging furiously. He looked at the men, growled, then headed back again.

Nate followed, slashing twice as hard, not bothering to hesitate until they reached the spot near the streambank where the dog pawed at the ground.

They stopped cold. In the shadows along the shoreline just in front of them, a long dark object lay in the water, hidden in the shade.

A caiman.

It was difficult to see the monster clearly as it was partially concealed by thick brush. After several moments, Nate heaved a branch at the quiet killer. No reaction.

"Cover me." Cautiously he drew closer for a better look. With a long branch he brushed aside the bushes covering the inert beast.

"It's safe, Gunn."

"What is it?"

"We found you a canoe." Nate pointed to the craft they'd mistaken for a predator. "And it looks like Pax has made some new friends."

CHAPTER 45

THE RIVER

The dugout had been trapped for so long that vegetation had grown around the skulls and exposed rib cages of its two unfortunate passengers. Nate ran his palm over the gunwale of the canoe. "Maybe a hundred years old or more; not uncommon to still be afloat," he observed. "This is our passage out of here, Gunn."

William studied the two skeletons. Arrow remnants, dumb evidence of their doom, remained lodged in the sides of the canoe. "They're certainly not going to object. And judging by their armor," William noted, "I'd say Portuguese. Decades old, more like."

Nate poked at the remains. "Guess they needed more armor."

"Or more luck."

A single white orchid grew from the forehead of one of the skeletons; its eye sockets stared vacantly. Under the rusted armor, a few shreds of clothing clung stubbornly to yellow bones.

Nate said, "They must have come down the main tributary."

"The Spaniard would have taken the same route," William pointed out. "Let's hope he winds up a pin cushion like our two friends here."

"He hasn't made any mistakes so far. If Capac, before he died, gave the Spaniard the correct directions, we're going to be hard pressed to catch up with that murdering papist before he gets to the orchids."

A sudden trembling in the earth set their teeth on edge. They braced, but the noise and vibration subsided as quickly as it had begun.

"She's at it again," Nate said with a nervous smile. "How long to this Sacred Land of yours?"

William recalled that Jussieu was a man of few words when it came to travel details. He pulled out a stiff piece of paper and unfolded it.

Watching Gunn examine the old parchment, Nate restrained the impulse to rip it out of the officer's hands and have a look for himself. He resented as much as ever being kept in the dark, having to depend on the Brit.

"From the map and from what I can recall," William said, "we should enter a larger stream in several weeks or so. That junction's our first objective. When we get there, you'll get more information." Nate favored him with a sour look.

By late afternoon, the dugout was dry and they loaded their gear. Nate said, "You realize this canoe may be our home for quite a while."

"What do you mean?"

"There's no going back, Gunn. Once we're on the stream, the only way out is down the Big River to the Atlantic coast of Brazil. And whatever you do"—Nate figured he'd give the Brit something else to worry about—"don't forget the penis fish."

"They never mentioned a penis fish in my lectures," William said stiffly.

"They wouldn't, would they?" Nate gave a devilish grin. "Never forget, there are fates worse than death lurking just beneath the surface." Seeing he couldn't bait William, Nate explained, "It's a small fish said to be able to enter anyone in contact with river water." The American was enjoying the Brit's discomfort. "There are even stories of the fish swimming up a stream of urine to enter an unsuspecting body."

"Let's get going, Yank." They bid farewell to the former occupants and heaved their remains overboard, before shoving off into the stream. William unconsciously clasped his hand to his crotch.

The canoe was long and deep enough to accommodate the men, the dog, and their packs. Pax watched from a spot in the center of the dugout, not really trusting this new means of travel. Sitting in front, it didn't take long for William to become comfortable, once the American showed him how to balance his weight.

It was brighter midstream, away from the dense jungle. The canoe cut easily through the blood-warm waters bordered on either side by the unbroken forest. Without the protection of the forest canopy, the sun could radiate uninterrupted waves of heat. Enveloped in this sultry landscape, the explorers glided noiselessly downstream.

The convoy of black caimans following the dugout ensured they didn't become overly relaxed.

Most nights the travelers rested for a few hours ashore. If there was enough moonlight, they would leave well before daybreak. A fog often clung to the river in the early morning. Only the chatter of quarreling kingfishers penetrated the thick mist. Floating soundlessly down the broad waters, the vapors would close about the dugout, the only evidence of their passing the silent bow wave spreading toward shore.

After almost a week on the river, there came an evening when there was no break in the dense undergrowth on the bank. It was impossible to find a place to camp ashore. With submersed sandbanks and snags all but invisible in the moonless night, they were forced to tie up to a large tree that stood half-submerged in the river. The swarms of insects were horrendous, but the current would challenge the caimans should they attack. This did not mean they wouldn't try.

In the middle of the night, a loud thump jolted the side of the canoe. They tipped precariously before the vessel swung back.

Nate stood and shifted his weight in the swaying pirogue. Guessing where the massive reptile would emerge, the American braced his right leg against the gunwale, raised his blunderbuss, and took aim.

Approaching rapidly, two bubble eyes broke the surface less than ten yards away. The water rippled with the speed of the twenty-foot-long beast's approach.

The yellow-white flash was blinding, and the sound reverberated through the jungle like thunder. As the smoke cleared, they could see that the narrow spread of shot had pulverized the attacker's head. The momentum of the huge carcass carried it forward to bump harmlessly against their canoe.

Nate lay down and pulled the netting across. "Wake me up if more come." He instantly fell asleep.

The song of the tropical night resumed, and to his surprise, William felt himself drifting off.

"You know, Bidwell, this is quite odd." Assisted by the current, they raced downstream, drawing ever nearer to the Sacred Land and the black orchid. With the American steering, the British officer had plenty of time to study their surroundings while he paddled.

"What's odd?"

"Every so often there seem to be large patches of palm groves mixed among the kapoks and teaks. I've recognized at least two different varieties of fruit palms, both in separate stands."

"What's so strange about that?"

"Single-variety palm groves are planted by men." William swiveled his head. "We haven't seen a single person, or a sign of a person, since we entered the Amazon."

Focused on avoiding sandbars and submerged obstacles, Bidwell grunted indifferently.

William gazed about. The number and variety of orchids were staggering. "There certainly are plenty of orchids. It must be because the rain forest is too dark and the topsoil too thin to support plants. Orchids live in the treetops because up there they can absorb everything they need directly from the air."

"And?" Nate figured it would keep the Brit relaxed to let him drone on.

"In his notes," William persisted, warming to the subject, "Humboldt mentions rumors of a black orchid found deep in the Amazon, possessing incredible healing powers, but he doesn't provide any particulars. The scientist heard this tale not once but several times over, from various native tribes. I'm starting to believe a plant like the black orchid might occur *only* here."

"Alexander von Humboldt: the great naturalist explorer of South America," Nate said. "A lot of people are waiting for him to publish his journals, if he ever gets around to it."

"You've heard of him?" William was astonished.

"Sure. Before he returned to Europe, he visited Jefferson and helped him define our border with New Spain."

Hiding his surprise, William carried on, "Humboldt warned of the extreme danger of searching for the black orchid. Most unlike him, he implied that somehow the plant was protected by an all-powerful entity. He finished with a mysterious caution: 'None ever returned.' Doesn't sound at all scientific, does it?"

Without thinking, Nate said, "*Nemo umquam reversus.*"

"Impressive," William said, adding skeptically, "for a woodsman."

"I saw the original," Nate said wryly.

William leaned on the gunwale. "Being as I'm only a mere gardener's assistant," he said, "it appears you may have the advantage on me, Bidwell." He resumed paddling and thought that there was a lot more to the Yank than he was letting on.

Nate stopped paddling. He thought, *Sure, and I'm Marie Antoinette. He's probably forgotten I heard everything he said to the Spaniard while I was dangling from that bridge.* He started to stroke again. *There's a lot more to this Brit than he lets on.*

William wanted to keep going to make up for lost time, but Nate insisted they pull over to replenish their depleted stores. The Yank had a knack for seeing food everywhere, supplementing their supplies with cassava root, bananas, figs, and other fruits growing next to the river as well as turtle eggs and alligator eggs dug from sandy areas along the shoreline. Pax would contribute the occasional crested curassow.

The nights and days passed slowly; the ceaseless riverbank slipped by uninterrupted except for the occasional entrance of a small tributary. The monotonous dip of their paddles marked time.

They soon began to feel the effects of rowing for eighteen hours a day in a narrow canoe, much of it in the full sun. Muscle cramps and constant dull headaches plagued them.

Late in the afternoons, drenched from the steamy heat, his entire body aching from the relentless paddling, William's mind would drift, at times reliving past battles, or lost in thoughts of his wife. Only when he focused on Sarah did he paddle with renewed vigor.

On one particularly sultry afternoon, the American was sculling half-asleep in the stern. In the front of the dugout, William suddenly straightened. Wordlessly, the Brit laid his paddle aside. With great design, he picked up the blunderbuss and began to raise it.

Nate quickly scanned ahead. He saw nothing unusual, just the flat, brown surface of the water and the occasional log.

"Rotten bastards," William said. He stood and braced his foot against the gunwale with the gun snug against his shoulder.

"What do you think you're doing?" Nate asked, half-amused but partly concerned his British keeper-of-directions had lost his mind.

The officer stood stock-still for a moment before looking around quizzically. "What?" he said, seemingly wakened from a dream. He slowly sat, then placed the gun behind him. "Shadows." He took his hat off and shook his head. "Never mind."

"Have a drink of water, Gunn, and throw some over your head while you're at it." Nate steered for the near shore. "We're going to rest in the shade for the remainder of the afternoon."

William insisted, "No, I'm fine—keep going. We've got to get to the orchids before the Spaniard. We don't know what problems he'll cause if he gets there first, but it's certain he *will* cause trouble."

"We don't know what we'll find when we get to this Sacred Land of yours, and it'll do neither of us any good if we're exhausted when we arrive. We need to be sharp." Nate pulled alongside the bank.

The American insisted on short rest stops from then on. William argued against it until Nate threatened to abandon him if he didn't agree.

Once William was rested, he realized that Bidwell was right. They continued to paddle through most of the night and day but took regular breaks.

On a clear morning, after traveling two weeks in this way, a huge tea-colored river entered from the west.

Looking at the map and trying to accurately recall what he had read, William said slowly, "Once the rivers mix, Jussieu's directions were to look for a small bay on the true left bank. Entering the bay, a beach and a landing should be visible. From the landing, the Frenchman wrote to proceed inland to a clearing." He offered, "My guess is we might find the guardians at either the landing or the clearing. That's where the path to the black orchid supposedly starts."

They continued downstream until the two rivers blended to a muddy brown. "We don't want to miss the blasted inlet," William said with concern, "it'd take forever if we have to paddle back upstream."

Back-paddling to slow their advance, they scrutinized every bit of shoreline. For the first couple of miles the jungle was an unbroken mass of green.

"There." Nate pointed with his paddle at a barely noticeable indentation in the left bank. They pushed past the rushes growing at the entrance and a wide bay opened before them, bordered by a light-brown beach.

"This has to be the place," William said eagerly.

"I don't know," the American said uncertainly, "seems overgrown to me."

Giant jade lilies as big as tea-tables covered the surface of the still cove.

"Incredible," William said. "We could walk on these if we wanted to."

"You were worried about pissing in the stream," Nate reflected, "and now you're talking about walking on lily pads." He steered between two of the oversized water plants. "Have you forgotten about the penis fish?"

A strange swirl in the water near the shore, followed by the top of what appeared to be an enormous snake, caused the green mats to rhythmically bob about.

"Anaconda, Admiral," Nate said, "largest snake in existence. They like to hunt in the water. Drown their prey."

William thought, *Penis fish. Man-eating snakes. One just can't accept everything this Yank throws out there.* He said scathingly, "Back in England, I was never briefed on any such animals, they were never mentioned."

"They'll be able to rewrite the curriculum if you ever get back."

They grounded on the sandy beach, and Pax was the first off. "If you're right and this is the place, and we manage to get what we came here for," Nate said, "I have a sneaking suspicion we're going to need the dugout again in a hurry." They dragged the heavy canoe further up the bank into the thick underbrush.

"I hope you're right about those directions," Nate said, "it doesn't look as if anyone has been here."

"It's the place," William said with a confidence he didn't feel. "But I agree with you. Jussieu wrote as if this place were a major river landing."

Nate started to cut vegetation but stopped when he struck something hard. He called out, "Give me a hand clearing this."

They cut roots and scraped thick moss away, uncovering large stone blocks sitting one on top of the other, forming a pillar.

William stood back. "It's definitely a man-made pier of some sort. At least now we can be sure this is the right place." He placed a hand on the stone, as if to reassure himself that it was really there. "How the hell did they build something like this here?"

Nate said, "They must have floated the stone here from the hills."

"That's hard to believe." Looking closer, William said incredulously, "There's a carving of some sort. Looks like a lion's head on the body of a horse."

Nate glanced around. "My guess is it's been abandoned for a while."

"Let's work our way inland and see if we can pick up the path Jussieu mentions."

The work would have been difficult enough without the presence of poisonous snakes, but they were everywhere. It took until late afternoon to hack their way through the thick undergrowth to the less dense rain forest beyond. Exhausted, they collapsed against the base of a small hill. The buzz of insects, the distant resonant howl of a monkey, and the high trilling of tropical birds filled the close humid air. They shared a drink and ate some fruit, along with the remainder of a bird they hadn't finished at breakfast.

"Be nice to have a cup of real English tea again," William said wistfully.

"My coffee doesn't measure up, Gunn?"

William ignored him and wiped his sleeve against his face in a futile gesture to keep the stinging sweat from his eyes. He said, "When God banished the snakes, they must have all landed here. I didn't think there were that many of the bloody bastards on the entire planet."

Nate shook his head. "I'd say snakes were more the devil's work. That is, if I believed in any of that."

"Not a God-fearing man, Yank?"

"I'm a man-fearing man." Nate took another long drink. "As I thought you'd be, Admiral, with all you've seen." He recognized the leaves of a small, unexceptional bush by his side as similar to those described by the old shaman in the Magdalena valley and plucked off a couple of small twigs with the greenery still attached. He put them in a side pouch of his bag.

Silent for a moment, William cleared his throat. "Back there, Bidwell, cutting those vines, I would have stepped right on the damn thing had you not said something."

Nate smiled. "Guess they didn't brief you on that back in England either. Viper. Probably came down on one of the vines. Bite from one of those is like watching yourself perish. You bleed from your mouth, your eyes, your ass, lose your mind from the pain—then you die." He stood wearily. "We should get going and find that path your Jussieu talks about. Make the most of the remaining sunlight."

William stretched and gazed around. The land was quite flat almost everywhere except for the slope they had been resting against. "This knoll is certainly strange," he observed. The British officer scratched away some of the debris covering the mound. Obscured under a thick cover of moss, soil, and tree roots was a stone step with deep grooves. "This is no hill," he said, shocked.

Scrambling to remove more of the overlying detritus, they gradually uncovered a series of stone steps with parallel grooves that appeared to run entirely around the mound.

"This is man-made too," Nate breathed, awestruck and mystified. He examined an image carved on a wide vertical stone. He hazarded, "Perhaps a temple or a tomb."

"Incredible," William uttered. Reflecting on their long journey downstream, he added, "It's beyond me how anyone could build something like this in the middle of nowhere."

"Look." Nate pointed.

From their new vantage point halfway to the top of the mound, they could see a derelict road not more than twenty yards away. It emerged from the twisted undergrowth in the direction of the river and continued straight on toward the clearing. It was at least thirty feet wide.

"If that track and this temple have become so overgrown with vegetation," Nate observed, "it's no wonder all that's left at the river is that stone pier."

"I wonder what happened to the people who built this."

"Maybe they've all gone on a holiday," Nate quipped. "Where's the dog?" Pax was nowhere to be seen. "Looks like that dog of yours is off looking for another meal."

William said, "He'll show up in his own good time." William wiped his brow again. "This old road is looking quite attractive."

"Took the words right out of my mouth, Gunn. Let's go." They followed the ancient path, and the relatively easy walking soon led to the edge of the clearing.

"Even though Jussieu's directions held true," William said, "I question why he didn't mention these structures or roads."

"Intentional oversight?" Nate said with a shrug.

They followed the path up a small rise to the edge of the open ground. Across the grassland a series of poles was visible in the waning light.

William said, "Looks like another Amazon-style greeting."

"Let's hope these are Jussieu's native guardians. We'll do exactly as we planned: offer them gifts with the promise of more if they lead us to the orchid. But it's hard to forget that Jussieu was the first and last white man to make it out of here alive."

William frowned. "You don't have to do this, Bidwell. I can continue on my own."

Sheer exhaustion, combined with the tension that had been building since they had left the river, compounded their irritability.

Nate replied, "And let you have the black orchid and the emerald for yourself?" The American stuck his chin out. "I'm afraid not, Gunn— you're not getting rid of me that easily. No one comes halfway around the world for a plant that most likely doesn't exist on the off chance it's the remedy for some obscure sickness. You're up to your neck in something else." He straightened. "Just don't get in my way when it comes to that gem."

The British officer bristled. "Look who's accusing me of being a sham—the great friend of the natives who's trying to steal their sacred gemstone. You're a hypocrite. If I don't survive," he fumed, "at least I'll know it was for a good reason."

"Hypocrite?" Nate seethed. "That emerald was taken from the Muzos in the first place, so the way I see it"—he stuck a finger in William's face—"it's up for grabs. But like I said, Admiral, don't get in my way."

Someone shouted. The American held his hand up for Gunn to be quiet. He cupped his hands near his mouth and shouted back.

"Are you insane?" William hissed.

"A stealthy approach in the Amazon would indicate an attack," Nate explained, "the more noise, the more likely the party has friendly intentions."

They stared intently across the field into the dark forest. Dim figures flickered vaguely at the margin of the jungle.

William's eyes narrowed.

Nate cautioned the officer, "Don't move. Take out that fancy medal the natives seem so impressed with, then keep your hands where they can be seen." He stared at the jungle. "I'll do all the talking, just like we planned."

There was another shout.

"The hell with that," William said, rising up. "I'm not going to sit here like a pigeon waiting to be plucked." He reached for the rifle. "What the . . ." The Brit's voice pinched off; he sat down and stared at the forest floor.

"Damn!" Nate arched against a sharp sting in the middle of his back.

Amazon wasp was his first thought. Halfway to the affected spot his arm froze and refused to obey his command to find the stinger; at the same time, his legs abruptly weakened and turned wobbly.

When the British officer crumpled to the ground in front of him, Nate knew. He would soon be unconscious as well. He managed to pull out his bear claw necklace with his other hand and became dizzy, then his vision narrowed. Small, black dots filled his sight. He couldn't breathe. Fruitlessly groping the air, he lost his balance, toppled backward, and rolled until he hit a tree. He couldn't move.

The last thing he remembered were voices speaking softly in a strange language.

CHAPTER 46

THE SACRED FOREST

William's heartbeat hammered painfully through his skull. Warm spittle ran from the corner of his mouth. Someone was shaking him awake, speaking words he didn't understand. *What in God's name is going on?* The last thing he could recall was speaking to Miriam, in the kitchen at Chatsworth. He attempted to sit upright. All he managed to do was to drag his face in the dirt.

Strong hands yanked him to a sitting position. He opened his eyes.

He looked into the grinning face of the American, who had already been moved to a sitting position when he awoke a quarter of an hour earlier. Bidwell's arms were bound behind his back.

"Smile, Gunn, and keep smiling—good-natured like," Nate said cheerfully, "as if we're on a holiday."

There were at least a score of Indians milling about, a good many of them women, armed with bows and arrows and blowguns. Nate and William were not going anywhere. A couple of large tapirs were carried past, hanging from poles.

"We're in luck. It appears we've stumbled across a group of hunters rather than a war party."

"What's so lucky about that?" The British officer didn't feel particularly lucky at the moment. His head was pounding.

"It means we're not dead."

"Correct me if I'm mistaken," William pointed out, "but according to the old leper, the other side of that coin was they bring us home and cut off our heads to stick them on a post somewhere."

"There's no point—white men don't have a spirit that's worth taking. Can't protect or bring luck to their village, so why bother?" Nate continued smiling broadly. "So far everything is going according to our plan. Meet the natives, get them to take us to your orchid. Well, I agree the introductions were a bit rough, yet here we are. Stop complaining and keep smiling."

The men and women were taller than any of the Indians of the Andes and the Magdalena. Many were at least the same size as the American and the British officer; others were taller. Their hair was also different, streaked with red dye, coarser and styled in a thick bowl cut and lightly plastered with clay. Their high cheekbones and long straight noses were painted ochre, while the bright yellow that was around their eyes and mouths gave them a fierce appearance.

Along with feathers and wildflowers, intricately designed ornaments of indigo adorned their olive-brown skin. Their clothing consisted of a short bolt of cotton they tied around their shoulders to cover their chests; loose cotton breeches reached just above the knees. A few had smallpox scars.

A muscular woman approached the captives. The tallest of the group, she was set apart from the others by a woven band of colorful plumes fastened about her forehead. Moving with an easy confidence, she was clearly the leader of the hunting party.

"Now we're getting somewhere," Nate whispered. He addressed her in the common language. "We come to trade for healing plants."

Either she did not understand, or she ignored him. She barked an order. To their shock, they were swiftly and efficiently stripped to their bare skin.

"What the hell?" William was embarrassed and confused. Standing naked in front of the assembled natives, several of whom were women, was awkward for them, but especially so for the Englishman.

"No problem, Gunn," Nate whispered out the side of his mouth, "probably looking for pox." Although in the warm jungle they had become used to seeing Indians in various stages of undress, this was very different. This was the first time *they* were undressed in front of a group of people.

She finished examining them and seemed to be satisfied. They were positioned in the middle of the armed troop and led across the field, passing between the rows of posts, each topped with a shriveled human head. Once past the posts, there was no mistaking the meaning of the line of bullhorn acacia bushes running along either side of the trail.

Of all the species of acacia, the bullhorn is armed with the longest and sharpest of thorns and is home to an extraordinarily large and aggressive ant possessing a legendary sting. Having a mutual relationship with the plant, the ants fiercely defend the acacia from every real and perceived attack.

The tribe had found a unique use for the bush. Almost every shrub contained a grim ornament of human remains in various stages of decay. Prisoners had been impaled; their flesh snared on the bullhorn's enormous thorns. Unable to escape the stinging, biting ants attacking their wounds, the cruelly twisted shapes were evidence of their agonized deaths.

Two of the acacias were empty.

For over an hour their captors marched them naked through the forest in the deepening evening until they came upon a fort built atop an embankment. A protective twelve-foot-high log wall enclosed the garrison and contained portals through which arrows could be fired.

"God Almighty, Gunn," Nate whispered, "this is different from anything I've ever seen. Indians in the jungle usually rely on natural camouflage to remain invisible, which makes this fort damned peculiar." A sharp blow from behind almost knocked him over and cautioned him to keep his mouth shut.

They entered the fortification through a gate and were greeted by several guards and a pack of dogs. A large gray dog separated from the others and ran up to lick William's hand.

"Pax!" William said. When they were prodded onward, the big dog rejoined the pack.

"The loyalty of a British mutt," Nate ventured out the side of his mouth.

They passed a row of round thatched-roof huts that ran along the inside perimeter of the compound. A couple of minutes later they reached a large oval hut at the far end of the fort. Many Indians were congregated around a nearby cooking pit, smoking and talking while preparing a meal. A variety of shrunken heads dangled from several poles close by. The newcomers and those assembled exchanged greetings, the captives momentarily forgotten.

"Some of those heads seemed to be white, Yank."

"Fashions change."

Two of the guards abruptly pushed the captives forward to be put on display. Those gathered kept their distance, though, and Nate couldn't be certain, but thought he felt disdain from them. Then the guards placed William and Nate inside the oval hut and unbound their arms. Their clothing was returned; soon after, plates were brought along with food on a large platter. Several armed Indians were positioned outside.

William turned over a finely decorated plate. "How did they come by these all the way out here?"

"I'll admit it's puzzling," Nate replied, holding up a ceramic dish that contained a small smoked fish. "But that's not the only strange thing. This fort has to be protecting *something*."

"Like a black orchid?" William suggested. "But they don't seem at all like the tribe the Frenchman described," he said thoughtfully, "or like people who build great monuments in the jungle." He shook his head. "This fort is pretty simple; plus, there are only warriors here. I estimate at least two score of them, but it looks like it was built to hold at least three times that many. There are no children, so I have to believe this is a guard post. What do you think?"

"We must be on their frontier." Nate scrutinized William for a reaction. "Strange your friend Jussieu didn't record any of this—or say why they kept him alive."

"I've been wondering why they're keeping *us* alive," William said. "I'm not so sure I want to hang around to find out."

"Let's sit tight for the time being, Admiral. We really don't have any choice: we don't have supplies and they're guarding us too closely. Believe me," Nate stressed, "we'd already be dead if they didn't like what they saw when they stripped us back there." He was thoughtful. "If this *is* a guard post, as you think, they must be acting under orders. Since we passed their initial test, I'm betting we'll be taken to their superiors, and that should lead us to your plant. I have a feeling the leader understood what I said back there about wanting to trade." Nate didn't bother to add that he expected the emerald could also be found where the orchids were. "Also, if we behave, when it does come time to escape, they won't be keeping as close an eye on us."

"As much as I hate to admit it," William said with some reluctance, "you're probably right." He figured there was no need to tell the American that Jussieu's diary or the map didn't contain any directions from here on. All the Frenchman had written was that the guardians guided him through the Sacred Land. And these natives gave the impression of guardians more than anyone else they'd run into so far. "Seems like we're stuck with them."

The ground shook, but the vibrations ceased as suddenly as they had begun.

"Should we be worried about these?"

Only when he exhaled did Nate realize he had been holding his breath. "I'm not sure what they mean. Nothing much we can do about them anyway."

The next morning, the leader arrived with a company of guards. Using sign language, Nate indicated that they came in friendship and wished to trade. Again, she ignored him and signaled for the guards to bring them along.

"You're not getting through to them at all," William mocked. "Do you really have even the foggiest idea of what you're doing, Bidwell, or are you just making this up as you go along?"

With studied innocence, Nate winked.

The guards led their captives to a lodge in the middle of the compound. Inside, a circle of poles was decorated with the pervasive shrunken heads. Nate said, "I'm beginning to think there are more of these than there are people left in the Amazon."

Under the canopy of woven palm leaves that overhung the front of the lodge, an elderly Indian sat. An ancient wisp of a man, he wore an elaborate headdress and heavy rings dangled from his ears, stretching the lobes. Vertical yellow and red stripes decorated his cloth wrap. Like other rare Indian survivors of smallpox, his face was badly pitted, evidence of the infection brought by European explorers. He held a rattle made of human hair, bird feathers, and claws. The warrior captains of the stockade assembled around him.

Nate signed his intentions but was once more ignored. William glared at him.

The leader signed at them, and Nate said, "I believe it's time to strip again. Whatever the reason, we'd better be fast about it."

The guards slowly turned them around while the leader ran her hands lightly over both their bodies.

"Bloody hell, what are they looking for?" the British officer said, not only because this was the second time he'd been exposed, but because of the careful scrutiny of this examination.

"Beats me."

She stopped and lingered at the scars on their shoulders. She pointed out the marks, which prompted a heated exchange with the shaman. This ended when the woman lifted Nate's bear claw necklace over his head and put it around the shaman's neck. The polished bear claws shone white against the wrinkled walnut skin. This pleased the old priest. The Yank continued to smile cheerfully.

William asked unsurely, "Why do you think they were looking at our inoculation scars?"

Nate said, "It beats me."

Their untouched baggage was placed on the ground in front of them. A warrior stepped up and rummaged carelessly through the American's gear, disdainfully kicking aside Nate's blunderbuss and pistol.

The shaman sat and fingered his rattle while the captains debated over the white men's belongings. The old man stared intently at the gold medallion hanging from William's neck. He indicated for William to draw closer. Not near enough for his liking, the old man stood unsteadily on spindly heron legs and hobbled over to the British officer, never taking his eyes off the Saint Christopher medal.

The shaman lifted the gleaming medallion. He carefully turned the gold relic over and held it aloft to a shaft of sunlight. Fascinated, the old man loudly proclaimed something. He let the medal fall back on the British officer's chest.

William said quietly, "He's obviously an admirer of the patron saint of travelers."

"Either that," Nate added, "or he's seen it before."

To the British officer's great relief, the leader indicated they were to get dressed. When they were ready, she brought them to the midday meal, where she sat them on the ground to either side of a small but ferocious-looking chap.

William whispered, "Looks like he's eaten something disagreeable."

The surly Indian's meal was interrupted when the guards placed two native prisoners in front of him. The two prisoners differed from their captors in their much smaller stature, patterns of body paint, penis sheaths, and lack of clothing.

One of the prisoners was clearly terrified, his shoulders slumped, his eyes downcast. He sweated profusely and was nauseated. The other stood straight, head held high, defiant. The frightened man had a wound on his upper arm that was mercilessly buzzed by insects.

The shaman arrived, accompanied by a young woman holding a ceramic basin and a young man carrying what looked to be a long pipe. The holy man approached the two Indian captives and scrutinized each in turn, then held his new necklace and started a circular shuffle dance around them.

He stopped abruptly in front of the blistered and bleeding native. Shouting in his face, he clapped him hard on the wounded arm. The man screamed and fell to the ground. Attempting to intervene, his companion was immediately clubbed into unconsciousness.

Still moaning, the wounded Indian was dragged to a pond and unceremoniously pitched headfirst into the water. The man screamed and attempted to claw his way out. Shocked, Nate and William watched the water foam around the prisoner.

The shaman joined the scowler and both men enjoyed their meal, bantering with the other Indians resting on the ground nearby. No one paid the least attention to the thrashing, shrieking man in the now red water. The ferocious little man traded pleasantries with the shaman and offered food to the foreigners.

The screams reached a crescendo, then quieted as the victim's head slid slowly under the surface, an appalling fleshless arm cast dreadfully toward the sky in a final futile protest, before disappearing entirely beneath the seething surface.

"No question about what's in *that* pond," Nate muttered, having seen starving river piranhas strip a boar to just bones in minutes.

Nate tried to communicate with the two men, but the glowering native clearly signed that the American and the Brit would be leaving. The shaman smiled and put a finger in his nostril.

Nate appeared concerned. "Gunn, be prepared to have some powder blown up your nose, because you're not going to have much say in the matter."

William asked, "Why?"

"I believe they've decided to pass us up the chain of command, only they don't want us to know the way. Recall the Frenchman's hazy description of the Sacred Land?" Nate muttered, "I'm thinking he couldn't see a hole in a ladder by the time they led him through this place."

William shifted his attention back to the shaman, who had finished eating and was now chanting, his hands held over the potion in the basin. As the old man droned on, Nate coughed and slipped into his mouth the twigs and leaves he had plucked from the bush near the ruins. He began to slowly chew. *With luck,* he thought, *this should keep the visions in check. Long enough, anyway, to note the way back here for our escape. It's my turn to lead this show.*

The old priest ceased his chanting and placed a portion of the mixture from the basin into the bowl at the end of the pipe stem. He signed for William to come closer.

With a last look at the Yank, William leaned in. The native priest inserted one end of the device in the British officer's nose, then forcefully blew on the other.

The intensity of the blast caught William by surprise. He would have fallen over if the shaman's assistant hadn't caught him. While the assistant held him, the shaman blasted another bowlful up William's other nostril. When they released him, the British officer fell, then vomited several times. The pain in his nose faded to a distant ache.

He didn't hear the laughter of the assembled warriors, nor did he know if his eyes were open or closed. A pleasant shimmering violet color ran throughout his body. A being surrounded by a radiant golden halo offered him its hand. Accepting the warm hand, he floated through a kaleidoscope of changing patterns, shapes, and hues.

William never remembered the guard leading him away. The American would only later tell him that he looked like an idiot.

When it was Nate's turn, he swallowed the liquid from the chewed twigs. The pipe was inserted, and the shaman blasted the snuff up the American's nose; the Yank threw his arms out like a rag doll, fell flat on his back, and rolled back and forth several times, mumbling incoherently, all to the great amusement of those watching.

Half a dozen warriors and the shaman's two assistants picked up both captives and started through the jungle into the heart of the forest. The position of the sun showed they were heading northeast, directly away from the river. In front of him, Nate could see that a trickle of dried blood ran from the dark hair of the surviving Indian prisoner and down his back. The man's hands were bound, but he was neither blindfolded nor drugged. This did not bode well for his future.

Several dogs accompanied the band, Pax among them.

William entered the familiar space of their Chatsworth kitchen and stood watching for a few moments: Sarah was helping her mother prepare a meal. She was much taller than he remembered. Miriam stood near the open window, humming her favorite tune, her hair dazzling in the afternoon light. With a flash of understanding and excitement, he realized light was color. He'd have to tell Miriam and Sarah—they would surely want to know this.

He called loudly, but they were either unwilling or unable to acknowledge him.

An immense dark shadow fell over the vision. Distressed, William's stomach churned in the darkness, and he struggled to catch his breath.

The guards increased their pace. As best he could, Nate noted landmarks along the way. Cisterns were located wherever another path joined theirs, and they were always on the west side of the path. There was an immensely broad tree at the junction with the main thoroughfare, and it became apparent that the route they had started out on was not a main road at all, but merely a side track. The thoroughfare was wide, paved, and obviously well-used, not unlike the Inca highway. They joined the main road and passed several companies of warriors going in the opposite direction, their voices subdued in the somber stillness. The ever-present withered heads fastened to the tops of the poles they passed remained mute observers of the company. Judging by the sun, Nate figured it was about noon when they overtook several imposing mounds covered with moss and vines, similar to those they had seen near the river landing. Smaller paths continued to occasionally enter or intersect the road.

Late in the afternoon, they walked through a remarkable forest of stately gray trees. Like solemn cathedral arches, their massive graphite roots extended dozens of feet above the ground, an occasional fig tree dispersed among them. At the far edge of the forest, under a particularly colossal giant, the leader stopped and ordered them to sit. Nate would never forget the sight that greeted them at the edge of that vast wood.

Across an expanse of cultivated fields was a city. Judging by the bulk and length of the surrounding palisade and the lofty tops of some of the structures just visible above the fortification, it might have been the largest city they had seen in South America.

Situated on an elevated man-made plateau, the city was high enough to remain dry even in the worst of flooding. The material used for raising the foundation must have been excavated from the deep moat running around the exterior of the high wall. Over this water-filled trench, a drawbridge led to a main gate. Further along, dugouts entered and departed the city on a large canal which crossed the wide fields before disappearing into the jungle beyond.

A smaller channel ran along the edge of the forest, between their group and the city. During the dry season, this conduit might have provided irrigation to the fields through a series of parallel ditches.

The British officer tried to shake the ache out of his head, but that only made it worse. It took several attempts to open his eyes before he could see.

"Where are we?" William blinked in the late-afternoon light. He tried to swallow. His throat felt like he had ingested sandpaper. If he had not been propped against the hard surface of a tree trunk, he would have fallen over.

Nate gave the Brit a close glance. A pair of clear blue eyes met his. This was encouraging, an indication the potion was wearing off.

"We're deep in the Sacred Forest. And you've never seen anything like this, Admiral, in your life. And probably never will again. Look."

Seemingly hewn out of the very jungle, the ramparts and spires of an immense settlement rose above the clearing. William shook his head. The apparition remained.

"Is this another vision, Bidwell? Are we still grogified?"

"I don't think so. Appears real enough to me. Somehow," Nate added thoughtfully, "I don't think a few trinkets are going to impress these folks."

In the early-evening light, warriors from the city arrived and warmly greeted the frontier Indians who had escorted the captives. They gave several bundles of supplies to the border guards and spoke together, pointing at times to the two white men. After a few minutes, the border guards picked up the supplies and left.

Instead of drugging Nate and William, the newcomers bound their wrists and prepared to blindfold them.

William nodded toward the captured Indian. "Looks like they trust him more than us."

The defiant Indian's eyes were not covered and his hands were untied.

"We'll see about that," Nate said gravely. "Just remember, I'll do all the talking. Our story is we come only for trade, and we're not staying."

"Sure," William said sarcastically, "that's worked really well so far."

They started off. Nate could sense they were not going toward the city but were going around it to the other side. It seemed to take forever to get past the fields. At one point, it was apparent from the water sounds and boatmen that they were crossing over a rather large waterway, most likely the canal they had seen earlier in the distance. Blindfolded, they could only tell they were in the forest again by the sickly sweet aroma of vegetation.

The soft path took a gentle upward slope. The splashing of a stream drowned out the banter of the guards. The ground became firm, and they were compelled to lift their feet as if ascending a long flight of steep stairs. A distant rumble grew louder. The sound of rushing water echoed as if coming from a narrow space. They shivered in a moist breeze.

Orders were shouted over the roar of crashing water, and they came to an abrupt halt. Strong hands seized their arms. The very air vibrated with the beat of deep, pulsating drumming.

The pounding suddenly stopped.

Their blindfolds were removed.

William and Nate stared into an unwavering forest of eight-foot-long lances, so close that the small burrs on the razor-sharp metal tips of the weapons were clearly visible.

CHAPTER 47

JUNGLE SOVEREIGNS

Even though they were standing, the American frontiersman and the British officer had to crane their necks upward to see those holding the lances.

These warriors were different.

The powerfully built men and women facing them wore bandolier-like leather straps across their chests. Over small cotton garments similar to an apron, short swords hung in leather scabbards from each of their waists. It was as if these imposing warriors had dropped out of the sky to alight in the midst of the Amazon. Reinforcing this impression were their metallic weapons, an oddity in a jungle, where metal objects were rarely found. No one moved or spoke.

"Still a good sign?" William whispered out the side of his mouth.

"I'm not so sure," Nate ventured, "we may be right stewed."

The natural flagstone base of the small clearing was wet with spray from the waterfall thundering into the emerald pool behind them. The deep water was so clear that the boulders on the bottom of the basin were plainly visible in the flickering torchlight.

Without warning, the drummers behind the warriors beat on their jaguar-skin drums, the rhythm and intensity steadily increasing. The tall warriors stood to attention, their long lances held upright at their sides.

The native prisoner wrenched free from his guards and flopped down, arms outstretched, face pressed against the flagstones. The guards kneeled and touched their foreheads to the ground.

"What the blazes?" William said.

A curt blow from a lance forced them into a kneeling position.

Between the two rows of warriors, backlit by strategically placed torches, the rulers of the Sacred Land appeared. The queen stood beside her king. Her dark braided hair was secured by a cap inlaid with sea-green beryls. A thick gold torc, an ornament consisting of a band of twisted metal, was fastened about her neck, and a jagged white scar on her forearm contrasted with her brown skin. A boar's tusk amulet left no doubt as to her skill with a bow and a blade.

Naked from the waist up, the king wore a striking high headdress with a bright lime fringe and a circlet of canary and crimson festooned with alternating blue and scarlet toucan feathers. Under the plumage, his thick black hair was shot with silver streaks. Shimmering golden armbands encircled his firm biceps and forearms and a colorful woven shawl was thrown over one shoulder and hung over his chest and down his back.

Clad in leather aprons, with long swords at their sides, they were tall, majestic, and grim-visaged and had an elegant, aristocratic bearing. They were like mythical icons from a time that had been lost in Europe since Arthur and Guinevere.

"I don't know which I should feel most—amazed or terrified," William uttered.

Nate whispered, "Probably both."

With each stride, torchlight reflected off the polished bands encircling the arms of the king and queen, piercing the darkness with golden echoes. The chiseled features of the sovereigns betrayed little emotion.

The drums grew louder.

The queen stopped in front of the bound captives, one hand on the hilt of her sword, the other on her hip. Her dark eyes bored into them.

The drumming reached a climax, then ceased.

The king gestured for them to rise. Prods from the warriors' lances brought the captives promptly to their feet. The sovereign turned, approached the pool, and beckoned them over. Bordering either side of the booming waterfall was a stand of tall red trees that shimmered with silvery leaves: cinchonas, the fever bark tree.

One enormous cinnamon-colored tree stood at the edge of the pool. As they neared, the light reddish-brown color of the broad trunk resolved into every hue of the rainbow. William wondered, *Is this it? The singular tree described by Jussieu, host to the plant which prompted this impossibly dangerous journey?*

The king pointed upward—his calloused hand was missing two fingers.

Halfway to the top of the tree was a large limb with a wide black scar. The burn damage started at the junction with the trunk and continued up the limb for ten to fifteen feet.

The remnant of an old lightning strike. Jussieu's words came flooding back: "where an old lightning strike had most damaged the bark."

Anchored to the damaged limb and barely visible in the early-evening twilight, damp in the spray of the waterfall, magnificent midnight-black flowers crowned a profuse group of silver-green orchids.

"We're here," William said and sighed. The object on which rested all his hopes for his daughter's recovery lay almost within his grasp.

"I guess I owe you an apology, Admiral," Nate said. "There they be." The sight of the fabled orchids and their prior discovery of the artifacts of an earlier advanced civilization made him feel that something very strange was happening, not just here, but throughout the Amazon. "These people aren't going to hand anything over, Gunn, especially to us."

Frustrated, William gestured extravagantly at the orchids, then at the monarchs, before Nate smacked his arms down. "What do you think you're doing?" the American chided.

The king ignored them, but the queen nodded to one of her servants.

A warrior, the servant had a noticeable blemish running along the back of her leg. Carrying a black lance with a nasty triangular tip, she stepped forward and turned a menacing eye on the prisoner who remained prone on the flagstones. She jabbed him with the blunt end of her weapon and indicated for him to climb the tree. Only when she lowered the sharp end of the spear to the center of his chest, did he slowly rise and turn toward the tree, picking up his pace after being given a sharp kick of encouragement.

William whispered, "That's what I was doing, Yank—getting through to them, and a lot better than you did."

"We'll see."

The prisoner grasped a branch of the tree and started to climb. A faint, unfamiliar buzzing filled the air. Halfway to his goal, the man froze. Around the next tree limb above him curled a small venomous snake. The green triangular head peered down while its yellow tongue tasted the air. The prisoner looked to the ground. Several of the guards had notched arrows and were beginning to raise their bows.

With lightning speed, the man jabbed out and clasped the asp by the neck, the writhing snake coiling about his arm even as he popped the head off with his thumb. Shaking free the decapitated snake, he resumed his ascent.

The humming increased and continued to grow. Almost fifty feet off the ground, the climber approached the orchids. From the foliage directly above, a swarm of monstrous black insects erupted, each as long and as fat as a man's thumb.

"Good God!" William said.

The rippling black throng descended on their victim. Shrieking in pain, arms flailing frantically, he fell backward, howling like a tormented animal. With a thud, the flailing figure struck the rocks at the water's edge. The giant wasps continued to sting the corpse relentlessly, the shattered body rapidly swelling to a grotesque shape. The huge insects only retreated when the guards approached with smoldering torches and drove the swarm back into the tree.

CHAPTER 48

NEMESIS

"We're here, all right," Nate mused, and added, "best of luck with those wasps, Gunn." Accustomed as William was to the horrors of war, this was altogether different.

Warriors took up positions behind them. The prisoners' hands remained bound.

The king stepped forward, accompanied by the queen. Nate glanced up and received a swift whack from behind. He got the message and averted his eyes.

To their surprise, the female servant emptied the contents of their packs in front of them. They hadn't seen any of their gear since the previous evening and figured that everything was gone.

The queen gave their items a desultory push with her foot, followed by an arrogant sneer. The king nodded to his wife, who raised William's head by his chin.

Her eyebrows arched when she saw the gold Saint Christopher medal; she looked to the king, searchingly. The king spoke to the servant by his side, who left immediately.

"They've seen that thing before, Gunn," Nate whispered. "This could either be bad for us, or extremely bad for us."

"What do you mean?"

"If they think we're something other than men, say spirits or such, we'll not get to see another sunrise."

"They don't seem to be the type to be overly concerned with spirits."
A kick silenced them.

The servant, returned from his mission, spoke to the rulers.

The king walked over and stopped directly in front of Nate. His face almost touched the American's. He stood unmoving, his mouth down-turned, and stared into Nate's eyes. Nate felt this was a critical moment; his mouth went dry. He clenched his fists to stave off the tremor that tried to run up his spine. William labored to loosen his bindings; they chafed his wrists as he worked at the stubborn cords.

After several tense seconds, the king drew out a long, finely honed blade. He held it beside the American's face.

With a single, swift motion the blade flashed.

The bindings on Nate's wrists parted.

Next, William's hands were released. The British officer rubbed his sore wrists.

The monarch waved dismissively. Without another word or a glance, the rulers of the Sacred Land departed, accompanied by their royal guards.

"They must have found the other medal, the one the Sheridans gave their son," William ventured quietly. In the absence of the royals, the warriors didn't seem to mind if the captives talked together. "He must have made it this far."

"Gave them pause, Gunn, seeing the same exact amulet. I've told you that this sort of thing's very strong medicine."

"I've decided, Bidwell, you have not a single benighted idea what you're talking about."

The guards pushed them roughly along the path, away from the waterfall and the orchids. Torches along the high palisades of the Amazonian city illuminated the road leading back to the settlement.

Outside the entrance to the city, a line of the dreaded acacia bushes was visible in the faint torchlight. Just past the bushes, the guards led them over to a deep black hole surrounded by a low wall. One of the guards dropped a torch into the pit and signed for them to come closer. The bottom of the hole quivered with countless snakes slithering away from the burning torch, over one another and through piles of yellow bones.

"You really shouldn't have gone to the trouble," Nate said to the guards.

They received sharp prods from the blunt end of spears to get them moving again. William winced. "Your signing is useless, Yank; these people speak with jabs and kicks."

A broad avenue led through the main entrance gates; gray ramparts overgrown with vegetation loomed above them.

"These walls are amazing." William whistled softly. "And I've only seen stone like that once or twice before—in Europe."

Just inside the city entrance, at the end of an ancient boulevard, stood an imposing sand-colored stone pyramid three stories high and at least four hundred feet in length at its base. The three levels of the edifice were terraced to a smaller flat space at the very top, upon which stood a vast stone carving. The remains of the weathered carving resembled an enormous feline, perhaps a jaguar or cougar. Elaborate carvings also graced the building's multiple entrances but were far too eroded to reveal the sculptor's intention.

"There must be a score of these buildings," William exclaimed.

Nate stared, overwhelmed. "Our plan to trade for the orchids and then get out of here is going to need some serious rethinking."

William said, "Never was much of a plan in the first place. The most important thing now is where they're taking us."

"Hopefully for a meal. Now that it seems we're safe for at least another day, I could eat a full-grown tapir." He signed at one of the guards, using what he hoped was the universal sign for food. He was prodded forward for his effort.

"Good try, Bidwell."

"Look at that building."

The structure immediately in front of them had fared little better than its carvings. Almost a third of the entire left side was ruined, the ground strewn with blocks of rubble and broken lintels from where the walls had caved in.

The guards continued to lead them through the city. They passed many other stone structures, most of which were in the same disrepair, although portions of some appeared to be in use, and showed signs of activity.

"Things seem to have taken a definite turn for the worse here," William observed quietly.

"That's an understatement, Gunn."

"I wonder what this is," William said of a large round stone lying flat on the ground with regular notches and raised edges.

"Probably used to tell the seasons," Nate guessed, "and that round tower over there was some sort of observatory."

William frowned at the American but didn't say anything.

"What?" Nate said, pretending to be offended.

"You're making that up," William said derisively, "you have no idea what that is."

But whether tombs or temples, most appeared abandoned. Several buildings constructed of regular masonry blocks were still intact and closely guarded. These caught the American's attention. He thought, *A look inside one of those could prove very interesting.*

In between the scattered stone constructions were brick houses of the upper caste, and the adobe and thatch cottages of the laboring class. Some of these appeared to be occupied; the inhabitants stared at the strange white men being marched past. The warrior-guards ignored the commoners, but traded pleasantries with other warriors along the way, occasionally stopping to chat.

Overall, the city seemed vaguely underpopulated, leaving the definite impression that a simple rural settlement had been thrown together among the stately ruins of an earlier, more noble city.

"I'll admit I'm out of my depth in this Sacred Land," Nate breathed. "I've never seen anything like it. Earlier today, before you came to your senses, I saw a lot more on the way in. Something strange happened here."

"Are you talking about how few people there seem to be?" William asked.

"More than that," Nate continued in a whisper. "On the way here, we passed crops you wouldn't expect to see. Like a plantation of cacao trees and a field of ripened maize. Just before the forest ended, there were rows of very straight trees. They were dripping a white fluid from cuts made in the bark. And where the soil was being tilled," Nate said, awe in his voice, "it was black and deep. It had to be man-made.

"There were also channeling systems providing irrigation for the fields, along with canals, roads, and more of those strange mounds. I saw old kilns, almost overgrown, which must have been used for making bricks. And think about it: the volcanic tuff and limestone used for the city walls and structures had to be transported all the way from the foothills. I'm telling you, with this sparse population, there's no way they could do all this."

"How the hell did you see so much? I was barely conscious."

"For God's sake, Admiral, pipe down before we wind up like those two prisoners." The American added, "I may have forgotten to mention that I took something that lessens the effects of most of these potions."

"Then why didn't you give *me* some?" William was red in the face. "I still haven't stopped puking from that stuff they blew up my nose."

"Because now, Gunn, I know the way out of here and you don't. So, when you get those orchids, remember who's in charge."

"You son of a bitch, I should have come on my own when I had the chance."

"Perhaps, but then you would never have made it this far, would you? And you most certainly would never get to see dear old England again."

William detested the thought of having to depend on the American for their escape but didn't see any way around it.

"C'mon, Gunn." Nate grinned. "Lighten up. We're here as planned—the promised land. Look." Nate nodded and drew his attention to several immense buildings, which could have been temples, situated around a small lake. An outlet stream controlled by a weir ran to a canal. There were many such canals, lined with stone and spanned by small bridges, passing through the city and into the jungle.

"I hope you're taking all this in, Bidwell. You're supposed to be our guide."

"Not to worry, Gunn, I have it all under control."

"That's what I'm worried about."

Nate's instincts as a tracker hadn't abandoned him. He'd easily kept a mental record of landmarks along the way, including waterways, the roads they had used, and the distance they had come.

He stared at the flowing water. He reasoned that the canals had to be fed from a river someplace upstream and must empty into an even bigger river somewhere downstream.

The guards led them over a bridge that spanned one of the larger waterways. Steps hewn into the stone embankment on one side led down to a landing on the canal where several dugouts of various sizes were moored. On the other side of the bridge, a short way down a wide path, was a long brick structure resembling a warehouse.

Flanked by several warriors, a woman emerged from the building. She carried a silver platter on which rested silver flasks and an array of golden objects. She gazed at the captives and caught William's eye. She stopped abruptly, and the warriors around her immediately came to a halt, their stoic countenances betraying no emotion. For the briefest of moments, she stared at the yellow-haired stranger before continuing on.

"Where do you think all this came from, Yank?" William wondered. "And where did the people go?"

"Our concern at the moment is that there are enough warriors to make our escape interesting," he remarked. "So, let's just keep our eyes open and figure out a new plan for how to get what we came for, and how to get out."

The guards led them through a gateway in a thick hedge to a long sunken courtyard. In the vivid light of torches, several long tables were visible, nearly covering the open area. Two chairs ornately carved with intricate animal characters were prominently positioned at the head of the first table. Tall warriors with short metal swords at their sides arrived; they were adorned with gold and jewels, and soon almost all the places at the tables were taken.

When the Brit and the American entered, many curious eyes turned to them. Nate and William were led off to one side, close to the first table, not far from the ornate chairs, but were seated on a rough-hewn wooden bench.

"Seems we're not exactly the guests of honor," William remarked.

The sonorous beating of drums announced the arrival of the queen. All conversation ceased. Preceded by a half dozen of her personal guard, she strode in, head held high, projecting proud authority in every measured step. Silver bangles ornamented her bronze forearms and a huge colorful headdress interwoven with rare bird feathers offset her heavy gold hoop earrings. The gold pendant hanging from her neck danced in the light of the torches—a gold Saint Christopher medal.

Preceding her, straining on a thick leash, a midnight-black panther coldly calculated its surroundings through green eyes. The queen took her place by the chair at the head of the table, the jaguar at her feet.

Then the king entered, accompanied by a companion.

"What the bloody hell?" William blurted.

Nate was speechless.

Accompanying the king of the Sacred Land was Captain Ernesto Rodrigo Marquez.

Almost as shocking as seeing the Spaniard who had tried to kill Nate was the sight of the enormous emerald hanging about the king's neck. Far exceeding the American's wildest expectations, the precious gemstone was larger than a man's fist. It was set in gold and glistened a deep, bright green.

William whispered, "Your emerald, I presume?"

Nate gave William a hard glance. He had no idea how the Spaniard had arrived before them. This was indeed a dangerous moment in a dangerous game. The American smiled.

"*Salud, amigo*," Nate called out.

The queen's guards immediately drew their short swords. Speaking out of turn in the royal presence at such an event was punishable by death. The leader froze at the queen's light touch on her arm. To the amazement of William and Nate, the queen said in Spanish, "That won't be necessary, Ismerai."

The king added in Spanish, "You already know each other. Good." He said solemnly, "We feast tonight, a celebration to welcome our new friends." He lifted his cup. The green jewel shifted on his chest, scattering sparkling rays of emerald light.

The queen held up her drink. "Your sovereigns offer *salud* to everyone."

The Spaniard glared at the American and the Brit.

When the monarchs sat, everyone followed suit, the Spaniard on the king's right. A young server placed ceramic bowls on a small table in front of William and Nate.

William asked the server in Spanish, "How is it you speak our language?"

"Men from river stay, teach," the young man replied.

"They must stay a long time to teach you."

"Some stay, some go." He waved dismissively and moved on.

"I'll bet they go," Nate said dryly. "Right into the snake pit."

William examined the table settings. "That's odd. The last time I saw delftware like this was in a duke's drawing room."

"It's what's on those plates that interests me." Nate felt like there was a hole where his stomach should be. He emptied something that appeared to be chicken onto his plate and reached for another bowl.

At the head table, they saw Marquez scowl.

"What's he so annoyed about?" William whispered.

"Probably delighted to see us again," Nate said.

The Spaniard lifted his cup and toasted the sovereigns so loudly that heads turned at the far end of the furthest table. "To the future friendship of our two great countries."

"You'd think he was trying to be heard in Madrid." William picked up a bowl of something that looked like monkey brains.

Marquez and the king drank deeply, quickly emptying their cups. The queen merely lifted hers, then put it down. They chatted and ate and paid scant attention to their new captives.

The Spaniard rose and approached William and Nate.

He greeted them in English. "I told you I would beat you here. Actually"—Marquez laughed gaily—"I never thought I'd see either one of you again. Like some animals, you heathens must have many lives."

He shoved a tortoise egg in his mouth. "While you were struggling to get here," he said quietly between chews, "I have been courting these people, as I said I would." He swallowed, then drank. After wiping his mouth with the back of his hand, he straightened and continued in English. "Once I baptize these pagans, they'll become our slave kingdom in the jungle, for my sovereign to do with as he pleases." His smile broadened. "It's unfortunate you won't be alive to see it. I'll make sure of that."

When the sovereigns glared in their direction, the American and the British officer laughed as if they were having the time of their lives.

Marquez walked back to the head table and, with a flourish, disrupted the conversation by offering the queen the neck fat of the howler monkey, a prized treat. She accepted the interruption with a thin smile, allowing the delicacy to be placed on a side plate. It sat on the table untouched.

William and Nate ate like men who hadn't seen food in weeks. It had only been a day and a half, but after being drugged, William had left most of the contents of his stomach by the side of the path. They were almost finished when they overheard the Spaniard.

"You see," he said, with a laugh, "they even eat like beasts. These are dangerous men, Your Highness, not to be trusted. They are infidels, unbelievers."

William's lip twitched. Nate put a hand on his arm and answered in Spanish, "Merely a sign, Your Majesties, of the appreciation we have for the excellent food you have served us."

William chimed in, "My king's table would be honored to have such wonderful fare. I send you King George's greeting and his offer of eternal friendship, along with his invitation to visit our country as his guests."

Nate said under this breath, "Well done, Gunn." He raised his mug. "To your continued good health, Spaniard. May we meet again."

Ignoring him, Marquez pronounced, "My Queen, I wonder that your border guards brought them here. These men could have brought the great sickness."

The queen shared a knowing look with her husband, who nodded to Ismerai. "Have our new friends join us."

Surprised to be seated at the queen's side, William and Nate were even more taken aback when she offered them the piece of neck fat Marquez had presented to her earlier.

CHAPTER 49

⊙URSELVES ᴬLONE

At one time the great empire of the Amazon with its vassal kingdoms stretched from the foothills of the Andes to the Atlantic Ocean with a population numbering in the millions. They maintained a vibrant trade with their neighbors, the Incas, as well as with their distant Mesoamerican cousins, the Aztecs. But even before either of these great civilizations came into being, the Amazonian empire had emissaries in the courts of the early Mayans.

Crowning the valuable export crops of the empire was the rare black orchid. The Amazonians nurtured and protected the plant, grown in their Sacred Land, the heart of their empire. The orchid was treasured as a cure for all known illnesses—that is, until the white man came.

The first European explorers in the sixteenth century introduced new diseases to the previously unexposed indigenous population. Sickness spread uncontrollably in the warm, moist climate of the rain forest. Native remedies were completely ineffective against the new maladies. Both young and old of every class died horrible deaths; the few that survived were disfigured for life.

The rulers were forced to take extreme measures. A strict isolation was imposed: any explorers entering the Amazon were killed, as were any infected tribesmen. Indeed, anyone who showed the slightest sign of disease was put to death. Men, women, children—none were spared.

Still, the decimation continued until their once-great civilization withered to a single, decaying city.

The empire of the Amazon was teetering on the edge—one small push was all it would take for them to become just another lost legend of the jungle.

The king and queen entered their quarters in a small, well-kept section of the royal palace that had remained intact. The entire far side of the top floor of the once-stately stone structure had collapsed in one of the frequent quakes, crushing the two floors beneath giving it the appearance of a single story. The partially dilapidated building was a mere shadow of its former splendor.

The leader of the rulers' personal guard checked the watch posted outside, front and back.

"Thank you as always, Ismerai, for your service," the queen said, dismissing her. "The king and I will discuss your counsel regarding the barbarians."

When her personal guard had left, the queen said to her husband, "Ismerai tells me they captured one at the border yesterday with the sickness, a cousin to the Jivaro."

The king stood opposite the entrance and looked out over the royal gardens lit by the rising moon. When he spoke, his voice wavered. "The sun went its way for countless years, and our people flourished. The rains came and went and came again, and still we tamed the jungle and all its beasts." He considered the smallpox scar on his arm. "Except one, it seems."

The gently waving fronds of the tall palm trees surrounding the grounds cast faint moon shadows against the far wall of the royal bedroom. Sentries on their rounds strode past the broad stone stairway leading down to the garden.

"We were celebrated by our allies and feared by our enemies, but we have become a whisper of ourselves, struggling to survive in the ruins of our great works." The king cleared his throat. "In the dark, I ask why. I am stunned by the silence."

The queen had heard this lament from the king many times before—too many times. She gently touched his arm. "My husband," she said patiently, "it is best not to ponder too much those things that don't make sense to us. We must focus on what we *can* do."

"But we are desperate," the king protested. "We can't keep the sickness out forever. It's in the water; it's in the air we breathe. We don't have much time left." He sighed.

"You are overly troubled, husband," the queen reassured him. "We *will* find a way to protect ourselves from the scourge of the white men. The arrival of these new captives may be a sign the gods have not entirely abandoned us."

"I don't know why you think these invaders are any different from the others."

"These men look different and act different," the queen explained. "I had them watched as they came down the river. It's said the gods of old who first visited the people of the mountains had hair of fire and gold, like the Englishman."

"He seeks the god-plant," the king said thoughtfully, "and he wears the golden talisman."

The queen said, "He also carries red fever powder. He may be a shaman. And the dark one is more like us than any that came before. Ismerai's spies tell her he's a friend of the forest; he may even come from the land of the old ones."

"Your grandfather allowed the Frenchman to leave when he promised to send more men who didn't have the sickness. Perhaps the Frenchman sent these?" the king asked.

"I don't think so, that was too long ago," the queen pointed out. "But the Frenchman might have sent the other one."

"Do you mean the young one who came before, whose companion brought us the god-stone?"

"Yes," she replied. "The young man sought the god-plant like these ones. He also wore the same talisman."

The king shook his head wearily. "That was unfortunate."

"What happened had nothing to do with us. Fear drove him to his death. He must have listened too closely to the stories," the queen said. "But take heart, My King." She took his hand. "The greatest sign is that our captives have only one mark from the sickness."

"What does that mean?"

"It means"—she kissed his hand—"our people's suffering may finally be over."

"Then we don't believe what the Spaniard says?" the king asked.

"The evil one speaks through that fool. All that nonsense of the great father in this place he calls Rome, and his special god." She sighed, letting the king's hand drop. "But stay with the Spaniard, and give him drink to loosen his tongue. We need to learn more from our enemy before we are finished with him."

The king said, "I'll have Ismerai appoint a woman to the Spaniard as well. He will try to impress her, and she can keep a close watch on him."

"A good idea," she said, "but the others are the key to our survival. I can feel it." They stared, silent and thoughtful, at the garden bathed in pale light.

The king abruptly threw up his hands. "If our priests spent more time with cures instead of indulging the superstitions of a terrified people, we wouldn't need them at all."

Below, the changing of the guard took place.

"Our religion used to make sense," the queen agreed. "Not anymore, My King. Our priests and healers have fallen into delusion. And since we see the gods so seldom, it is up to *us* to decide what to do next."

"Do you remember," the king asked, "when our grandparents' grandparents listened to the priests and consumed the flesh of the first invaders who didn't have the sickness or the scars? Even though it was against everything they believed, there was no benefit. The sickness spread."

"Husband," the queen said firmly, "I no longer believe what I can't see. The secret to the survival of the invaders must be carried within them," she said determinedly, "and we'll find it, even if we have to take them apart, piece by piece. But before weakening the Englishman with bloodletting, I wish to try potions made from his golden hair. We'll use the other one first."

She smiled, and again took the king's hand. "Did you see their faces when the swarm appeared?"

The king laughed and shook his head. "Yes," he said, gently embracing his queen, "a sight I shall never forget."

She slid her arms about him. Then, with a fierceness that surprised the king, she drew him close, and kissed him.

CHAPTER 50

THE BEST-LAID PLANS . . .

Not far from the main canal, William and Nate were confined to an adobe hut patrolled by two guards.

"We've been over this a dozen times before," Nate said. "The only way to escape would be at night, by the light of a crescent moon. Any brighter, and we'd surely be spotted; any less, and we'd be groping around in the dark."

They'd been under constant observation for almost two weeks. They left the hut just once a day: each morning the American was taken to a temple and bled by the priests, and in the afternoon the Brit was taken nearby to have his hair clipped.

William was concerned about the American. Bidwell was becoming increasingly pale and listless, completely unlike his usual irritating self. William needed the man to lead them out of the Amazon, but if they kept taking his blood, there wouldn't be much left of him to guide anyone anywhere.

William said, "We have to think of something quickly. They're bleeding you out, and I figure they'll soon start on me."

"I don't know," Nate offered, "I think your new hairstyle is quite becoming. Could set a new fashion for British officers."

"Focus, Bidwell—this is important. In the mornings you go further across the city than I do. Are you sure you haven't spotted anything that can help us?"

"I've already told you: once we climb the steps to the main part of the temple, the guards are always there. As for taking a stroll on my own, the place is always surrounded by patrols."

William said, "We can get out through the roof at night, then make our way out." They had found a weakness near a partially supported joist and had made a hole wide enough to crawl through.

Nate asserted, "Our best chance to escape was when they brought us food that first night. The moon was perfect, and we were healthy. At the moment, we'd have a problem taking on anybody, never mind any warriors we might run into." He snorted feebly. "I'm fine, but you look like hell, Gunn."

"We weren't ready that night," William pointed out. Truth was, when they were first brought there, the British officer hadn't figured out how to get the black orchids.

The American rubbed his eyes. The headache that pounded behind them was a constant reminder his body was being drained a little more each day.

"Listen to me, Bidwell," William persisted. "That Spanish bastard may still have influence, especially with the king. In fact, the last time I saw him, he was with a woman. She wasn't a guard."

Nate looked up. "Then we *are* in trouble, if he's taken up with one of them."

"I told them about inoculation," William said, "so they'll soon try to treat someone with the sickness. Think about it: If it works, they'll no longer need us. If it doesn't work, then we're really in the thick of it." William stressed, "We need a plan, *right now*, to get out of here."

"Don't worry, I'll think of something," Nate said, then promptly passed out.

The next morning, Nate peeled the skin off a banana. "At least they've been feeding us well." The bones of several fish were piled on a plate.

Somewhat revived by twelve hours' sleep and breakfast, he offered, "Listen. Forget the hole in the roof—we need weapons. So, after dark, you pretend to be sick, and when the guards come in to see what's wrong, we ambush them, take their weapons, get the orchids, and bolt."

"They must have drained the blood from your brain, Bidwell, because that's the daftest plan I've ever heard."

Nate replied, "Hey, I'm a guide, not a damned wizard."

"Here they come," William warned. "We'll figure this out when you get back."

To their surprise, the guards took William, not Nate, and went toward the area where the ruling and religious castes lived. They continued until they arrived at a tidy brick building with a sturdy timber roof. After a few moments, the high priestess came out. The warriors bowed deeply and with great deference.

To his surprise, William recognized the priestess as the woman who had met his gaze on his first day in the city several weeks earlier. She instructed the guards to remain outside and leave her alone with the British officer.

"Welcome," she said in Spanish, and indicated for him to enter. William had expected to see the same assortment of animal skins, shrunken heads, and dried herbs that seemed to be the décor of shamans, but the dwelling was quite orderly and plain. There was one large entry room and a smaller room at the back, through a doorway.

The priestess pointed to a hammock strung by a small table containing an empty ceramic bowl and a wooden basin half full of water. "Lay down," she instructed. When he was supine, she sat beside him. "My name is Kantuta. Your friend needs rest. Today, we take small blood from you instead. I do this without pain."

"My companion was taken to a temple," William said, puzzled. "This doesn't look like the same place."

"Today, my home," the priestess said simply.

William couldn't help but like her. She was gentle, and the wounds she made in his arm were small and clean. She spoke continuously while working. He learned that Kantuta's husband had died at the queen's side on a royal hunt, gored to death by a large boar. Now the family was just Kantuta and her young son, whom she treasured.

William said, "I remember you from the first day I arrived. You were carrying a silver tray and stopped to look at me."

"You are not like the others. Our stories tell of a shaman with yellow hair from far away. I think this when I see you."

Kantuta was cleaning the incision, when she was startled by the sudden appearance of a young boy at the doorway to the inner room. She leapt up and quickly led him back inside. But not soon enough. Wet with sweat, the child had the smell of sickness, and William's skin prickled at the sight of the pale pink spots covering his head and upper arms.

"My son," she said when she returned. "He is home with broken leg."

William thought, *She believes he has the pox. She brought me here because she didn't want to leave the boy alone, in case he's seen.* He said, "He doesn't have a broken leg. He has the sickness."

"You must understand. We are a dying people," she said. "I tell you this because you are shaman. There are two who bring death: the sickness and the goddess who shakes the earth. Most of our caste believes that keeping the heads of our enemies will protect us from both."

She shook her head. "I feel they are wrong, as do our rulers. The king and queen say the gods no longer answer us and the strangers bring more and more sickness. That is the real danger, not the earth goddess." She carefully dressed the small wound. "With more people, we can be strong again, make new roads, plant new trees, remake our cities. But without a cure, our people will continue to die. Then, when the earth goddess decides, we will finally be no more."

William realized that was why she felt abandoned by her gods. He shifted so that he could look directly at her. "I can help."

Frightened, the priestess held the incision knife to the British officer's throat and shook her head. "No! Tell no one!"

The cold, sharp blade was like ice against his bare skin. "When I first came here," William said somberly, "I saw a man with the pox thrown into the piranha pond."

She nodded sadly. "If they know, they will kill my son too."

"I can prevent that," William said.

She lowered the blade.

He rubbed his throat. "We can help each other."

CHAPTER 51

A GOOD STEW SPOILED

Marquez brooded over recent events as he lay in an unguarded hut not far from the royal palace.

In order to pursue the emerald, he had delayed reporting to his superiors the deal the British had made with Bolívar. El Jefe was to be his justification for this transgression. But now those two meddling infidels had brought an ideal opportunity to the brink of ruin.

The king of the savages had been quite friendly from the start, expressing a desire to learn more about Spain and Spanish royalty. Marquez recently felt he was also winning the queen over and getting very close to baptizing the pagans. Afterward, it would be a simple matter to convince them to give him the emerald to present to the Spanish monarch as a sign of their good faith. Then Spain would claim this part of Brazil from the fractured Portuguese empire, enslave these native brutes, and obtain the land and resources in the name of His Most Holy Roman Catholic Church. His neglecting to immediately report the Bolívar deal would be forgotten.

But now, with the arrival of the two heretics, there'd been a noticeable change in the attitude of both the Amazonian monarchs. He didn't have the easy access he'd once enjoyed, and the king no longer spoke freely with him. He regretted more than ever not killing the Brit and the American when he'd had the chance.

But these savages have made a grave error. The young native woman the king had assigned to be his companion had fallen under his spell. In secret, he'd baptized her, assured her of everlasting life, and promised her she would accompany him to the Old World as his consort. He had no intention of honoring his word, of course, but he did succeed in learning from her that his life was in danger from some sort of human pox trial.

Once again, he was one step ahead of them all. Tonight, he would take the prize from these pagans and carry it to Spain as a sign of the riches to be taken from the jungle kingdom. The Spanish monarchs would almost certainly present the treasure to His Holiness the Pope. Perhaps His and Her Majesties might even mention to His Holiness that Captain Ernesto Rodrigo Marquez was the loyal servant responsible for such beneficence. Then the Vicar of God on Earth might not only grant him every possible indulgence, but make him inquisitor-general, or even assign a religious order into his safekeeping. The Jesuits would do nicely, for instance; or in a pinch, perhaps the Benedictines.

But enough daydreaming—it's time to act.

CHAPTER 52

ḢELL ḢATḢ NO FURY . . .

Late that afternoon, William was put back inside the hut. The outside beam was replaced across the door, shutting them inside.

When the guards were out of earshot, he blurted to Nate, "Tonight, we escape!"

"What are you talking about?"

"The high priestess, Kantuta, is going to help us."

"Why would she help us? What's in it for her?" Nate asked skeptically.

"Her son has a sickness. She believes it's the pox, and I didn't correct her." William took a deep breath. "She's worried they'll find out about her son and kill him. She's going to help us escape, and in return we'll help them get out of here. For some reason she trusts us to lead them to safety. She says it's because of my hair, but there must be more at play."

Tired, Nate was slow to respond.

William said, "Your plan had holes I could march a regiment through. Think about it—without a solid strategy, we'll both wind up as ornaments in one of those acacia bushes. But now we have help from the inside."

Nate reconsidered. "But why tonight? I could do with another day's rest."

"There's enough moon to see by, but not enough for anyone who's awake to easily see us. Plus, I don't want the boy to get better while we wait around and have her realize she doesn't need us anymore. Listen, Yank," William stressed, "the extra time we bought by telling them about inoculation has just about run out. The priestess told me they've found someone with active pox. You know as well as I do, Bidwell, that inoculation doesn't always work. The moment one of them dies, which is bound to happen, we're fish food for certain."

Nate thought for a moment. "Tonight could work. But you're sure she can get you to the orchids?" Nate asked. "Even if you were King George, they wouldn't allow you to just waltz in and take those flowers."

Despite sitting on thick mats, they felt a trembling of the ground accompanied by a deep rumble. The noise and vibration lasted longer than previous tremors. "These things are nerve-racking," William said, "I don't care how often they happen."

Nate waited until the rumbling stopped. "What exactly is your plan?"

"Kantuta says the guards are frightened of the religious caste and will do anything she orders them to. She has arranged to change places with the priestess blessing the food of the late-night guards. She'll give them a little something extra to make sure they're out for a while. Next she'll unbar the door and help us get to the orchids; then we'll fetch her son, who'll be at her house. By the time the sun comes up, we'll be long gone—back the way we came."

"We'll never get out the way we came in once they discover we're gone. Listen, Gunn," Nate added, "I've been watching every canal we've crossed, and they're all flowing. And flowing canals have to empty into even larger waterways someplace downstream. In due course that has to be the Amazon. So, here's the plan: after we get what we came here for, we meet at the large canal, grab one of those dugouts, and slip away in the darkness."

"That's the thing," the British officer said, intentionally not looking at the American.

"What's the thing?" Nate said warily.

"They're coming with us—all the way."

"You're joking." Nate's eyebrows lifted. "You're not joking."

"What do you think would happen to Kantuta and her son," William asked grimly, "when they discover she helped us? I'll tell you what: the piranha pond. The boy can't be more than ten years old." He thought of Sarah. "They come with us."

"I guess I hadn't thought that far ahead. We'll get a bigger canoe."

He must be growing a conscience. All that ever led to was trouble. "Well then, Admiral, it seems we have a plan."

Now all Nate had to do was figure out how to get the emerald. That could prove interesting, especially if it was still around the king's neck.

William awoke in the night. He fought off the fog of sleep. With the loss of blood, they had both dozed off.

Had Kantuta awakened him? He gradually became aware of screams from somewhere in the distance. In the dark, he couldn't tell if he was actually awake or not.

"Kantuta?" he whispered. There was no answer. He looked over at the American.

He could just make out the dim form of Bidwell, lying on his right side, deeply asleep. William heaved the American into a sitting position, then shook him.

The British officer wasn't prepared for the Yank's response. William instantly found himself on his back, pinned to the ground, being choked by a sleeping man. He tried to kick his way out, but the American's weight on his chest was too much. His fingers desperately sought Bidwell's eyes, when the noise outside reached a peak.

The American shook his head. "What? What was that?" He only noticed then that his hands were around the Brit's throat.

"Get the hell off me, Bidwell," William rasped, "and I'll explain."

"Is it time?"

"No, it's too early." Rubbing his neck, William said, "Something's going on, there's an incredible commotion." He hurriedly added, "I know we've heard all sorts of things in the jungle at night, but this racket is crazy."

Fighting his way through the fog of a pounding headache, Nate ventured, "The Spaniard?"

"Who knows?" William shrugged. "But maybe."

Unnerved by intermittent shouts and cries, the guards outside paced with a restless energy.

"It would be just like that bastard to complicate our plans," Nate pointed out. "Whatever he did, he's woken the whole city."

After several minutes the noise was interrupted by a lonely, high incantation, austere and solemn, a gentle humming and droning that provided a constant whistling background which built in intensity and then slowly lowered. The chanting was more unnerving than the clamor that had preceded it.

"It's the shamans singing the song of the dead," Nate said.

"You know they're not singing for that Spanish bastard," William remarked.

"Change of plans, Gunn. We're getting out of here—*now*."

Too late: The door swung open. In the shadowy radiance of the torches, flanked by her guards, the queen stood. Crimson streaks across her face lent an ominous, malevolent aura to her gaze. In spite of the tropical warmth, the frosty stare she directed at the captives rippled over them like an icy wind off a frozen lake.

William suppressed a shiver.

"Outsiders breathe evil," she spat. "You come. And we die." Her eyes changed in an instant, filling with grief and anger. "The king welcomed the foreigner. Death and thieving are our repayment." The queen glared at William and Nate. "When Inti first appears, your hearts and flesh will become part of the tribe. You will be sacrificed. The priests will say it is to the god of the sun, but know that you die for me, because it is what *I* command."

The queen gazed with a glassy stare, unseeing in her pain. "We will find the Spaniard, and his slow passing will not be so worthy."

Surrounded by her guards, she left, returning to the night.

William and Nate were blindfolded, gagged, and marched through the darkness to a stone building next to the canal. They were tightly bound hand and foot and thrown inside. The door was barred. Well-armed warriors stood guard outside.

The distant humming and droning started again. The song of the dead. It would end with the coming of Inti, the sun god.

As would their lives.

CHAPTER 53

&SCAPE

The drums continued to beat, growing in intensity until the very air shuddered.

A vague scrabbling noise close by roused William. Lying blindfolded and bound on the dirt floor of the jail cell, he had no idea how much time had passed. He felt something soft pick at his hands. *Snake—or rat!* Revolted, he squirmed.

"Stop moving," Kantuta hissed urgently. "Be quiet."

She cut through his bindings. William removed the blindfold and the gag. The meager torchlight that slipped through the cracks of the closed door revealed a big dog panting in his face.

"Pax!"

He twisted to look at the priestess. Despite the pain in his head, he'd never been happier to see someone. "How did you get in here?" he asked her.

"A potion for the guards," she said as she untied Nate, "to calm them. They are nervous and angry. Their king is dead. Quickly now," she added. "Guards will sleep, but not for long." She helped William get to his feet. He rose unsteadily.

Nate sat up and removed his blindfold. Somewhere in the back of his throbbing head a drum was beating to quarters. Pax sniffed at the American. "What's he doing here?"

"The dog digs a hole over there, outside." Kantuta pointed to a dark corner in the back of the room. "But when I come, he stop and come in with me."

"Kantuta," William asked, "where's your son?"

"We go for him after orchids"—she smiled—"like we plan."

William picked up his rucksack, which the guards had thrown into the cell to be burned with the captives. "Are you sure you can get us through the city to the orchids?"

She said, "No worry. There is much madness because of the death of the king. No one will notice. And if they try to stop us . . ." Kantuta held out two large daggers. "Take these."

"You go with Kantuta," Nate said, "and I'll meet you at the big canal, like *we* planned."

"Where're you going?"

"I'll go for her son," Nate replied, "otherwise we're going to run out of time." He neglected to mention that he intended to go directly to the warehouse first. If the emerald was stored anywhere, it should be in the heavily guarded warehouse. Plenty of time to get the boy afterward.

William described where Kantuta's house was. "It'll be difficult for you to get there without being noticed."

"I've thought of that, but I have an idea. Let's get those guards in here."

Kantuta peered outside. The first faint shreds of dawn streaked the eastern sky. She led them to the guards lying unconscious in the shadows at the side of the jail. They bound and gagged them, then dragged them inside. Nate stripped one guard and put on his gear.

William and Kantuta exchanged glances. "Maybe," she said. She adjusted Nate's tunic, then pulled his hair back tight in the fashion of the royal guards.

"It'll have to do," William said. "Let's get going."

"I'll go with you as far as the bridge," Nate said.

The high priestess looked out, then nodded. William said, "Good luck."

"You too, Gunn."

Once outside, they replaced the beam that barred the door.

Kantuta led the way to the bridge. William walked behind her, head hanging despondently, his wrists crossed as if bound. Nate marched behind the prisoner, holding a torch aloft in one hand and spear in the other, in the royal fashion. Several groups passed them, some carrying wood, but as soon as they spotted the high priestess, they averted their eyes and bowed.

They reached the bridge over the large canal without incident. In the distant torchlight a large congregation was amassing at the plaza at the foot of the principal pyramid.

"They will make fire to send our king to the other world," Kantuta said, "with his servants." She pointed at the British officer and the American.

"Not if we have anything to say about it," Nate said.

William took a black packet out of the rucksack and left the bag at the bridge. He looked at the American and nodded once. Gunn turned to go, and Nate called, "What's the kid's name?"

"Cauã."

Kantuta led William and Pax over the bridge into the darkness on the other side.

Nate detoured around the crowd forming at the temple and approached the warehouse from the opposite direction.

From a distance, he might look like one of the royal guards, but he thought it best not to test the deception too closely. He avoided a well-lit street, and made his way along a quiet, dark avenue. The warehouse was a short way down a lane to his left. Once there, Nate clung to the shadows of a tall palm grove bordering the square in front of the building; from there he could observe the guards without being seen.

The area was bathed in torchlight, and there were at least three patrols. Even if he managed to take one out, there would be still two to contend with. And he had to first get across the square without being seen.

He recalled how the Brits had successfully marched straight up to the Spanish across the parade ground in Tunja; in desperation he was about to do the same, when a deep muted boom shook the air like thunder, but lower in timbre, accompanied by a rolling tremor that buckled the ground. Branches crashed down from the palm overhead. It was far worse than any tremor he had ever felt. He steadied himself against the trunk of a tree, fully expecting the earthquake to pass. This time, the rolling tremors didn't stop, but grew rapidly more violent, as if an enormous beast were squirming beneath the ground. A chasm opened directly in front of him, then closed just as quickly.

Kantuta's son. He deliberated for a moment. If they were to keep Kantuta's help in getting out of the Sacred Land, he'd better try to get the boy. *I must be nuts. This place is falling apart.* Abandoning the shuddering warehouse, he hurried as best he could over the surging ground, hoping it wouldn't be too late.

No one paid any attention to him; everyone was too busy trying to stay alive. He dodged falling tree limbs and stone blocks until he came to the house. Miraculously, it stood almost intact, although the door hung at a crazy angle. He yelled into the dark interior.

"Cauã!"

From the shadows within, a young boy approached. Although his skin glistened in the dancing light, he didn't appear very frightened. The small blemishes on his skin might have been bright and pink, but they weren't infected. Gunn was right, this kid wasn't that sick—in fact, he was looking pretty good.

Kantuta had prepared him well. She had told him they needed to leave that night with the outsiders, and he held a small bag in his hand.

"I sure hope you speak some Spanish, kid," Nate said, "because we don't have any time to waste."

Cauã asked in Spanish, "Where is Mother?"

"She's waiting for you," Nate replied. "Come."

A tremendous convulsion unlike anything they had yet experienced knocked them to their knees. The brick walls split, and pieces of the roof crashed to the ground; dust filled the air, making breathing difficult.

Nate stood and braced unsteadily against a broad piece of timber. *Where did that come from?* He looked up and saw stars: The roof was almost completely gone. The dust settled, and he could see the entire back part of the building had collapsed.

The booming shakes persisted. He climbed over the debris to where the far wall once stood and found the boy safe under a thick roof support.

"Somebody's really vexed the dragon's wife this time," the American said softly to himself in English. "Let's go, kid." Nate helped him stand, and together they staggered out of the rubble through the remains of the shattered door.

Kantuta led William toward the waterfall, the path just visible in the dim light. Behind them, the keening moans of the shaman's song coming from the city filled the humid night air.

They arrived without incident at the opening in the rock face leading to the black orchids. The priestess gripped the British officer's arm and whispered, "I will try to have the guards bring torches. They are royal guards and answer only to our rulers; should they resist, we must kill them."

William nodded. "Let's send Pax in first." He had seen how the Indians valued their dogs—Pax would distract them. The big dog slipped through the cleft in the rock.

The British officer concealed in his sleeve the knife Kantuta had given him. She loosely bound his wrists again. A moment later they entered the flagstone clearing. Lit by a single torch, a guard knelt in the semidarkness not thirty feet away and spoke to Pax. Her spear lay on the ground beside her. An archer stood close by, holding a longbow.

William limped in with his head lowered, dragging his left leg. The archer started to notch an arrow but hesitated at the sight of the high priestess.

Kantuta issued several forceful commands to the warriors. Instead of immediately obeying, the guard with the spear stood slowly, one hand on her hip, and calmly replied. William sensed these guards weren't cowed by the religious order, nor were they going to comply. With their attention focused on Kantuta, the British officer very slowly let the knife slip out of his sleeve until the hilt was in his palms, the blade concealed by his shirt and forearms.

The guards traded words with the high priestess but ignored the lame and bound prisoner. William shambled to within striking distance.

In a flash, he grabbed the archer by the arm; the notched arrow flew wildly. With a powerful upward stroke, he drove the metal blade of the knife under the man's rib cage and into his heart, killing him instantly.

The other guard whipped about, her spear drawn back for a killing thrust. Instead, her eyes opened wide in surprise. Her weapon clattered to the stones, and she crumpled to the ground. Behind her, Kantuta returned her dagger to her belt.

William rubbed his forehead, and his hand came away covered with blood. Kantuta smeared an ointment on the wound where the arrow had grazed him, while William ripped cloth from his tunic and fashioned a bandage to help stanch the flow. He started toward the majestic cinchona tree.

"Wait," Kantuta called and hurried along a small path behind the boulders that ran along the edge of the pool near the entrance. While waiting, William took advantage of the time to replenish his store of red bark.

He stripped several pieces from the trunk of the cinchona and stowed them in the pouch tied around his waist. The priestess returned with a lit torch. It had a glutinous foul substance covering the top and gave off a stinking black smoke.

"You use this, the flowers are guarded."

He nodded and took the smoking torch.

The massive cinchona tree sat on the edge of the pool at the base of the waterfall. Climbing with one hand would be challenging under the best of circumstances, but attempting it under the threat of attack by giant wasps was a truly daunting task. A father's desperate love for his daughter, with time running out, compelled William forward.

He reached for the lowest branch and pulled. He found a footing. He passed the torch from one hand to the other, and continued up, working his way from one branch to another.

When he was about twenty feet off the ground, a low groan rumbled through the cove. He raised his head, expecting to see the night sky filled with black, roiling clouds and flashes of lightning. Or swarms of giant wasps. Only hazy stars appeared overhead.

The deep roar continued; he looked down. *Why is Kantuta kneeling?* When the tree swung in a great creaking arc, he realized it was because she couldn't stand.

Earthquake!

Terrifying, undulating shock waves crashed from deep within the earth. The roaring increased in volume and intensity. Wave after wave struck, heaving the ground like a massive serpent coiling and uncoiling beneath the earth.

Climbing was next to impossible. William wrapped his free arm around a stout branch. He wouldn't let this stop him; he had come too far. Looking at the rocking tree above, the British officer recalled the boatswain's mate of the *Voyager* guiding him up the ship's rigging in an eight-foot swell, lessons William would never forget.

With the back of his hand, he wiped blood from his eyes; the cut had started to bleed again. He adjusted the bandage on his forehead, then reached for the next branch and pulled. His foot found a secure support. He passed the torch from one hand to the other, then carefully repeated the sequence.

William was forty feet off the ground and almost to his goal, when a thrumming from above blended with the deep rumbling of the earth below.

Nate cast the spear aside. He grabbed the boy's hand and lurched into the night. They stumbled down the path, the earthquake rolling the ground like waves in an ocean. A surreal nightmare of fire and noise confronted them—the wreckage of buildings, shouting, screams of pain, panicked animals, and above all, an overpowering, deep grating boom. Nate felt as if he were in the hell the New England preachers had ranted about every Sunday when he was a boy.

The fierce undulations continued. He steadied himself against the trunk of a swaying palm tree that somehow continued to stand. Branches and leaves rained down around them. A wooden structure across the way fell to pieces; flames and sparks leapt high into the sky. Searchers could be seen trying to enter the debris, outlined against the glow, shouting for their comrades—an extremely risky activity considering the still-undulating ground beneath their feet.

Not far from the main canal, they careened down a side street. Through the swirling smoke, the long outline of the partially damaged storehouse could be seen not far ahead.

"What the hell, kid," Nate said in English, "there's time for a quick look. No sense in leaving this place empty-handed." Cauã seemed confused.

A warrior, either stubbornly or stupidly, remained at the entrance. Her eyes wide and glazed, she glanced about continuously, as if hoping for relief. Nate lurched up to her, yelled some gibberish while pointing up the path, and shook his head with a serious expression. She looked at the boy, then at Nate, nodded once, and ran off.

With his free hand, William clung tightly to a branch. His foot slipped as he tried to gain leverage on the limb below.

Wherever the bark of the tree was damaged, black orchids grew profusely. The plants vibrated with the trembling of the great tree. The lowest orchids, some in full bloom, were almost within William's range. The buzz from the giant wasps had grown louder.

At this height, he was so close to the nest that the noise of the stinging swarm surpassed the roar of the tremors. The tree swept through an enormous arc, swinging the British officer like a dog shaking a rat. It was as if the tree were trying to dislodge an unwanted parasite. Branches and leaves fell from above as he desperately inched along.

Just a little further. Holding the torch as best he could, he wrapped his arm around the trunk, pushed off with one foot, fully extended his other arm overhead, and managed to grip a branch at the very edge of his reach. Seared from an old lightning strike, the limb just above this contained several flowering black orchids.

He reached out.

The deafening crescendo of the giant wasps abruptly ceased. A furious dark cloud descended. William released the tree trunk to bring the smoky torch closer. Only his grip on the branch overhead kept him from falling to certain death.

The ground rumbled with the violence of a sudden tremor that shook the tree to its roots, the tremendous energy again sweeping the trunk in a great arc. With a crack like a gunshot, the branch beneath William split and fell away; he dropped the torch just in time to grab the bough overhead with both hands. When the tree swung back, the partially severed branch he was holding pivoted on a strip of bark that held it to the trunk. William was flung outward toward the waterfall, still desperately clinging to the damaged tree limb.

The weight on the broken strip of bark was too much. The limb holding William pulled away from the trunk in a clean break.

William fell.

The American was deflated. What had he expected? To see the emerald displayed at the entrance, lit by a dozen candles?

No, that was ridiculous. At first glance there didn't seem to be much of value in the storehouse. Peering through the smoke, he could make out some wooden spears, blowguns, darts, and vials of colored liquid on wooden shelves.

This was the first time Nate admitted to himself that he wasn't going to leave with the gemstone. It wasn't in a storehouse or any other place: an incomparable treasure of this magnitude the king would keep with him at all times. The realization hit him like a cold slap—the Spaniard had killed the king and had taken the emerald.

I'll track that bastard until I find him.

A burning timber crashed to the ground only feet away. He was glad the boy was outside. A gust of wind briefly parted the smoke in the undamaged portion of the storehouse. He quickly snatched what he could see. A few gems, several small gold and silver objects, including the gold medal the queen had worn to the banquet, and what appeared to be red cinchona powder. Near the exit he seized a blowgun and a few poisonous darts and dashed out.

He stopped in the plaza outside the warehouse to load the weapon just as the structure collapsed behind him. He instinctively ducked, sparks shooting skyward and pieces of smoldering thatch swirling in the air. Burning embers began to fall around them. They skirted the falling debris and only stopped to cough and clear their lungs of smoke. Nate brushed a glowing ember off Cauã's shoulder. To keep him distracted, Nate gave the boy the darts and blowgun to carry. Then he grabbed Cauã's hand, and together they ran for their lives.

Debris was strewn along the path, the air full of stone dust, smoke, and floating leaves. Making their way by the light of the fires, they approached the canal. Miraculously, both the canal and the span over the water were still intact, but the steps down to the landing were now rent with large fissures. The bridge was partially ruined with one abutment cracked.

When he spotted the guard from the storehouse standing by the dugouts, Nate stopped at the top of the steps. He signed for the boy to hand him the blowgun.

Whether she was guarding the dugouts or simply trying to decide whether to take one and flee did not concern him. Without hesitation, Nate let fly with a dart. The poisonous needle found its mark; the guard wavered slightly, then fell forward.

Nate staggered down the steps to one of the larger canoes and signed for Cauã to join him. The boy stood frozen by the sudden violence.

Oh hell. Nate picked his way up the steps. He lifted the boy, carried him down, and placed him in the dugout.

"Where Mother?" Cauã shouted.

"Soon," Nate lied. There was no time to explain. It would have to wait.

He looked up at the partially ruined bridge and tried to peer into the murk on the other side. Ash fell from the sky like a gray snowstorm.

Where in damnation's that Brit?

Then it came to him with a start—he didn't have to wait for William;

he already had enough trinkets to keep him going while he tracked down Marquez and the emerald. The odds were certainly in his favor to survive the journey out of the Amazon. And the kid would be an asset should he run into any more locals.

He swiftly stowed the pack.

Approaching the ruined palisade of the city, Kantuta half dragged, half carried the unconscious British officer. Pax pulled at his pant leg.

When William had fallen from the tree into the pool at the foot of the waterfall, he had smacked his head on a floating tree limb and been knocked out. Pax and Kantuta had fished him out of the water. In the wavering light of the burning city, his forehead was visibly swollen.

By time they reached the bridge, the priestess was exhausted. She didn't even notice the heavy damage the quake had inflicted on the structure, now on the verge of collapse. They struggled over, barely managing to reach the center of the span, when Kantuta had to stop to rest. Pax barked encouragement. William managed to struggle to awareness. Consciousness brought back the realization of his failure to obtain the orchid, and of a lightning bolt ripping through his skull. He surrendered to the vortex of oblivion.

Not long after, a strong shock caused the bridge to completely disintegrate, and fall into the canal below.

The American paused before launching the dugout, knowing for certain that without his help, the British officer had no chance in heaven or hell of making it home to save his daughter.

These thoughts evaporated when three familiar figures emerged from the smoky mist, slowly making their way over the bridge, stopping every few feet.

"Stay here!" Nate ordered Cauá. He made it to the top of the bridge just in time to catch William from Kantuta's exhausted arms. She wasn't much help as he tried to pull the British officer off the fragile bridge, but Pax seized William's leg, and together they managed to move the paralyzed officer to the other side. Nate scarcely had time to breathe a sigh of relief before the entire span fell into the canal.

At the dugout, Kantuta hugged her son tightly and held his hand. "Thank you," she said to the American. He lifted Gunn into the dugout, and Pax lay down beside him. A quick look at the Brit's badly swollen forehead told Nate all he needed to know. Kantuta said, "I go for medicine."

"There's no time," Nate warned, seeing the warriors hastily approaching through the smoking ruins.

She saw them at the same time. "The royal guards," she said anxiously. The high priestess's face assumed a look of grave resolve; she gave Cauã's hand a squeeze. "Take care of my son," she said to Nate. Letting go of the boy's hand, she left the canoe and strode up the steps.

Knowing there was no way he could change her mind, Nate shoved off, propelling the dugout into the middle of the canal.

"*Where Mother?*" The boy's eyes probed the smoke. Nate yelled at Cauã, "Look at me!" He handed him an oar. "Paddle! Quickly."

Over and over, the American dug his paddle into the brown water and ignored the boy's pleading cries. Only when he had gained some momentum did Nate venture to look back. He couldn't tear his eyes away from the unfolding drama.

At the top of the steps, in the light of a nearby blazing storehouse, the high priestess held an icon aloft. Uncertain, the guards hesitated. An intense tremor brought down the flaming building, and a huge ball of smoke and flames enveloped the scene, sending a cascade of cinders soaring into the night sky to mingle among the stars overhead.

"Keep your eyes on me!" Nate shouted to Cauã. He stole another glance over his shoulder. The warriors appeared at the top of the steps to the landing. Through the dissipating smoke, the priestess could be seen behind them, standing alone, arms flung wide, unmoving for what seemed an eternity. Slowly, she knelt as if in prayer, head raised to the heavens, seemingly intent on the sparks spiraling upward until she was shrouded in haze.

Nate looked at the British officer; William's complexion was extremely pale. An arrow whizzed past. A wicked *thump* sounded on the gunwale as a long shaft embedded itself in the heavy wood. There was no time to fuss. Nate and Cauá paddled furiously.

The warriors were at the edge of the water. Nate wished he'd had time to sink the other canoes. Too late now. The warriors had several paddlers for each of the dugouts and would soon be on the fugitives.

We really could use another paddle in the water. "Gunn, can you hear me?" he yelled, and scooped water onto William's face, hoping the Brit would come around. Too bad Pax couldn't paddle. A more immediate danger then caught his attention. A shadow, darker than the night, sped along the earthen top of the channel toward them.

"Suasuarana," the boy said, his eyes wide.

"Right, kid." *The queen's pet jaguar, coming to say hello. What next?* "Here." Nate leaned forward and handed the blowgun to Cauá. "Load a dart." As ineffective against the black panther as it might be, the weapon was their only option. He pulled on the paddle for all he was worth.

The black shadow was nearly on them. But then he saw something odd. The Indians had not entered their canoes to pursue them but had retreated to the top steps of the landing. They held the ropes of their pirogues and gazed upstream.

Then he saw why the pursuers had delayed. Behind them, the water in the canal was rising fast. Very fast. A great brown swell came racing down the canal toward them, outpacing even the dark shadow. An upstream weir must have given way under the earthquake and released the main river into the narrow channel.

"Hang on!" was all Nate could yell before the swell picked up the stern of their dugout; he leaned as far back as possible to keep them from being flipped over. Perfectly balanced just below the crest, they rode the wave, rocketing down the waterway. Nate steered as best he could, the jungle on either side a dark blur.

"Good thing they built this canal fairly straight," he muttered to himself, "or we'd wind up in the jungle." He yelled, "Got out of there in the nick of time, didn't we, kid?"

By the time the wave blew out, the dark shadow was gone and no dugouts could be seen behind them. He began paddling again in earnest. Nate knew they would be coming.

The current remained fast. In the early-morning light, the jungle around them began to take shape. William stirred but was still unresponsive. Pax nuzzled the officer and licked his face.

The American glanced behind. "They're coming again!" He could just make out the pursuers in the distance. There were at least a dozen canoes with several warriors in each, and they were gaining rapidly.

The boy turned and looked at him. Nate would wait until he had the time to properly tell him that his mother had given up her life to save them. Maybe embellish it a bit. That is, if they got out of there alive.

He took the medal he had found in the storehouse and placed it around the boy's neck. *Two Saint Christopher medals in the dugout—there's got to be some magic there.*

Up ahead, the light began to grow.

"Captain Gunn," he shouted, "I am ordering you to get that paddle in the water."

William heard his name and an order issued to him. He struggled to sit up, his head swimming. He felt terrible, but was stirred by the insistent voice calling him, commanding him. Opening his eyes, the jungle slid by on either side. The big dog licked his face. He felt light-headed and nauseated. He puked.

"Grab that paddle, Gunn, or we're going to be in that snake pit before noon!" The American kept looking back as he paddled.

Through the fog of pain, William grasped their predicament— he didn't need any encouragement. Weak and pale, the British officer plunged his paddle into the water and began to pull as hard as he could.

Moving his arms at first was difficult, like trying to drag them through molasses. His skull felt twice as large as normal.

Nate called, "How's your head?"

"Nothing a few weeks in the English countryside won't cure." He saw the young boy in front of him. "I'm glad you brought along another good man," William said in Spanish, loud enough for Cauã to hear. "Where's his mother?" he asked in English.

"She sacrificed herself to give us a chance to get away," Nate replied.

William was silent.

The light in the distance continued to grow. Without warning, they shot out the end of the sluice into a vast river, their momentum carrying them well into the current.

The river was immeasurably larger than any they had ever seen, and it flowed directly east into the rising sun, where bright gold clouds illuminated the surrounding jungle.

The sound of drums reached them from the near shore. On the bank, dark human shapes flashed indistinctly against the dim border of the forest.

"Good God, they must have run all night," Nate said. "They must think we're partially to blame for the king's death."

Unsure whether the knock on his head might be causing delusions, William shaded his eyes and stared.

On the bank, almost a hundred yards away, two striking forms stood in a patch of glowing sunlight. Their bows were slung over their well-toned shoulders, and they balanced their long lances languidly in their graceful hands. The queen and Ismerai—and they were gazing steadily at them. In the distance, thick plumes of smoke rose, evidence of the destruction of the city.

A flurry of arrows from the warriors in the forest splashed close by.

Nate said, "I suggest we move further into the middle, where the current's most rapid, and get out of range as soon as possible."

They dug as hard as they could. William could feel his head about to burst.

"Oh, great," Nate exclaimed, "we've got company."

William endured the pain to look around. A flotilla of canoes in the middle of the river was quickly gaining on them.

William said, "Pull, Bidwell, pull!"

"What do you think I've been doing, Gunn, while you've been sleeping?"

The current picked up. Nate searched for the fastest part of the river, trying to eke out every bit of speed they could muster to outrun their pursuers. They expected to be boarded at any moment and didn't dare stop paddling to look behind.

After several minutes, Nate took a quick glance over his shoulder. Their pursuers were no longer in the middle of the stream. Inexplicably, they were hugging the bank and no longer gaining.

"Gunn."

Painful as it was, William turned around. Even as he watched, the canoes seemed to lose ground and fade back. Meanwhile, the current in the middle continued to increase and propel them even further ahead.

A few arrows dropped harmlessly short. The current picked up still more dramatically. The warriors receded into the distant mist.

"Seems we're in the clear," Nate said when there had been no sign of their pursuers for at least a few minutes.

His arm numb, William said, "Perhaps we can rest for a while. Doesn't seem much point paddling in this current anyway, does it?"

Nate looked around. The banks were a solid green wall of jungle on either side. And although the banks were quite far away, the dugout moved swiftly past. The current *was* quite strong.

"Probably saved our lives. But I agree, perhaps it's time we rested."

They laid the paddles across the gunwales and leaned on them. Only then did Nate realize how tired he was. "Did you get the orchids?" he asked.

William hesitated. "What the hell, Bidwell. There's no way to sugar-coat it. I failed, Yank. I failed. No orchids." He choked out, "I left my young child to the care of others, came all this way through countless dangers. What for?" He shook his head. "I had them within my grasp— almost in my hand. Goddamn it anyway."

Nate hadn't seen this despondent side of the British officer before.

"We found the plants once, Gunn, we'll do it again." They floated for a few minutes in silence. "The boy needs us."

William thought of the young Indian boy whose mother had sacrificed herself for them and his sense of responsibility answered. "At the moment, Bidwell, the question is why did those blokes break off the chase just when it seemed they had us?"

Nate was glad that the Brit was back with him, but he felt uneasy. Something was not right. He scanned their surroundings. The current was incredibly fast.

"Cauã, do you know this river?"

"No, never leave village," he said, frightened.

Thinking aloud, Nate said, "This isn't natural."

A strange hissing sound. "Do you hear that?" William asked.

They looked at each other.

Nate swore under his breath then picked up his paddle. "Gunn, switch places with the kid and pull hard for the shore—our lives depend on it! Rapids!"

A low rumbling roar rent the air.

Nate felt his skin prickle. He bellowed, "WATERFALL!"

Too late he realized the plumes of mist rising ahead were coming from a high waterfall. They had to do something fast or they'd be dashed to bits on the rocks below. Nate used every stroke he knew to get to the shore and away from the raging rapids. "The left side, Gunn—deeper, dammit, and draw toward you with everything you've got!"

No matter how deep they dug or how hard they pulled, they were caught. They bounced like corks, barely in control.

The stream was riddled with rocks, the swirling waters breaking over many of them. But there were enough big boulders to give them a chance—their only chance.

"We can't make it straight to the side," Nate yelled. "Head for the water behind the bigger rocks. Go!" With any luck they could swing from rock to rock and out of the current to the shore.

William missed with his paddle when he tried to grab the first boulder. Nate slowed them at the next rock, and William was able to grab on. But the back of the canoe swung out, causing them to slip down the rapids sideways.

"I'll stop us," Nate shouted, "then you latch onto the closest rock."

Looking ahead for the next large rock, Nate noticed the sharp edge of the horizon drawing close, the gray plumes rising beyond. They were approaching the brink fast. This might be their last chance.

William saw the same thing. "This has to be it!" he yelled.

Nate swung the prow around to the upstream side of a huge boulder. The canoe hit perfectly. They clawed at the rock with their bare hands, trying with all their might to swing the heavy canoe around to the quieter water. They just managed to get a grip on a chipped ledge.

Their fingers clung desperately to the narrow fissure, their forearms straining to the utmost. It took every ounce of their remaining strength and determination to hold on. Slowly, almost imperceptibly, the heavy dugout canoe began to swing out of the current.

Cauã shouted and pointed. Rushing toward them, barely visible, was the submerged brown trunk of a waterlogged tree.

"Hold, dammit," Nate yelled. "HOLD!" His eyes were glued to the enormous projectile hurtling along on the current. "Hold fast for your life!"

But it was too late. A wicked jolt rocked them and ripped away their tenuous grip. The boulder was gone.

Paddling was futile. The most they could do was swing the canoe's prow around to face downstream and pray.

His voice edged with fear, Nate shouted to Gunn and Cauã, "Lay back, stretch out, and whatever you do, stay in the dugout!"

William thought of the young boy behind him, just having lost his mother, facing this new terror. "Cauã, stay with Pax!" the Brit hollered.

The noise surrounding them swallowed Pax's yelp. The big dog instinctively hunkered down beside the boy. They lay back, thoughts frozen, every muscle tense, nerves ready to snap. The gray sky passed by overhead. They could feel droplets of mist settling on their cheeks.

The water beneath them suddenly disappeared.

They were over the edge and plunging weightless into space, the only sound the thunderous cascade crashing, far, far below.

BRAZIL

ATLANTIC
OCEAN

AMAZON Manaus
Amazon R.   Amazon R.   •Belém
BASIN

BRAZIL

ANDES MOUNTAINS

PACIFIC
OCEAN

Rio de Janeiro

SOUTH
ATLANTIC
OCEAN

1⁰⁰

CHAPTER 54

𝔇ELIVERANCE

The coastal packet cut smartly through the warm cobalt waters off the Brazilian coast; the sheets and rigging overhead slapped as the ship tacked in the evening breeze. It was quiet—most of the passengers were asleep, either on the foredeck or in their cabins.

Veeborlay leaned on the gunwale enjoying a late smoke before he retired. Stuck in that Amazonian hellhole port of Belém for almost a week by the horrendous weather, he was sure he'd be late for the king's reception in Rio. But the teeming rain and low black clouds had finally lifted long enough for the packet to get underway. He gazed at the passing shoreline, relieved to see that the coffee-colored waters of the Amazon had been completely absorbed by the tropical Atlantic, which indicated that the packet was almost back on schedule. It was likely he would not only make the reception but, most important, be in time for the departure of the Dutch East India Company's ship to Spain. He knew the ship's captain wouldn't wait for him, not with the kind of cargo they were transporting. If he wasn't on board, all would be lost.

"Veeborlay." A middle-aged man with a smart Vandyke trimming his chin limped toward Dutch from the stern. The man continued in Spanish, "You old scoundrel!" He was short and barrel-shaped and a beret of sorts almost, but not quite, covered the bald spot on the man's head.

"Rossi, you old cutthroat," the Dutchman replied with a noticeable lack of enthusiasm. Abel Veeborlay had successfully avoided Vinco Rossi ever since he had spotted him coming aboard in Belém. It was impossible to forget the horse's ass who had nearly gotten them both killed in that Barbados scam.

"Where are you going?" the merchant asked. Not used to receiving replies to his prying questions, Rossi persisted unabashedly, "To Rio, like myself, I'd say. But what manner of business brings you so far from your Barranquilla lair, huh, Dutch? King's business, I'll wager. But which king?" he quickly added with a knowing wink and a sly grin.

Abel Veeborlay restrained his desire to choke the bastard. Instead, he replied, "I've been invited to the reception." That should be enough to keep the man peeved.

"You have an invitation to the Portuguese ruler's reception?" Rossi asked incredulously. "I find that hard to believe."

"Believe it. You'll have to excuse me, nature calls."

"I'll wait for you right here." The merchant called, "Perhaps you can wrangle an invitation for me as well? Old friends and partners, and all that. We may never see him again if he goes back to Lisbon."

"You won't see me either, if I have anything to do with it," Dutch muttered, hoping Rossi overheard him. Turning toward the bow, he bumped straight into a fisherman in an orange hat and oversized jacket.

"I beg your pardon," Veeborlay said in Portuguese. The man had apparently been leaning on the gunwale right behind him. The stranger nodded curtly and disappeared in the shadows toward the stern.

Dutch made his escape from the nosy merchant. There was simply too much at stake in this trip to Rio. He had two very promising major opportunities for a windfall: the Spanish inquisitor and the Brazilian king.

If his arrangements to get Marquez and the emerald out of the country and back to Spain on a company ship met with success, the grateful Spanish monarch would reward him handsomely.

In addition, as an agent of the Dutch East India Company, he intended to secure an exclusive trade agreement with the Brazilian royal couple. It didn't really matter that the company couldn't back up any of Veeborlay's promises, so long as he came away with the assurance of a trade deal. That would earn a hefty bonus from the directors of the company.

And not to be overlooked was the fact that he was still on the British payroll. If he reported to the British any information he picked up in Rio, they would provide significant recompense as well.

It was a complicated and dangerous game, but one that Abel Veeborlay was well accustomed to playing. If he played this hand right, it could turn out to be very, very profitable.

They were alone in the dark, leaning against the starboard rail not far from the ship's bow. Under a clear sky and a fair breeze, the ship cut neatly through the tropical seas. Off to starboard, flashes of silent lightning reflected off the dark-gray clouds hovering over the far-off western hills; along the shoreline, low mangrove forests slipped by under the faint southern stars.

William scratched his unkempt blond beard, causing the bells affixed to the sleeves of his ragged blue shirt to jingle. William's hair was so dirty it could no longer be called blond, and the beard covered a nasty, recently healed scar along his cheek. At his feet, a large gray-brown dog lay asleep; an Indian boy was curled up beside the dog, one arm thrown over the animal. "Thanks for stopping me from throwing that Dutch bastard overboard."

"Someone might have seen," Nate pointed out. "And we'll get information simply by my tailing him. I've already overheard that the king is returning to Lisbon. And that he's having a reception at his palace the night before they depart."

"That's good to know." It was imperative that William meet the royal couple, who should know above anyone if there were black orchids in the area. "It'll also be better to corner Veeborlay in Rio. That's the most likely place for him to meet the Spaniard. And it's a good thing the Dutchman's never met you, Yank."

"Are you kidding?" Nate laughed softly. "After the Amazon, no one would know us from Adam anyway. Believe me."

William considered this and, as much as he hated to admit it, Bidwell was right. They had lost everything in that terrifying plunge over the falls. But several days after, fortune finally smiled on them and they had found the blowgun at the side of the river. A completely healed Cauã showed them how to cobble together enough darts from palm leaves to enable them to cling to life on small game. But with the coming of the rains, the river rose fast and the current became unmanageable. The rough raft they had made was about to come apart when they intercepted an expedition of starving Portuguese explorers who had guns, a little dry power, and dugout canoes. Between them they barely managed to make it to the military outpost at Manaus, and from there to Belém.

Not only had their long struggle in the jungle changed their appearance, but they'd been away for so long that William was sure everyone in the duke's support network in South America had to assume they were dead. However, seen in a different light, this presented an ideal opportunity.

Before leaving England, there was military discontent in Portugal over the lingering British presence after the Peninsular War. Two years later, William had no idea of the current political or military situation, either in Portugal or in Brazil. With his altered appearance, he could make his way to Rio posing as a traveling minstrel. The Indian boy and the dog rounded out the disguise.

The American interrupted William's musings. "Good thing no one's asked us to perform yet."

A thin white scar tracked across Nate's brown forehead; his face spouted a patchwork of black hairs. The Spaniard's trail had grown cold upon reaching Belém several weeks ago. Nate had only asked to become part of Gunn's little troupe on the ship only at the very last moment, when they spotted Veeborlay on the packet. Nate figured that only the emerald could drag Gunn's Dutch friend all the way from Barranquilla to Rio.

"I don't know about that," William replied, "my card tricks are quite entertaining, even if you don't think so. Those Portuguese soldiers certainly did."

"They were drunk."

"At least my card playing won these clothes. If you're so clever, what extraordinary talent do *you* possess?"

"I figure that trick with the knife is worth something."

"You mean where you stab yourself in the hand and bleed all over your audience? Yes, very entertaining, Bidwell, kept those chaps in Manaus in stiches."

"That was *one* time, Gunn.

"Anyway," Nate said, "the news the king is leaving must be of use to you."

William replied, "Things must have really heated up since the duke's briefing almost two years ago for the king to now depart Brazil and return to the troubled politics of Lisbon." He wondered who the British were backing, and he was glad he was in disguise.

Nate said, "Veeborlay is planning on being at the king's reception—said he has an invitation. Do you think we can get in?"

"I'm counting on my contact in Rio. He should be able to get us there."

"Do you know anything about who's running the colony?"

"Before I left Britain," William replied, "I was advised that the entire Portuguese royal court arrived in Brazil from Lisbon in 1808 on a fleet of thirty-six ships."

Nate said, "I recall hearing something about that, but don't really remember why they left."

"Napoleon. The prince regent Dom João ruled the Portuguese empire in place of his insane mother, Queen Maria, and made the decision to abandon the home country. Brazil was a natural refuge for them."

William felt it couldn't hurt to be frank with the American. A simple bond had been forged in the Amazon between him and Nate which, though not entirely devoid of friendship, certainly included trust. "The British navy escorted the struggling convoy across the Atlantic. Our countries have been close ever since. When his mother died, Dom João became King John VI. Brazil used to be the largest colony on the continent, but Dom João made it an equal partner in the Kingdom of Portugal."

William added, "Part of my mission was to quietly meet, if at all possible, with King John on behalf of Great Britain. Wave the British flag, shore up our markets, and all that."

Nate shook his head. "I have to hand it to you Brits, always looking for the next market for your biscuits. Damn, you're almost as bad as we are."

William considered that, then said, "This must be tough for you, Bidwell, having missed your chance with the emerald."

Nate said, "So now you're convinced the treasure the Spaniard took *was* the black orchid and not the emerald?"

"Why not? As you said, the queen wasn't specific, and they treasured the orchids above everything. Guess we'll just have to wait and see."

They stared at the acrobatics of the blue-gray dolphins riding the ship's bow wave, which glowed with marine phosphorescence.

"What do we do with the boy?" Nate asked.

William said simply, "He stays with me."

They were quiet for a few moments, Nate lost in thoughts of their journey out of the Amazon, and William worried he was far too late to see his daughter alive again. The sliver of the moon cast a dull light on the wide, restless ocean.

"I have been away for a long time, Yank. Orchid or no orchid, I have to get on the first ship out of Rio for Britain."

"You know," Nate said, "I was wondering, How close did you get to the plant?"

William replied, "When our clothes were shredded by the waterfall, you could see for yourself. The cinchona bark I had in the pouch around my waist comes from that very tree. They were within my grasp, Bidwell. I was there." William looked away, the frustration in his voice impossible to hide.

"Why do you keep that bark anyway? We don't need it anymore."

"I guess it reminds me of just how close I got."

Regretting he had asked, Nate changed the subject. "If you'd seen what I took from that storehouse and put in the pack, you'd have wanted to search for it below the falls for a while longer."

"If *you'd* seen that waterfall coming," William snapped, "we'd have avoided this whole mess. This jungle business *is* supposed to be your area."

Nate was defensive. "I'm a guide, not a fortune-teller."

They were on the last leg to Rio and due to arrive early the next morning. Although the red bark was all William had to show from the Amazon, the ship's hold held a case of orchids he had managed to collect during a brief layover in Recife. The strange and beautiful plants would please the duke, but there wasn't any sign of black orchids.

"I'm starting to believe the black orchid can only grow on damaged bark," William said, "where the tree's sap is concentrated—that's what makes the plant so potent."

Nate shrugged.

The officer persisted, "If you recall, the orchids we saw were on a damaged part of that tree. And those giant wasps—I'm thinking they might be the key to the orchid's reproduction."

"So?"

"If those wasps exist only in the Amazon," William concluded miserably, "that might be the only place on earth the plants are found as well." If what the British officer said was true, the black orchid was much more singular than anyone could have ever imagined. And much more valuable.

"I'd like to keep everything that happened in the Sacred Land close to the chest, Bidwell; no need to tell anyone we saw the orchids."

"And no need to say anything about the emerald either, Admiral."

William said, "Not to worry. And once we get into the reception, I can ask the king if there are any orchids in Brazil. That'll also be our chance to get the Dutchman alone."

"You certainly have a lot of confidence in this contact of yours in Rio. They haven't been much use so far, from what I can see."

"This merchant has been doing business there for a long time. He'll get us in."

The ship abruptly changed tack and steadied into the breeze. The sails slapped loosely. In the moonlight, a small fishing boat drew alongside. A short, stout fisherman leaned over the rail and had a brief, guttural conversation with the captain of the packet, after which the fishing boat drew away. The captain steadied the vessel on its previous course. The sheets filled and snapped taut.

"*Senhores!*" one of the mates they had befriended called excitedly, working his way forward from the aft of the boat.

"Yes, what is it?" William answered in Portuguese.

"A fisherman from Rio spoke with the captain. There's big trouble there."

"What kind of trouble?"

"Rebellion!"

"What did he say?" Nate asked.

William was grim. "Enough. Our plans may be in serious jeopardy."

CHAPTER 55

℞IO DE ℐANEIRO

The pilot champed on a cigar as he guided the ship between the head-lands and into the harbor of Rio de Janeiro.

The first thing William intended to do after the ship docked was to look for the contact provided by the duke, a local merchant named Canning. He was an Englishman, which William hoped made him more trustworthy than Veeborlay. The British officer desperately needed an invitation to the king's reception. This was the key to uncovering the whereabouts of the Spaniard and, possibly, the black orchid.

William also needed to know when the next ship would depart for England; in addition, he required funds, and a report on the local political situation.

From the sea, the city of Rio de Janeiro appeared grand. It was surrounded by impressive, forest-covered mountains and a shoreline fringed with vegetation that was occasionally interrupted by coves of sandy beaches. On the outskirts they passed plantations of coffee and sugar cane that competed with virgin woodlands thick with colorful orchids. Within the city boundaries churches, forts, and glittering white houses topped every hill.

But as soon as they set foot on the pier, this bucolic impression evaporated. Squalor, intensified by the excessive humidity, assaulted their senses. Piles of decaying trash littered the waterfront. In the fish market near the port, the afternoon shoppers casually competed with the rodents for the day's haul, occasionally brushing away a particularly aggressive competitor.

Two squealing rats wrestled over a fish head. Pax growled.

"We'd be eating these things in the Amazon," Nate said ironically.

"Somehow," William said with disgust, "city rats aren't as appealing."

When the prince regent had landed in Rio over a decade earlier, he had opened Brazil's ports—ports that had been formerly closed to all shipping except that from Portugal. Now vessels from all nations competed for berthing space. Despite the rats and the slave trade, Rio was not only the principal city but by far the most cosmopolitan city in Brazil.

After several inquiries, a storekeeper directed them to the address of a prominent British merchant just a short distance from the port. The Brazilians they passed wore every manner of clothing, from a wisp of material covering only the essentials to gaily colored turbans and swaths of brilliant cloth wraps. Many women wore simple skirts with vibrant cotton shirts. With such a kaleidoscope of colors, Nate's and William's outlandish outfits didn't draw much attention; Pax and Cauá fit right in.

William's contact resided in a two-story whitewashed stone house on the corner of a busy street. In response to William's thumping, a servant opened the cheery canary-yellow front door. The servant gave the odd company a sideways glance and told them to wait outside. William brushed past him and led them inside, leaving the noisy street behind. The servant followed, wringing his hands fretfully, his brow creased with worry.

Halfway down the stairs, the startled merchant froze when he saw the two men, the native boy, and their large dog in his foyer. Assessing the oddly garbed, deeply tanned pair, the businessman quickly recovered. "It's fine, Henry," he said, addressing the servant, and turned to his guests.

"Traveling troubadours, I see," he said lightly. "If you gentlemen will proceed outside and around the back, you'll be treated to a fine meal."

"Mr. Canning, we're plant hunters in the employ of the Duke of Devonshire, on behalf of His Majesty."

At the mention of the duke, the man's eyebrows lifted and he put a finger to his lips. "Inside," he said, with a nod of his head, indicating the next room.

The late-afternoon light streamed through partially shuttered windows. The sago palms resting in oversize planters complemented the local furnishings.

"Please," he said and indicated for the men to take a seat on a blue divan bordered on either side by miniature bamboo plants. The merchant smiled when the boy settled on the rug next to the dog. A middle-aged man, Edward Canning had thinning gray hair and a friendly disposition.

William said, "We arrived on the coastal packet just a short time ago and came directly here. We'd been in the Amazon for a long time"— he sighed—"too long, before we joined a party of Portuguese explorers heading downstream."

Canning listened intently. The British officer explained their appearance there, describing their mission as plant hunters on behalf of the British king.

"Right, and I'm the Queen of Brazil," Canning replied.

"What are you saying?" William asked.

"I know my good duke likes his gardens, but he likes his intrigues ever so much more. Well . . ." The merchant took out his pipe and began to slowly fill the bowl and tamp the damp tobacco. "There's more than enough scheming here at the moment to satisfy him."

The servant returned, bringing hot tea for the guests, cocoa for the boy, and a bowl of water and sweetbreads for Pax.

"You gentlemen have arrived at a very touchy time—to put it mildly," Canning said as they settled with the refreshments. He continued tamping his pipe as his visitors drank. "In hope of avoiding turning the Portuguese empire into a bloody shambles, King John is planning to go back to Lisbon to endorse a liberal constitution. In fact, at this very moment, I believe the king is attempting to quell a mutinous rebellion by the Portuguese troops stationed here."

"Do you expect bloodshed?" William asked.

Canning chuckled. "You don't know our king. He'll probably ride out tomorrow with the queen to meet the mutineers. They're at the regional barracks not very far from here."

He leaned back in his chair, lit the pipe, and took a long draw. The smoke melted slowly out his mouth when he spoke.

"I tell you these things, my plant-hunting friend," he said and smiled through the curling blue haze, "to give you some leverage with the king, if you're fortunate enough to be granted an audience. Our consul hasn't had that privilege. You see, officially, we're personae non gratae, just so the king can please the other side for the moment. But I'm sure a quiet, unofficial meeting might be possible, even welcome. And I'm certain such a meeting would make our duke very happy. But first, may I say that a bath, shave, and change of clothing would not go astray."

They spent that evening at the merchant's house. At about nine o'clock Nate took his leave, saying he wished to get some fresh air.

"Mind yourself on these streets," Canning warned, "Rio can be a dangerous place, particularly after nightfall. Take my cudgel lying by the door. Just the sight of it should dissuade any potential troublemakers."

Nate made his way to the port. About halfway down the wharf he found the ship he was looking for. An American flag flew from the staff. He exchanged a few words with the quartermaster, who went below and returned with another man. Nate engaged him in a brief conversation, saluted, then handed him a packet addressed to the secretary of state. Hopefully, this would ease his way home.

Leaving the American ship, Nate's attention was drawn to the preparations in progress across the quay for getting a vessel underway. *Strange, at this time of night.* Then he realized the ship was a well-armed Dutch East Indiaman.

Things are starting to make sense.

No one troubled the tall American, either going or coming.

The next morning, Canning confirmed it would be at least another six weeks or more until a ship left for England.

Distraught, William declared, "I'll swim there if I have to."

"That won't be necessary, Captain. But you'll have time to meet King John, if it can be arranged."

"I haven't come through hell and beyond to wait for anything at this point," he said, picking up his borrowed jacket.

"What do you intend?" Canning asked.

"Once you give me directions, I'm going straight to the plaza and demand an audience. The king has to acknowledge a direct representative of His Britannic Majesty."

"That's a terrible idea, Captain," the merchant said. "Be a shame for you to meet your end in the plaza after coming all this way." Canning took a sip of tea, swallowed, then sighed. "And so close to returning home. I'm sure your loved ones would miss you."

The merchant's words found their mark. William said soberly, "I'm listening."

Canning said, "You must not approach the monarch directly—that would be interpreted as a grave offense. Going to the plaza will only work if you quietly and respectfully petition the captain of the guard for a brief word once there's a break in the negotiations. John may be amenable to seeing you, particularly if his parley with the rebel officers is going well. In fact, I agree that you should leave for the plaza immediately; the king is popular and usually concludes these things rather rapidly, especially if his son, Dom Pedro, is there."

"Why his son?"

"Pedro is a favorite, not only with the soldiers, but with everyone."

William took Canning's advice and set off for the plaza accompanied by Bidwell; Cauã and Pax trailed behind. It seemed the only ones walking in the heat besides themselves were the poor. The preferred mode of transport for the gentry appeared to be carriages pulled by horses or litters carried by slaves. Those in bondage were everywhere and engaged in all manner of activities: carrying parcels and drums of fresh water, sweeping the sidewalks, and selling fish and vegetables from small roadside stalls. Slave overseers lounged in the shade, truncheons and whips close at hand.

Within minutes, Nate and William came to the square that served as the major market site in Brazil for the sale of slaves. They skirted the market and saw that preparations for an auction were in progress.

Confused at the sight of shackled people shuffling along under the beating sun, including children his age, Cauá paused and stared. "Let's go, Cauá," William said gently, wanting to avoid any trouble that might call attention to them. At his side, Pax growled at the slave drivers and bared his teeth.

Although the slaves had been bathed in preparation for sale, a faint residual odor wafted toward the men. Childhood memories of the stench from the slave ships moored on the Boston waterfront washed over the American.

"Human misery," Nate said grimly.

Several coaches of customers waiting for sales to begin were drawn up on the opposite side of the plaza; countless others were still arriving. One particularly formal carriage, accompanied by guards, was forced to come to a halt by the traffic. The passengers, a striking woman dressed in a gray riding suit and her young companion, appeared uncomfortable and out of place.

At that moment, a slave child in chains sighed and collapsed with exhaustion. The overseer approached her.

Nate fixed the man with a loathsome glare; tension crackled about the American like a living thing.

The slaver brought his whip back as far as he could and growled in English, "Get up, you lazy little cur," then struck the child a nasty blow. She shuddered and curled hard into herself, further provoking the man's wrath. "I'll teach you how we does things here!" He raised his arm to strike her again.

The blow never came.

A hundred and ninety pounds of lunging American hit the slaver in the small of the back: The blow knocked the wind out of him and drove him to the ground, skittering his whip across the square. Bidwell rammed his knee into the shocked man's crotch, leaving the brute writhing in pain.

Breathing heavily, the American rose; behind him, another slaver was preparing to strike him in the back of the head with the butt of a pistol.

Two years in a Brazilian prison. Sarah will understand. William grabbed the man's arm and twisted violently back until the pistol clattered to the ground. Pax joined in, savaging the man's ankle. Cauã picked up the weapon.

"Stop!" ordered the commander assigned to patrol the slave market, his saber poised inches away from William's chest. "Raise your hands over your heads! Now!" Beside him, half a dozen Brazilian soldiers had their weapons leveled.

The overseer who had hit the girl continued to lie on the ground, moaning.

Rubbing his arm where William had twisted it, the other slaver complained, "You saw it, Lieutenant," he said, and added in a broad Yankee accent, "They was interfering with us controlling the merchandise."

The rubbing ceased and the slave driver squinted at Nate. "Hold on there," he suddenly exclaimed, his eyes widening. "I know you— you're Simon Bidwell's son." He turned to the Brazilian soldier. "This man here's wanted for murder in America! You've got to arrest them!"

The officer said to William and Nate, "You're under arrest for interfering with a business operation and for attacking a merchant. And you, sir," he addressed Nate, "to answer the charge of murder."

"Officer, you will release these men!" At the edge of the square the beautiful woman in the open carriage frowned indignantly. Accompanied by an armed cavalry escort under the banner of the queen's household guard, she insisted, "It's illegal to harm a child, slave or not, Lieutenant, and that brute was whipping that girl. You'll release them into my custody immediately."

"Julia?" Mouth agape, Nate stared at the woman attempting to save them from being thrown in prison. With an almost imperceptible nod, Julia cast her eyes down.

William nudged the American; Nate followed the British officer's lead and bowed his head.

"I cannot do that, Lady," the officer said respectfully. "By law, I must detain them until a magistrate determines their fate. And this man stands accused of murder."

"Has he been accused of murder here or elsewhere in our country? No." Julia paused. "All you have is the claim of this swine. Do I need to send word to the queen herself?"

"I will not release them, my lady. You may accompany us to the plaza to see the king's captain of the guard. I answer to him. He can decide their fate."

"Very well. Unshackle that child and place her in my carriage, along with her parents; we will visit our king and queen together."

The lieutenant and his soldiers marched Nate and William to the plaza; accompanied by the "Lady" Julia and her entourage, they made quite the parade.

Nate spoke out the side of his mouth. "My apologies, Captain." William smiled—it was the first time he had addressed the British officer by his correct rank. "I saw red back there."

"Nothing else for it, Yank. It's only too bad those bastards can still walk."

They arrived at a plaza flanked on three sides by military barracks. Companies of soldiers stood at ease. The troops stood in small knots, talking quietly; a group in the far corner was playing cards in the shade of a tree. Around a table under a white canopy in the center of the square, there was an ongoing discussion of some sort. It appeared that the king was in the midst of a meeting with military officers. Nate and William were onlookers to King John and Dom Pedro's parley with the rebels.

There were several uniformed officers standing around the table, and perhaps two or three civilians. There certainly didn't seem to be much tension, and at one point laughter could be heard from the group.

Pax decided this was as good a time as any to make his move. He launched himself at the officer who had arrested them. William yelled and made a grab for the big dog but tripped and knocked over the soldier next to him. Julia covered her face, embarrassed, while Nate dragged Pax away before the dog got shot. Cauã hugged Pax, stroking and whispering to calm him.

The commotion at the edge of the square didn't go unnoticed.

Looking at the source of the disturbance, the king was amused. His wife, Queen Carlota, sat on his left; a young man sat on his right. Several other officers were off to the side having a discussion under the shade of the canopy.

Having successfully concluded negotiations with the officers, King John said, "Dear, I see your ever-alert companion Julia has found a couple of wild-looking fish. They appear to be of a different sort. I wonder why they've been taken into custody."

The attractive queen was dressed in finery, and her long hair hung loosely about her shoulders. "John," she whispered to her husband, "why don't we see why my bodyguard has brought these men here?"

At a signal, the captain of the guard escorted the British officer and the American across the square, accompanied by Julia.

"What have we here, Julia?" King John asked his wife's bodyguard with a kindly smile. Even in the warmth of the square, the clean-shaven king wore a regal white uniform jacket buttoned up to his neck and a red sash. He certainly wouldn't be called handsome, but his eyes were intelligent and kind.

"Your Majesty." Lady Julia offered a deep bow. "These men are simple adventurers. One is British, the other American. They were on their way to see you when they had a disagreement with a slave overseer mistreating his people at the market. They intervened."

The captain of the guard interjected, "Your Majesty, one of the slavers said the American is accused of murder in his country."

"Captain," King John said politely, "no crime has been committed in Brazil. And seeing how we are presently surrounded by hundreds of my troops, I see no immediate threat from these two men."

The king's son, Dom Pedro, laughed, "Your Britannic Majesty is truly favored when he commands such noble men as you, who tour the world to entertain us. Surely you men are traveling minstrels?"

About the same age as William and Nate, Dom Pedro was handsome and clean shaven, with hazel eyes and dark-brown hair. He wore simple nankeen trousers, a high-necked white cotton shirt, and a striped tan jacket. Protected by the shade of the canopy, he had rested his straw hat on his lap.

Before William could answer, Pedro added, "Does your dog do tricks?"

William looked up. "No, Your Majesty, Pax is a hunting dog . . ." While William was speaking, King John had lifted his hand, and Pax sat. Then with a brief whistle, the king had him roll over.

"Bravo!" the queen said, and clapped her hands.

Astonished, William finished, ". . . and our constant companion. The boy is an orphan from the jungle, now in our charge. And please, Your Majesty, excuse our appearance. We've been in the Amazon for many long months and these ill-fitting garments were hastily borrowed."

"But what could compel you to undertake such dangerous journey?" John was incredulous.

"I am searching for New World plants for the king's repository, with the purpose of securing those of a particularly curative nature."

The penetrating look of her bodyguard, Julia, intrigued the queen. She whispered to John that perhaps it was time to take leave of the military men with whom he had been negotiating.

The king addressed the gathered officers: "I thank you for your time, gentlemen, and your willingness to put aside your arms and speak on the friendly terms that we have always enjoyed. My minister will draw up the papers and present them for your signatures in the next few days."

The rebellion was over.

From the outset of his regency, King John had demonstrated his adherence to the principles of the enlightenment. It was not unusual that he should end a rebellion without bloodshed, yet both William and Nate were impressed.

The king and queen stood.

"Captain, you will kindly arrange a carriage and escort the foreigners to the palace as our guests."

CHAPTER 56

THE KING AND QUEEN

São Cristóvão Palace, home of the rulers of Brazil, was located several miles outside the city center on the top of a small hill. Builders were constantly at work on the palace and outbuildings, the subjects of countless renovations.

The captain of the guard and his mounted troop accompanied the elaborate carriage as it trundled along the paved road. The passengers traversed farmland and fruit groves before coming to the decorative portico that fronted the palace, a gift from the English Duke of Northumberland.

"What's the bother, Yank?" William asked. "You look as though you've eaten rotten fish." He had never seen the American so agitated. "You should be overjoyed that we're not in some hellhole of a Brazilian prison," the Brit reminded him, "instead, we're in a charming coach on our way to the palace."

"It's probably nothing."

"Come now, spit it out. You can trust me."

Nate considered for a moment. "There's more to this Lady Julia than meets the eye, Gunn."

"What are you talking about?"

"I've met her before."

William laughed. "Next you're going to tell me you slept with her." William continued laughing, giving Nate the opportunity to join in.

Nate remained silent.

"No." William was aghast. "It's simply not possible, man. We've been in the bloody jungle for I don't know how many months." He looked at Nate. "Tell me you left matters on good terms."

Nate grinned.

"Never mind," William spoke quickly, "just tell me I have nothing to worry about."

"You have nothing to worry about. Probably."

William gave a hollow laugh. "Oh, yes, a double-dealing former flame who may or may not have an axe to grind. I'm sure with our luck, she'll tell the queen to throw us a parade. They'll build a statue and name a day for us."

Inside the palace, servants took Cauã and Pax to the kitchen so the staff could fuss over the young boy and the dog. The British officer and the American were led down a long hall cushioned with a light-green carpet. At the end of the hall, they descended a winding staircase to a lower level, where they were shown to guest rooms next to each other. The tall, open windows in both allowed in the light and a fresh breeze. Lunch was brought, along with wash basins and linen towels.

William had just finished eating when a servant arrived and led him upstairs to meet the king and queen. He wasn't surprised to be going alone. He figured the queen—or her husband—couldn't be overly excited about seeing the American.

Once on the main floor he was led to a room used for informal functions. The light blue walls, white ceiling, and wide windows framed from the outside by a line of tall trees that shaded the side of the palace, created an airy atmosphere, while the sky-blue carpet underfoot, plush chairs, and cut flowers in tall vases made for a cozy room.

"Come in. Please make yourself comfortable," the king said in English. He dismissed the guards and waved his hand toward a settee across from the couch on which he sat with the queen. A servant placed a silver tea service on a low table in front of them.

John said, "I understand you are Captain William Gunn of His Majesty's Dragoon Guards. Carlota's bodyguard, Julia, has told us of your most noble mission to bring, through great personal adversity, a secret offer of assistance from your king to General Bolívar. Your king must have great faith in you to trust you with such a mission."

"Your Highnesses—" William began.

John interrupted, "First of all, William, we'll have none of that in here. In this room, I am John and my wife is Carlota."

Carlota poured tea, handed a cup to William, and said, "How on earth did that little Indian boy come to be with you?"

"His mother perished helping us to escape a difficult situation. I promised to keep him safe."

"You certainly have no intention of taking him to England, do you? You're welcome to leave him here at the palace. He will be well educated and cared for."

"With all due respect, Your Majesty, I consider myself under an obligation. The boy will remain with my family as long as I draw breath."

"Very well, William. I must compliment you on your loyalty. We so admire a man who keeps his word." She smiled. "Especially to his last breath."

John spoke again. "We have chosen to meet you in our family room because we consider England to be part of our family. Our two countries have always enjoyed a close relationship."

Charmed by their familiarity, William was also wary. He had enough experience with nobility to know such magnanimity would last only so long as Nate and he agreed with them. He took their silence and expectant gazes as a cue to speak.

"Yes," he began, very carefully, "a very close relationship. And it is the express wish of our king that this close connection continue. To be specific, the king would like to renew the Treaty of 1808."

"That might very well happen," said Carlota, "but there are strains on our empire of which you may not be aware."

William was alert. "Strains?"

John replied, "The bankers and merchants in Portugal are insisting I return to Lisbon to endorse a constitution they have concocted in the name of enlightened liberalism. It may remove much of the absolute power of the monarch, but it is also a thin disguise to return Brazil to the dark ages of being a mere colony of Portugal."

Carlota added passionately, "Brazilians have enjoyed free and open trade ever since John arrived here as regent. And my husband guaranteed these rights when he declared Brazil to be an equal partner in the Kingdom of Portugal. Now the Cortes wants to force Brazil back into colonyhood, excluding trade with anyone but Portugal. They also refuse to endorse John's support of the abolition of slavery across Europe."

"We desperately require British assistance," John interjected, "so that I can resist the most extreme of these measures. So far, your British king insists his public is in no mood for any more war adventures. But I'm prepared to offer Great Britain very generous terms if your king can be persuaded to provide covert military aid to us. The main problem, you see, is that we have no champion in the British court to convince him to do this."

"However, if your duke supported us," Carlota said, "we believe your king would reconsider and send us British assistance. All we ask for is clandestine support, much like Britain is giving Bolívar."

"And you somehow think I can help in this?" William was mystified at this totally unexpected turn of events.

Carlota and John traded glances, but it was the queen who spoke first. "Everyone has their spies, Captain Gunn."

"Tell me if I have this correct," William said. "You will consider renewing the treaty only if Britain secretly assists you in resisting the more extreme measures of the Cortes—measures which would return Brazil to its former status as a colony and deprive her people of the full rights of citizens."

"William, William," John said with a conciliatory tone, "you are being harsh. All we wish is for you to convince the duke to represent our interests to the king."

William was frustrated. "You vastly overestimate my influence on the duke. Before my mission, I was merely one of his gardeners, and he has a multitude of those. His Grace rarely tipped his hat in passing. I'm afraid I wouldn't be of much help even if I could approach the duke."

Carlota and John shared a long glance; a current of understanding passed between them. She put her teacup on the table.

Emboldened by their overtures, William asked, "You would do me a great turn, personally, if any of your naturalists know of the presence of a black orchid in your country, or anywhere in your empire for that matter. It is of utmost importance to me, and more important for you, it is of importance to the duke as well."

Carlota said, "I learned of your search from my companion. You were unsuccessful in finding your black orchid in the Amazon?"

"I'm afraid I never found the plant," he lied. "Maybe it's just a myth, like everyone says."

"That's truly a shame, to have traveled such a long way and come up empty-handed. We will make some inquiries. Is that satisfactory?"

"I would be most grateful, Your Majesty."

"With your long absence," she said, "your daughter's health must weigh on you."

"Time has always been my enemy," he replied, shifting uneasily. "I *must* see my daughter. But there's no ship leaving for home for at least six more weeks. If I could, I would have left yesterday."

John said, "You don't have to wait, Captain."

"I don't understand, Your Majesty. I was told the next ship to England wouldn't leave for almost two months."

"Perhaps merchant vessels. But a ship arrived here this morning. I believe you know her captain quite well: Darius Acton. He has orders to quietly transport the queen and myself to Portugal ahead of the rest of the royal court. But I'm certain he would be more than happy to afterward bring you back to your duke. You may want to take advantage of this opportunity, particularly if our inquiries regarding your plant are futile."

William was speechless.

"We leave on the morning tide," John continued, "so it's best if you spend the night here, in the palace. There's an official reception this evening, should you like to attend. There'll be some interesting people there, including Captain Acton."

William said, "I look forward to it."

John said, "Perhaps as repayment for our arranging your swift passage home, you will at least consider stressing our need to your duke. You may exert more influence than you realize. Your reappearance alone will surprise many."

It was Nate's turn to be interviewed by the monarchs, but this time Julia was present as well. "Your Majesties," Julia announced as Nate entered the room, "this is Mr. Nathanial Bidwell of the United States, also known as Yankee."

Nate looked into the room before entering. Julia rolled her eyes. John, trying to put the man at ease, said warmly, "You're here as our personal guest," and indicated for the American to sit in a chair next to Julia.

Affecting a casual air, Nate made a small bow and took his seat.

"I believe you're already acquainted with my bodyguard and companion, Julia Mendoza?" The queen indicated Julia with a nod of her head.

Nate's eyes went wide, but the queen interjected before he could speak. "I understand your confusion," Carlota said, "but please try to forgive us for our deception. We deemed it essential to forge a strong bond with General Bolívar, but it was critical we send the proper emissary. My bodyguard, Julia, who was raised in New Granada, volunteered. Because this was a secret assignment, she had to travel covertly and could not reveal her true identity to anyone but him."

Nate nodded, pretending to understand. "I understand."

Queen Carlota said, "The strong alliance she created with our new neighbors to the north made her absence easier to bear"—she smiled—"but only by a little. You see, she is also my closest female companion."

Julia spoke, "I told King John and Queen Carlota about the fabled lost emerald of the Muzos, Yankee, and said that if anyone could find *El Jefe*, it was you." She cocked her head and asked, "So, Nate, do you have *El Jefe*?"

He was surprised and wary at this line of questioning. "The prize was close, my lady, but *El Jefe* slipped through my fingers." He was not going to mention Marquez.

"We would pay a great deal for such a gem," the queen offered, testing him. "Traveling with such a treasure would be most dangerous for you, while a letter of credit in your name from the Brazilian king would be so much more secure."

The veiled threat didn't escape him. He said, "Your Majesties, I got there too late. That's it. The emerald was gone." He paused thoughtfully, then the penny dropped.

Julia manipulated me into chasing down the emerald for them! It had nothing to do with Bolívar's regrets over my dismissal, it was all about my finding the emerald for her queen.

The threat was still unmistakable, so instead of venting his anger, Nate let out a deep breath and said, "What's the rest of the plan?"

The king responded, "In Lisbon the Cortes, supported by the bankers and business interests, wishes to roll back my father's democratic reforms and return Brazil to a land of destitute colonials. They also hope to block any efforts to end slavery.

"Events are moving most quickly, Mr. Bidwell. The queen and I intend to sail to Portugal tomorrow. But without outside support, I am afraid I will fail in preventing the return of Brazil to subjugation as colony. The only nation capable of lending the support we need is Great Britain, but all our formal overtures to the British monarch have been rejected."

"What does the emerald have to do with all this?" Nate asked.

"We desperately need a powerful friend in Britain, someone who has the king's ear, and his confidence. That person is the man who sent Captain Gunn on his mission to Bolívar, and that emerald is the key to getting his help."

"The Duke of Devonshire," Queen Carlota finished, "happens to be an avid gemologist and collector of precious stones. For such an incomparable gift," she stressed, "the duke would have to at least consider intervening with the British king on our behalf."

Nate said, "I'm sorry, but none of us win. As I just said, I simply don't have it. There's no one who wants that gem more than I do, but wishing it is not going to make it happen."

"Just know that should you come by the emerald and see fit to entrust it to us, you would be ensuring the freedom of Brazil and the ban on slavery in a major portion of the world."

The king drew up. "I will return to Portugal and do everything in my power to ensure Brazil remains a country free to determine her own future. Not unlike your own young country. The tides of freedom cannot be halted, Mr. Bidwell."

"If you say so," Nate replied.

CHAPTER 57

THE LORD LOVES A TRIER

Nate stopped by William's room and found the British officer resting on the four-poster bed. "They're playing us, Gunn, just like that awful Brit game."

"If you're referring to cricket, I don't see how," William said. "They're in a very difficult situation, Yank—impossible actually. They're just trying to do the right thing but need help to succeed."

"You didn't tell them about the orchids, did you?"

"Of course not."

"Then I don't know why they're so convinced I have the emerald."

"I don't know that they are convinced," William said. "They're just desperate. But the good news is I'm leaving with them tomorrow on the *Voyager*—the very ship which brought me to South America."

"You're going to join their cause?"

"Don't be ridiculous. Captain Acton was assigned to bring the king and queen to Portugal. After he drops them off, he'll take me to England."

"Well, I'm happy for you."

"You don't have to go back to America, Bidwell. Back home I can put in a good word for you, if you'd like. The people I work for could probably use an occasionally handy fellow like yourself."

"Thanks, Admiral, but I have some loose ends in the States that need tidying up. And in any event, no one would ever forgive a Yankee who turned lobsterback."

"Come to the reception tonight anyway. You can watch me throttle the Dutchman."

"Wouldn't miss it for the world."

Later that evening, Nate was in his room preparing for the reception, trying on clothes the king's tailor had provided, when there was a knock on the door.

"Come in," he called out.

Julia entered. She glared at him. "I am certain you have *El Jefe*," she said without preamble.

"That's a fine how-do-you-do, my lady," Nate said with a mock bow.

"It was Bolívar's idea to have you search for the emerald," she said. "He was certain the treasure existed. He said if anyone could find *El Jefe*, it would be you. But neither of us ever actually expected to see you again."

"Sorry to disappoint you, Julia. But no emerald." Nate gave her an intense look. "So, if I just happened to survive earthquakes, ambushes, headhunters, rapids, and waterfalls, not to mention an endless green hell filled with more ways to meet the devil than can be imagined, I was supposed to just hand the gem over to you?"

She persevered. "You don't want to understand, because you feel used. Listen to me," she pleaded. "Without British assistance, we lose our fight. And if we lose, our people will sink into an abyss of slavery, inquisitors, and poverty."

He said, "You're a simple schemer."

He deftly avoided the knee intended for his groin, but never saw the hard backhand slap that ripped across his face.

He rubbed his cheek, which took on the blush of undercooked beef. "Now *that's* the Julia I know."

She shook her head. "After all you've been through with the British captain, I expected more. I thought you would have learned something from him about loyalty."

"Loyalty?" Nate asked. "I'm surprised you know the word."

"I get it, American, you don't have the emerald. Thank you for nothing, and may God forgive you." She stormed out, leaving Nate alone with his cherry-red cheek.

CHAPTER 58

OLD FRIENDS

That evening at the palace, King John VI and Queen Carlota Joaquina were in the brightly lit entrance hall, greeting their guests: the wealthy and influential of Rio, along with those other lucky few who had managed to secure an invitation to the reception. The waiting line ran from the entrance to the bottom of the marble steps fronting the palace, where ornate carriages continued to deposit passengers. The music from the orchestra wafted through the open windows to welcome the arrivals. This final soiree of the royals before they departed for Portugal was not an event to be missed. Soldiers at the foot of the steps relieved the invitees of any weapons before allowing them to enter the queue.

Nate was still in the anteroom when the Brit entered.

William said, "Are you sure you won't be joining me in England?"

"Not this time, Gunn, I'll take my chances on returning to the States."

They could vaguely hear the names of the guests being announced outside.

William said, "Time to join the party."

The reception was held in the palace ballroom, a vast sparkling white room with a vaulted, decorative ceiling. Well-lit by countless candles, the spacious area was filled with the intoxicating scent of jasmine drifting in through the oversized windows facing the garden.

A man in the dress uniform of a British naval officer threaded his way through the guests, his head visible above the crowd. He touched William's elbow.

"Captain Acton!" William said.

Darius Acton took the British officer's hand and shook it warmly. "Being unsure of your status here, Mr. Gunn, I believe a handshake instead of a salute is the best choice."

"Considering this crowd, you choose wisely," William said. Recalling Acton's cold demeanor on their parting in Barranquilla, William was surprised by his warm greeting. "I must say, I'm most delighted to see you again, Captain. I hope you arrived in that fast brig of yours to whisk me back to England?"

Darius Acton glanced at Nate and hesitated to answer.

William steered Acton and Bidwell to a relatively quiet corner of the room.

"My apologies, Captain," William said, "this is Nathanial Bidwell, my very experienced American guide." Turning to Nate, William said, "Two years ago, Captain Acton was kind enough to drop me off in Barranquilla."

Nate shook Acton's hand. "You weren't doing him any favors," the American quipped.

Captain Acton grinned and relaxed somewhat. He said to William, "It's a miracle you managed to survive the Amazon."

"It's safe to say I wouldn't be standing here without his help," William said, indicating Nate. "But how is it you've come to Rio, and at this time?" he asked Acton.

"I had secret orders to transport the royals to Portugal posthaste. Our disguise as a merchantman would allay the suspicions of even the most curious. Then one of our coastal mail packets in Belém picked up a Portuguese trader out of Manaus. He told a strange tale of two skeletal white men upriver, one with a strange accent claiming to be a British officer. I figured it could only be you."

A Brazilian officer interrupted and offered his apologies. He detached Captain Acton and led him away to meet a group of men on the other side of the reception.

Under his breath William exclaimed, "Son of a bitch!"

"What?" Nate asked.

"Abel Veeborlay."

"Bless my soul," the Dutchman said, "if it's not Captain Gunn, of all the people I never expected." The perspiring, overweight businessman pasted on a broad smile. He approached the men with one hand extended, the other holding a hat.

"Stow it, Dutch," William scoffed. "Do you think I've forgotten about Marquez? That murdering bastard tried to kill me twice."

"A fanatical papist in the direct employ of the Catholic monarchs of Spain, whom I have absolutely nothing to do with. An honest to goodness son of a bitch, I agree. I am truly sorry you had to cross paths with him."

Veeborlay looked hard at the rangy young man next to the British captain. The Dutchman stuck out his hand. "I don't believe we've met. Mr. Yankee, is it? Or Bidwell? I get easily confused in my old age."

"Best clear up that confusion if you want to get any older." Nate smiled coldly and didn't extend his hand.

Abel Veeborlay was no fool and knew not to trifle with these men. "My apologies, Mr. Bidwell, that was uncalled for." He extended his arms as if to encompass them in a distant embrace. "You should know I'm a great admirer of you both. There was rumor some time ago an American went missing in the Muzo area, a Nathanial Yankee. And no word from you, Captain Gunn, since descending into the abominable Amazon. Yet here you both appear, healthy, and in the thick of things, so to speak."

William asked casually, "What brings you to Rio?"

"There's no need for any drama, gentlemen," Veeborlay said, "my plans are no great secret. I wanted to meet the king, and there's been speculation he may leave for Portugal."

William looked around. The room was becoming quite full. Their conversation could easily be overheard. He looped his arm through Veeborlay's and pulled him closer. He said, "Something, or things, managed to drag you out of New Granada. We're going for a short stroll, and you're coming along. You're going to tell me everything I want to know, Dutch."

The Dutchman tried to disengage. "I'm afraid I really must protest,

Captain, I have people to meet—" A sharp jab cut him short. Nate had positioned himself to hide the object he held firmly to the Dutchman's side. Veeborlay's normally amiable expression took on a definite air of distress.

They walked Veeborlay toward the balcony. Once outside on the empty veranda, William closed the doors behind them. "Is it part of your job description to oust our British merchants from Brazil? Going to revive the Dutch East India Company all on your own?"

Veeborlay shrugged. "How could I refuse to serve the company after you dispatched their only man in South America almost two years ago? Their best agent, I might add." The sharp object dug deeper. The first prickle of panic ran along his spine. He replied softly, "My good Captain, did I not provide you with excellent information when you needed it, and good companions? And," he added desperately, "had I not restrained Lieutenant Rodriquez, you and your men would either be at the bottom of the Magdalena or stuck in a Barranquilla jail."

"What have you offered King John?" William asked.

"The company extended substantial aid to the king in his upcoming struggle in Portugal, in exchange for favorable treaty conditions. But I strongly suspect the king knows it's an empty offer. The company simply doesn't have the resources—not yet, anyway."

He let them digest that before saying, "I'll be sailing back to Europe to report, then I'll return to South America. You'll be pleased to know one of my reports will be to Whitehall."

"It looks like you're playing everyone this time," William said brightly. "You should be able to retire, Abel, if this gamble works out for you."

Veeborlay stiffened. "Why does anyone come to the Americas from Europe if it is not to steal what they have and bring it home." The Dutchman stuck out his jaw. "I may be a pirate, but so are all who sail these shores. Take the knife out from between your teeth before you look to take a sanctimonious tone with me, plant hunter."

Nate tightened his grip on Veeborlay's arm. He caught William's eye. "This isn't a cavalry charge or a pistol duel." William nodded and Nate pulled the Dutchman to the side. "Would your itinerary include a stop in Spain first? Think carefully before you answer."

Veeborlay saw the hard look in the American's eyes. This man was capable of anything. Veeborlay's shoulders slumped. He nodded.

"Where are you meeting the Spaniard?"

"Is that all you want to know?" Dutch didn't hesitate to answer, his life was worth more than any fanatical papist. "On the ship."

"Which ship?"

"The Dutch ship *Prins Willim II* bound for Cádiz."

"When does *he* board?" The hand tightened around his arm. "If I don't like what I hear the next time you open your mouth . . ." The blade pinched. "Quick!"

"No need for the dramatics, please," he gasped. "He'll board late, when it's quiet and he won't be observed. Just before departure. He'll go aboard then."

"When's departure?"

"On the late tide, tonight."

"Not a word, Dutchman," Nate threatened, "to the Spaniard or anyone else. Or you're dead."

William bent toward him. He said softly, "Abel Veeborlay, if you wish to partly make amends, keep your British stipend, and not have to worry about how or when I will even the score, I would have you do something."

The businessman eyed the British officer with great respect tinged with an element of fear. He said nervously, "If it is in my power."

William placed something in his hand. "Give these to the Sheridans, and tell them I am truly sorry."

"Consider it done. On my return to Barranquilla."

William opened one of the doors. With the relieved Dutchman gone, the weapon had disappeared under Nate's jacket.

William looked at him with raised eyebrows.

Nate reached into his jacket and held up the object which had encouraged the Dutchman. It was the sharp end of a stiff quill pen. He shrugged and smiled. "Closest thing I could find," he said, and tossed it off the balcony.

"I'll be seeing you, Gunn. There's a score that I need to go settle."

CHAPTER 59

Getting What You Deserve

Leaning on his crutch for support, the ancient sailor shuffled onto the planks of the darkened pier. In all likelihood, an old mariner unable to sleep and taking a late-night stroll, recounting memories of former sea voyages as he wandered a well-worn route among the docks.

The wharf was lit by oil lamps from the boarding decks of the three vessels with their gangways still extended. The quay was mostly quiet at this time of night, save for the noises typical of wooden ships tied alongside a pier and the sound of scuttling rats. The few rodents that didn't flee at the old man's approach received a smart blow from his crutch.

Marquez chuckled whenever he managed to send one of the vermin flying. Hunched under a frayed blue coat, his face concealed by a long beard and wide-brimmed hat, the Spaniard made his way slowly toward the Dutch East Indiaman at the far end of the dock.

Well aware of the Brazilian hostility toward the Spanish, he had hidden his identity ever since arriving back in civilization. His prior arrangements with Abel Veeborlay for a secret transfer from Rio to Cádiz were about to be realized. If word had leaked of this arrangement, the loaded Chaumette pistol held in his free hand under the old coat would soon discourage any interference.

He hobbled along, the treasure secure in a satchel underneath his coat. He restrained the urge to quicken his pace.

The inactivity on the waterfront pleased Marquez, not that he expected much to be happening at this late hour. Aside from the rats and a drunken sailor locked in soulless fornication with a tart in the shadows, all was quiet. He had been assured by the Dutchman that as soon as Marquez was aboard the *Prins Willim II*, the ship would depart on the early-morning ebb, directly for Spain.

With his intimate connections to the Spanish court and the Vatican, the inquisitor was valued cargo. And the treasure he carried in his shoulder pack ensured he would be most welcome in those stately European palaces.

He spotted the East Indiaman, the gangway extended and lit for his arrival. The sight urged him onward. His shambling quickened.

Marquez paused. Possessing the instincts of a wild animal, he withdrew his pistol; he spun, and impulsively jerked backward from an object swung at his head. Instead of rearranging the side of his face, the heavy cudgel glanced off his arm.

Stumbling from the blow, Marquez fired off balance; the shot grazed Nate's face. The Spaniard yelled, "Thief! Thief!"

The American was dressed as a common sailor; the prostitute he'd hired for the ruse was nowhere to be seen.

Shouts and activity could be heard coming from the Dutch ship. They would be here in moments, and the contest would be over.

Bidwell allowed the cudgel to swing in a wide arc, not giving the Spaniard time to recover, and swung the heavy head of the club up between Marquez's legs.

With a grunting expulsion of breath, the inquisitor went down in a heap. The American tore the blue coat off the Spaniard's back and cut the straps holding the satchel. He looked at the groaning Spaniard on the pier, weighed the cudgel in his hand, then glimpsed the men rushing toward them. *No time.*

"Your lucky day, Spaniard."

There was no escape down the pier the way he had arrived; he crossed to the other side of the wharf and halted at the edge between the two docked ships. He glanced back: Marquez moaned, trying desperately to crawl after him. The sailors from the Dutch ship were no more than a couple of dozen paces away and closing fast. Several raised muskets.

Bidwell looked past the pier and the docked ships, out at the black ocean beyond. Hefting the satchel he had taken from the Spaniard, he turned, gave a jaunty salute, and dropped over the side into the darkness below.

CHAPTER 60

PARTING OF WAYS

Bidwell landed with a soft thump in the dinghy, which floated at the bottom of the ladder. *Good thing the tide's in.*

Shouting, interspersed with the sounds of running men, filled the night. Several musket shots rang out, the rounds singing in the air overhead. One tore into the dock, kicking up splinters that showered the men below.

"Sounds like all hell's broken loose up there," William said, rowing strongly. Nate grabbed the second set of oars and pulled. Muffled with swaths of wrapped cloth, the oars were noiseless. William said softly, "We'll keep in the shadows and pull for the ocean-side of the *Voyager.*"

They rowed parallel to the pier. Nate timed his pull to match the British officer's. The shouting from the wharf was muted by the bulk of the docked vessels that came between them and their pursuers. Hidden behind the ships, the small dinghy was soon consumed by the night.

William asked in the same quiet voice, "Well?"

Nate stopped rowing, secured the oars, and opened the satchel he had taken from the Spaniard. He clenched his hands to stop their trembling. He carefully went through the items inside the bag—a small pistol, sheath knife, bandana, and money clip—before he found what he was looking for. Wrapped in an oilskin was a teak box. He lifted the lid of the box and opened the silk bag within. His heart pounded at the emerald sparkle from a dark-green gem the size of a man's fist.

"Sorry, Gunn." The British officer's last remaining hope for his daughter's cure had just been dashed, and Nate tried to dilute the elation in his voice. He tied the bag, wrapped the box, and put it back in the satchel.

William heard the sharp clang of a ship's bell. He coughed back a tightening in his throat and let out a deep breath, "Well done, Yank." He heaved powerfully on the oars.

Later that night, Nate was alone in his room in the palace. He was grateful that Captain Acton hadn't asked about the gunfire on the wharf and thankful that Acton had roused the ship's surgeon to tend to his wound. Fortunately, the American and the British officer hadn't met anyone on their way back.

Now that Nate had some privacy, he carefully unwrapped the parcel. To his surprise, his hand shook. *Didn't realize I was the nervous sort.*

He drew a sharp breath.

The gem was enormous, larger than he recalled from first sight. He held it up. Even the candlelight streaming through the emerald was enough to throw shards of deep-green fire around the room.

He exhaled in a soft whistle. For Nathanial Bidwell, *El Jefe* was the end to all his troubles. His luck had finally turned. He could not only buy his way back into the States but buy anything else as well.

There was a light knock at the door.

"One moment," he said, and hurriedly stowed the gem. He held a pistol behind his back and opened the door.

The young girl who had been whipped at the slave market stood there, holding a mug of hot cocoa. She took a couple of tentative steps forward and shyly held the drink up to Nate. The dress that Lady Julia had given the child almost hid the welts, but not entirely.

Knowing she must have waited for hours to perform this act of kindness, Nate's breath caught at the thoughtfulness of the little girl. He managed to say, "Thank you," but then choked up without really knowing why.

She smiled a beautiful, bashful smile for him, nodded, and backed out.

Nate put his pistol down and cupped the warm mug in his hands. He stared at the closed door for a long while.

The next morning, the American and the British officer rode toward the harbor together. Cauã sat behind William, while Pax ran alongside. The servants in the palace had opened their hearts to the orphan and his canine protector and had taken great care of them. The young boy had seen so much that was new to him that he was beyond being surprised at anything, even riding a horse.

Nate asked the British officer, "What did you give the Dutchman yesterday?"

"The Saint Christopher medals. The Sheridans should have them."

They were both quiet for a few minutes.

Nate broke the silence. "That slave girl who was whipped, Gunn . . ." Nate shook his head. "Do you know that smell when the slave ships pull into the docks?"

"Can't say that I do, Yank."

"The scent of death, Gunn. It never leaves you."

William said soberly, "If you're wanted for murder, Bidwell, I know the bastard deserved it."

Nate seemed to make his mind up about something and pulled his horse up. "What the hell, Gunn: my woman died, and I killed a man. He more than deserved it, and she didn't. And had I stayed, many more innocent people would have been hurt."

"I figured you for an honorable man"—a smile creased the Brit's sunburned face—"deep down, that is." He asked, "And you've reason to believe all is forgiven now?"

Nate appeared distracted. He said mysteriously, "If I play my cards right with this emerald, I'll come out on top in the end."

William didn't say anything for a beat. Weighing the good of the many was a fine topic for drawing-room conversations, but they were both too experienced to entertain any delusions that their actions could affect the fate of countries. Freedom was a fine word, but it was hard to see the sense in fine words when every day was a fight for survival. Nate had caught a break, and William couldn't begrudge him for it.

"I don't doubt it for a moment, Yank."

They rode down the wharf to the *Voyager,* where even at this early hour there was quite a bustle. There was a notably vacant space toward the end of the wharf, where the *Prins Willim* had been berthed.

Nate said, "Let's hope your duke's as generous as you believe. With everything you've done for him, there should be no question of his funding another search for the orchid." The American gave Cauã's shoulder a squeeze, then leaned over and rubbed Pax under his chin. When he stopped stroking, the big dog gave a yelp.

"And for God's sake, Gunn, teach that dog how to bark."

Jimmy, the cabin boy of the *Voyager,* met Cauã and Pax on the wharf and escorted them aboard. He was thrilled to have someone he could show around, not to mention the bonus of a big dog for company.

William followed them onto the gangway of the British brig-sloop. He turned and shook Nate's hand.

"Somehow, Yank, I have a feeling we haven't seen the last of each other."

Not long after, King John and Queen Carlota arrived on the dock alone, save for Lady Julia, whom Nate asked for a moment alone with. The queen gave a questioning glance, but Julia nodded and released her arm.

Nate walked Julia apart from the others and gripped her by the shoulders.

Julia was startled. "What do you think you're doing?"

"Just listen, please," Nate said fervently. "I've had time to think. Your king was wrong. The tide of freedom *can* be stopped. I've seen it— stopped dead in its tracks . . . by people like my father."

He took her hand and placed a heavy object wrapped in brown paper in her open palm, "Take it."

She looked from the object in her hand to the American.

"Don't say anything. I just know that if I don't do this, I might not regret it at first, but someday, I'd realize my mistake." He gazed at Julia and recalled the first time he'd seen her, lying half-drowned on a stream-bank on the side of a mountain.

The shock on her face was quickly replaced by doubt, then pure and simple astonishment when she opened the paper. "I never thought—"

Nate interrupted. "Someone once told me that doing the right thing regardless of whether anyone will ever know is what makes for greatness. I may be an idiot for doing this, but this may be my last chance to make that choice. What are the chances that this will work?"

Julia smiled, and then kissed him on the cheek.

"That's what I thought. God help the Portuguese when *you* hit Lisbon." He had never known her to be speechless before, but as the realization of this most extraordinary turn in their fortunes sank in, it appeared she was on the verge of tears.

She sniffed, regained her composure, and said with a crooked grin, "Sure, Yankee, me with my duck-foot pistol, right?"

"I suggest you leave now," Nate said, "before I change my mind."

She wiped the wetness off her cheek, squeezed his hand, then joined the king and queen at the foot of the gangway.

Captain Acton welcomed the Brazilians aboard. At the top of the gangway, John glanced back at Nate standing below on the dock and nodded once. Then the king put his arm around his wife's waist and went forward. Julia hesitated.

The walkway was drawn up and the lines cast off. Under the pull of the ebb and reduced sails, the ship moved slowly away from the dock.

The tidal flow gradually increased. Drifting out of the land shadow, a full complement of sails was set. A fresh breeze snapped the sheets taut, and the *Voyager* picked up speed.

The wharf emptied. The American alone remained, staring at the ship that slowly disappeared beneath the eastern horizon.

He felt the weight of the jungle pressing in behind him and counted the years that were left ahead.

He spoke aloud to himself, "I should at least have kept the dog."

CHAPTER 61

A PROPER CALLING CARD

Once *Voyager* cleared the harbor and secure quarters were piped, the hands battened down the ship, shifting from tasks associated with leaving their dockside berth to final preparations for a cross-Atlantic voyage.

"Mr. Evans, the deck and the conn are yours," the captain said, then turned to his guests, the Portuguese monarchs and Julia. "Perhaps you'll join me in my cabin."

The queen looked to her bodyguard, but Lady Julia hesitated. "I'd like to stay up here in the fresh air for just for a while longer, if that's all right. Captain Gunn will keep me company. I'll rejoin you shortly."

William Gunn and Lady Julia stared quietly over the taffrail at the rapidly widening gap between the *Voyager* and the green land. Julia realized she didn't know herself as well as she thought she did. She had been prepared to risk everything for Bolívar's success, including killing the man who was now responsible for enlisting the powerful Duke of Devonshire to their cause—if she could just convince the British officer to accept the emerald and to pass the gem to the duke.

William drew her attention to the wharf, rapidly shrinking toward the horizon. "I can still see him, just barely."

Julia strained. "Yes, I believe I can as well."

After a moment she said, "I'd have thought he'd be the first to leave the dock, headed for some scheme or the other."

The lone figure gradually diminished to a mere speck, then vanished.

They were quiet, content to weigh the lonely call of gulls mingling with the flutter of luffing sails. William pondered the strangeness of his partnership with the American.

She broke the silence. "How did you first meet Bidwell?"

"We fought at Boyacá together, under Santander."

"They say a bond forged in battle, Captain, is often unbreakable for life."

"In our case, my lady, I'm afraid the bond took a bit longer to forge than one battle. In fact, I came close to killing him once"—William grinned—"well, maybe twice."

"He does seem to have that effect on people. I know Bolívar wanted to be rid of him."

"There did appear to be quite a few people waiting in line."

"I was one, but I'm certainly glad I was unsuccessful."

"Perhaps he'll live longer, Julia, now that you and I are leaving the continent."

Lady Julia smiled, then grew serious. "On the matter of the black orchid, I wish to say again how sorry I am that there's no evidence of such a flower in Brazil." She laid her hand on his shoulder. "But the king and the queen both stressed that you are most welcome to come back to Brazil anytime to explore, with their full blessing and support."

"I appreciate their kind offer." William's words couldn't hide his disappointment.

Staring out to sea, the officer reviewed all that had happened over the past two years, burdened by the knowledge that he had failed his daughter. But at least he was finally heading home. He fervently hoped his daughter was alive and well so they could have a few more years together.

He straightened and looked around; it was the first time he really noticed the shipboard activity, the sailors' accents, and the quiet sea chants of their work. Suddenly William felt he was back in old England.

Julia moved from the port rail and leaned on a bulkhead to steady herself.

"Take this, Captain," she urged and held out a wooden box.

Intrigued, William took the box and turned it over in his hand.

Weighty for its size, the box was attractive—dark wood inlaid with ivory and mother-of-pearl.

"Please open it," she said.

Inside was a letter addressed to the Duke of Devonshire sealed with the king's stamp. There was also a royal-blue silk bag containing a roundish object.

"Please," she said, "be careful."

The British officer handed her the empty box, upended the bag, and dropped the item inside into the palm of his hand. His eyes widened.

"I want to say this is an emerald," he said slowly as he studied it, "but it's much too large."

"In fact, Captain Gunn, it's the largest uncut emerald in the world."

Struck by the priceless treasure in his hand, William was momentarily speechless. He considered the queen's bodyguard. "*El Jefe?*" he asked. "Bidwell sold you the emerald?"

"He gave it to us."

"*What!*" William couldn't keep the astonishment out of his voice.

"No one is more surprised than I am, Captain. A change of heart—for what reason, only he knows. But don't you see? This gives all of us hope."

William again considered the treasure he held in his hand.

"Our salvation, you might say, William, if only you will agree to present the gem to your duke. Please tell me you will do this on behalf of King John and Queen Carlota. We know this will impress His Grace with the need of all Brazil and the desire of her people to remain free."

"Why don't you just give it to him yourself? Why me?"

"Please try to understand. None of us can go anywhere near England. Nor can we send an open emissary. Your government cannot be seen to be aiding us. Everything we do must be in secret." She took his hand in both of hers and folded his fingers over the gem. "I firmly believe it is by the grace of God that you are here."

She dropped her arms to her sides; William's hand remained clasped over the sparkling jewel.

"I suggest you put that someplace safe. Then let us go below and join the others. All will be right soon, when we have both returned home."

CHAPTER 62

PARTING SHOTS

"Sail! Directly astern!" the lookout on the mainmast hailed the deck. Lieutenant Stephen Evans worked his way up to the lookout's station and gazed through his spyglass. A large three-masted ship appeared, hull-up with a bluff bow, stern raised above the main deck, and flying a full complement of sails.

The ship should have been spotted long before, when she was hull-down. Too much in-shore work and not enough blue-water sailing these past months had blunted the vigilance of the lookouts. It would be seen to, but not until the interloper was dealt with.

Evans recognized her lines; that ship had departed from Rio much earlier than they had and shouldn't be overtaking the *Voyager*. Something was not right.

"Keep an eye on her and let me know if anything changes."

"Aye, aye, sir."

The lieutenant returned to the deck and beckoned to a young midshipman. "If you please, inform the captain an East Indiaman directly astern of us, perhaps seven miles distant, is maintaining a constant bearing. She wears a full complement of sails and is gaining on us. Do you have all that?"

"Yes, sir," the boy replied and bounded below. Flushed with excitement, the midshipman flung open the door to the captain's cabin. "Sails spotted, sir!"

Inside with his guests, Darius Acton's eyebrows arched, and his lips twisted slightly downward. "It is customary, young man, to knock before entering. Please excuse the interruption," he said to the king, the queen, and William.

Embarrassed, the young middy shut up like a clam.

The captain favored the repentant youngster with a kindly glance. "Take a deep breath. Where away?"

"She's directly astern, sir!"

"Anything else?" the captain asked patiently.

"Yes, sir," he stammered. "Mr. Evans says she's an East Indiaman, perhaps seven miles distant and gaining on us."

"Very well. Tell Mr. Evans I shall be there presently."

He asked William, "Mr. Gunn, the name of the ship Veeborlay was to board?"

"The *Prins Willim II*, I believe."

"Well then, let's have a look, shall we?"

"Captain on deck!" the watch officer announced.

"Mr. Evans," Acton said, acknowledging the first lieutenant, "our situation?"

"The East Indiaman bears down on us, Captain," he reported. "If she maintains course and heading, she'll close within the hour." In a more confidential tone, the lieutenant added, "Sir, she's not as low in the water as one would expect a merchantman recently departed from Brazil."

The captain raised the spyglass. "You're right, Lieutenant. She must have left in a hell of a hurry." He stared through the glass for a long moment. "Her lines and her figurehead are familiar." He added softly so that only his deck officer could hear, "The bugger was waiting for us." He put the glass down and turned to his passengers. "We are being run down by your Dutchman, William." Darius Acton paused and smiled. "Not an entirely unexpected turn of events, considering the prominence of our passengers."

"I have to admire your nonchalance, Captain," King John said, "the *Prins Willim* must have a great many more men than the *Voyager*, and is more heavily armed, if I'm not mistaken."

The captain raised the spyglass again. "We have some surprises of our own, do we not, Stephen?"

The first lieutenant grinned. "Aye, sir, that we do."

Under a full spread of sails, the *Prins Willim II* ploughed through the dark-blue water. On her quarterdeck, Captain Hendrik de Jaager scrutinized his target through a spyglass. The English brig-sloop *Voyager* was clearly visible, dead ahead. Behind Jaager, Captain Ernesto Marquez paced impatiently, and Abel Veeborlay clung to the quarterdeck railing.

Marquez spat, "What are you pissing about for? We'll never catch them at this rate." The theft of the emerald gnawed at the inquisitor, his desire to recover the gem and kill those who'd stolen it increasing the more they neared their prey.

Jaager snapped back, "I have no need for your advice, sir." He should never have let this Catholic fanatic convince him to attack the British sloop. Now it was too late. He countered, "Every bit of available cloth is filled at the moment, unless you'd like to unhitch that blouse you're wearing. This is the best approach for a boarding."

Marquez said irritably, "I must be certain of your commitment, Captain Jaager."

The captain didn't reply but turned to the Dutch businessman. "Abel, you say you're absolutely certain they're on that ship? Everything depends on it."

Abel Veeborlay did not look entirely comfortable with either the swaying ship or the conversation. Veeborlay feebly assured him, "I guarantee you, my dear Captain, the king and the queen are returning to Portugal on *that* vessel." He managed to free one hand from the rail long enough to point at the sails in the distance. "And once they arrive, they intend to sign a democratic constitution."

The Spanish would pay handsomely to prevent the arrival of King John in Portugal. Ferdinand of Spain had only a loose hold on power and feared the appearance of a liberal state on his doorstep.

Marquez said to Captain Jaager, "Naturally, there will be no survivors?" It was as much a statement as a question.

"Is that prudent?" Veeborlay asked.

"Absolutely," the Spaniard said. "As far as anyone will ever know," he added flippantly, "they sank at sea, in a storm. No witnesses."

Captain Jaager considered this. They were a merchant vessel: Piracy and kidnapping were *not* what the company was ordinarily about. But these *were* special circumstances. In addition to a handsome sum in gold, Marquez had guaranteed Captain Jaager that, once the king was turned over to the Spanish, they would consider the Dutch East India Company as their primary trading partner.

With this daring move, Jaager alone could be responsible for resurrecting the company from the ashes of its former glory. The directors would canonize him. And since the *Prins Willim II* was the most heavily armed ship to ever fly the flag of the Dutch East India Company, a swift victory over the lightly armed British sloop was assured. Once he obtained a favorable trade agreement with the Spanish, the company would overlook what happened here.

"Don't worry, Abel," Captain Jaager said, "this will be over in a flash." The Dutch captain shot a glance at the Spaniard and grinned. "Storms happen at sea all the time."

Veeborlay said nothing.

On the *Voyager*, Captain Darius Acton spoke to his royal guests. "Please go below and assist in the infirmary for the upcoming action. It's the safest place during a battle."

"Consider, Captain," King John responded, "I'm an excellent shot and would be much more useful on the deck with a rifle."

"I, too, am no stranger to risk," Carlota said, "May Julia and I occupy positions on your deck with rifles as well?"

"I'm afraid, Your Majesties," the captain replied, "the Dutchman's deck is far higher than ours. Any small arms fire from the deck of the

Voyager would have little effect. But my plea for assistance in the infirmary was genuine—we're down a surgeon's mate at the moment."

John replied, "Below, tending to the wounded, I would probably do more harm than good."

The captain replied, "If there's no chance of dissuading you, Your Majesty, another sharpshooter on the deck wouldn't hurt."

"Very well, then," Queen Carlota said, "we will retire below under protest, to hopefully discover some nascent healing ability that we may possess."

"Thank you, Your Majesty." He nodded. "Julia."

"William," the captain said, "you're not under my direct command, but you may join the crew for the upcoming action if you like. I seem to recall you made quite a mark as a gunner's mate."

"You couldn't keep me away, Captain."

"Good man, I expect no less from one of the king's own. A word of caution: We didn't drill this sort of thing two years ago on our way to Barranquilla, so expect a bit of messing about."

The British officer broke into a slow smile. "I see. By your leave."

The Indiaman was now a point off their stern and gaining rapidly.

Captain Acton pressed his senior deck officer: "While in Rio, Mr. Evans, you had a chance to observe her armaments. What do you suggest?"

"She carries only nine-pounders, more for show and to scare off Malay pirates than anything else." Lieutenant Evans raised his spyglass. "No topmen, no snipers. An obvious lack of respect for her quarry, the Dutchman bears down on us with little caution. To him, we're a smaller, unarmed ship manned by a sorry lot of lubbers. She intends to board us with little or no resistance. Even fully laden, her gun deck would be well above our own." He briskly lowered the glass. "I suggest a Frenchman's feint."

The captain rallied the crew. He called out, "Men, that vessel has been lying in wait for us. She is an Indiaman manned by a Dutch crew. They bear down believing they are the lion and we a tasty morsel." Acton paused, looked about, then raised his voice. "Gentlemen, are we going to allow a load of shopkeepers to stop and board us?"

A great angry roar arose from the deck. Lieutenant Evans never ceased to marvel at Captain Acton's ability to rouse his very professional crew to murderous action with just a few words.

"I thought as much." Acton smiled. "Then let's deal them a bargain in English shot. But first, a feint it is: sail like Frenchmen until we're astern."

"Mr. Burke," Lieutenant Evans said to the quartermaster on the helm, "battle stations, but quietly."

The old quartermaster, who missed the sights, sounds, and smells of desperate action, was smiling fit to split his craggy old face. Instead of piping out the order, he softly passed the word, "Battle stations! All hands, all hands battle stations!"

The gun crews immediately made their way below to the gun deck, and skylarking ensued topside. Hats were put on backward, and impromptu jigs danced on the deck. The fun was in deadly earnest, as the crewmembers had no doubt that once those aboard the East Indiaman got what they wanted, they intended to send the *Voyager* and all her crew to the bottom of the ocean.

The lieutenant glanced at the topsails. "Considering the wind and her bearing, I recommend crossing our Dutch friend's stern."

"Make it so, Mr. Evans."

"Helm," the lieutenant raised his voice to be heard above the activity, "maintain current heading, but spill some wind from the sails, in as lubberly a fashion as possible."

For his shipmates' ears, Evans ordered, "When the Indiaman is half a mile away, you will back sails and work your way starboard-side around her stern, at which time we will engage her with our starboard smashers."

Below decks, the crew went into a controlled frenzy. Hammocks were rolled up and positioned around the gunwales to help reduce the risk of injury from flying splinters. The partitions on the gun deck were knocked down and stowed away, freeing the deck of encumbrances.

Assigned to the second starboard gun, William helped the gun crew select the least-pitted cannonballs for the first couple of shots. Powder bags were filled with premeasured amounts of gunpowder. Shirts were removed and bandanas tied around heads. All that remained was to raise the porthole covers and run out the guns when ordered. The odor of their slow-burning fuses would soon spread throughout the gun deck.

The ship's surgeon set up his shop down below the waterline, assisted by the queen and Julia. The cabin boy led a protesting Cauã into the cramped space of the surgery.

"What's this, Jimmy?" Dr. Gibson asked.

"Mr. Burke ordered me to escort Cauã to the surgery to assist you. But he doesn't want to be down here; he wants to be with me on the gun deck. But I'm afraid he'd get hurt, sir, he hasn't the know-how yet."

"You're dead right, Jimmy. You best be off to your station. And you," the doctor said to Cauã, "stop your squirming and spread the sand in that bucket there."

Queen Carlota asked, "What's the sand for, Doctor?"

"So we don't slip on the blood," he said, but quickly added, "not to worry there though, Your Highness, the only blood spilled today will be on that ship across that small strip of ocean." Through the porthole the Dutchman could be seen quite clearly, closing fast.

A boom accompanied by a puff of smoke came from a topside cannon of the *Prins Willim II*, closely followed by a geyser of ocean spray off the *Voyager*'s starboard bow.

On deck, the crew's antics and sloppy ship-handling continued.

When the Indiaman came within hailing distance, Captain Darius Acton picked up the horn and called, "What is your business with us?"

"Heave to. Prepare to receive a search party. Any resistance, and we will sink your vessel."

"I will heave to, but under protest. This is piracy of the lowest kind."

A second shot flew over the *Voyager*, this time tearing a hole in the forward staysail.

"We beg your patience," Acton called again, "we are unaccustomed to being accosted at sea and are inexperienced. Allow us time to close with you."

His voice dripping with derision, Marquez said, "Look at those morons. A crew of Spanish schoolboys could set sails better than those jackasses."

Jaager frowned.

Drilled in this maneuver, the experienced crew of the *Voyager* allowed her to wander near enough to the Dutch ship so as to come beneath the enemy's deck guns. With no headway, the starboard side of *Voyager* slipped backward past the port side of the *Prins Willim*.

"Watch your drift, man!" the Dutch captain called out to *Voyager*. "Fill your main, for God's sake!" He watched helplessly as the crew on the wallowing brig-sloop did exactly the opposite and backwinded the sail. "Those damn idiots are going to wind up behind us."

On *Voyager*'s gun deck, William focused on the whispered commands of the third mate: "Cast loose your guns . . . Level your guns . . . Out tompions . . . Run out your guns . . . Prime . . . Ready at the port holes and ready on the gun tackle. Well-timed and well-aimed for her rudder. We need to cripple the Indiaman's steering."

With minimal sternway, *Voyager* continued to inch backward until her starboard bow gun was directly behind the Dutchman's rudder.

The Dutch captain was becoming very uncomfortable with the vulnerable position of his ship, regardless of how harmless the schooner appeared. *Voyager*'s sails snapped taut, abruptly ceasing her backward motion. Jaager saw an odd movement in the foremast and mainmast shrouds. "Good God!" he breathed in Dutch. He shouted, "Helm, hard to starboard!"

On the gun deck of the *Voyager*, the third mate's commands rang out, "Right smart fashion, lads, open the ports, *fire as her rudder bears!*"

And in one heart-stopping instant, like a genie's magic, gunports appeared where there shouldn't have been any, pointing directly at the stern of the *Prins Willim II*. The seamen working the *Voyager*'s tops brandished hidden rifles. The awkward landlubbering of her sailors disappeared, replaced by grim, deadly intent.

Too late, the Dutch captain rued his foolish carelessness. The lumbering *Prins Willim* was excruciatingly slow to respond. His shouted orders were drowned by the roar of *Voyager*'s sixty-eight-pound bow carronade, followed by screams of pain and the sound of splintering wood.

Gaining headway, *Voyager*'s remaining starboard guns came into play. The mate shouted, "Continue to shoot singly as we pass by her stern-post. After firing, reload with cannister!" William stood by the second starboard cannon. The acrid smoke from the first gun bit his throat; his ears rang through the cotton stuffed in them. The muffled yells of the first gun crew as they repositioned their cannon sounded as if they came from a great distance.

Patiently the seconds ticked by. From above them came the pop of *Voyager*'s sniper fire and the report of their bow and stern chasers. Any musket fire from the stern of the Dutchman was instantly suppressed by a fusillade from *Voyager*.

The cannon William was assisting with began to bear on the *Prins Willim*. The ships were so close that William felt he could reach out and touch the other ship's rudder. Through the hole carved in the stern by the first smasher, movement could be seen inside the enemy ship. The gunner adjusted line and elevation slightly, then touched the lit fuse to the big cannon.

Boom! The second smasher leapt off the deck, belching forth smoke and fire. The sixty-eight-pound projectile tore through the *Prins Willim*'s rudder and continued on into the ship, ripping apart bulkheads, spraying deadly splinters and iron shards in its aftermath. A gun barrel appeared in the hole left behind—the muzzle flashed, and the gunner in front of William jerked backward, bleeding from his neck. He crumpled to the deck and lay still.

The smaller brig, with its outsized cannon, continued to blast the stern of the behemoth. The third smasher followed, causing more damage to the Dutchman, daylighting the interior of the ship. After the fourth round pummeled the inside of the Indiaman with a direct hit, a deep groan rumbled across the narrow watery chasm separating the vessels.

Like a partially felled redwood, the Dutchman's mainmast began a ponderous plunge, creaking to a halt at a steep angle just above the deck. In its wake, a tangle of spars, shrouds, and sails tumbled down. A brief moment of silence was followed by the awful screaming of the

Prins Willim's wounded, quickly drowned out by the cheering of the *Voyager* crew.

William helped reload the carronade with canister. He looked through the opening of the gun port, waiting for the next chance to strike a blow. He had a direct view of the devastation wreaked upon the *Prins Willim II*, when up popped a head from behind a bed in what must have been the captain's cabin. "Veeborlay!" William shouted. "You cad! What are you doing there?"

The Dutchman's eyes were as big as saucers, his skin as white as crisp, clean linen. He offered no response. The *Voyager* pulled ahead and Veeborlay disappeared.

On the command deck, the lieutenant calmly urged the helmsman, "Hard a-starboard, keep under her guns." The ship's forward momentum again brought her parallel to the Indiaman, enabling the reloaded starboard guns to unleash their deadly canister calling cards.

The Dutchman fired her swivel guns on the back side of a large swell, raking the *Voyager*'s deck. A sniper fell from a lower spar and bounced off the railing.

"Mr. Poole," Captain Acton acknowledged the ship's bosun. Poole had assumed the helm after the helmsman was hit. "Not to worry, Captain," Poole said, crimson streaming down his face. He used one hand to tie a large, rolled handkerchief around his head.

Three of *Prins Willim*'s nine-pounders were still active and had found their mark on the downswell: Two cannon balls holed *Voyager* just above the waterline. The third passed clean through the top deck, showering the gun crews below with splinters; fortunately, the spent ball caused only minor injuries.

Voyager answered, bow and stern chasers pouring deadly fire into the enemy's gun crews, the Dutchman's guns becoming eerily silent while the screams from their wounded filled the afternoon air.

The smaller ship then unleashed a broadside of canister shot at close range into the portside hull of the larger ship, holing her along her entire length at the waterline. As she settled, water rushed into the Dutchman's stern and port compartments.

The engagement was over.

The *Prins Willim II* left behind a trail of broken timber, pieces of cordage, and bodies. Rivulets of blood swiftly mixed with the open sea.

"Bastards! Soulless heathen bastards!" Marquez shook his bloody fist at the back of the departing Englishman. Next to him on the quarter-deck, Jaager lay dead, the scarlet stain on the white chest ruffles of the Dutchman's shirt—he had made no attempt to disguise his captain's uniform—mute testament to King John's skill with a rifle on the downswell. Behind him, the lifeless body of *Prins Willim*'s helmsman was draped over the spokes of the now useless helm.

For all their skill and deception, it had been luck that had won the day for the English. At the very onset of the engagement, a fortuitous roll of the ships had allowed *Voyager*'s deck carronades to rake the higher command quarterdeck of her opponent.

His left leg shattered, the Spaniard clutched the deck rail. Marquez wiped away the crimson wetness from a splinter wound on his forehead; the blood mingled with tears of rage flowing from his eyes. There was no pain—the hatred in his gut obscured all feeling. He shook his fist and cursed them again. He swore to God there was no place on earth they could hide from him. After this he would hunt the dogs down and bring them to their knees. They would pay.

On the command deck of the *Voyager*, the lieutenant ordered, "Secure from battle stations." Across the open ocean, a muffled explosion reverberated from the stricken vessel in their wake.

"Captain," Lieutenant Evans reported, "no damage below the water-line, and the carpenters have already started on repairs."

"Nicely done, Stephen. Double ration of grog all around this evening."

"Thank you, sir." The lieutenant beamed. "I'll pass the word."

"Casualties?"

"One dead I'm afraid—Gunner's Mate Johnson—and four wounded, one seriously."

"Very well." The captain swallowed. "He was a good man, Johnson, served on *Redoubt* with me. Service in the morning."

"Of course, sir."

"Resume course. The deck and conn are yours, Mr. Evans. I'll be in the surgery."

Acton called back to the bosun, still on the helm, "See to that scratch, Mr. Poole."

"Aye, sir."

With trimmed sails and a red sun sinking into the dark sea behind her, *Voyager* continued on her journey.

CHAPTER 63

HOMECOMING

Robert Turner, master gardener of Chatsworth, was accustomed to rising before anyone else on the estate. This morning, like every morning, Turner was on his early rounds. Coming to the front of the manor in the dim light, the old Scot could just make out a pair of clippers under a hedge, wet with the night dew. "I'll twist that young buck's ears," he muttered, "leaving tools at his arse like this."

His exasperation evaporated at the sound of an approaching carriage—quite unusual at this hour. Curious, he peeked inside the open windows of the coach as it slowed. "By God"—the shears clattered to the ground—"it's William Gunn!"

Turner yelled to the sleepy footman at his station at the front door, "WAKE UP, YE DAFT EEJIT, IT'S CAPTAIN GUNN, COME BACK TO US!"

Shocked awake, the footman bolted inside the mansion, decorum thrown aside, "It's Mr. William, he's back! He's alive!"

Before William had a chance to emerge from the carriage, Turner swung the door open and reached for the soldier's arm, "Out with ye, lad! There's no time to waste!"

William disengaged his arm from his old mentor, "What's going on, Mr. Turner? Is it Sarah?"

"It's a bit of a story, William. The doctor will give you the details soon enough. But right now," he insisted, "it's best if you come along smartly."

The night before, Darius Acton had invited William to share his coach to Chatsworth and had arranged for a very early departure, knowing how desperate the soldier was to see his daughter. Acton called out the carriage window, "You go, Gunn, I'll brief the duke."

Turner started them down the path behind the manor toward the workshops and the tradesmen's quarters. William asked, "Where are we going?"

"Sarah's below, with the head blacksmith and his family." The blacksmith's lodge was on a side lane behind the manor house.

William's voice had a hard edge. "What's she doing with Porter?"

"The duke didn't want to lose Porter to the new factory," the old gardener said, "as there's nay enough blacksmiths to go around these days. So, when Porter said his wife would care for Sarah for a consideration, His Grace agreed, just to keep the blacksmith at Chatsworth." The old Scotsman stopped to catch his breath. "The duke thinks he's paying them to care for your daughter."

"A consideration? Sounds more like blackmail."

"Aye," Mr. Turner agreed, "blackmail it was, pure and simple." He shook his head. "Up till then your daughter had been doing so well in the big house, Captain, never a bother."

They started off again. "Mind you, we didn't see much of Sarah once she went to Porters'. At the beginning, the staff looked in on her, but the blacksmith's wife soon put an end to that. The women continued to send over food and baking, but with that load of gussies, it's doubtful your daughter ever saw any."

It didn't take long to get to the blacksmith's lodge. The outside of the cottage was unkempt: assorted pieces of ironmongery lay about the yard, and the vegetables in the garden had surrendered long ago to a horde of invading weeds. Twisted vines almost completely covered the outside walls. A lone zinnia managed to thrust through the onslaught of thistle choking either side of the path to the front door.

William surged ahead of the old Scotsman. Turner called, "Upstairs, end of the hall on the left. I'll leave you to it." William bolted through the front door and up the staircase, several steps at a time. There were four bedroom doors on the corridor at the top: The two on the right were slightly open; several pairs of young eyes could be seen through the narrow gap.

He opened the last door on the left. His daughter lay on the bed—the same Sarah, but rail-thin, her hair darker, much longer, and slick with perspiration. Her eyes were shut, her breathing shallow, her skin a ghastly ashen hue.

Dr. Ferguson held the child's wrist, taking her pulse; on the other side of the bed, the assistant gardener's wife, Mrs. Hudson, sat holding Sarah's hand. "Good Lord, William, you're back." Mrs. Hudson leapt to her feet, rushed over, and hugged him. "You're alive!"

The doctor interrupted, "There'll be time enough for that later; for God's sake man, if you've found anything in that jungle, let's have it *now*—your daughter's in dire need!"

William drew out the packet which contained the red bark, the only evidence of how close he had actually gotten to the black orchids, and handed it to the doctor.

Ferguson carefully opened the package, then looked at William with a questioning glance.

His face grim, the British officer shook his head.

The doctor took a piece of the red bark out of the packet and scrutinized it. Apparently satisfied, he casually rewrapped the bark and, without a word, put the packet into his medical valise.

William said, "Mr. Turner remarked that Sarah had been doing very well."

The doctor put his valise down. "Yes, fairly well," he replied guardedly. "However, about a week ago, your daughter came down with what appeared to be a seasonal chill. Then a strong fever unexpectedly came on that simply won't break. She's drifted in and out of consciousness ever since."

William took his daughter's small hand in his. It was cold to the touch; her swollen knuckles were raw and calloused. The pale blue tinge inching from her fingertips toward her heart chilled him to the bone.

Ferguson said, "Mrs. Hudson and her girls have been here night and day, tending her. Your daughter's never alone." He felt Sarah's forehead.

"Since your search for the orchids was unsuccessful, I must dose her with something as soon as possible. But I have to caution you, Captain, it is doubtful it will have the desired effect." He picked up his bag. "I'll be back as quickly as I can," he said and left.

Mrs. Hudson sighed. "With no word of you for ages, William, God forgive us, we thought the worst. It's truly a miracle you're back." She wiped tears from her eyes. "Just last evening Sarah had violent shakes—we thought she was going to leave us." She stifled a sob. "But she's a fighter."

William gently stroked his daughter's hair, the brown curls so much like his wife's.

Mrs. Hudson whispered, "You should know our being here doesn't set at all well with the Porter family."

William looked about for the first time. The inside of the house was dismal. The windows were so dirty that the rays of the rising sun could hardly penetrate, and the walls cried out for a fresh coat of paint.

Wakened by the fuss, Porter, the dark-eyed blacksmith, filled the doorway with his bulk. He bellowed, "WHAT THE BLOODY HELL'S GOING ON HERE?" He was balding, with a permanent scowl covering his red face, and his massive arms hung at his sides. William sat on the bed, his back to the man. Porter roared again, "And who do you think you are? Barging in here without so much as a by-your-leave?" He added, "First thing that doctor does, is take over my boy's room for your little pup. And you," he sneered at William, "not a word for years, then you show up and start throwing your weight around."

By this time, Mrs. Porter, dressed in her bedclothes, had arrived. Resembling a buff tent, she peeped from behind the corpulent frame of her husband. "The girl was lazy, never did what she was supposed to," the tent exclaimed. "Gave her the best room in the house, we did, with little thanks."

The gravitational pull of the enormous parents must have attracted their offspring, who were now crowded about them.

William never shifted; nor did he give any sign that he'd heard. After a brief moment of silence, he rose with great deliberation, his back still to the couple. At his full height he was perhaps not as broad as the blacksmith but was at least a head taller. He slowly turned to face the pair. His knuckles were white on the silver grip of the cavalry saber Captain Acton had presented to him as a battle token. Tucked into the dark battle sash encircling his scarlet uniform jacket, the metal handle of the long knife the Amazonian priestess had given him glittered in the candlelight; beside it, an elegant pistol the queen had received from Bolívar and gifted to the British officer kept the blade company. Barely controlled fury contorted William's features, the livid scar on his face flushed bright red.

He hadn't uttered a word or made any threatening gestures, but the pair reeled backward, as if struck. "Lay a hand on us, you'll answer to the duke, William Gunn," the wife said faintly. Porter added weakly, "This is my house, and it was only fair the girl earn her keep, as was right."

The British officer advanced on Porter until their faces almost touched; pressed against the corridor wall with his wife pinned behind him, the blacksmith was unable to back up any further. He farted.

William spoke softly, "You've been well paid to care for my daughter, but she's been neglected here, treated as a common servant." He prodded the blacksmith in the chest. "I hold you responsible for her condition. Should the worst come to pass," he leaned in and breathed with quiet vehemence, "I will come for you."

William went back to the room. "Gather her things, Mrs. Hudson." He lifted his daughter off the bed, disturbed at the terrible, insubstantial lightness of her.

Mrs. Hudson covered Sarah with a blanket and picked up her scant belongings. "Where to, Captain?"

"Chatsworth House."

In the downstairs kitchen of the manor house, the doctor had almost finished preparing a tonic for Sarah when the Duke of Devonshire swept in. He sniffed, "A rider arrived at dawn at Gladdenbury, Ferguson, with a message that I return at once." He removed his hat. "I haven't even breakfasted. Just what is so urgent?"

"This, Your Grace."

Ferguson moved aside. On the tabletop next to a black packet were several pieces of blood-red bark. Jesuit's bark.

The duke's lip twitched. "Is that what I think it is?"

The doctor nodded.

"How? Where?" Cavendish was genuinely puzzled.

"William Gunn."

"*Gunn?* He's here?"

Dr. Ferguson nodded. "Arrived early this morning, escorted by Captain Acton."

"Indeed." The duke's eyebrows lifted. "William Gunn and Darius Acton." For a man who was used to manipulating outcomes, this was disconcerting. Neither of these men was supposed to be here. Gunn had been forgotten long ago, just another dead soldier. Acton was ordered to go to Portugal, then directly back to South America. The duke did not like the unexpected. And apparently Gunn had returned with red cinchona. *The devil to pay now.*

"We're beyond desperate for that bark, Ferguson; you know better than most that that bloody cinchona is the only remedy for the marsh fever decimating our troops. The gray cinchona is absolute trash." He said solemnly, "And now we have someone who knows firsthand where to get red cinchona."

"Your Grace, there's something you should know."

"Yes?"

"Gunn's daughter has gotten worse: she's close to death. And he blames you for removing her from the care of the manor house."

"Blames me? If I recall correctly," he said dismissively, "we pay quite a good sum for her care."

"It appears the child was not well kept by the blacksmith and his wife."

"Is that so?" He was momentarily reticent. "Perhaps, in hindsight, we could have been more vigilant." He asked thoughtfully, "Did Gunn manage to lay his hands on any of those imaginary orchids he was wandering about looking for?"

"Unfortunately, no."

"Will you be able to help the child?" the duke asked.

"The next few hours will tell, one way or another."

"Will the red bark work?"

The doctor explained, "Gunn's daughter may be afflicted with a fever unrelated to malaria, but we must try the red cinchona—it's all we have."

"Do your best, Ferguson." The duke stressed, "We may once again need the services of our intrepid Captain Gunn." He tapped the side of his nose. "Does he have any idea of the value of the red cinchona he's brought back?"

"I don't think so, Your Grace, at least he gave no indication."

"Where is Gunn now?"

"With his daughter at the blacksmith's cottage."

A commotion sounded from the main entrance.

The duke said wryly, "I do believe our good captain may have arrived."

Upstairs on the main floor, William had stridden past the dazed butler and straight down the hall to the wide staircase leading to the upstairs bedrooms, his daughter in his arms, swaddled in the blacksmith's bedsheets. Mrs. Hudson followed. The servants, alerted earlier to the arrival of the British officer, lined the balcony overhead to get a glimpse of the apparition that now mounted the stairway. Dim gasps of recognition drifted up and down.

"So much older."

"Ye wouldn't know him."

"Good Lord, would you look at the great bloody white mark on his face."

"A scar that is."

"Proper hero he is, done up in his finest rig."

"Look at the poor wee child. How pale."

"There'll be a reckoning now, someone'll get a comeuppance for sure."

They parted to allow the British officer through. He kicked open the door of the first room he came to. Mrs. Hudson entered after him and pulled back the bedclothes on the large bed; William gently laid the wispy child down.

Mrs. Hudson addressed the servants now crowding the doorway,

"Stop your silly gaping and get some cold water, compresses, and clean towels. Straightaway."

Dr. Ferguson pushed through and eyed the boot print on the door. Anna, Mrs. Hudson's eldest daughter, followed him. Grace, the younger daughter, trailed behind carrying a small pitcher on a tray. The doctor said to William, "I was told you were here. I've prepared a tincture which hasn't been attempted before for these symptoms. But we must try something."

William reluctantly let go of his daughter's hand and stood to allow the doctor to approach. "Her breathing is so shallow, Doctor," he said anxiously, "at times she seems to stop altogether, but then, with a start, she begins again."

Ferguson said grimly, "I won't mince words, Captain, this is a most perilous time." He removed a vial of light-green liquid from his bag.

"Mrs. Hudson," the doctor directed, "if you would be so good as to slightly raise her head and shoulders off the bed." William lent a hand, though he hardly needed to; his daughter was featherlight. "That'll do," Ferguson said. He opened the vial, poured a measure of the tincture into a spoon, and lifted it to Sarah's pallid lips.

"Keep her raised, a bit higher there, missus. Water, please." Anna handed him a glass. He spooned a little water from the glass into Sarah's mouth.

William wasn't much given to prayer, not even on the eve of a battle; nevertheless, he found himself silently pleading with the universe. *Don't punish her for my not being here. She's just a child and has only known hardship and loneliness.* He hung his head. *Much of which, I fear, is my fault.*

They waited in time suspended for the entire day. The house functioned with an almost funereal air, the upstairs servants quietly going about their duties, the normally raucous downstairs kitchen staff preparing meals in silence. The pendulum of the longcase clock audibly ticked off time, while the top of the hour chimes pealed unimpeded throughout the mansion.

Sarah's labored breath continued, and her skin kept its sallow hue. The sun rose ever higher, and the shadows falling on Sarah's bed retreated across the room. William continued to hold his daughter's hand and whisper to her; Annie softly hummed a child's tune while drying Sarah's fevered forehead. Shortly after lunch, the crunch of carriage wheels on gravel signaled that Captain Acton was leaving to rejoin his ship.

In midafternoon, Dr. Ferguson returned to check on Sarah. He took her pulse and looked up. "No better . . . but no worse either. Though I fear her exhausted heart won't be able to sustain the battle much longer. I will dose her again, and, Mrs. Hudson," he instructed, "have the girls apply a fresh cool compress every quarter hour. And tell the servant to open those windows."

Ferguson pondered the wretched drama: the desperate father, who had searched in uncharted wilderness for almost two years to no avail, danger his constant companion; the assistant gardener's wife and daughters, praying so fervently for the small child; and the little girl in bed clinging to life, her every breath a struggle.

Ferguson said, "The next hour will tell." He glanced around for a place to sit, and a servant immediately materialized with a chair. The doctor placed it beside the bed, close to William.

William's mind raced. *Was it all in vain? Was I on a fool's errand all along?*

No one moved or spoke, each lost in similar thoughts: Could they have prevented this? Had they done everything possible? They focused on the small figure on the bed, as if force of will and concentrated effort could bring the child back from the brink.

Mrs. Hudson broke the interminable silence. "Grace, another fresh compress."

Chatsworth was in candlelight, the sun having long fled the room, when the gong of the big clock in the downstairs library struck seven. At the sound, Sarah appeared to hold her breath. The doctor lightly touched William's forearm to encourage him to loosen his tight grip on the little girl's hand; Mrs. Hudson inched to the edge of her chair. The child slowly exhaled, long and easy, then drew another slow breath.

Ferguson checked her pulse. After a moment, he felt her forehead.

The corners of his mouth drew up ever so slightly. "I do believe, Captain Gunn," he choked, then coughed self-consciously, "that you may have saved your daughter's life."

William rose, wanting to believe, but afraid to. Incredulous, he said, "Are you certain, Doctor?"

Ferguson nodded, and said evenly, "Absolutely. Her fever's broke, her pulse is strong and steady, and her breathing is regular and clear. She's now sleeping peacefully." Mrs. Hudson gasped and covered her mouth with both hands; tears streamed down her face. Her girls hugged each other for joy. The doctor added thoughtfully, "Perhaps it was the cinchona. Or perhaps just your presence, Captain, may have been the deciding factor. For the moment, at least."

The good news of Sarah's recovery flew throughout Chatsworth.

Ferguson said, "Mrs. Hudson, let's leave Sarah in the very capable hands of your daughters for a few minutes. I'd like to speak outside with Captain Gunn and yourself." The doctor closed the door behind them. He pointedly addressed the few servants in the corridor still milling about, pretending to be working, "If you please."

When they were alone, he said, "In cases like this when we have so little experience of the malady, we can never be certain how the patient will fare in the long-term. William, you must ensure your daughter remains in the manor house under Mrs. Hudson's care. Would you object to that, Mrs. Hudson?"

"You know we would care for Sarah as one of our own," she replied warmly, "and the girls already love her like a little sister. But, if I may be so bold, will you be abroad again so soon, Captain Gunn?"

William couldn't understand what the doctor was driving at. "Perhaps the good doctor knows more than I do," he said sharply. He had no plans for going anywhere and intended on rejoining Mrs. Hudson's husband as a gardener.

The doctor said gravely, "If I spoke out of turn, forgive me. I'm sure you have much to discuss with His Grace."

I certainly do, William thought.

While William was conversing outside with the doctor and Mrs.

Hudson, inside the room William's daughter had awoken from her deep sleep. She had an untroubled smile for Annie, who was still cradling Sarah's small hands.

"Annie, I was dreaming," she said excitedly, "my father had come back to me. He was holding my hand. It was so real. He was here." Annie raised her eyebrows in disappointment. "Oh, Annie, you know I'm always happy to see *you*."

Before Annie's younger sister, Grace, could blurt out the news of William's return, the door opened.

Sarah sat up, her eyes wide with shock. "Daddy," she breathed. Then louder, "Daddy, it really is you, you're back, just like my dream!" Nothing could stop her from struggling out of bed to fall into William's open arms. He held her in a great hug, and said, "Yes, Sarah, I've returned, just as I said I would." He repeated over and over, softy, into her hair, "Yes, I'm really here."

William waited until Sarah had fallen into a deep sleep before answering the duke's summons to a meeting in the study. He stopped at the servants' quarters to retrieve Pax and Cauã. He continued to think about the events of the past day—in particular, Ferguson's interest in the red cinchona, which he had used to dose Sarah. William suspected the bark might be of more importance than he had ever guessed.

The head butler intercepted them at the door to the study. He sniffed, "I'll take the cur and the indigent in tow, Captain, and leave you and His Grace in peace."

"That's thoughtful, Smythe, but they stay with me."

They entered the room. William Cavendish, Duke of Devonshire, sat behind an oak desk surrounded on three sides by bookcases. The fourth wall was home to a fireplace.

The duke put down a letter he was reading. "Ah, Captain Gunn, I've been waiting. So good to see you again." In an attempt to summarily deflate the Porter business, the duke said, "Before I propose a toast to your success, William, an explanation and an apology are due from me." He hesitated, distracted by the dog and the Indian boy on the rug in front of the fire.

Cavendish had never before tolerated a canine in that room. And an Amazonian Indian had never even been seen in the entirety of the East Midlands, no less entertained in a duke's study. The boy snuggled beside the dog in the warmth of the small blaze, and both were soon fast asleep.

The butler poured two brandies for the men, set them on a side table, and left the room. The duke sat at the table and indicated for William to take the other chair.

"Only today did I learn of the neglect of your daughter by that blacksmith and his family. We had no notion the man was a rogue who would pocket the handsome sum I paid for Sarah's keep. Although it'll be a devil of time replacing a blacksmith, I'm happy to say that they've been run off the estate. The cad was fortunate to get away without a whipping."

William gazed fixedly at the aristocrat. "After giving your word that my daughter would be well cared for in Chatsworth House while I undertook your mission to Bolívar, you turned around and used Sarah as a bargaining chip to induce a tradesman to remain on the estate. I wonder what would have happened to my daughter had I not returned. And you used *me* as well."

Cavendish found the British officer's cold stare unsettling. "In the service of the Crown, we are all used, William—willingly used. You should be proud. Your mission to Bolívar was a resounding success: we received the general's emissaries months ago." He lifted his glass. "Here's to your achievement, and to your daughter's recovery and continued good health."

William raised his glass. "I will drink to my daughter's health. But I don't give a damn about your mission." The officer swallowed the drink in one gulp and placed the glass on the table.

"I understand your distress, Captain Gunn, and will ignore your remarks since you have proven time and again you are the king's man." Cavendish leaned forward. "Don't forget, William, it was the Crown's benevolence which allowed you to search for the orchid."

Cavendish stood, and noted that Gunn remained seated. The duke changed tack. "I still haven't congratulated you on your Brazilian success." He walked to the sideboard and refreshed their drinks. "Those stunning orchids you've brought back. I've been told some have actually survived." He continued conspiratorially, "Orchid collecting is on its way to becoming quite an obsession, you know, both here and on the continent.

"By the way," he said offhandedly, returning to his chair, "Acton mentioned you weren't alone in your quest for the black orchid." It was a statement of fact, not a question.

"That's true," William replied. "After my native guide was killed at Boyacá, a woodsman—one of Bolívar's foragers—lent valuable assistance. In fact"—he decided this was as good a time as any to introduce the topic of payment—"this gentleman should be compensated for the service he rendered over the year and a half we were partners. He saved my life several times. I don't know that I could have made it back without him."

"Well, we had better see if we can make this happen. Who might this 'partner' of yours be?"

"An American. His name is Nathanial Bidwell."

William witnessed rare surprise in the Duke of Devonshire.

"I see. Well, that's something to think about."

The duke decided to change course, perhaps probe a bit. He twirled the amber liquid in the glass. "Do you wish to disclose something, Captain Gunn? It doesn't take a sleuth to notice that you've been fondling an object in your jacket all evening."

William's hand drifted to the pocket of his jacket. He still hadn't entirely come to grips with the fact that Nate had willingly relinquished the incredibly valuable gemstone. No need to reveal the emerald yet, however.

Instead, William produced King John's letter to the duke and set it on the table between them.

Cavendish carefully broke the official seal, unfolded the linen paper, and read King John's handwritten plea for assistance. Not once, but twice. He betrayed no emotion but asked pointedly, "How is it they came to believe, William, that *I* would have any influence in such an adventure?"

"I told them nothing," William replied, "but the queen is particularly resourceful." He shrugged. "I have no doubt that either the general confided in her or she divined your influence on her own."

The duke drummed his fingers on the table. He said pensively, "What you say is entirely plausible. And like ourselves, King John has his spies as well." He turned the letter over in his hand, then set it back on the table. "I believe you, Captain, and appreciate your bringing this message to me."

"But will you represent them, Your Grace?" Insolent or not, William would not hand over the emerald until he ascertained which way the duke was leaning. By rights, the stone belonged to the Yank.

The duke replied bluntly, "It is absolutely impossible for us to get involved in Portuguese internal politics." The duke put his brandy down. "Captain Acton was good enough to give me the gist of what transpired in Brazil, but now we have much to discuss—particularly, that scarlet bark you brought back."

William asked airily, "What about it?"

The duke confided, "That bark is the only remedy in the world for marsh fever, which is decimating our troops. That's because the only bark which has been available to us up to now comes from gray cinchonas, which are totally useless. The source of the pure red cinchona has been a mystery to every European government."

So that was it. They needed red cinchona, desperately.

The duke smiled tightly, "Dr. Ferguson confides that you can locate additional cinchona of this type."

"It's difficult to say," William replied vaguely.

"Ah, I see." The duke uncrossed his legs and leaned forward. "It is absolutely essential you return to South America. After a suitable period, of course"—he tried to sound reasonable—"to enable you to once again become acquainted with your daughter."

Nothing like cutting to the chase, William thought. He wanted to say, "You're mad," but held his tongue and carefully considered his next words. "You're asking much, considering my daughter was on her deathbed just hours ago, due in no small part to the estate's neglect. The way I see it, my mission is done and over with. I expect to resume my gardening duties under Mr. Turner. I've earned the right to remain and ensure my daughter is properly cared for."

The duke clarified, "You don't fully understand. The importance of quickly acquiring the red Jesuit's bark cannot be overstated. The situation for the empire is dire. Britain desperately needs a steady, reliable supply of red cinchona or we will have to abandon our existing colonies. This would be an unprecedented military and economic disaster for Britain."

"I will *not* leave my daughter again and return to South America."

Taken aback by the officer's unyielding tone, the duke took a closer look at the young man sitting by the firelight. Actually, not so young anymore. William's face betrayed a world-weariness that had not been there before; the brown skin was now deeply lined, and his furrowed brow framed tired and distracted eyes.

"I am not accustomed to having my requests refused."

William thought of Nate and smiled.

The duke was unnerved by the smiling officer. Perhaps the jungle had made him simple.

"It is not me you would be helping, Captain Gunn, but your fellow soldiers. If they die, and you know of a possible cure, their blood will be on your hands."

William stood. The duke remained absolutely still. Slight movement in the shadows betrayed the butler, Smythe.

William Gunn pointed. "Your Grace, I'm a little man. I've traveled far enough now to know that my blood does not belong to me any more than those soldiers you speak of are my responsibility. We are owned by men like you, sir, who push us around a chessboard too big for us to understand.

"No man wants to leave his family. No man wants to kill, like those boys have been asked to do, before they even know what dying means. If I got your cure and you did use it to save the lives of a few soldiers, it would only lead to a thousand times more deaths in other places we have yet to know the names of.

"Maybe you know that—but I prefer to think Your Grace's head is buried in the sand."

The duke leaned back and stretched out his legs. Although the aristocrat was ordinarily inscrutable, through his anger William was amused to detect *impertinent bastard* written all over the duke's features for a brief moment. But William was *their* bastard, and the only one who knew where the red cinchona forests were.

The duke had experience with the ones who managed to return. Some were hardened and often eager to go out again. They missed the danger, which became addicting, and led to recklessness. Others counted their lucky stars and swore they would never go on another mission. Still others were more obviously ruined.

But this young man was of a rare sort he'd only encountered once or twice before. The haunted look in the eyes wasn't there, nor was the nervous tic of the unsettled. If he saw anything, it was a fierce resilience backed by keen intelligence and courage tempered by experience.

Wellington had chosen well: this man remained most useful. But he must be kept in check, on a tight leash.

William had come to a decision. With great deliberation he reached into his jacket pocket, this time removing a blue silk bag from an attractive teak box inset with ivory and mother-of-pearl.

William walked slowly over to the table. The curtain in the shadows shifted slightly as if by a sudden breeze.

"I know the kind of person you are, Your Grace," he said. He upended the bag, and the emerald dropped onto the table in front of the duke. "A gift from King John, ruler of the United Kingdom of Portugal, Brazil, and the Algarves."

It was the first time Captain Gunn had ever witnessed William George Spencer Cavendish, the sixth Duke of Devonshire, rendered speechless.

"The Portuguese envoy in London is John and Carlota's man," William said. "He'll arrive here quite discreetly after dark tomorrow evening, and will leave shortly thereafter, either with a secret agreement for the British navy to support the Portuguese king, or with the emerald."

"William . . ." the duke began, but when he looked up, the room was empty.

CHAPTER 64

TROLLS

The footman opened the door to the main entrance of Chatsworth House to admit the visitor. The big man entered and handed his coat to the butler but glared when the servant reached for his cane. "Not on my watch, sunshine."

"That's fine, Smythe," the duke declared, ever hopeful his deprecating tone would irritate his caller. "We must endeavor to accommodate our guest's special needs. Whiskey, perhaps, after your long journey?" he asked. "It's the only drink for such a beastly day. And you must definitely stay for dinner."

"I'm here to conclude our arrangement, Devonshire," the visitor replied rudely, "not for anything else."

The duke's gaze remained fixed on his adversary. "One whiskey then, Smythe. Nothing for our guest; it seems he's not drinking this evening. I do believe he's anxious to proceed."

"The last time I remember being *anxious*, Cavendish, was when one of your man-o'-wars chased me up the coast, trying to blow my ass to hell. *Anxious*," the man said scathingly, "in the library of a British gentleman?" He looked around. "Although I suppose I should be anxious in *your* library."

"Come now, Simon, our latest agreement has worked out perfectly fine for all of us—except perhaps, the Spanish." The duke shrugged. "But they never were part of our little arrangement, were they?"

"Oh, they were part of it all right, Chatsworth, they just didn't know it." Simon Bidwell delighted in addressing the duke in every informal manner he could think of. He stretched. He walked to a bookcase and peered at the titles. "The way I see it, America agreed not to aid Spain in her struggle to keep her South American colonies. We also agreed to recognize preferential trade rights for Britain in Gran Colombia once your boy Bolívar kicks the Spanish out." He looked over his shoulder at the duke. "Remind me again what *we* get out of this."

The butler returned and set the whiskey down on the table next to the duke.

"Come now, Simon, your memory's not grown feeble, has it?"

Simon transferred his weight to favor his cane, the stories of which even the duke had heard.

Cavendish shifted in his leather chair. "If you recall, we agreed not to interfere with your secretary of state's negotiations to purchase Florida from the Spanish. Negotiations that included Adams sending an American agent to offer a deal to Bolívar."

Bidwell sneered, "You knew our sending a man anywhere near New Granada would only drive Bolívar *further* into the British camp."

The duke picked up the whiskey glass. "Be that as it may, Mr. Bidwell, you now have Florida. For sugar cane, Caribbean ports"—the duke took another sip of his whiskey—"and another slave state."

"Don't patronize me, Cavendish—the only reason the British don't need slaves is because they have colonies."

The duke would not be baited by this uncouth American. "As we also agreed, in return for American recognition of Britain's preferential trade rights with Gran Colombia, His Majesty's Royal Navy will enforce any future policy President Monroe might announce that prohibits foreign powers from interfering in your hemisphere." Almost as an afterthought, the duke added, "Oh, I almost overlooked one small item. Lest you forget, Simon, we've avoided boarding your slave ships"—he paused—"at least, until now."

Bidwell stopped and pointed with his cane. "You buy cheap cotton from us for your mills—cotton grown and picked by those same slaves."

The duke said offhandedly, "That *is* true. Now, on a related matter . . ." He took another drink. "It was thoughtful of you to send your own son to South America."

Simon Bidwell was startled. "How did you know that?"

"Come now, Simon, you're behind the times. Not only do I know that"—the duke sniffed—"but I have it from a reliable source the young man was manipulated into fleeing your country in the first place. Something about an attack on one of your Indian villages. Terrible loss of life, I understand."

The big man glared, closed one hand over the handle of his cane, and began to twist.

Seemingly out of thin air, Smythe appeared between Bidwell and the duke. "Sir," he said calmly, "I respectfully request you stay your approach, lower your walking stick, and stand down." The butler's hand disappeared inside his waistcoat and stayed there.

"Simon, my old friend, you misunderstand me," the duke said evenly. "I meant no disrespect: *au contraire*, my motto has always been 'the end justifies the means.' In fact, had it not been for your son, His Majesty's agent in South America would not only have failed in his mission, but he would not have lived to tell about it."

Simon Bidwell lowered his cane and relaxed, the menacing stare fled just as quickly as it had appeared. "How certain are you? I had news the boy met his end some time ago."

"I'd be surprised if there are two Nathanial Bidwells running about down there. In fact, at the moment I believe he's looking for passage back to the colonies. For some reason, he believes Mr. Adams will obtain a presidential pardon for him."

Pleased he had taken the American by surprise, the duke continued, "It would be advantageous to us both should your young man find himself mistaken."

Bidwell unconsciously tapped his cane on the floor, his brow knitted in thought. "What do you mean?"

"I knew you would stay for dinner! Smythe, set another place for our guest."

Simon Bidwell was wary. This was something entirely new, perhaps the start of another negotiation. He changed tack. "You're not that much older than the boy."

"And yet"—the duke gave a dismissive wave of his hand—"here we are."

"Indeed."

Cavendish said, "You have slaves and cotton, Simon, but *we* have mills. I'm quite aware of your humorous efforts to steal the specifications for our machines, but I'm offering you a more straightforward solution."

Bidwell was quiet for a moment. Then he sat down and said, "You can bring me that whiskey now, Hart."

The duke winced at the American tycoon's use of his childhood nickname.

CHAPTER 65

FRYING PAN

Early on a warm September morning, Nathanial Bidwell browsed the canvases of the art show assembled on the square across from the wharf, just beyond the customs booth. The square was almost empty at this early hour, the population of the nation's capital still preparing to meet the day.

Forced to wait for weeks in the Caribbean for a ship, it took much longer to get to Washington than he had calculated. The coastal trader he finally boarded in Jamaica had taken its time, making many ports of call on the way. Nate had disembarked just that morning and was in no hurry to get to the secretary of state's office. John Quincy Adams probably wouldn't be in yet anyway.

Although returning to America had always been a risk, things looked to be weighing in his favor. Nate was confident that the information he would provide to the secretary would earn him a pardon. In addition, he was sure Adams would find Nate's newfound friendship with the king of Brazil to be useful.

It was growing warm, even in the shade of the canopies set up to protect the canvases. He had seen enough. Bored by the portraits of people he'd never heard of and the syrupy romantic renderings of landscapes, he was turning away when something caught his eye.

At the very end of a group of floral paintings, he spied what appeared to be a painting illustrating the wide leaves and exposed tuber of an orchid. Coming closer, his quickening pulse beat in his ears—the profuse flower of the orchid was black as coal. The script in the corner read *M. Southwell.* He must find out more about this painting.

Two pairs of strong hands pinned his arms from behind. "You're under arrest on the orders of the secretary of state, for murder and treason, while acting as an agent of a foreign power."

Despite Nate's protests, he was hustled into a closed carriage waiting at the curb. Before he knew what was happening, they were speeding through the early-morning streets of the wakening capital. Two of his abductors sat facing him in the carriage, along with those still gripping his arms. His captors wore civilian clothing. They did not speak. The curtains were drawn.

"That's a fine 'welcome home,'" Nate said, right before they gagged him.

William took his evening tea in the garden of the spacious detached cottage the duke had assigned to him. Each day he had spent as many hours with his daughter as possible, trying to make up for lost time. Their housekeeper, like a fond aunt, cooked and cleaned for them. William's daughter really didn't remember her mother. But William wasn't worried. Sarah never wanted for company—the families on the estate had adopted her as one of their own, and Mrs. Hudson and the girls were always nearby. She was fully recovered and thriving with all the attention.

However, this evening William was unsettled. There were stories. A recently hired gardener, a former soldier not long out of India, had told of the high number of casualties throughout the empire—men dead or dying from fever. It was rumored that over a third of the military was incapacitated, and almost another third already dead. There was concern that not enough remained to man the empire. The new gardener himself was recovering from a long bout of illness.

William didn't know how he felt. The next morning, he was overseeing a team of men pruning fruit trees when he heard a cough from behind.

"Mr. Turner, I beg your pardon, I didn't know you were there."

"Oh, I was here all right," the master gardener said, noticing the faraway look in William's eyes, "but where were you? That's the question." The old Scotsman scrutinized the British soldier. "Aye, laddie, ye'll be off again, soon enough," he said, shaking his head. He walked away and called over his shoulder, "His Grace wants a word. Don't keep him waiting."

Cavendish was standing in the library holding a cup of tea.

"How is your daughter?" the duke asked, looking at William closely. "And how are you settling in?"

"Well. But you haven't asked me here for that, Your Grace, have you?"

"I admire a man who cuts to the chase, Gunn. And the answer is no, of course not. You will be going back to South America." Before William could refuse, the duke said, "Your associate in South America—tell me his name again."

"Bidwell, Your Grace, Nathanial Bidwell."

"That's right. Bidwell. Of course." He carefully placed the cup and saucer on an immaculately polished walnut table. "Pity about Mr. Bidwell," he said with a sigh, "but the fortunes of war and all that."

"What are you saying, Your Grace?"

"The man's life is forfeit—arrested, to be hung as a traitor, I believe."

William's mind raced. This time he recognized the game was on, but once again, the duke held all the cards. Stalling, he said, "Not only is he not a traitor, but if the Americans hang him, you'll never get your red cinchona."

Cavendish's eyebrows raised a fraction. "How's that?"

"Bidwell furnished the bark; he's the only one who knows where the cinchona comes from. He got the directions from an old medicine man in the upper Magdalena."

"Captain Gunn, you misunderstand me. I know what the American means to me. The real question," the duke pronounced smugly, "is what is the value of his life to you?"

ᴅELIVERANCE

A tiny patch of blue sky was just visible through the hole that served as a window into Nate's cell.

He'd had no visitors in the weeks he'd been confined somewhere on the outskirts of the capital. Not that he had expected anyone.

Just the same routine: orderlies brought food; he was allowed out once a day to rinse his pot and have a brief walk around the yard. At least the food was decent. It beat Nate why they fed a condemned man good food. What did it matter? *It's the gallows for me tomorrow.*

He wasn't afraid. He really hadn't known fear ever since *she* had died. He did feel a sadness he couldn't explain—sadness that it had all come to this in the end.

Somewhere down the hallway, rusty hinges screeched in protest as a cell door swung shut, followed by a loud clang and the scraping of a metal bolt sliding into place. The footsteps of the departing guards echoed hollowly on the hardwood floor, the sound diminishing to an empty silence.

This was his favorite time. In the mornings, he could hear the birds singing outside. If he closed his eyes, he could be anywhere else.

A strange sound punctuated the birdsong—strange, yet familiar. It was a peculiar howl, perhaps the bark of a large dog excited at the return of its master.

Nate smiled.

AUTHORS' NOTE

To write historical fiction requires the author to be as much historian as novelist. Which leaves the question, how much of any historical fiction is actual fact, and how much of it is fiction? As for *The Orchid and the Emerald*, we devoted enormous research to ensure historical accuracy, ranging from Bolívar's South American revolution to early treatments for malaria (marsh fever) and to high society's love of orchids. We trust the reader will indulge the occasional departure from historical fact in order for the writers to maintain a suspenseful story line.

Preface: The background material on orchids is accurate. J. H. Chesterton was an actual nineteenth-century adventurer and plant hunter who passed away in Colombia. The background information about Joseph Jussieu is factual. He did keep a diary and stored his large collection of scientific specimens in his trunks, which he took everywhere. He had a manservant who stole the trunks while Jussieu was away arranging to depart South America. His journey into the Sacred Land is fictitious. He did die in an insane asylum in France.

The Old World: The dialogue throughout the book is imaginary. The Battle of Waterloo, in which William was an aid to the supreme commander—Arthur Wellesley, the Duke of Wellington—is recognized as a decisive moment in world history, a turning point which ended a series of European wars and ushered in a relatively long period of peace. The historical sixth Duke of Devonshire was an interesting and powerful aristocrat much devoted to horticulture; his role as spymaster and his portrayal as a cold, masterful manipulator is fantasy on our part. The description of the orchid house is factual. Although the brig *Voyager* and her crew are fictional, the ship is based upon the schooner *Pickle* that saw duty at the Battle of Trafalgar and was the first ship to bring word of the battle to England. Information about New England's support of the slave trade is accurate.

South America 1819: Bolívar's crossing of the Andes is accurately portrayed and the Battle of Boyacá is true to the actual timeline, terrain, troop movements, and commanders involved. The geography and political situation in South America are accurately presented. The weapons described were in use during that time. When orchids are mentioned—except for the black orchid—the locations ascribed to the particular species are accurate. The indigenous tribes cited existed in the locales mentioned during that period. The Dutch East India Company was dissolved in 1799, but there was an attempted revival two decades later—during the period of our story. Numerous British volunteers fought with Bolívar, and the famous Albion Brigade is factual.

The Wilderness: The information about emeralds and the Muzo mines is accurate, and information regarding the Devonshire emerald is correct. It is the world's largest and most famous uncut emerald, weighing 1,384 carats. The fight with the jaguars presents factual information about South America's apex predator. In the Valley of the Lepers, William and Nate are overcome with toxic fumes emanating from a volcanic seep. This harkens back to the ancient Oracle of Delphi. Gas seeping out of the fissures in the cave where the famous mystic sat, caused her to have visions. Archaeologists who inspected the geology of the area found two fault lines converging just under the temple through which the "vapors" the Oracle breathed most likely seeped. The dissolving limestone along those fault lines gave off ethane, methane, and ethylene—all gases which render the sniffer euphoric and can cause hallucinations.

The Amazon: The information about the Amazon is factually presented. Recent discoveries about pre-Columbian Amazonian civilizations reveal that a significant number of the trees in the Amazon belong to domesticated species, including the Brazil nut, the Amazon grape tree, and the ice cream bean tree. These immense groves bear striking resemblance to plantations, both in their size and proximity to known human settlements, and would have been necessary to support a pre-Columbian civilization. In addition, "black soil of the Indian" is a type of very dark, fertile man-made soil of special composition found fairly recently in the Amazon basin, of unknown origin, resulting in extreme soil improvement lasting centuries, allowing cultivation in the thin, sterile rain forest topsoil. This new evidence reveals advanced and complex societies and a network of roads that stretched far beyond the known boundaries of the Inca Empire. Many contend there were Amazons present even at the court of the Olmecs who prospered in ancient Mexico from 1200 BC to 400 BC and would account for the pyramids, rubber, obsidian, jade, and other advanced artifacts found in the Amazon. In fact, in the 1990s a long-lost section of the Inca road system was discovered running from Machu Picchu in Peru directly to the Amazon.

Brazil: The queen's bodyguard, Julia, is fictional: There is no evidence of such a bodyguard or that she ever visited Gran Colombia or personally knew Bolívar. In addition, King John VI and Queen Carlota were accompanied back to Lisbon by their son Miquel, but we have omitted this information for the purposes of brevity. (Miquel only made a nuisance of himself anyway!) John's main purpose in returning to Portugal was to endorse the constitution. He may have been interested in the banning of slavery throughout Europe, but the road to emancipation for slaves in Brazil was a long one; it wasn't until the reign of Dom Pedro II, John's grandson, that slavery was finally abolished. The Devonshire emerald resides with the Devonshire estate to this day, from time to time on loan to the Natural History Museum of London. Perhaps coincidentally, or perhaps not, the British navy would opportunely appear on those occasions when King John most required support.

Stay tuned for Book Two, in which William and Nate's mission to South America unravels, resulting in a pursuit to the Far East threatening to upset the fragile peace and send the world's great powers spiraling into chaos.

ACKNOWLEDGMENTS

A great debt of gratitude is owed to my wife, Sheila McNeill, for suggesting that we write a novel about the orchid hunters after our visit to the Biltmore Estate in Asheville, North Carolina. Sheila was a source of inspiration while she was with us; her influence persists even after her departure from this life.

We are indeed fortunate to have on our side a fabulous agent of unparalleled experience in Mel Berger of WME, who not only agreed to represent a trio of unknown writers but is a constant source of encouragement and advice. And for her patience and incomparable guidance in collaborating with us, we are indebted to our editor, Madeline Hopkins. We are delighted our novel landed in her skillful hands. For our stunning cover art, we are grateful to Kathryn Galloway English, Lead Designer of Print Books at Blackstone Publishing. We'd also like to extend our warm appreciation to Michael Krohn, Blackstone's copyeditor who had the laborious task of proofreading our draft manuscript; his thoughtful suggestions and corrections greatly improved our work. Much thanks as well to Josie, Megan, and the other supportive folks at Blackstone Publishing who ushered our book through the publishing process.

We are most grateful as well to the readers of our draft manuscript. Their warm encouragement and input were not only welcome but essential. The brave souls providing us with extraordinary and timely feedback included Michael Whelan, the first to take the plunge and who provided the initial boost to our confidence; Jim McGuire, whose Hibernian literary talent and invaluable comments added much polish to a rough gem; Sam Berman, whose knowledgeable and attentive eyes found many areas for improvement; Judy Ellis and Bob Pitts, for freely sharing their insights and general historical knowledge; Bill Mirabile, for generously devoting immediate attention to fine-tuning our draft; Jim Mallahan, our Gonzaga connection, forced us to rethink William's Barranquilla confrontation; Lynne Lamprecht for her thorough review and discriminating edits; Michael McNeill and Rachael Tennant for their loving support; and much appreciation to John O'Grady in New Zealand whose feedback added to our conviction that we had achieved our goal.

Big thanks as well to our Cherokee shaman, Earth Thunder, who generously rendered key guidance on the behavior and habits of the big cats of the Americas.

A warm nod is due to Alastair and Jackie Smith-Maxwell, our kind Arabian companions, whose friendship and timely advice on life in general contributed greatly to our continued existence through many subsequent adventures.

ABOUT THE AUTHOR

Timothy David Mack is a relatively recent figure on the literary scene, known mostly for his nonfiction publications on military subjects and on avian science.

The reclusive author is winner of the Houdini Award for Nonfiction for his series on the Malayan Emergency, and the Mascarpone Book Prize for his account of the Chindits during the Burma campaign. Mr. Mack is also credited with a study on the endangered Mascarene petrel, published in several scientific journals and books, including the definitive work *Joseph Johns: Pelagic Birds*. His one-man play *Sisyphus Revisited* won grand prize at the Edinburgh Festival.

Although not authenticated, information available on the solitary author indicates he was born on a blue-water schooner anchored in the Portuguese port of Macau to a Scots-Irish mother and an American father. By necessity, he was homeschooled during his early years as his parents traveled the world, his father pursuing his profession as a mega-project construction manager. The records indicate Timothy graduated secondary school from Eton in Berkshire, followed by a stint at Yale University, dropping out in his third year to become a merchant seaman.

In addition to spending several years at sea, the writer reportedly acquired Special Forces training during this interval; in addition, he has been an explorer, scientist, photographer, and businessman. It appears he has acquired a working proficiency in several languages, being credited with a pioneering translation of the Upanishads into Gaelic, and the translation of select Japanese literature into English.

An accomplished sailor, the author won the around-the-world Joshua Slocum Solo Competition in 1987 and is known to appear at presentations for charities. It is reported he is an avid black powder gun collector and scuba diver.

A devoted contemplative, Mr. Mack spends several months a year on retreat in a remote Benedictine abbey in the French Alps. The last interview he gave was in 1986.

The Orchid and the Emerald is a collaborative effort of the authors Kevin McNeill, David McNeill, and Tim Wendland.

Timothy David Mack, a purely satirical concoction, is a pseudonym and registered trademark of the authors.